GAR

# THE NORTHERN WAVE

## BOOK 2

Michael Terence
Publishing

First published in paperback by
Michael Terence Publishing in 2022
www.mtp.agency



ISBN 9781800943247

*This book is dedicated to the memory of John Davidson and all the Burghead Salmon Fishermen who crewed the bothies along Burghead Bay. We spent most of our school holidays there with characters who influenced all who encountered them. Too many to mention have passed, and so few remain.*

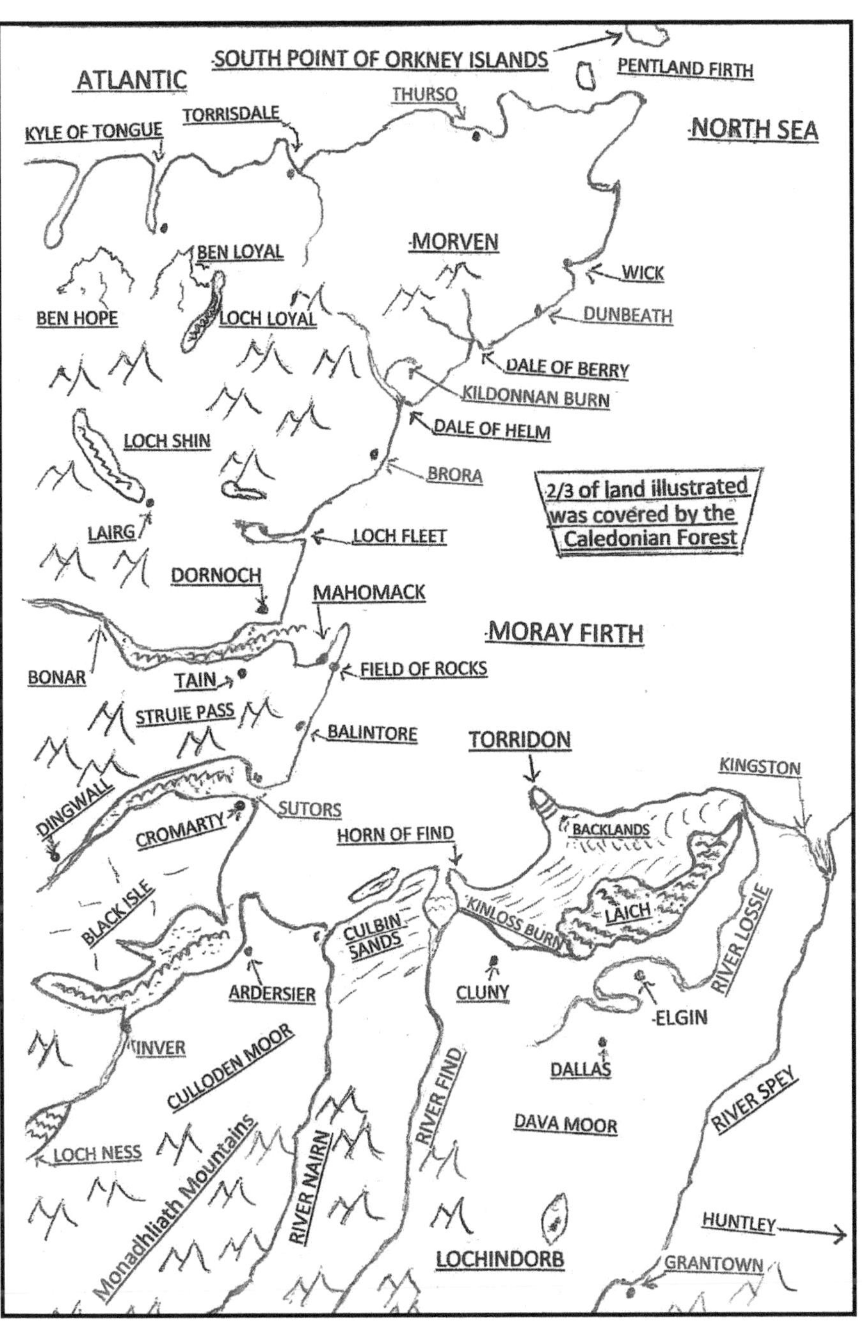
SOUTH POINT OF ORKNEY ISLANDS
PENTLAND FIRTH
ATLANTIC
THURSO
TORRISDALE
KYLE OF TONGUE
NORTH SEA
MORVEN
BEN LOYAL
WICK
BEN HOPE
LOCH LOYAL
DUNBEATH
DALE OF BERRY
KILDONNAN BURN
DALE OF HELM
LOCH SHIN
BRORA
2/3 of land illustrated was covered by the Caledonian Forest
LAIRG
LOCH FLEET
DORNOCH
MAHOMACK
MORAY FIRTH
BONAR
TAIN
FIELD OF ROCKS
STRUIE PASS
BALINTORE
TORRIDON
KINGSTON
DINGWALL
SUTORS
CROMARTY
BACKLANDS
HORN OF FIND
BLACK ISLE
CULBIN SANDS
KINLOSS BURN
LAICH
RIVER LOSSIE
ARDERSIER
CLUNY
ELGIN
INVER
CULLODEN MOOR
RIVER FIND
DALLAS
RIVER SPEY
DAVA MOOR
LOCH NESS
Monadhliath Mountains
RIVER NAIRN
HUNTLEY
LOCHINDORB
GRANTOWN

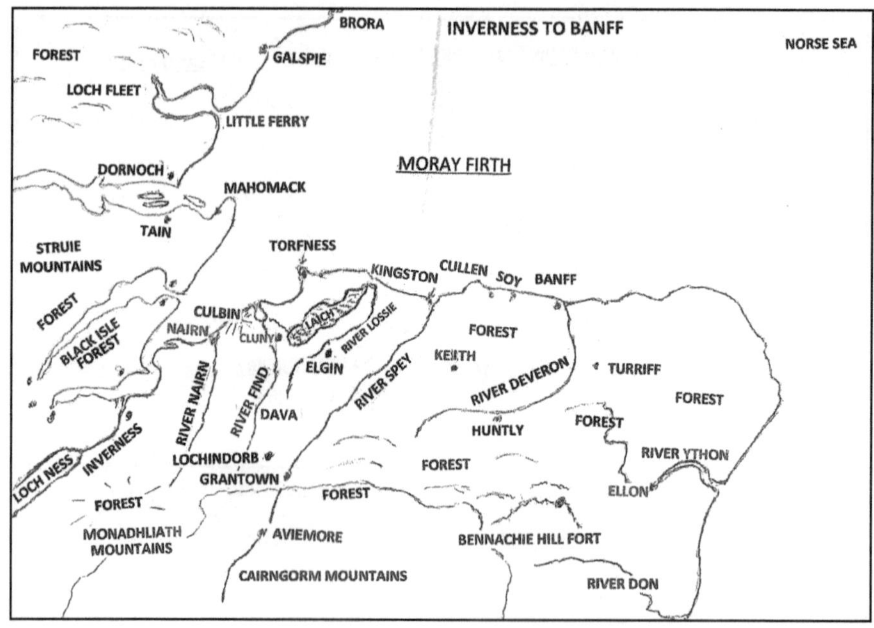
INVERNESS TO BANFF
NORSE SEA
BRORA
FOREST
GALSPIE
LOCH FLEET
LITTLE FERRY
DORNOCH
MORAY FIRTH
MAHOMACK
TAIN
STRUIE
MOUNTAINS
TORFNESS
KINGSTON
CULLEN
SOY
BANFF
FOREST
CULBIN
LAICH
NAIRN
CLUNY
RIVER LOSSIE
BLACK ISLE
FOREST
FOREST
ELGIN
KEITH
TURRIFF
RIVER SPEY
RIVER DEVERON
FOREST
RIVER NAIRN
RIVER FIND
DAVA
FOREST
HUNTLY
INVERNESS
LOCH NESS
LOCHINDORB
RIVER YTHON
GRANTOWN
FOREST
ELLON
FOREST
FOREST
MONADHLIATH
MOUNTAINS
AVIEMORE
BENNACHIE HILL FORT
CAIRNGORM MOUNTAINS
RIVER DON

# Chapter 1

Scotland was already in turmoil even before any facts were known about the fall of Torridon. Only days after the Fort fell the Norse had reinforcements from Norway and Orkney. Over three thousand warriors now held the Fort and two thousand more were camped at Backlands. Any thoughts of taking Torridon back and driving the Norse into the sea were dismissed by those who knew the defences. The mystery of how the Fort was attacked from inside only deepened with conflicting reports from those trapped inside. Some said a hundred Norse, others said two hundred, but all were adamant that no boats had landed on the flat rocks or anywhere close to the Fort, further adding to the mystery of where they had come from.

Like those across the Firth in Mahomack, the conclusion was reached that wherever they came from they must have been close enough to see the King's army leave the Clarkley and head towards Cluny. Timing was such a critical factor and so too the number of warriors who had remained inside the Fort. None had survived and their numbers were also contested. Even a body count on the battlefield was denied as nobody would go near there.

The chiefs knew the bitter taste of defeat. The impossible had happened, Torridon had fallen, their King killed in battle. Tusk confirmed that, but no one knew the fate of Sheena the Queen nor of Bran, the King's brother. Throwing thousands of warriors against Torridon would only result in certain defeat and destruction. Surprise of any kind didn't exist. They had no hope of storming the Fort or putting it under siege as the Norse had access to endless supplies of food and warriors from the sea. Even Tusk and Gordon along with Anderson, Munro and Grant had to face the cold reality that they might be next and they quickly set about building up their defences; all but Tusk, who had prepared his well in advance. The Chiefs agreed on one thing, the enemy had planned this attack with ruthless precision and used the element of surprise to create total confusion, securing their triumphant victory.

They dispatched messengers in all directions, putting every warrior along the Moray Firth on high alert and all the way south as word spread. The news that the King had died in battle became a rallying call. None feared facing the Norse in open battle, but open battle was unlikely as the Norse had nothing to prove. Outsmarted and defeated, Picts retreated in disarray towards the great Fort on the mountain-top of Bennachie where they would rally, but without leadership, they feared for the future.

Meanwhile, to the north, Frazer and Forbes rode quickly from the Stockade at Brora, accompanied by a warrior who had brought the news that a headless corps had been washed up on the beach not far away and judging by the tattoos, the warrior was Lugi.

When they reached the beach, they found a group had gathered who pointed them east. About a bow shot east the smell hit them and they covered their faces with their arms as they inspected the bloated body. His tattoos were indeed Lugi and seeing two interlocking circles on its right thigh and the head of an Eagle on its right shoulder they both knew his identity immediately. The name they gave, Sanda, matched the hair he didn't have. That was what the warrior with them thought, and they hastily retreated. They stopped by the group and confirmed the body was one of the messengers sent to alert Sinclair. It was Sanda, the younger of the two.

Frazer called the council on his return to the Stockade and they digested what finding this body meant. How long it had been on the beach nobody knew as this part of the beach was seldom visited. Old Callum suggested it could have come from the Helm. Much debris that came down the river ended up on this beach depending on tide and wind. Stroma listened in silence; she had no local knowledge.

"I think we should send somebody to the Helm," said Forbes. "If he had his head, he could have drowned crossing the river but with no head, and if he came from the Helm, some sign of what happened might show?"

Frazer agreed with him and so did the others. They would send twenty warriors to the Helm the next day and Frazer suggested Stroma should go with them. She had fretted for days and needed something else to occupy her mind. The loss of Bran was the main reason for her depression, but she didn't admit that to anybody. Frazer suspected as much and said so to the council. Anything they could do to snap her out of it was encouraged. They didn't expect the trip to the Helm to yield much; rain would have wiped away any tracks, but any distraction was welcome.

They set out at dawn and reached the vicinity of the Helm before noon. They all knew they must cross the river and went inland to look at the Ford. The river was raging as they knew it would be, but they had seen it higher and decided to send three warriors across, three who insisted they had crossed in far worse. They were right and crossed without incident. Mounted on horses from the King, Stroma and Frazer went next and crossed successfully. The others followed and they assembled on the east bank. Stroma's mind was now focused, and she remembered that Embo had crossed here. Her thumb stroked the orange stone in her Dirk and Fraser noticed.

"In the dark, it wasn't so easy," he said, reading her thoughts.

They mounted and headed downriver following a well-used animal track. The foliage on this side of the river looked thick with bushes and silver birch but they knew as they neared the flood plain on the east bank, the foliage would get less. It didn't get less, it disappeared altogether revealing ground strewn wood chips and small tree stumps. Close to where the Kildonnan burn reached the river, Frazer called a halt and surveyed the scene for a moment in silence.

"Dismount," he then instructed quietly and went to Stroma. "We leave the horses here," he ordered and drew his sword.

"What is it?" she asked, softly.

"I'm not sure. We go ahead on foot. Half of you come, the rest stay with the horses."

They passed his words down the line, while he went ahead with Stroma close behind him, her sword in one hand and shield in the other. They cleared the last of the cropped vegetation and ahead could see where the burn met the river. After pausing to search the area ahead for any movement, they went on to the Burn and discovered a sheepskin lying on the bank as if cast aside. A quick look up the burn revealed more, weighed down with rocks and untouched.

Stroma looked at the skin briefly but like Frazer and the others her focus stayed on the flood plain and what lay across it and she frowned. The entire flood plain had been trampled flat and what looked like molehills were dotted all over it. They went to the first and discovered it was a small fire pit with tinder already placed and ready to light, the same with the next and each one they checked.

"Spread out and don't touch anything. Leave no tracks," ordered Frazer and together with Stroma, he headed along the river bank towards the mouth, keeping off the sand and moving fast.

They saw fresh tracks of otters and foxes but no old tracks. The rain and tides had washed all that away, but otters and foxes didn't set fires. They stopped at the end of the flood plain where it re-joined the river.

"Norse!" said Stroma.

"And many of them," replied Frazer.

They waited until the rest of the warriors joined them. Every fire pit stood ready to light; every fire pit had ashes below the fresh fuel and all were built the same way.

"Go back to the horses," Frazer ordered. "Spread out and if you see anything on the way back hold the line and we will look, but don't touch anything no matter what."

They spread out as instructed and halfway to the Burn a warrior raised his hand and yelled. The line halted and Frazer went with Stroma to look. The warrior pointed and Stroma took a step forward with her hand outstretched.

"A sword!" she exclaimed but Frazer's hand stopped her in her tracks.

"Don't touch it! Leave it where it is," he hissed.

"Why? It's a sword.".

"A Norse sword, but was it dropped or left?"

"Why would anybody leave a sword?"

"Neither weather nor animals can remove a sword," replied Frazer, "only people. If we leave it, they won't know for sure if anybody has been here. If we take it and the Norse return, they'll be left in no doubt. They probably left it deliberately."

"You think they'll come back?" she gasped.

"That's the unknown like everything else, but if they do come back, we can be ready for them," Frazer grinned.

She smiled back reading his thoughts. Embo had failed in an

ambush here. She wouldn't make the same mistake and vowed to seize the potential by the horns.

"We leave everything as we found it. Now get out of here," urged Frazer.

Stroma and many others wanted to stay; wanted to assess the situation and come to terms with the obvious, that they had found the site of a large Norse army camp. They did not doubt that. Now they knew where the Norse had launched their attack on Torridon. It could only have been from the Dale of Helm. Frazer insisted they should go, leaving no sign of having been there. Reluctantly Stroma followed his lead. She had so many questions to ask by the time she came up alongside him, but with their horses galloping, speaking became impossible.

They reined into the Stockade at Brora as the light began to fade and felt a drop in temperature that made them shiver. They wasted no time in arranging food and assembling the council. Frazer explained what they had found to a stunned audience. He turned to Stroma.

"Now, is the time to think. Now is the time to discuss and now is the time to plan. We'll take our time and cover everything we know in great detail. The Norse might just have made their first mistake," he grinned and she got the message, but the questions escaped her lips immediately,

"Why were all the fire pits set and ready to light? Are they coming back?"

Frazer looked thoughtful; those were the questions that bothered him the most; he had spent hours in the saddle looking for answers and found one.

"I believe the fires were cooking fires," he responded, "and like us, they wouldn't light them in daylight because with that many, the smoke would have been seen from far away. At night with cooking pots on top, the light would have difficulty getting out. I think the fires were made ready but something happened before dark that prevented them from being lit. I think we know what happened to our messengers, they were heading for the mouth and would have run straight into a Norse Army."

He reached for the soup and they all followed, the silence only broken by the slurps of Callum and the appearance of the Cook.

"Snow and the wind's getting up," she announced, and they all groaned in unison.

Soon after dark, the Gab hit Torfness with a vengeance. The wind howled from the north with such ferocity, it turned the sea state white. Soon the longboats at rest on the beach came under threat from the waves sweeping around the back of the head and crashing along the ledge as white water. Two boats anchored close to the low water mark began to pound on the hard sand as if dropped onto solid rock.

Hundreds of warriors raced to get boats out of the water to the safety of the beach but with the tide flooding, the race was lost before it began. The wind and sea took charge of six longboats, driving them before the tide towards the beach end of the promontory. They crashed into each other and warriors ran for their lives in the dark with snow and sea-spray lashing their eyes. Kael ran to Sigurd and urged him to get as many boats out of the water as possible. All the Skiffs were easily dealt with and seven longboats made safe, but Kael threw something at Sigurd he couldn't ignore.

"If the wind shifts north-west, the boats on the beach will be destroyed. They must be pulled up higher," he bellowed against the howling wind.

"Sound the alarm," replied Sigurd immediately. "Get every warrior to the beach! And you, you stay here," he roared, seizing Kael by the arm and thrusting the old navigator onto a bench with a warning shake of his finger.

Then seeing Frode and a band of warriors assembled at the gate, awaiting orders, Sigurd joined them.

"You stay here to protect the fort," he commanded. "The others go and help get the boats higher out of the water. Open the gates!"

Warriors, male and female streamed from their camp at the Clarkley and all night the Norse struggled to salvage their fleet. As Kael predicted, the water came up to the beached boats not because of the wind direction but because of the tidal surge caused by the wind. Not only Norse warriors came to the rescue, but help also arrived from the most unlikely source of Ro-Sheen and Kayra.

The four great Dale of Clyde horses had remained stabled, with warriors looking after them like they were four pots of gold. Never had they seen horses this big. They were destined to go to Norway, but when the warriors were ordered to get them to help move the boats higher, they had no idea how to control them. They screamed in Norse to get them to move but the great beasts just stared back at them.

Sigurd was told they couldn't do anything with the dumb animals and his quick thinking sent a messenger back to the Fort, telling Kael to find Ro-sheen and Kayra and take them to the horses. He found them on the battlements with Frode and both women Smertaes raced to the stables, laughing loudly. They had never seen these horses before but from the description knew they were Dale of Clyde, the same as those in Tongue and they had watched them being worked.

Hearing commands they understood, the great beasts looked eager to comply. Leading two each, Ro-sheen and Kayra came to the beach and harnessed horsepower to that of man. In no time the boats were dragged clear of the water. They also managed to haul two additional Longboats up onto the sand, clear of the broken water. Snow blinded and froze everyone to the bone. When daylight flooded the grey sky, Sigurd discovered the scene of devastation was far less than he expected. Only the two longboats caught at the low water mark were sunk and sunk they could remain; no more damage could be done if they didn't pound. There was nothing left that could be achieved and people were ordered to clear the beach and seek shelter.

In the mountains, the situation was worse. Many trees had blown over along the side of the loch, but the Stockade held firm and Tusk cursed that the Gab hadn't come sooner. How long it would last didn't matter now, but he hoped it would last a long time. In Mahomack the boats were still on the shore and being mostly sheltered, the wind only succeeded in blowing the thatch from rooftops.

Urquhart and Ross sat beside a roaring fire for a private discussion about Sheena. They were in no doubt that the Norse would come for her and kill her. She was the Queen and as long as she lived, she would rule, not them. Sheena had to die, disappear or rule. The only person who could make that decision was Sheena.

They had no idea that Sheena shared the same thoughts but for different reasons. She knew she had panicked when Cluny was attacked. It was her who pleaded with the King to go to Cluny. She feared the attack was a decoy and the main advance would be on

Mahomack and Tain. The King had led the army to their deaths to please her. Her guilt ran deep and, in her mind, she had caused the downfall of Torridon. She didn't deserve to be queen. Only Enya and Ross witnessed her panic. Neither had raised the subject since nor had she.

Sine had now become a warrior and flashed her tattoo of the Bull at every opportunity. She had gone to Mahomack and the Field of Rocks and thanks to Krike, the word had spread and a new game evolved. Effigies of Norse appeared, complete with Norse helmets and chain mail. Spearing them became a popular pastime for warriors, young and old.

# Chapter 2

Torridon was given the new name of Torfness, but the view from the battlements remained the same. Frode looked out in every direction and all around appeared white. The sea was white also but not from snow and he knew how lucky they had been. If the Norse fleet had been caught in this storm it would have been destroyed, even if it lasted a short time. The sea state was such that out in the deep he knew the broken water would have swamped heavily-laden boats, Norse built or otherwise.

Towards noon the wind shifted to the east and shelter prevailed on the west side of the promontory. The wind became less but still strong enough to move great swathes of sea foam from the east beach and spew it out onto the west beach, shrouding everything in sight. Towards nightfall, the wind died as quickly as it had risen and an uneasy calm descended on Torfness.

Sigurd was by the great fire in the kitchen when Frode arrived. He heated his hands then sat opposite Sigurd. The Cook put soup and bread on the table and Frode ate heartily.

"How lucky were we?" asked Sigurd.

"Very lucky. That storm was the worst I've ever seen. I think it's blown itself out. The wind has died."

"Tomorrow we might get a chance to bring the two Longboats to the shore," said Sigurd.

"Launch my other three first," replied Frode. "Then we can worry about repairs."

"You have a plan?" asked Torf.

"I don't need a plan; I just need to be seen."

Sigurd threw Frode a look. He knew he meant the Longboats but the way it came across it was he, Frode, who had to be seen. Before Torf could get his teeth into Frode, Sigurd spoke,

"As soon as the weather clears, I'll lead the army inland. Torf will hold the Fort and your longboats can create havoc to the north. A lot of horses have found their way back from the battlefield but until we clear our enemies back towards the mountains, we can't burn the dead."

They knew their limitations and they knew the Picts would be watching for any mistake. If they could get between Sigurd's army and the Fort, they could surround and destroy the army and there would be thousands more Picts than Norse. That was his fear, one understood by all. In open battle, they would be massacred by a Pict army. Their losses at Kinloss had driven that point home and being a captive inside a Fort wasn't what Sigurd had in mind. He had to move south towards the mountains, and drive all before him.

Two days later, the sea lay calm and the sun shone out of a clear sky. They launched Frode's Longboats, using the Dale of Clyde horses, raising great excitement amongst Frode's warriors. The ledge became a hive of activity for loading supplies and checking rigging. The boats came in turn and then went to anchor. When the three were ready to leave, Frode announced that fifty warriors should get in each boat, the rest to go with Sigurd and they could sort out who was going where, between themselves. He gave them until sunset to do that.

On schedule, three sails were set and heading towards the setting sun. Frode wanted to see what lay to the west before turning north. With him came the navigator Kael and the experienced master, Magnus, who knew Pictland-Fjord better than anybody else. Sigurd left Torf to deal with the damaged boats and assembled his army to head south. They would traverse the high ground away from Cluny. His scouts had reported a crossing was possible to the east where a river turned west close to the sea and fed the lake. They crossed there and like the west beach at Torfness, the beach was sand as far as they could see.

Once across the thin strip of sandhills they followed the river and came into the forest. A well-worn track evolved from the sand and they followed it as it turned west. The forest looked dense and Sigurd ordered fifty mounted warriors to scout ahead. Two riders returned a short time later to tell him the forest gave way to open fields not far ahead and the army moved forward. Swathes of land had been cleared here but no dwellings were seen and they followed the track on high alert expecting to encounter Picts at every turn. The river came close again and Sigurd ordered five hundred warriors to cross and sweep the forest to his right. Seeing riders approach from ahead he waited for the arrival of four scouts and frowned seeing one horse was double mounted.

He stared at what sat behind one of his warriors, it was an old Monk. Ro-Sheen rode up to him.

"Who are you?" she demanded, slightly bewildered by the monk's appearance and he by her voice.

"I am Brother Giles. Tell the Norse they approach Elgin. Only the old remain and the settlement must be spared. There will be no resistance; all the warriors have gone," shouted the Monk.

Ro-Sheen interpreted his words and Sigurd stared at the monk for several moments before speaking.

"He will lead, and he will be the first to die if he lies," he said quietly to Ro-Sheen.

She passed the message on and the Monk reassured her he would live.

Sigurd read the signs that appeared all around him. The fields shone with new green shoots and much of the land had been cleared to the south. Thousands of trees had been felled, many thousands; no small settlement could support such an effort but all the dwellings were far away and widely spread.

Ahead stood a hill the shape of which alarmed Sigurd and the sight of a stockade on top radiated conflict. The hill stood almost sheer on all sides and getting a clear view of the Stockade was impossible. A defensive position of great merit if ever he saw one. He and the others fixed their gaze on it, trying to detect any sign of movement. They saw none but as they approached, they realised many dwellings existed below the mound. Sigurd ordered a halt. He had no intention of leading his army blindly into whatever lay ahead and he sounded a horn to alert those in the forest to stop.

Two riders appeared from the trees on the opposite side of the river and he gave orders for the five hundred to scout ahead and get behind the Stockade. The army would follow on the south of the river at a safe distance.

"I'll speak to the Monk," said Ro-Sheen and walked forward, something stirring in her memory.

"Where are your warriors?" she demanded.

He glowered at her and pointed up.

"Most of the warriors of Elgin lie dead at Kinloss. They died with the King. Others have scattered into the forest with the families of the dead," he shouted, although he did not need to raise his voice.

Ro-Sheen conveyed this information to Sigurd and his expression remained unchanged. Until proven otherwise they were on the hill ahead and he waved the army forward. When they reached two bow shots from the dwellings and three from the steep hill, he halted them and waited by the side of the river. With water on one side and clear land on the other, an attack could only come from ahead.

It seemed to take an eternity before movement was seen on the hill-top and a murmur ran through the observers when bodies appeared on the battlements of the Stockade. More bodies appeared and spread along the top of the hill but whether they were Norse or Pict was unclear.

Ears not eyes answered that question when a Norse horn was heard by all and the signal was four blasts.

"Answer them!" roared Sigurd and four blasts were returned.

When three came back, he smiled.

"Forward, watch for treachery," he yelled into the mounting war cries.

They didn't charge they walked; Sigurd would never charge with Ro-Sheen by his side.

"Elgin is bigger than Torfness," observed Sigurd.

"Now I remember," said Ro-Sheen, suddenly. "Imogen told me that in winter, many of the warriors of the standing army at Torridon were from Elgin. She couldn't ask where it was for fear of arousing suspicion."

Sigurd said nothing but his eyes took in much. This was indeed a prize to hold and destroying it for no reason might be something he would regret. He summoned Knud his commander and gave him orders.

"Let the army loose; they can plunder but don't destroy. Kill only those who resist."

Warriors within earshot didn't wait for Knud to relay Sigurd's orders. A sea of Norse warriors swept through the dwellings and some came streaming down from the hill. Four figures remained on the crest of the hill below the walls of the stockade and each had a Norse Sword in his back. Sigurd dismounted and ordered the Monk to be put on the ground.

"We wait here. The leaders will report to me," he said to Ro-Sheen. "Ask the Monk where all the livestock have been taken."

Ro-Sheen went to him.

"The pens are empty," he grunted and turned away from her.

Sigurd frowned. He could see that for himself. These were no small pens and would hold many animals. This place was a market, a large market, and it would be his. Any thought of destroying it was quickly erased and he fired a question at Ro-Sheen.

"Ask him what they call this hill?"

She grinned at the Monk's lengthy reply and left out the threat of eternal damnation when she translated.

"It is called Lady Hill. An Abbey is inside the Stockade. It is the Abbey of our lady the virgin Mary, the mother of Jesus," she said, whirling in alarm as a loud shout from behind made her jump.

"Gudrun comes!" said Sigurd, laughing at her reaction.

The commander galloped towards them and shouted to Sigurd,

"There is a bridge across the river behind the hill. We saw no sign of Picts. A track continues west and looks well used."

Sigurd left Ro-Sheen with the monk, Giles, and went to Gudrun. Knud followed and they had a discussion.

"Why did they run? Why didn't they hold the Stockade?" Ro-Sheen asked the Monk.

"To fight another day. They saw what happened to the Stockade at Cluny. This one is the same. Fire! They can't fight fire with more than half their warriors dead. Many families came from Torridon, saved by the cross and brother Aethan. Whoever burns this Stockade will destroy the Abbey of our Lady and will feel the wrath of God," he stated decisively.

Now Ro-Sheen did decide to warn Sigurd of the threat of divine intervention. He didn't laugh. He read the sign from the blood-covered cross he found in the fort at Torfness, a sign that demanded caution.

It was near noon before the warriors finished their looting spree. Their rewards were frugal. The Picts had enough time to evacuate with anything valuable including their livestock. Orders to follow the track across the bridge were given.

An assortment of Picts had been rounded up and stood with the Monk. They were of the same vintage and of no value. Knud held back many warriors to occupy the Stockade. Gudrun took the lead towards the bridge. Sigurd had lost his sense of direction and felt quite surprised to see water beyond the trees to his right after he had come through the forest of oak. He cursed and stared north across the water. He soon realised he was on the south side of what the Picts called the Laich and he called a Lake. He summoned the map makers.

Now he knew they were close to the battlefield and a pang of guilt swept him. It was short-lived. The dead could wait, his duty was to ensure they did not die for nothing. Sigurd was pleased with the look of this land. When the track reached Cluny, many carrion crows rose noisily from the bodies of the Picts who still lay where they had fallen. The sight and stench around the defence made them move quickly. They set up camp further west beside what he judged to be the river where his army had landed, that the Picts called the Find.

Outriders had reported bear and wolf but no Picts. They had travelled for most of the day and ended up only a short distance from Torfness. At this rate, it would take an eternity to reach the mountains and Sigurd had to re-think his strategy. However, he was satisfied with this day's revelations. Knud would secure the stockade and send for more warriors from Torfness to occupy it.

He gathered his chain of command and they agreed that the only way to make progress was to follow the tracks of the Picts leading south. They were few but had to lead to settlements. Travelling fast they could catch them off guard and kill them. Fifty warriors would lead and fifty would cover their backs. All had orders to move fast but not to get too far ahead of the main army following on foot.

At daybreak, the first fifty left their camp. They were followed closely by the second. All set off at the gallop back in the direction of Cluny and found the same track taken by the people of Cluny. They headed south with Sigurd's words ringing in their ears:

"Scout and find the rest of this King's army. If you find them get back. If you find only farmers, kill them if they resist and if they don't resist, take them prisoner."

Ro-sheen went with the scouts. Sigurd knew they needed the means to communicate and reluctantly let her go. When they came across a fork in the track, they looked for a sign and the most-used track led to the left, so they followed it at the gallop.

Without warning they came across the first village and charged, scattering livestock and screaming children who ran into thatched dwellings. Adults appeared with drawn swords and spears. Ro-Sheen screamed at them to lay down their arms or everybody would be killed. Many Norse arrows were notched and she raised her arm.

An old man appeared behind the warriors and walked towards Ro-sheen; he was unarmed.

"Tell your people to throw down their weapons or everybody will be killed, women and children also," she pleaded, seeing the hatred in the eyes of the armed and fear in those who stared from doorways.

He didn't speak just waved his arm and they lowered their weapons. He snarled at them and weapons were dropped.

"What do you call this place?" asked Ro-Sheen, lowering her arm slowly.

"Dallas," the old man replied and stared as the second wave of Norse arrived with thundering hooves.

"Get everybody out of the dwellings and assemble them over there," Ro-sheen ordered and her request was understood.

More women and children came out and the warriors ushered them towards a stone wall. It was a small band, only ten dwellings. Some aged warriors and families, but it was a start and she shouted in Norse for warriors to march them back towards Sigurd's force.

With most of his warriors on foot, Sigurd rode at the head with his commanders at a walking pace. When he saw prisoners approach with mounted warriors on either side, he called a halt and waited.

"They're from a village on the edge of the forest. The others are waiting there," said a warrior.

Sigurd wasn't impressed by the look of the prisoners; too old and too young.

"Take these prisoners back to Torfness," he roared and spurred his horse forward.

Before noon the last of his warriors arrived at Dallas and Sigurd took a close look at the place. No burning if it could be avoided, he didn't want to warn anybody they were coming, and his orders had been obeyed. They would burn this village later as an example. Looting it was for the moment and he let his warriors loose.

The land here had been cleared and planted. A large field of green shoots met his gaze and the mountains looked closer. Rested, they carried on as before following a track that led directly towards the mountains, but it wasn't long before the lead horses came into moorland thick with heather. Here the track was joined by another then both vanished, apart from deep grooves made by carts, which had filled up with water. The ground grew softer as they went. Soon a great hole filled with water appeared, where a cart had been dug out and then another. It continued like this until they reached firm ground and stopped. They had seen nobody. Plenty of deer and also grouse that startled the horses by exploding into flight under their hooves.

Although they had seen nobody, somebody had seen them. A hunting party arrived breathless at Lochindorb and sounded the alarm. Tusk came running from a longhouse on the shore.

"Norse! An army of Norse have crossed the Dava," the hunters chorused, their eyes wide in panic.

Many people flocked around Tusk and he raised his hand for silence.

"Wait!" he yelled and then addressed one of the hunters, his voice more under control. "How many Norse?"

"Many, about fifty horses," replied the warrior and Tusk smiled.

"That's not an army, that's the scouts. Where are they now?"

"They stopped when they came off the moor."

Tusk looked at the sun and ignored the murmurs.

"It will be nearly dark by the time they get here if the army is on foot. You've practised this many times; now get everything onto the island," he ordered and people scattered.

The livestock and some horses were on the west side of the Loch and there was very little food here; just some deer hung and some wild goat. They were quickly cut down and sent to the island. In a very short time, people were being rowed out to the Stockade, Tusk followed last.

Innes came running to meet him her eyes wide in alarm. Tusk let her rave while he and three warriors pulled the boat out of the water and carried it into the stockade. She was still trying to get his attention when the gate shut, and the beam was put in position. He could ignore Innes but not the hundreds of faces that surrounded him. Tusk wasn't going to speak to everyone individually, daughter or not, he had to address the mass.

"You built this stockade, now you know why you built it. Everybody calm down. The stockade at Cluny was old and dry, the timbers here are mostly fresh and green. We have enough food to last a year; we have enough water to last until the end of the world and we have boats. The Norse have no boats, they can't attack the stockade unless they swim. They can do nothing except burn the longhouses; even if they put us under siege, there is nothing they can do," Tusk announced and the atmosphere changed from fear to defiance. "We won't show them our full force. They might attack if they think we're weak. That will be your only chance to kill some because they won't attack twice!"

People scattered in all directions eager to claim a space and there was plenty of space. Three hundred warriors now swelled Tusk's band and they were armed to the teeth. So much so, that even the young warriors, male and female, bore real weapons and they stormed the battlements to wait. This gave Tusk an idea.

As expected, the scout force arrived, looked at the scene, whirled around and went back the way they had come. Sigurd was glad to get off the moor and when the Scouts returned at speed, he knew they had found something important.

"Don't tell me, show me," he instructed and spurred his horse.

Behind him, orders were given to increase the pace and they responded eagerly seeing their leader gallop into the distance. Sigurd slowed at Ro-sheen's signal and she came beside him, pointing at the longhouses.

"It could be a trap," she said.

Sigurd agreed and warned the warriors to stay away from the dwellings.

"We will wait here where they can see us, and we can see them," he said as he dismounted.

He was well out of bow shot but walked closer towards the loch to get a good view of the Stockade. He nodded his head and muttered to himself. This wasn't good. Whoever built this had left nothing to chance. Even if his army had boats, they would have nowhere to hide, the timbers were so close to the water. A killing zone surrounded this stockade, and he knew it couldn't be taken without losing hundreds, if not thousands of warriors."

They waited and heard cheering coming from the island, they sounded like children and even looked like children.

"That's children calling come and fight," Ro-sheen informed Sigurd.

"They won't shout for long," he answered, seeing the army coming closer.

It was as he said and the children went quiet when the endless stream of warriors came into sight. Sigurd raised his sword and brought it down heavily on his shield. The signal was read, and a great roar erupted from his warriors as they slapped their swords against their shields, like the sound of thunder.

"Now that's an army!" shouted Tusk and grinned as the children ran for their lives in terror.

The warriors swept through the longhouses and every building in sight but found no trap and no humans. The sun was getting low and Sigurd ordered them to camp in the dwellings and use their fires to cook. As the light faded, a rise of trout hit the surface of the water and a food supply was revealed. The loch was tranquil and to add to the tranquillity, a piper started playing a lament that drifted eerily across the water.

Sigurd smiled to himself; whoever was over there was either a fool or knew he was safe. He settled for the latter, but he wouldn't play his game. He ordered guards to be placed and headed into a longhouse. He found a sleeping platform and lay down.

"Call me when there's something to eat," he barked and closed his eyes.

# Chapter 3

At sea, Frode watched as the dark land closed on his longboats from both sides. Since leaving Torfness the tide had changed and they were going with it at an alarming speed. He sounded his horn four times before he heard a reply. He checked the stern light and ordered the boat master to hold the position. From the darkness, one boat loomed alongside and they waited for the third. It came and lines were passed from the centre boat to one either side. It was flat calm and they didn't have enough wind to manoeuvre against the tide. He didn't like the situation they had blundered into, neither did his boat master, Tarbat, who ordered sounding lines to be used.

Frode had intended to be close to the land at daybreak, close enough to put any observer into a frenzy of panic. Now it was himself and his warriors who were in a panic. A loud shout of "Rocks ahead!" sent shivers through everybody and warriors grabbed oars they couldn't use with boats on either side and suddenly water started splattering up between the hulls as the boats pitched and banged together. They braced for impact, but nothing happened. Everybody stared at the sea it looked alive with jabble! Small waves rose and sank everywhere and hissing spray shot up between the hulls, then it was over.

His heart pounding, Frode looked at the now calm water and let out a roar,

"Tide rip, the tide has turned!" he yelled to a great cheer and they knew they were safe.

Frode shook his head. He wouldn't make that mistake again.

"Single up, we row back the way we came!" he yelled and watched the three craft being untied.

"It will be daylight soon. Don't take us into the unknown again in the dark," whispered Frode and slapped his boat master on the back. The latter had warned him when they left Torfness to wait for daybreak and growled in reply.

The calm didn't last long and a breeze got up from the southwest when the first rays of light appeared; they were alarmed by how close to the shore the boats had come. The boat master altered to starboard and the two behind followed. Stern lights were doused and Frode stared up at the land then at where they had come from. He could only see land behind, not a passage, but he knew there was one. The oars were taken in and the great sails hoisted to everybody's delight and the longboats picked up speed.

The land loomed high and tree-clad as they traversed it with lookouts posted for any sign of obstructions ahead. Warriors curled up on thwarts and slept; they had been awake all night and had rowed for a long time but Frode was wide awake and drew their new land on sealskin. The boat master poked him on the shoulder and pointed ahead.

There the land was parting and Frode knew immediately where he was.

"This must be the gap we can see from Torfness," he said quietly and the master agreed.

Something else got his attention and it wasn't with his eyes. They listened as a deep thumping sound reached them. Boom, Boom, Boom. It reverberated to their souls and got louder as they approached the opening in the land. Those who slept opened their eyes in wonder and all eyes were fixed on the direction of the sound. Slowly the land parted, but they still couldn't see through the passage. It was wider than it looked from Torfness. On the east side, they picked out the first sign of life; a rider galloped up and over the top of the steep hill and disappeared.

The boats passed the high cliffs of the west side and the gap opened up to reveal a great waterway heading North West. Trying to ignore the haunting beat of the drum above them, they took bearings and marked the centre. Soon they could see smoke along the west side but no sign of life. Nothing but sound came from the west side.

"We go and look?" asked the boat master but Frode shook his head.

"No! Reduce sail and keep going. The rider will announce our arrival. Don't go faster than him," Frode grinned.

They watched as the gap closed and again smoke rose but this time from ahead, a lot of smoke and suddenly the drum-beat stopped.

In Balintore all hell was breaking loose and the sight of the great sails of the Norse passing the Souters triggered a mass exodus. Panic seized what remained of the population, mostly mothers, children and old people. Younger warriors from Nigg, Balintore, Invergordon and all the small villages had massed at Mahomack and Tain.

If the sight of the Norse boats induced panic, the direction they came from caused utter shock. Where had they come from? They knew they would come, but never from the west. People streamed out of the village and headed up to the high ground. The galloper from Nigg had alerted Balintore. The great Drum on Cromarty had alerted Nigg, sending gallopers to Mahomack and the Field of Rocks.

The people stared from the high ground as the three Longboats came abreast of the village and all breathed a sigh of relief when they continued slowly east.

In Tain and Mahomack warriors mounted and on foot, streamed towards the Field of Rocks. The mounted dropped off, two at a time and went back for more.

Krike held them on the high ground and there they spread across the hill; several hundred were joined by another thousand and they passed the paint around with abandon. The dots to the west grew bigger and by the time Sheena and Ross arrived they looked like boats.

"We stay away from your father," said Ross and pushed her mount with his to the right.

She threw him a look but went with him to where Krike stood on a large rock.

Urquhart and Sine stood downhill, proud of the army. There they watched the boats approach and they came close. Frode had seen the movement on the hill and ordered the master to come to port then resume his original course. The two behind followed suit and the warriors on all three boats could be clearly seen.

"Your enemy is putting out feelers, Sine," said Urquhart.

She was staring transfixed by the boats, her knuckles white gripping her spears and she didn't take her eyes off the Norse when she asked,

"Will they attack, father?"

"No! They won't attack unless they're drunk. They've come to look, just to look. They scout the coastline, make maps and find places defended and undefended. Then they will plan first before they attack. Daughter, when they come, there will be more than three boats, thirty more like."

Frode marvelled at the blue mass on the hillside and the sight of many Norse Shields among them triggered a response he had not foreseen.

They came closer and Krike broke the silence,

"Their sails are at half sheet; they're not in a hurry," he said and Ross frowned. If this was them going slow, he dreaded to think of the speeds they could achieve.

"If one of them came after us we wouldn't have gone far," he said to Sheena but like her sister, her knuckles were white. She held the hilt of her sword and stared at the Longboats.

"Shields!" ordered Frode.

His men took them from outside the longboat. He slapped his sword against his own shield and they followed. Warriors in the boats close behind did the same and the noise reached the observers.

Urquhart lifted his sword and shield and a thousand warriors did likewise. The crescendo of steel and war cries rose deafeningly against the oncoming Norse who banged their shields harder and louder, screaming. Some female warriors went into cat mode and Frode feared they would jump into the sea. Some warriors bit their shields and the boats listed alarmingly.

The master grabbed a hunting horn and gave a mighty blast. Frode screamed at them to stop and get away from one side of the boat. Water poured in through the oar holes and the boat listed alarmingly. They stopped and spread out but stared in silence at the great swathe of noise and warriors on the hill.

"I won't do that again either," said Frode.

The master smiled at him sarcastically. "That's two mistakes in one day you've made," he said and Frode grinned.

He marked the map and traced his finger east, to where the land ended and the entrance to another Fjord began. Smertae had drawn the map and he would correct it.

"Full sail!" he commanded and warriors leapt into action.

From the shore, they saw the huge sail billowing in the wind and the hounds of the sea responded quickly. The warriors on the hill stared in admiration as the Longboats picked up speed and kept heading east. They let out a final roar and shook their weapons at the retreating enemy.

"Back to Mahomack!" shouted Urquhart.

"I'll come with you!" announced Krike, jumping onto the back of Ross's horse.

Sheena rode to her father and Sine. Ross followed with Krike muttering about how many lobster traps he could get on a Longboat and Ross didn't know if he was joking or not.

"We stay in Mahomack tonight," said Urquhart and nobody argued.

Meanwhile, at Lochindorb, Sigurd had spent the morning surveying the scene and he had a plan of the loch and island drawn up. His scouts had rounded the loch to the west side and some had followed a track east; it appeared the stockade was the same from the other side, but the gate was there. All information he could use but Sigurd knew he was being used. If he tried to take the stockade, his army would be exposed and he had no intentions of taking such a risk, but he would try to communicate. Before heading east towards the smoke, he sent for Ro-Sheen who arrived quickly.

"Take a white flag and tell them if they surrender, we will let them live," Sigurd ordered.

Ro-Sheen laughed, and then fell silent.

Tusk had kept the children on the battlements tormenting the Norse since daylight. But during the night, every warrior inside the stockade manned the battlements. The children were getting braver. A young warrior ran down and told Tusk a warrior on a horse was waving something and Tusk hurried to the battlements.

"They want me to send a messenger," he said, frowning and looking carefully.

The Norse warriors had all withdrawn well back from the edge of the loch and their leader sat on his horse in front of them.

"Launch a boat!" commanded Tusk and a murmur ran through the children.

Innes looked at him, not quite sure what he intended to do.

"How many arrows have you made?" he demanded.

She stared at him biting her lip.

"Tell me!"

"Five but-,"

"Five is enough. Get Cian into a boat and come behind me. Tell him to stay well back. If I raise one arm and drop it, he has to fire one arrow over the messenger; two arms, hit anything he can," Tusk barked and yelled again for a boat to be launched.

Innes went to find Cian. She carried the bow of the Angles and five long arrows her father ordered her to finish, as she was good at putting on flight feathers.

Sigurd grinned when he saw the people on the stockade. They were bigger and they were many. From behind the island, a small boat appeared and came towards Ro-Sheen. She walked her horse knee-deep into the water and waited as ordered and watched as a second boat come into view well behind the first.

Two people sat in the first boat. One rowed, while the other on the front held something brown. As the boat neared, she realised it was a hide stretched over a frame. It would be a large shield if needed; this man wasn't taking any chances.

The boat stopped within speaking range and Ro-Sheen knew it wouldn't come any closer. The second boat also stopped far behind the first.

"Tell your Chief if he tries anything, you'll get an arrow through you," growled Tusk.

She hesitated.

"Tell him!"

Ro-Sheen did as he asked and laughter erupted through the ranks. The army and Ro-Sheen were well out of bow shot from the stockade or any boat, but Tusk's boat wasn't far from the Norse. Any wrong move from Tusk would result in a shower of arrows.

"You laugh. Tell him not to laugh, just watch!" roared Tusk and Ro-Sheen relayed his message.

Tusk raised his arm and let it fall; Cian loosed an arrow from the mighty longbow of the Angles and they gasped as it sailed high above Ro-sheen and buried into the ground halfway to Sigurd. Even Tusk was surprised but he didn't show it.

"They don't laugh now," said Tusk. "What do you want?"

"If you surrender, Sigurd Jarl of Orkney will let you all live," replied Ro-Sheen quickly. She didn't like being a target.

"You go back and tell Jarl Sigurd to get off my land and if he comes back, he might not live! Now, turn your horse and go back."

She obeyed quickly.

The hide Tusk held was raised again and the boat went backwards a long way before turning to face the island. Innes breathed a sigh of relief.

Ro-Sheen was shaking; she was a teacher, not a warrior. She reached down and plucked the arrow from the ground before heading for Sigurd.

"He says you must leave his land," was all she reported, fearful of antagonising Sigurd.

"What else?" Sigurd smiled.

"Not to come back or you may die," Ro-sheen replied and bit her lip.

"Give me that," he said pointing to the arrow and she handed it to him.

"It would take a mighty bow to fire that!" he said and handed it to eager hands of onlookers, one being Astrid.

"We head east. Our scouts have seen smoke. We follow the tracks and we will find more settlements. He wants to stay in a stockade, we will give him some guests. Don't burn these dwellings, we may need them," Sigurd laughed, and his scouts took the lead.

He stared at the stockade on the island and its jeering occupants.

"You! Whatever your name is, will answer to me," he glowered and spurred his mount forward.

Tusk watched them leave, his face set in hate.

"They head for Grantown, father," said Innes and Tusk grunted.

"They won't find many in Grantown and their messengers will warn Huntly," he replied.

A settlement on the banks of the Spey was the source of the smoke but more importantly, it was also the location of a bridge across this wild river that both north and south of the bridge could not be crossed. Like Elgin, the place was abandoned but showed signs that horses had left going east very recently. Scat was still warm and Sigurd ordered his scouts to follow at the gallop.

As at Elgin, the settlement was looted but left intact. With the army safe across the river, Ro-Sheen learned from some olds left behind, that the river was called the Spey and the settlement named Grantown. Before noon, Norse scouts returned to the army as it continued east along the track.

The Scouts had overtaken ten Picts double-mounted and killed them at the cost of three Norse warriors. They had five more horses and believed they had stopped messengers from warning others ahead. This inspired Sigurd. Now there was a chance to surprise his enemy and he urged the army on through the dense forest that seemed to stretch forever.

For the next four days, Sigurd's army swept east as far as Huntly where they had a battle with eighty Pict warriors trapped in an unfinished stockade who wouldn't surrender. In victory, the Norse moved quickly east. Mapmakers were busy and noted every outstanding detail. Rivers, mountains, forest and moor they crossed all and found very few Picts. Many villages and every dwelling they found, they plundered. A few prisoners were captured and herded along with much livestock and Sigurd decided to follow the river east. It seemed the Picts were keeping out of his way and if he couldn't find them there was no point in looking for them. A small stockade where the river met the sea, a place called Banff was abandoned and burned, not by the Norse but by the Picts.

Following the battle at Huntly, Sigurd decided to send five hundred warriors north on what looked like a well-used track. The vanguard of the five hundred came upon a large village built on either side of a small river and surrounded by strange-looking buildings. At first, they thought they were smokehouses for fish but inside they smelt of anything but fish, and barrels could be seen within buildings with slats on the roofs.

Warriors found a sealed barrel and broke it open. It contained the spirit of the Picts and to prove it, they drank some and screwed their faces up with the taste, which was horrible, but soon they felt on top of the world and shared more of it around. They found more barrels and the command knew they had to stop this before the warriors went mad.

The temptation to set fire to every building and break open every barrel was rampant. Especially when the liquid hit the flames of cooking fires and ignited.

Commanders had their orders and meeting with little or no resistance the need to set an example lessened. The Picts had fled and Sigurd's orders were to move quickly. Before nightfall, they came across a great, fast-flowing river and found a crossing where the track led. Bears were seen along its banks. This valley had large flood plains and the soil was rich. Many dwellings and much land had been cleared here. Fields of green shoots abounded and again the Picts had fled into the forest. All along this valley they pillaged and herded what livestock they could gather. On the east side, there were no dwellings and the forest reached the river bank Their orders were to find a large river, follow it to the sea, and wait.

Along the coast, Sigurd had swept the area clean and taken some prisoners. He sent five hundred warriors inland to secure his flank and plundered all before him. This land was better than anything he could have dreamt of. Fertile and mostly flat he would flood this land with settlers and warriors. They kept heading west and passed many settlements around natural harbours and the inhabitants, mainly fishermen and families were gathered up along with everything they owned including their boats. Eleven boats followed his progress. Warriors more used to Longboats were glad to be on the sea instead of their feet.

Scouts reported a large river ahead and part of the Norse army camped on the far bank. He sent the scouts to gather the five hundred on his flank and kept marching.

The entire army assembled at the mouth of the river, which Ro-Sheen had found out was called the river Spey. It bore the same name as the one high in the mountains, not far from Tusk's stockade. This revelation was greeted with great reverence by the map makers. Now they had a direct link to the base of the mountains and from here they could also see Morven across the sea and took bearings on it. They had much information to work on when they returned to Torfness and had predicted the distance from it to the mouth of the Spey was less than one day's march.

They used the fishermen's boats to ferry the army over to the west side of the Spey and swam the horses. They knew this river would yield many salmon. A Pict settlement was built here and like the others, it had been abandoned. The river flowed fast, but it spread at the estuary and only deep channels had to be crossed. However, at high tide it would flood a large area and Longboats could get here.

The map makers' predictions were accurate, and the scouts came to the river that bordered the high ground leading to Torfness at noon. By the time the light started to fade the entire army had returned to great cheer. Prisoners were herded into the lower stockade and livestock penned at Backlands.

Sigurd had assigned Ro-Sheen to find out the name of the man who defied him.

"His name is Mael Brigte," she grinned after questioning some prisoners and laughed when Sigurd tried to get his tongue around it.

"Brosme Tann, Buck Tooth, is the name they use for him?"

"In our language, they call him Tusk, it means the same," Ro-Sheen smiled.

"Tusk is good! I will also know him as Tusk," Sigurd smiled back at her "I saw you with tears in your eyes when the music came over the water. Why?"

"It was a lament. Music for the dead," she replied.

"You can go and join your friends, Ro-Sheen," he said and she took her leave of him.

Sigurd gathered his command and most agreed the expedition had been a great success. However, questions were raised as to why the stockade on the island wasn't put under siege or why they didn't burn everything in sight?

"It's what he wanted," responded Sigurd. "Make us angry and angry men make mistakes. If he stopped my army there, he would have given the Picts time to assemble theirs and cut us off from Torfness. We didn't stop and they fled before us, all except the warriors at Huntly. We killed them and burned their stockade. The man you speak of is known among the Picts as Tusk. We will deal with Tusk when the time is right. He won't be going anywhere. You ask why we didn't burn their dwellings? Why burn what belongs to us? If we destroy what they left behind, the Pict farmers won't come back to gather their harvest. Do you want to gather it?" Sigurd smiled at the expressions of those used to rape and pillage raids as they tried to digest his meaning.

He banged the table with the handle of his Sword and yelled,

"Now, we have a duty to perform! A duty that won't wait any longer. Two thousand dead warriors lie on the battlefield. Tomorrow at dawn take these monks to the battlefield. I want to see the sky black with smoke before noon. It's time!" Sigurd bellowed to great cheer.

# Chapter 4

Enya was with Frazer at Brora when the Norse boats passed the Field of Rocks. They knew nothing of their approach until a galloper came from the beach in a frenzy. Stroma, along with her council made an instant decision to head for the Helm with a hundred warriors as fast as they could ride.

Stroma and Enya rode side by side with a warrior behind each. Only fleeting glimpses of the boats were seen as they followed Frazer who led them inland, insisting they should keep out of sight.

"Let them enter the Helm then we can attack them. If they see us, they won't come into the river," he declared and that made sense to Stroma and Enya.

Callum assembled three hundred warriors after the horses left and sent them on foot towards the Helm. They found their rhythm, a sustainable hound gait and followed quickly.

The three Longboats heeled over to port and sliced through the water. The wind had increased a little and was in their favour. Horses followed them unseen but double mounted, they tired and slowed. Outriders reported the boats had gone out of sight behind the high ground close to the river mouth and close to shore. There was great joy among the chasers when they reached the river. Now they would go on foot along the west side that looked down on the river and leave the horses out of sight.

The master of Frode's boat was well pleased. Frode had put his name to a point of land they had passed. It lay to the east of where the Pict army was seen, Frode named this point Tarbat-Ness and Tarbat felt honoured. He knew exactly where they were now and could see the tide rip from the river stretching far out to sea. He brought Frode's attention to this, who told him to go around it. He was busy working on several maps with the navigator.

Stroma and Enya were among the first warriors to reach the crest of the high ground and bellied through the heather to peer down on the Helm. A bear with cubs sniffed the air and walked leisurely along the riverbank. The Helm was empty. They sighed and turned on their backs. The Longboats had gone past and were heading towards Sinclair at Dunbeath; there was nothing they could do to warn him.

It was a dejected army that returned to Brora. Like Urquhart's warriors, they were pumped full of fight and painted for battle. Like Urquhart's warriors, they drank an antidote and proclaimed the Norse too frightened to land because they must have seen them.

Frode and indeed his little armada were enjoying their new role of creating turmoil and soon after passing the Helm, fishing boats were seen close to shore. The Longboats headed straight for them and there was great hilarity at the speed the fishers rowed and even more when they rowed straight onto the shore among the rocks and ran for their lives up the steep cliffs, abandoning their boats to the elements.

All along the shore, they chased boats while keeping their course north. They came close under a high cliff and the lookouts pointed to the stockade high above them. Sinclair was informed and came running. Panic ensued and he sent warriors to follow the boats. The same turmoil ensued at Wick but the Longboats kept going until they reached a point they knew well, the entrance to Pictland Fjord.

There, Frode had a decision to make; either carry on the short distance to Kirkwall or go through Pictland Fjord and create more turmoil. He consulted his navigators and they decided to head for Tongue first. They would go through the Fjord.

They waited for the tide to change twice. Frode wanted to pass close to the Pict stronghold that they could see from Orkney and he wanted to go close in daylight. Tactics had changed from stealth to blatant threat. Keeping up with the Longboats was impossible but when they held back, the riders not only caught up with them they passed them, and messengers reached Thurso.

Sinclair had sent Brody with twenty mounted warriors and seeing the Norse waiting for the tide, Brody concluded they were going through the Sea of the Dead. If they were heading for Orkney, they wouldn't have held back and they would have been much further out to sea. Where they were holding, they would catch the full force of the tide as soon as they rounded the headland. Brody and his warriors were exhausted by the time they reached Thurso to raise the alarm. Back at Dunbeath, Katrion was in hysterics that the Norse had come from the south and she feared for Stroma and her people.

Sinclair feared for his people and cursed the wet ground that lay between him and Thurso. There, warriors painted for battle had massed along the beaches, more than a thousand of them, staring east.

Pictland Fjord had been described to Frode as the ride of his life. The wind came off the land and they adjusted sails to capture it. They cleared the small island on the east side at the speed of a galloping horse while the sea seemed to be still all around them; it was going at the same speed as the boats.

Tarbat steered closer to the land. Kael knew where the Pict stronghold stood and aimed straight for it as soon as it came into view.

They came into view from Thurso also and a ripple of yelps ran the length of the warriors on the beach. The yelps increased to full-blown war cries as the boats closed the distance quickly and still, they headed straight at Thurso. Shields were recovered aboard the Longboats, a sign that the warriors were arming themselves and there was great hope they would keep coming. At the last moment, the lead boat went to starboard and sailed past close to the screaming Picts.

The Norse didn't go crazy like the last time but gave a good sign of intent with swords and shields, as each boat passed.

"We scared them away," scorned Grigor.

"We scared nobody. They never intended to land, they're playing games, that's what they're doing," Brody growled, knowing he and many more had near broken their necks for nothing. "They're feeling us out. Finding our strength and where we are, but why did they come from the south? It doesn't make sense!" he seethed, throwing his sword onto the table.

Frode was ecstatic and so were his warriors. Now they headed further out to sea, intending to stay there out of the strong tide until they headed into Tongue, which Magnus assured them they would reach before dark.

Their show wasn't over for this day. From Ben Loyal they were seen entering the Kyle and warriors sped back to Torrisdale in panic. They would set fire to everything and head for Thurso taking the old people with them. The turmoil to the south only matched what Drest had been dealing with for many days. His warriors were frustrated, had drunk everything in sight and were ready to wander. Drest was nearing breaking point when the Norse horns sounded in the Kyle and the Stockade gate was jammed with bodies trying to get out to go and look.

Great cheers met the Longboats and they saw a man they knew well standing on the bow of the first. Frode had never been here but he was impressed by the reception and Drest ushered his commanders into the Stockade with visible relief. He screamed for somebody to get Isla and she came quickly.

She listened to the leader and her jaw dropped.

"What's he saying? What's he saying? What's happened?" Drest yelled at her.

"The King is dead. The Queen is dead. Sigurd has taken Torridon," Isla translated quietly in a state of shock.

Drest jumped to his feet and ran to the battlements. He bellowed the news to the warriors and the world. He was so happy. He, Drest, had backed the right army and would be rich. His joy was infectious and great cheering erupted from his audience. They would all be rich, Drest had told them so.

After they ate a great feast with Drest and several of his leaders, Frode asked that the maps he drew be taken to the Stockade. He made a strange request to Isla that he wanted a Tattooist. Both arrived at the same time and Frode spread out the first sealskin. On it was his voyage from the inner Fjord to Tarbat Ness and he invited Drest to look but not touch. Drest took a little time to find his bearings. He had only seen things from the land, but he spotted the gap.

"The Sutors," he muttered. Then everything made sense.

He pointed to the left of the Gap.

"Eilan Dubh, Black Isle, tell them they were lucky they never went through there," he rasped.

Isla translated.

"Why?" asked Frode.

"He asks why," she told Drest.

Drest shook his head and looked at the roof as if in a trance. He flashed his eyes suddenly at Frode and pinched his own ear lobe. He wiggled it violently and let go. Then slowly raised and lowered his open hands above the Sealskin.

"Boom, boom, boom," replied Drest and stared around at all of them. They nodded in understanding and he smiled. "Tell them they heard the death drum of Cromarty. When you hear that you are going to die!"

He listened while Isla struggled to get his message across and realised, she would never manage it. He ran to the kitchen and returned with a rolling pin for making oatcakes and the Norse stared at him curiously. So too did Isla. What followed next was something between hilarity and agony.

Drest put both his hands together, "Prisoner!" he said and Isla translated.

He pointed to the Black Isle, then took the rolling pin and made moves as if sharpening it to a point; they nodded in understanding.

"Bend over," he snapped to Isla and she did so.

"They put grease on it and ram it up your arse," said Drest going through the motions.

They all followed this weird ritual with wide eyes.

"Then they stand you up and put the pole in a hole. Stand up Isla. Then the pole goes up your arse into your guts. You slide down it until it tears your guts to bits. But! Before you die, the bastards cut your head off. Don't go to the Black Isle, we don't go near it. The Picts are there," Drest declared and Isla tried her best to translate with a red face.

Now they understood but not the part about Picts being on the island. As far as the Norse were concerned, Drest was a Pict and so was she. That was a strange statement, but the rest was clear and they shuddered at the thought of what the savages did to prisoners.

Frode returned to the map and they spoke quietly amongst themselves for a short time then he addressed Isla.

"Tell the Tattooist to follow the lines on the skin. Everything that's drawn, follow everything!"

She did as he asked.

They took the next skin to another table and spread it out leaving the Tattooist space to work and viewed the next map. It was late into the night before they finished and Drest disappeared for a short time. He returned smelling like a pig, but he held a flagon aloft in triumph.

"The last of the Whiskey!" he announced and Magnus grinned. He was getting used to this drink and broke the good news to his companions.

By the time Frode reached Stromness to drop off Magnus and Kael, Sigurd had returned with his army to Torfness. Between them, they had created turmoil of epic proportions and Frode still had to undertake the return journey.

The Turmoil in the north was matched by the turmoil in the south and without leadership, the tribes were at odds with each other over what to do, so nothing was done. The window of opportunity, the power vacuum, would be short-lived. Sigurd knew it, his command knew it and unlike the Picts, the Norse worked together. Again, Sigurd demanded foresight. They were confident they could hold what they had with the army they had. To split his force and attack the north with only half and leave the other half in Torfness would be reckless. They needed another four thousand warriors to secure one front and attack the other. Two thousand remained in Orkney. Magnus would send them and Harold would send the rest.

When Frode returned they would have greater knowledge of the challenge. Frode would gather information and make maps. Until he returned, they had to continue to show their strength.

The shield maidens had laid claim to the entire building used by the Smiths and they were joined by Imogen and Kayra. When Ro-Sheen arrived, she had much to tell. The stock of charcoal was greatly reduced, the great hide bellows silent, but the place felt warm and comfortable.

Some went to the battlefield to burn the dead but returned quickly. They had little to say about what they had seen. Imogen thought about Sigurd's idea for some time before sharing it with Kayra, who wanted to go immediately. But Imogen knew the dangers and dwelt on them much longer.

Listening to the tale from a shield maiden about a lover she dumped and showing where his mark had been tattooed on her arm, Imogen's mind went into overdrive. She inspected the Tattooist's work closely; the mark had been covered over with flesh coloured ink. Something she had never seen before. The mark could still be seen, but only on close inspection and the shield maiden declared her new lover's mark would have covered it up had he not died on the battlefield.

Kayra had tattoos, Smertae tattoos, and so did Ro-Sheen. She only had a Celtic butterfly on her back and it could easily be covered by what she wore. Imogen's tattoo meant nothing to anybody, but the Smertae tattoos identified them as Smertae. Imogen had never worked alone, always with Halfdane. Now she had Kayra and they had formed a bond. Kayra learned quickly and her hatred was under control. Now Imogen saw a chance to remove the Smertae brand from her and discussed it with her.

Kayra was keen to do this and even keener after inspecting the work done on the Shield Maiden.

Imogen went to Sigurd and put her proposal to him.

"It's a start, but we don't have much time. You must get into the north quickly," he said.

She left him with his commanders, but Astrid followed and called her back.

"I have some of the colour you need. See here," she said and pointed to her bicep.

Imogen looked, then smiled. She had never noticed the tattoo on Astrid.

"Come," said Astrid, "I will give it to you but stay quiet and give me back what you don't use."

"I promise," said Imogen and followed her to the building of the Smiths.

Astrid recovered a small pot from her bundle and handed it to Imogen, putting her finger to her lips as she did so, then ran back to join the command.

The Tattooist didn't take long to cover the Smertae tattoos; they were only small, put on when Kayra was a young child and had faded with time. Ro-Sheen wanted hers covered also and reluctantly Imogen agreed as this ink was a precious commodity, sought by many. Imogen went back up the wall, leaving the two Smertae sitting on the steps of the great well, dug deep and carved out of the solid rock. She found Astrid and gave her the small pot back as promised.

Ro-Sheen felt left out and unsure of her role. Kael had gone. She had Mungo's bundle and his fish. Imogen had taken Kayra and she felt alone.

Imogen hadn't paid much attention to the prisoners. They were a mix of old and young, most of them fishermen and families. They were of little interest to her and she didn't go near them. Now she decided she would and was bundled among them with little ceremony other than a slap across the face. They stared at her then helped her to her feet. She knew what she wanted; the young wouldn't know so she went to sit by some older men and hung her head between her knees.

"Who are you?" asked one.

"Where have you come from?" asked another.

She didn't answer, just lifted a tear-stained face. She was good at that.

"I need to know the mark of the Caledonii," she sobbed and buried her head again.

A finger poked her on the shoulder and a man replied,

"The Caledonii wear a thistle, that's their mark," he said and Imogen hugged him before collapsing on the ground beside them.

They tried to revive her but couldn't. Then they screamed for the guards who carried the limp body from the slave compound and out of sight. One laughed as Imogen sprung to her feet. She had what she wanted; now she and Kayra had to get tattooed quickly.

A thistle was easy to draw; Ro-Sheen drew one using just the outlines and both spies returned to the tattooist. Within a short time, both had thistles on their right biceps. They asked him to do it lightly, to make it look older when the scab came off. He agreed.

"We will go west into Caledonii country then head towards Mahomack - the hard way," said Imogen.

"On foot?" Kayra exclaimed and Imogen laughed.

"That would take a long, long, time. We'll go and see Sigurd, come on," she said and pulled Ro-Sheen to her feet.

As soon as they found him, Imogen launched in immediately.

"The tribe to the west is called the Caledonii we have their mark. We must come from the west and we must have horses," she stressed.

"You're rich, are you going to buy them?" he jibed.

She grinned. She was getting used to his humour.

"Good ones or bad ones?" he asked.

"Not good, not bad, with no brand," she replied; she knew exactly what she wanted.

"Go and find what you want. Then after I finish with the commanders, you will brief me on your intentions. Is there anything else you need?"

"Yes! Why do you keep Ro-Sheen down there with strangers when she should be up here? If we leave, you will only have one translator left," she said and winked at him.

Sigurd smiled. She was giving him Ro-Sheen. This Irish warrior was like none he had ever known.

"When they leave, Ro-Sheen, you will come here," he instructed and she bowed.

# Chapter 5

Imogen had traversed this ground before and knew a great river lay ahead, a river she knew couldn't be crossed. The Smertae had told her it was called the Inver and came from a great loch to the west. The settlement she and Halfdane had skirted was also called Inver, the biggest the Caledonii had. This information was scant but stuck in her mind. She had a good memory and couldn't function without one, a fact she had conveyed to Kayra many times.

Six days later, they galloped along the sandy beach towards the River Find. It was early morning and the sun shone. They had equipped themselves with weapons from the battlefield. Two shields with sword damage, a Pict spear each and two dirks. Two black mares they rode had no brand and were quiet natured. Imogen knew they had to travel by day and rest at night. They had a great challenge ahead, but she had overcome the worst and removed the sealskin boots from Kayra. She had to get the shield maidens to pin her down while she did so. While Kayra felt less than happy wearing the boots of a fisherwoman, the fisherwoman felt worse forced to walk around barefoot. Ro-Sheen kept Kayra's boots safely for her.

They skirted every sign of smoke or movement and from high on a heather-clad slope, they looked across at the Black Isle and the settlement of Inver below. Now they would go towards the high mountains to the west and find this great Loch. They found a dip in the heather well away from trees and made camp. Wolves lurked somewhere, but they were confident no bears would appear. Wolves made noise and so did horses. They had no fire, but ate cold fresh meat, and would last for their journey, which Imogen thought could take four days, all going well.

As they feared, the river was running in spate like all the rest. They couldn't swim the mouth without being seen so they followed the river for a long way west, keeping to the forest that lined both banks. Ahead they could see a great swath of sky and the trees to their right peeled off to the north. They carried on for a short time and Imogen cursed. Ahead lay a great stretch of water so big they couldn't see the end of it but that wasn't the cause of her curse. The land rose steeply on their side of the Loch and that was also obvious for as far as they could see.

Imogen had one more option and that was to swim the horses across the Loch before it got too wide. There, the current would be much less than in the river, but she dreaded the thought.

As they neared the Loch, they spotted movement ahead through the trees on the opposite bank and stopped. They dismounted and led their horses. The river made enough noise to muffle their approach which was also hidden by trees. Suddenly a small boat came into sight and they froze. It went to their left towards their side and Imogen moved quickly.

From the cover of the trees, they looked along the Lochside. Two men with bows got out of the boat and pulled it up onto the bank clear of the water.

"Stay here," whispered Imogen and crouching low she went ahead, her heart beating fast. If they were hunters they would leave, and they could steal their boat. The other option was to kill them and steal their boat. One way or the other, the boat was hers.

It seemed to take forever for the men to walk the short distance and enter the forest. She knew by their actions they were hunters and she ran quickly back to Kayra.

"Give them time to get up the hill then we move fast. Pet your horse, stroke him and pet him, let him want to follow you," she whispered and showed Kayra what to do. The last thing she wanted was a frightened horse.

They moved swiftly, pulling the boat into the water and grabbing both horses by the reins. Kayra sat at the back while Imogen had the oars.

"Go!" said Kayra and the horses followed without a whimper. Almost immediately they were swimming and she tied both reins to the back of the boat. She grabbed their two shields and staring out between them, she waited for an arrow.

"You can put them down now, we're out of range," said Imogen and dug in with the oars.

They found two horses on the other side, tied to a tree and they landed beside them. Kayra released their horses and both came out of the water so fast the two women had no time to run before the beasts shook water all over them.

"So much for keeping dry," Kayra spat, then looked curiously at what Imogen was doing.

"Why are you pushing their boat out into the Loch?"

"They'll be more interested in getting their boat back than chasing us. If, that is they even saw us. We leave their horses," Imogen grinned and mounted.

They galloped away through the trees back the way they had come and didn't stop until they could see smoke from a high point.

"Now we must stick to the forest. Two more days and we will be in Mahomack," Imogen declared cheerfully.

Meanwhile, Frode had set sail from Stromness and gone north, intending to go around the island and keep out of sight of the Picts, as they had done when they left Tongue. The Picts would think they were still to the west. Magnus had his orders and Drest had his.

They crossed over the entrance to Pictland Fjord well out to sea and headed south. By daybreak, they could see Morven and sailed towards it. Now, he had to take a risk, a calculated one. Frode planned to go into the Dornoch Firth where Mahomack was situated, not far inside, just enough to put the fear of God into the inhabitants and map the interior.

They sailed close to shore and saw much smoke on the starboard side coming from somewhere south of the river they used to hide their fleet. He marked the position on the map and stared out to sea. The wind was coming from the land and it was sufficient to give them good speed, but they only had one point of reference, Tarbat Ness, and that lay to seaward at the end of the headland. Once past it, they would find themselves inside this unknown Fjord.

In Mahomack life stirred, slowly. Suddenly it flew into a frenzy as the alarm horn sounded repeatedly and all eyes turned seaward at the terrifying sight of three Norse boats heading straight for them. Everyone ran for their weapons. Frode grinned broadly when he heard the horn.

"It's all yours," he bellowed to Tarbat. "Turn when you want. I've seen all I need to see."

Several times he wanted to shout at Tarbat to turn but the man knew his boat and kept going until he only had room to make a sharp turn, by which time the boat risked coming into bow range from the shore. Frode sighed with relief when the boat turned quickly to port and those behind followed. Immediately the sail was hoisted to its full height and the Longboats raced towards the open sea.

Frode heard the yells and screams hurled at them from the shore and saw his warriors waving joyfully back as if at old friends and all of them were laughing.

"A lot of shit will be running down a lot of legs," he said.

Tarbat just smiled and cast a glance at Frode's legs.

"Round your headland and head for the gap," ordered Frode and looked at his map.

All this appeared prime land for invasion; the inner part of the Fjord, a huge plain on the east side, which he marked with a big cross. He had noticed many seals along the edge of this land and he knew seal colonies only gathered where they would feel safe from humans.

By the time Urquhart and half his army arrived from Tain, the Longboats were out of sight around the headland and he cursed them. In Mahomack everybody was in a great state of anger and confusion.

"We would all be dead by the time you got here. They were nearly on the beach!" they complained and Urquhart had little to say except to get him something to eat.

Ross arrived with more mounted warriors and looked around for Urquhart who was swamped by people. He rode through them pushing some out of the way and Sheena followed. Urquhart sat on a rock and hewed into some oatcakes and soup.

"We would all be dead by the time you got here!" he yelled at Ross and laughter erupted.

"We need to move the army here, father," said Sheena.

"The stockade is at Tain, not here. If we have to defend, we must hold the Stockade," he replied.

Ross took her by the arm and walked her clear of everybody.

"They play with us, Sheena. They want us to move the army here. No matter where it is - and they'll know where it is - they will strike somewhere else. They won't attack by boat. They'll land their army by boat and they need somewhere safe to do that."

She sighed, knowing he was right.

Sine and Enya arrived with more warriors on foot and they were breathing hard. They looked bewildered at the mass of warriors all sitting around.

"Tell her what would happen!" shouted Urquhart at the top of his voice.

"We would all be dead by the time you got here!" roared the warriors and laughed just as loudly.

"What are you thinking?" Ross asked Urquhart.

"I'm thinking they're looking for a landing place; somewhere they can land an army without being attacked and they can take their pick," he replied, sweeping his arm over the flat ground across the Firth. "We go over there, they'll land here. We stay here they'll land over there."

"Is that what you think father?" asked Sheena.

"That's exactly what I think. What would you do if you were them?" Urquhart threw at her.

"Go back to Norway," smiled Sheena and they laughed.

They stopped laughing when a rider came from the Field of Rocks and declared that from the high ground, he had seen many Norse boats far to the south, close to Torridon and they had come from the east.

"We prepare for battle!" commanded Urquhart immediately.

At Invergordon village, two riders came carrying spears and stopped briefly to ask the way to Mahomack. They were dirty and bedraggled and looked as if they had just left a battle. Their horses were spent and villagers offered them shelter and food, everyone eager to get news. After skirting Dingwall after noon, Imogen and Kayra had galloped their mounts until they were exhausted, then galloped them again to make sure they were exhausted. They accepted the offers of hospitality gratefully and enjoyed a good meal.

They were given ale and began to tell their story to a captive audience. Imogen explained how they had been travelling to see their uncle in Inver when the Norse attacked them on the shore of the great Loch. They had to ride into the water to get away from them and swim the horses across the Loch close to where it met the river. She went into such detail, even Kayra believed her and speaking without her Irish accent, Imogen sounded just like her and Ro-Sheen.

The audience were frantic; they wanted to know where the Norse were, how many, what were they doing, where were they going, did they cross the river?

However, Imogen was caught flat when they said they had seen them.

"What do you mean you saw them?" she asked.

"They came in their boats and crossed the Sutors," said an elderly woman. "The Drum was sounded on Cromarty and they kept going. They didn't come into this Firth. Then they went past The Field of Rocks and Urquhart scared them away there and we haven't seen them since," she spat.

Imogen had no idea where Frode had taken his boats, neither did anybody in Torfness. By the sound of things, he was creating havoc as ordered and she capitalised on this information.

"They must have dropped off warriors at Inver then gone north for more," she said, adding fuel to the fire.

Rested, warm and fed the two women decided to spend the night in Invergordon for the sake of their horses, especially since it would be dark by the time they reached Mahomack and everybody was on alert; far safer to stay there until daylight.

Meanwhile, Frode's Longboats were nearing the infamous Black Isle,

"You sure you want to go in there?" Tarbat grinned, rubbing his arse.

"Ah, don't listen to that fool," said Frode. "It's a trick to keep the Smertae from stealing. They're scared to death to go near the island. We go in, look around and get out, the same as we did in Mahomack. I want to see the land inside, on this side," he demanded.

They were close to shore, so close that when they passed Balintore the villagers ran up the hill again. Not until they were about to turn into the Gap did the drumbeat start and it was loud. Tarbat turned the boat to starboard and hugged the east side along the entrance, but all eyes stayed in the direction of the sound.

"That drum must be as big as a boat," said Frode.

"Too big to stick up his arse, but whatever they beat it with might fit," growled Tarbat.

The sound was unnerving. They could see no sign of life on the island, no screaming savages, nothing, not even a dog.

They passed a small settlement on their side of the Gap and saw people running up the steep hill which gave them some satisfaction. Then they spotted the village on the island. It had many dwellings along the shore that also extended into the thick forest. Tarbat steered more to Starboard; Frode spoke then paused mid-sentence. The Drum stopped but another started somewhere up ahead of them, distinct but not so loud.

Frode looked all along the east side and then the west side. Satisfied, he shouted to Tarbat to turn and go back out to sea. Something about this place made him uneasy. He knew eyes were on them, but why didn't they show themselves? Was the meaning of the signal picked up further along the Island? The surprise was over. It was time to leave. He had seen all he wanted to.

When the drum started on the point of the Black Isle called Balblair, all hell broke loose in Invergordon. People rushed from their dwellings, screaming and finding themselves caught up in the fracas, Imogen and Kayra ran too, not knowing where they were running to or what from.

"Norse, Norse!" people screamed and pointed.

When they saw the reason, they wanted to smile but stared in silence. So too did the villagers as the lead boat turned. Not a word was spoken until the third boat turned. Then, a great cheer went up and the drum stopped.

Imogen stared at Kayra. They could hardly believe what they had just seen, and Imogen crossed herself discretely; somebody was looking after them.

Those who had fought the Norse were more revered, the more the whiskey flowed, and soon the two female warriors had become heroes.

The three Longboats headed for Torfness. It would be dark by the time they got halfway but they would anchor in the bay and wait for daylight. Sigurd would get a surprise in the morning instead of the savages.

Meanwhile, in the stockade at Tain, Urquhart had assembled every leader he had and every settlement that sent warriors had a leader. As many as forty gathered in the great hall and stared at a huge cow skin pinned to the wall. On it was drawn a map of the immediate area, taking in Decantae lands from Invergordon to Tain. Across the water into Lugi country, only the coastline appeared drawn in great detail. One small fishing village called Dornoch that bore the name of the Firth was marked on the cowhide, it lay close and straight across the water from Tain.

"Are we all here?" Urquhart roared, and nobody knew if they were or they weren't. "You think the Norse are playing games? Well, you're wrong, very wrong!" he bellowed and silence prevailed. He held a spear and raised it high. "The Norse are gathering information. This is no game. They're scouting the coastline looking for places to land an army. They look for strong points and weak points, sandy beaches and rocky beaches and you can be sure they will be looking at exactly what you're looking at.

"This is a map the Norse have. Now get inside their heads and find the most suitable place to land an army. Nobody leaves this place tonight until we have an agreement on where they will strike!"

Urquhart made his way through the crowd and found Sheena.

"Is that what you wanted?" he asked, smiling. It had been Sheena who drew the map.

"If you're right father, we have something they have. That's more than I had last summer and I was seeing Norse in my sleep."

"That might be so but saying where you think they'll land isn't good enough. We need reasons why they would land there. Leave them. This will take time." said Urquhart and led her back to his quarters.

"Don't get involved any more than you have to. I want you here as my daughter, not as the Queen."

"Father, it's not going to be easy to hide a Queen, when a thousand warriors know where she is!"

"That's so, but the people won't betray you, Sheena. Go with Ross in the morning and bring Stroma and her council back here. We must plan for an attack and I fear it will come soon."

"Why don't we signal them?" she asked.

"Signals don't ask names and I want Stroma and her council here. The Queen can order that," he smiled.

"Where is Sine?"

"I've no idea. Possibly with Fiona."

"I'll go and find her, there's nothing more I can do here. I'll come back later," Sheena suggested and Urquhart nodded.

In the great hall, arguments and theories abounded. It seemed everybody present had a different idea of where the Norse would strike, but few gave reasons why. Ross and Krike were in the thick of things, trying to distinguish the outrageous from the highly unlikely, the probable from the improbable, and most difficult of all, allowing everybody who had an opinion to speak. Krike had Urquhart's spear and threatened to spear the next one who started shouting over somebody else, such was the uproar.

"This was Sheena's idea. We should have let her run with it," declared Ross, throwing his hands in the air.

"Go and get Urquhart!" Krike roared above the racket.

"You'd better come before a battle starts," grinned Ross and Urquhart laughed.

"It's what I told her would happen," he said and followed Ross out. "Did any of them pick the spot we picked?"

"Six of them," replied Ross. "The rest were all over the place."

Urquhart let out a roar for silence when he entered, and they all obeyed. He took the spear from Krike and went to the map.

"Six of you have picked here," he announced, pointing with the tip of the spear to the village of Dornoch. A wave of disagreement rippled through the onlookers and Urquhart raised his voice. "That is where the council has also chosen. Let me tell you why and while I explain, anybody who utters a word will be thrown out. I'm not going to yell, so listen," he said, looking around with warning in his eyes, daring anybody to defy him.

"They land here," he continued, "between us and the Lugi, with thousands of warriors. They can land without being attacked. If the Lugi attacks them, some can head to Brora in boats and take the Stockade. If we attack, we must be across the firth, and Tain would be undefended, so would Mahomack.

"They could get here from Dornoch faster than your mother could make soup. Dornoch! Or look the other way. They went into the Souters and came out again, so they would have seen the beaches behind Nigg. They could land a force there, and we would be drawn out to fight it. Again, leaving Tain and Mahomack undefended and a second force could take both or attack us from behind.

"Dornoch is the place we think they will strike and there isn't a damned thing we can do to stop them without sacrificing either Brora or Tain. Loch Fleet cuts off the beach to the Lugi and the Firth cuts us off from a charge. We leave on horse and foot, we can't get back. The Lugi leave on horse and foot, they can't get back.

"We are two thousand. If the Norse bring four thousand, a battle at Dornoch will have only one outcome and I don't need to tell you what that will be. We have to hold our ground. The Lugi have to either hold their ground or join us here. Sinclair won't come south. He fears they will cross the Sea of the Dead and hit Carnavii country with the Smertae that are massed at Tongue. We can't go north to help the Carnavii and the Carnavii can't come south to help us.

"If we hold our ground, we can kill many. Let them come to us and we will be ready. What say ye?" Urquhart roared, and a great cheer went up.

Ross looked at Krike, who smiled quietly. It was the outcome they had hoped for and nobody put up any objection. Ross left and headed for his quarters, to see Fiona and Sine. He was surprised to find Sheena as well there and welcomed her warmly.

"They agree with your father," he said. "Dornoch is the target and we hold our ground."

He smiled and gave Sine a kick with the side of his foot. "Are you coming to Brora with us in the morning?" he asked and she sprung to her feet with a great smile on her face.

# Chapter 6

Large swathes of farmed land stretched before Imogen and Kayra. The further they headed east the more distant the tree-clad mountains became and for the first time they looked at the mountains of the Struie from the low ground. Both shuddered with the memory of their crossing along the top. To their right, the land was in stark contrast and had been cleared for livestock and growing crops. The undulating lines of gently sloping hills filled this view, and they knew they were on rich terrain. They noted the landing beach they came close to shortly after leaving Invergordon and knew Frode would have seen it also.

Nearing noon, they caught sight of smoke coming from ahead. They were on a well-used track and stayed on it. Rested and fed, they still looked bedraggled and dejected. Ahead, a large camp came into view and the track ran down the centre of it. They steeled themselves for what lay ahead and Imogen instructed Kayra to loosen her top. It wasn't hot but the gesture had nothing to do with temperature. Imogen did likewise and Kayra opened hers more.

"Not too much, things will fall out!" Imogen shouted at her, and they laughed.

Warriors saw them approach but nobody rose to challenge them. Not until they passed the first of the fires did warriors stand and stare. A female jumped up from a cooking fire and came to them giving the males a dirty look first. She took hold of Kayra's bridle and stopped her. She didn't try to resist as Imogen had instructed.

"Are you hot?" the warrior fired at her staring at what she revealed.

"We have a fever," Imogen replied feebly and the warrior's eyes softened.

"Where are you going?" she asked.

"We don't know. We were told in Invergordon to come here. We're Caladonii. We fought with the Norse at Inver and escaped across the river."

Imogen sounded sick and Kayra coughed.

"Go straight ahead; you will come to a fork. Right leads to

Mahomack left to Tain but Mahomack is closest," the warrior instructed and let the reins go.

They thanked her and walked the horses ahead. Many warriors stood and watched them go.

"Mahomack!" said Imogen. As they reached the fork in the track and turned right towards another camp. This one was much bigger and the smell of food tantalised them. Again, the camp straddled either side of the track and they walked the horses through it, barely getting a glance but those who did glance ended up staring.

They came within sight of the sea and breathed a sigh of relief.

"Lace-up again. That was the hard part now we need to seek shelter," Imogen instructed her pupil.

Across the Firth at daybreak, it wasn't Sigurd who got the first surprise, it was Frode. He counted fourteen Longboats on the beach and four Knarrs were at anchor close to Torfness. Frode ordered the boats to pull anchors and proceed under oar towards Torfness.

Sigurd ran to the battlements when he was told Frode had returned with all three boats and watched as they approached.

"It's getting crowded in there," Frode muttered.

"Looks like home," said Tarbat.

"At home, you usually barge your way into a berth, so do that now. We're not going back to anchor," insisted Frode and scanned the beach. There was no sign of the two Longboats where he had left them to be repaired and he breathed a sigh of relief when he saw they were together amongst the other vessels. The only boats that were operational were the Skiffs and three stood alongside the Knarrs. The crews of the boats cheered a welcome as they passed.

Accompanied by two navigators and three masters, Frode climbed the steep hill towards the Fort and the gate opened to let them inside. Sigurd met them and stared at the pile of rolled-up skins they carried.

Food came first on Frode's agenda and they ate a hearty meal of roast sheep and soup. Then all were herded into the great hall to join the twenty or more masters and navigators already present. The greetings took a long time. Most were newly arrived from Norway and from all over the coast. Frode hadn't seen many for years, and by the time they settled down to the day's business, voyages long past had been re-visited.

Sigurd called for quiet and the maps Frode had brought replaced those already spread on the big table. They were laid side by side in sequence and the observers marvelled at the tattoo ink and detail on each.

Not until Frode was satisfied did he address them as Sigurd instructed and he started from the west.

"Here the Fjord narrows and the tide is great. This land is high with trees and known as the Black Island. We saw nothing on this island but they make a lot of noise with drums. The Smertae tell us they fear the savages on this island greatly, and so should we," he smiled. "If they capture you, they stick a tree up your arse, let it tear your guts and when it nears your throat, they cut your head off, then leave you to rot!"

This brought much hilarity. Frode waited till it died down then continued.

"This Gap you can see from Torfness is another Fjord. Inside on the east side is a landing beach and the high hills you can see from here don't go far then it's flat ground. That's why it's marked with a circle.

"To the east of the entrance there is nowhere to land an Army but we saw one, marked by a cross. Here two thousand savages were dancing on the hill. Again, you can see this land from here, it's very close, but you could never land an army there it's all rocks, all the way to this point which I named after Tarbat. This point will be our reference point, Tarbat Ness!" proclaimed Frode.

His gesture went down well. Tarbat was clapped on the back by many. They would all like to have somewhere named after them and it was the right of the man who discovered land to name it, not the right of royalty. Sigurd smiled; he was happy for Tarbat.

Frode went on with his voyage but there was a long way between Tarbat and the next land which contained the river they knew well. He went all around the coast to Tongue and back again via Orkney. Then Tarbat removed all the maps and placed a single map on the table. They all stared at it.

"Tarbat Ness!" announced, stabbing his finger at the small point of land.

Sigurd had one look and banged the table hard.

"Wait! say no more until I return," he commanded and hurried from the hall. Frode frowned and shrugged in response to the questioning looks he received.

Sigurd returned with Ro-Sheen and a rolled-up map. He grabbed some stones and spread the map out.

"Position your map with Frode's," he demanded.

Ro-Sheen blushed and looked around in confusion until Frode came to her rescue.

"Mahomack," he said, stabbing his finger at a circle.

"Ah, now I know where I am," she said, apologetically.

They watched with great interest as she lined her map up with that of Frode's. His showed the coast as a straight line. Hers showed bends and sandbanks and they looked at each other in wonder.

"Now you can see what you couldn't see, but why did you go so close?" asked Sigurd.

"Not me, him!" yelled Frode, pointing at Tarbat. "I handed command here, by the time he turned I near shit myself. So did the savages!"

They laughed aloud at this. Ro-Sheen's map butted onto Frode's but overlapped Mahomack and the land beyond towards Tarbat Ness. Apart from that, there was little between them. Frode gave her a look. He did not know her venture. Only Torf and Sigurd knew and Torf smiled.

"From here on the east side, a sandy beach stretches to where the Fjord turns north. as you can now see!" said Frode casting a look at Ro-Sheen. "This small gap is something we don't know; it might be the entrance to a river or a lake. Whatever it is, a strong current comes out of it. Here we saw plenty of smoke but no warriors. None came to the beach, but I think this is a large settlement," he pointed, again looking at Ro-Sheen.

"Do you know where this is, Ro-Sheen?" asked Sigurd.

"I don't know. I have never been there," she replied. "But it could be Brora. The tribe that owns the land opposite Mahomack are the Lugi. Their Stockade is at Brora; that's all I know."

"How many warriors can this Lugi raise?" asked Sigurd.

"About the same as the Smertae, I think. A lot less than the Decantae at Mahomack, I know that," replied Ro-Sheen and Sigurd indicated to Frode to continue.

"Here," he said, pointing to a position straight across from Mahomack, "the land is flat, the beach is good and we saw only enough smoke to mark a small village. This beach is good to land an army."

"What is over there? Did you see any settlement?" Sigurd cut in and spoke to Ro-Sheen.

"Nothing! There is nothing over there. It's just flat land without trees and we didn't see even smoke," she replied.

"We need to make one complete map out of two and make more to go on the boats. When we have one map, we can see what we're up against more clearly," suggested Frode, which was met with mumbles of agreement.

"Then bring skins and get to work!" ordered Sigurd.

Taking Ro-Sheen by the arm, he led her back to his quarters and ushered her into the adjoining room. She looked at him curiously.

"Find whatever clothes you want," he said. "It's the queen's chamber and Torf won't look good in her clothes," he grinned and left her spellbound.

Ro-Sheen was still rooted to the spot when a plump woman came in and startled her.

"My name is Else," she said. "Sigurd says I have to take care of you. Water is being heated. Now, let me see what you can wear?"

Meanwhile, to the north, the ride to Brora was the long way around and it took until noon before the party and escort of ten warriors reached Loch Fleet. Sine showed off her Bull, but little attention was paid to it. Like everywhere else, the small village was in turmoil. The Norse boats had been seen passing the mouth of the Loch and gallopers had been sent to Brora only to run into gallopers coming from Brora and by the time they reached the entrance together, the Norse boats were going out of sight around the headland.

Stroma and her warriors had returned to Brora quickly thinking it might have been a decoy to get them away from Brora; if it was, it had worked. The gallopers from Loch Fleet went with them using the beach and found no Norse. In a panic, she had sent twenty warriors to the Helm, and they had returned without seeing any Norse. That was a huge relief to everybody. The speed with which their boats cut through the water wasn't lost on those who saw them, and they marvelled.

Sheena ordered a messenger from Loch Fleet to get Stroma and her council. The travellers were weary and it was a long journey to get back to Tain. Sheena handed the messenger her Dirk. That was all the authority he would need.

In Mahomack, Imogen and Kayra, the battle-ravaged, sick and weary travellers were fed and given shelter by an old man and woman who lived in what they called their castle, close to where the boats were on the beach. They gave the women Toddy and they felt on top of the world but looked like they were at the bottom of it and behaved accordingly.

Imogen gripped her throat and rasped. She could barely speak but she could listen and the old couple spoke incessantly. They had been to the land of the Caledonii many years before and to Inver. They mentioned names and described things they had seen, and every detail was filed in Imogen's brain. She would question Kayra to see how much she had picked up when the time was right. Now, they had to lie low and let somebody come to them. Their story of Norse at Inver would spread quickly, Imogen was sure of that.

Back in Torfness, while navigators worked on the maps, Sigurd spoke to Frode alone and got a taste of the turmoil he had created across the sea. It was a lot and without knowing, he had also mobilised the entire Lugi army.

"Kael will come in three or four days with two thousand warriors from Orkney, three Knarrs and twelve Longboats. He'll have to squeeze them in!" Frode laughed.

"If he manages all of them, we will have nine thousand warriors. We only have boats for four thousand," Sigurd grinned. "Four thousand will be enough and leave five here. It's not far across the sea; they can go across and back in a day. If reinforcements are needed the Longboats can bring them. I'm convinced the area opposite Mahomack is the best landing site but we must all agree on that as we always do. This River or whatever it is to the east would make any charge on that flank hard to drive home."

"The warriors at Mahomack might read our minds and put warriors there," warned Frode, "but they will weaken their own defences. I think Tarbat showed them how quickly we can move from one position to the other, but I want to speak to your chart maker, she will know what's important; how fast they can get across without boats. I saw many horses on the hill, enough to be concerned about, and a charge from them and an attack from the east along the beach at the same time would greatly reduce our numbers. You know how they fight to the death?"

Sigurd didn't need to be reminded.

"That would take time and timing Strode," he replied. "You're right, Ro-Sheen will know where they can cross with horses. If the crossing is close or far away, it will make a great difference."

In Mahomack, the light was fading when Krike rode up to the old fisherman's dwelling and walked straight in. He looked at the shields and spears just inside the door and called out,

"Angus, it's me!" He sniffed the air and yelled, "where's mine?" as he entered the dwelling.

"Krike! I might have known the smell would bring you," the old woman chirped and went to a griddle hanging over a low fire.

Krike looked at the two Caledonii warriors, smiled and turned to Angus.

"Your sons will be warm tonight!"

"No, they won't, they're camped with the rest. Urquhart says they have to sleep armed and I'm damned if they're going to sleep here with swords and shields. The two lassies will have their platform. They're worn out," said a voice from the fireside.

Krike was presented with a bowl of smoked fish, slow-cooked in butter and milk. He accepted gladly. It was his favourite, along with the handful of oatcakes.

Imogen and Kayra had no idea who he was and smiled shyly as he sat opposite them and slurped juice from a dripping oat cake. They were enjoying this meal more than anything they could remember. It was beautiful and they ate without speaking. Krike finished before they did and handed his bowl to the woman.

"That was their seconds you ate. You're not getting any more!" she growled and slapped the back of his head.

"You two are unlucky. You ran away from the Norse and ran into them. They were here yesterday and we expect an attack any time. It was dark when they took Cluny and Torridon, that's why the warriors are ready for anything."

Imogen gripped her throat and mumbled that they had seen them from Invergordon.

"That's where they went. Did they land there?" asked Krike, concern on his face.

Imogen shook her head. She made a half-circle with her finger and Krike read it as in and out. He breathed a sigh of relief and spoke to Angus.

"Urquhart will want them in Tain. I'll come and get them in the morning if I'm still alive. I'll head back to the beach," he said and stood up.

"Well, you won't be wanting Toddy," the old woman chirped and Krike sat down again.

It was after dark when Stroma, Frazer, Forbes and Enya arrived at Loch Fleet and Sheena greeted them warmly. Stroma handed the Dirk to her and she put it into her belt. Sine was hanging onto Enya and keeping Ross away with her free hand. Enya laughed loudly, and so did everybody else.

"Go away brother, she's mine," Sine grinned.

After eating, they spoke well into the night and Stroma felt glad they had come. Frazer and Forbes weren't so sure. They had abandoned Brora to old Callum and they wanted to get back as soon as possible. When Sheena announced they all had to go to Tain, Forbes was adamant he had to return to Brora and Sheena reluctantly agreed.

"There's nothing I can add that they can't," argued Frazer. "If Urquhart has the Decantae on alert, the Lugi must do the same."

Nobody could disagree.

"We go at first light and reach there by dark," said Ross.

He ruled out using the boat crossing, even the one at Bonner, they had to go further inland. This news was met with sighs of disgust. Tain seemed so close but so far away unless you were a bird.

In Torfness, the discussions began in earnest and they stared when Ro-Sheen entered. She was dressed in the finest leather and looked radiant; her blond hair pinned back with a gold pin and the curves of her body evident.

Astrid came to her and hugged her. She got a smell of the roses from her and whispered, "Get some for me?"

Sigurd stared harder than the others but remained silent. She was indeed beautiful, but not uppermost in his mind.

Both maps had been joined as one and the tattooist had joined the coastline at Mahomack, leaving Frode's map intact to the east and Ro-Sheen's to the west. Now things looked different.

"We planned the invasion of Torridon twice," said Sigurd. "Each time took many days and wasn't agreed until we all agreed. Last time we went for a small force in the dark with the element of surprise. This time there will be no surprise and no small force. Four thousand warriors will go in daylight. Like the last time we planned, I want foresight, because there will be no chance of hindsight. Don't underestimate the Picts. We think they may number three thousand at most. Remember, seven hundred killed one thousand. They fight like mad bears and they fight to the death, so think carefully," he warned and raised his arm as a signal for them to begin.

Norse were a people of action and few words. Planning for action was as good as taking part and enthusiasm soared.

He went to Ro-Sheen. "You look like a queen; you smell like a queen as well," he smiled.

She blushed and looked down.

"Go among them and answer any questions you can," he said.

She went to join Astrid. Although she could speak good Norse, the conversations left her for dead. They spoke in many dialects and spoke fast. She followed fingers that pointed in all directions and each direction had ten or more comments. She gave up in the end and rested her head on Astrid's shoulder, while her friend continued watching and listening. Ro-Sheen only gave an opinion if asked, and that was unlikely, considering the people facing her represented the cream of Harold's commanders and navigators.

Suddenly she jumped awake when Astrid nudged her and she realised they were all staring at her.

"What is it, Astrid? Why are they looking at me?" she whispered.

"They want to know how quickly the army can move from Mahomack across to the other side," she replied.

"Ah, I must show them on the map."

As Ro-Sheen went to the table, the men parted to give her room.

"You can still see some snow on the mountains," she said. "The mountains you see are here. And if there is still some snow on the south side, there will be plenty of it on the north."

They nodded their understanding and she pointed to the map. The furthest west Ro-Sheen's map went was to the long finger of land sticking out into the firth. She grabbed a small piece of charcoal and drew both sides of the firth that curved around and narrowed, almost met, then opened up a little by which time she wasn't just off the map, she was nearly off the table. She pointed at the finger of land.

"Here, they can cross, but not now. Even if they could, they would go in small boats and swim the horses but the current will be too strong. Snowmelt will make crossing here at Bonner difficult or impossible, so they will have to go inland to find a crossing." She bit her lip in thought and made a decision. "From Mahomack, I think more than half a day."

They grinned broadly. Ro-Sheen found herself squeezed out immediately and re-joined Astrid.

"We go to the kitchen. If they want us, they can send for us," sighed Astrid and took her hand.

Sigurd called a halt when one of the cooks came and asked if they were going to eat tonight? They grumbled loudly and wanted to continue but he knew they were as tired as he was.

"Tired people make mistakes," he insisted. "Now, move!"

That sealed the discussions for the night and they went to eat.

Sigurd put his arm over Torf's shoulder and whispered in his ear,

"You'd better find somewhere to sleep. You've been kicked out."

Torf never batted an eyelid, he wasn't blind.

"Imogen!" he cursed, placing his hand in front of his groin and making a cutting motion.

Sigurd laughed. "It was her idea, not mine," he hissed.

# Chapter 7

Krike and one warrior arrived at the first light and banged on the door to get somebody up. Angus came running and threw the door open, pointing a spear at Krike's face and grinning a toothless grin.

"I thought you were a Norse," he grunted. "Come on in, lassies!" he called and Imogen came first.

He handed the spear to her and then her shield. Kayra received the same treatment and the old woman came behind them with her dog.

"How old's your dog, Aggie?" asked the young warrior with Krike.

"He's been a dog for ten winters," she replied proudly.

The youth shook his head and whispered to Imogen,

"We don't know what he was before he was a dog,"

She smiled briefly and went around the building. Their horses were there. Angus had saddled them, saying the women were too weak for such a task and they agreed. They rode after Krike and the young warrior, who was somewhat disappointed with the appearance of the two females. They looked half-dead as if they'd been running for their lives.

Imogen and Kayra took in every detail of their surroundings and made a rough count of warriors as they passed. After the track passed the fork, the number of warriors decreased. As they approached the Stockade at Tain, they couldn't fail to be impressed. Not easy to take by any army, but it was wood, and it would burn.

Imogen nodded to Kayra, who reined in her horse and slipped off the saddle headlong onto the ground, softening her fall with her hands. She rolled clear before lying on her back. The horse whinnied, looked at her and stood calmly by.

Imogen let out a loud shout and Krike turned in alarm. She was off her horse and tending to Kayra before the young warrior came by her side.

"What wrong with her?" he asked, staring at the lacing across her bosom.

"I don't know. She's passed out I think," snapped Imogen, trying to lift Kayra.

He pushed her aside and scooped Kayra into his arms.

"Put her in front of me," ordered Krike and they lifted into position.

He held onto her with one arm and walked his horse slowly towards the Stockade. The others followed with Kayra's spear and horse. The gates were opened before they arrived and several warriors ran to greet them. They had seen the warrior fall from the horse but had no idea it was a female. Krike handed her over to them once the gate closed and they took her inside quickly.

Urquhart glanced at her but turned to Krike with a questioning look on his face.

"Two Caledonii," he said. "They're sick. Had a battle with the Norse at Inver and swam the Loch to escape."

Urquhart caught his breath.

"Inver! The Norse are there?"

"Sounds like it. They saw them enter the Cromarty Firth then turn and go back out again. The drums were sounded," replied Krike, handing his reins to the young warrior.

Imogen noted that although she saw no warriors outside the Stockade, inside she estimated several hundred manned the ramparts. She followed after Kayra and heard Urquhart yell for somebody to get Sorsce.

"Sit her up," Imogen asked and the warriors complied.

Urquhart came behind and watched as she put a hand on either side of Kayra's face and repeated her name over and over, giving her a gentle slap on the face as she spoke.

Kayra groaned, her eyes opened, then closed. Imogen repeated her actions and eventually, Kayra opened her eyes and they stayed open.

"Where am I?" she asked staring around with big eyes, mainly focused on Urquhart.

"You're safe now; get some rest," he smiled.

He nudged Imogen, who stood up and followed him to a table.

"Sit down," he said, "and tell me about the Norse at Inver?"

She sat down heavily. This was going better than planned and her mind drifted to the Dirk in her belt. Here she was, alone with the leader of the Decantae. She could kill him now but that would mean certain death and Imogen had much to live for.

She started explaining where she and her band had come from but Urquhart interrupted,

"You speak strangely for a Caledonii."

"Everybody says that my grandmother was Irish, and she brought me up," she replied and coughed.

Urquhart found nothing unusual about that. Scotland was a melting pot of Picts and Celts and had been for generations.

Kayra closed her eyes and listened. She loved the stories Imogen told and she told them so convincingly, even Kayra began to believe her, but her voice rasped and Urquhart didn't push her for much detail. He knew the river and the Loch. He followed her journey in his mind and it was as he remembered it.

Sorsce arrived and glanced at Kayra. She came to Imogen and leaned over the table. Imogen looked at the tattoos on Sorsce and smiled.

"If she can walk, come with me, or we can get people to carry her," said Sorsce.

"We can try," replied Imogen, relieved that her interrogation was over; she wobbled a little when she got to her feet.

Kayra was pulled to hers and between them, they walked her out of the great hall into the open and towards Fiona's quarters. They laid her out on a sleeping bench and Sorsce felt her heart.

"It races," she said and felt Kayra's forehead. She nodded and went outside to mix a little whiskey with honey and hot water.

Kayra stared when the Smertae, Fia, entered with two steaming bowls. She handed one to Imogen and the other to Kayra, who was shaking when she took the bowl and this time she wasn't acting. Fia patted her leg and said she would be all right after she drank the honey.

Then she left.

Kayra hadn't seen Fia for more than three summers. The last time Fia had seen her she was plump and much younger. Now she had lost all her fat and was older. Kayra breathed a sigh of relief but her heart was still pounding. She took deep breaths. Imogen always told her to do that if she was stressed and it worked.

Sorsce came back and looked at the two Caledonii. They were sick, dirty, dishevelled and their clothes hung on them. She grunted and left. Cleaning them could wait, they were sick and needed rest, but she would find something to fit them, that didn't stink and she left them alone.

Imogen went to Kayra and smiled then put her finger to her lips.

"Feel better after you drink that!" she whispered and returned to her seat.

Kayra wanted to be away from Fia and gladly agreed.

The sound of a horse outside made them look towards the door when somebody framed it. Tall and with long hair, Fiona entered. She was dressed and painted for battle like all the warriors they had seen and they stared at her.

"I'm Fiona; this is my dwelling. What are your names?" she asked and came closer.

"I'm Imogen and she's Kayra," Imogen rasped and coughed.

"You're sick, Sorsce tells me. And Krike says you are Caledonii. You did battle with the Norse at Inver. You did well to escape and get here," Fiona smiled and threw her sword and belt onto a sleeping platform.

Imogen took note of that and nodded. She would let this one speak, she thought.

"We waited all night for the Norse to come but they didn't. I must sleep. I've been awake all night and I'll be awake all this night. Sorsce and Fia will look after you," said Fiona and lay down beside her sword. She pulled some furs over her and closed her eyes. Her guests looked at each other and shrugged.

Sorsce arrived next and placed a pile of skins on the table beside Imogen.

"Lie down and get some sleep," Sorsce whispered and left quietly.

Imogen finished the last of her honey. She took the empty bowl from Kayra and lay down on the sleeping platform beside her. Kayra cuddled into her back, wanting to hide her face.

"Sleep!" Imogen whispered. She knew they would also be awake all night.

Ross looked at the great swath of broom growing along the edges of the track and cursed. Flowers had bloomed and he turned to Frazer who rode beside him.

"The yellow's on the broom, Frazer, the Smertae will be champing at the bit."

"Aye, it won't be long before it's dry enough for them to move, but in what direction? That's the question, Ross."

Ross was wondering the same. They checked the crossing at Bonner because they had to pass it to get to the one further upriver. At first glance, the water level looked the same as it had the previous day but on closer inspection, they realised it had dropped. Two of their escort wanted to try to cross but Ross shook his head. It still looked dangerous, despite the drop in the water level.

"You want to try? Go ahead and try!" bellowed Sheena, raising a look of alarm from both Ross and Frazer.

The warriors let out a whoop and splashed into the river. Everybody hated the thought of going to the next ford. The terrain was largely unused. It was rugged, slow and anything but safe. Bear and wolves were a constant threat but not so much when travelling in a party. Nobody in their right mind would go there alone. They held their breath when the horses turned to face the rush of water. They moved slowly upstream and to their left. Water boiled under their bellies and the onlookers knew that if the water got deeper, the horses would be swept away.

Sine stared and bit her lip as they crossed slowly and precariously but cross they did and let out a yell of triumph that was echoed from the north bank.

"Go in pairs!" Sheena roared, taking hold of Sine's bridle with her right hand. "Do nothing; let my horse guide yours," she ordered and entered the water.

Again, the horses were turned and headed upstream and to the left. Four warriors came behind them, following closely. Ross threw his hands in the air and grabbed Enya's bridle.

"You'd better get wet Frazer, or a bear will catch you," he grinned, and Frazer grabbed Stroma's Bridle.

Wet but happy, they assembled on the south bank and rested.

"Desperate times require desperate measures," smiled Sheena. "We've saved nearly half a day. Now we can get to Tain well before dark."

However, Ross dashed her feeling of triumph.

"Now we know the Smertae can cross here," he said.

Cold reality soon dawned on the travellers. News of their coming reached Tain long before they did and they were cheered by many warriors along the trail between Bonner and Tain. Ross informed them they had crossed at Bonner and ordered warriors to guard the Ford. Urquhart rode out to meet them with Sorsce and by the time they entered the Stockade, the arrival of the two sick Caledonii was known by all. The news that the Norse held Inver was greeted with shock.

Urquhart turned that around when he speculated that if the Norse attacked the Caledonii, their warriors might come and join the Decantae. Two had arrived already and if more came it would strengthen their force.

Ross grunted, the Caledonii had another route to the west coast, and despite peace between them for many years, they had been enemies for much longer. When Urquhart went there it was to do battle and the Decantae were triumphant.

Saddle sore and hungry they reached the Stockade and went into the great hall where food would soon be served, Sorsce assured them.

Sheena went to her quarters and lay on her sleeping platform. She stared at the rack of antlers above her head. Her thoughts weren't on Norse, they were on Smertae and had been since Ross brought her attention to the yellow on the Broom. If they came, the Decantae army would be split. Fighting on two fronts would be impossible. Would they attack south, or west, into Carnavii country? Or attack the Lugi, the weakest of the three tribes and drive a wedge between the Decantae and the Carnavii? Would they attack anywhere?

She rose quickly and went to her father who was with the others in the great hall.

"Come, father," she said and headed towards his quarters.

Urquhart threw a look at Ross and followed curiously.

"Close the door!" Sheena said and stared at Urquhart. "I want three hundred warriors and all the horses. I'm going north to destroy the Smertae before they destroy us and everybody in the north," she said decisively.

"Have you lost your mind?" he scorned, taking a step towards her.

"Don't father! I've made up my mind. The Smertae caused the loss of Torridon and the death of the King. They are traitors. Traitors are killed. Don't argue, I've made my decision. The Smertae must answer for their treachery."

"We need more warriors to fight the Norse, not fewer, and horses?" Urquhart was incredulous at this sudden twist in their plans. "You won't need horses and you know it. You go around with horses and they will come across by boat, which could go on for an eternity. Any battle with the Norse will be on the beaches and if the Smertae come, they will come in strength."

"Father, we know where they are and they will move soon. They might have moved already. We can meet them on our terms if they move south. If they go east, I could hit them from behind but we must do something!" implored Sheena.

She didn't like pleading, she was the Queen, but she respected her father too much to order him to do anything against his will.

"You know how to put somebody off his food," Urquhart hissed and opened the door, yelling, "Ross, get in here!"

Ross came quickly. He had heard the raised voices and was concerned.

"Close the door. Your queen has come back to life. Tell him," growled Urquhart.

Sheena explained her thinking, this time without raising her voice and added,

"Don't you see, the Smertae massed to make us think the Norse and the Smertae would attack the Carnavii from two directions? We were focused on the Smertae and the Norse tricked us. Now we're focused on the Norse, the Smertae can attack us, or the Lugi, from the land. We must attack them. Even if the Norse attack here, we will know we only have one army to worry about. Right now, we have two from two different directions."

They knew she was right.

"Go and eat both of you and let me think," sighed Urquhart.

They left him and received many puzzled looks when they sat down to eat, but not even Sine questioned what was going on.

When the food arrived, Sorsce left and headed back to Fiona's dwelling. Fiona had woken and so had her guests. They said they felt much better and ready to stand watch all night, but Fiona insisted they washed and tidied themselves up, inviting them to try on the clothes Sorsce had left.

They washed quickly and held the leathers out to see who they would fit. Sine had grown out of her tops and Sheena remarked she would soon be wearing her clothes. The two guests tried on the leggings and they fitted perfectly. Fiona smiled and handed Imogen a top. She squirmed out of her laced-up top that was torn and threw it to the floor.

Sorsce arrived and grinned when she saw how well the leggings fitted. Then as Imogen turned to get another top from Fiona, she showed her bare back. Sorsce took a sharp breath and stared at the Celtic Butterfly. She reached for her sword instinctively, but she had no sword, neither did Fiona, hers lay on the sleeping platform with furs obscuring it.

The top slid down Imogen's body and the tattoo disappeared. When she went to turn, Sorsce dropped her eyes and seeing their cast-off garments on the floor she gathered them up. She froze when Imogen spoke.

"Fit for a queen, I've never felt clothes like this, so soft," Imogen praised in a distinctly Irish voice.

The thread of doubt Sorsce had was removed but now she had her wits about her and helped the other one to lace up her top.

"I'll get rid of this!" Sorsce laughed and went outside with the castoffs. "Dump this somewhere," she said to Fia and walked back to the great hall. She wanted to run every sinew in her body demanded she run but she grimaced and forced a walk.

Ross frowned when she grabbed Sheena by the arm without speaking and urged her towards Urquhart's private quarters. Sheena dropped a wooden spoon onto the table, looked at Ross and shrugged.

Sorsce shut the door behind them and Urquhart stared at her and then at Sheena who again shrugged.

"She's here!" Sorsce whispered, staring at Sheena through wide eyes.

"Who is here?" asked Urquhart, instinctively lowering his voice.

"Halfdane's partner. She's here. She's in Fiona's dwelling," Sorsce hissed.

Sheena grabbed her. "What do you mean? tell me!" she yelled but Sorsce put her finger to her lips.

"Don't shout!" ordered Urquhart. "Sit down, Sorsce, and tell us what's happened."

"The warrior who is supposed to be Caledonii, the one with the same hair as Sheena, we tried to find her in Torridon, but couldn't. Then she escaped with Halfdane. We questioned all the warriors who had slept with her because some saw her coming out of tents and some warriors came to the Monks and gave confession on the understanding they wouldn't be named. They drew a tattoo they had seen on the small of her back. Three of them drew the same tattoo, so there is no mistake. I showed it to Aethan, and he agreed with me it was a Celtic Butterfly. She has the tattoo and she's Irish and she has the same hair as Sheena!"

Sheena looked at her in stunned silence. So did Urquhart. He had only heard Sheena speaking about this partner of Halfdane, nothing about a tattoo.

"She's come to kill the Queen. That's what I think," insisted Sorsce.

Sheena and Urquhart's eyes met and neither spoke. This was indeed a development.

"If I had my sword with me, I would have killed her," said Sorsce, unapologetically.

Urquhart grunted and threw her a look; he had no doubt she would have killed her and explained why later.

"She's alive and she's here. We know who she is. So, we either kill her or use her," he said.

"Use her for what?" Sheena frowned.

"Give her wrong information and let her go," replied Urquhart.

"No! She dies!" snapped Sheena.

She stormed into her quarters and came out with her sword. "She wants to kill me, she's not going to stab me in the back," she growled. "Enya! Come with me, we've got a score to settle!" She waited for her at the door.

Enya looked curiously at Sheena, then at Ross.

"What score?" asked Ross.

"Halfdane's accomplice, she's here and she's going to die. She and her accomplice, so move!" Sheena roared and Ross jumped to his feet along with Enya.

"They're in Fiona's dwelling," said Sorsce nervously. "Fiona is in there with them."

Ross nodded and fastened his sword belt. Enya tied hers quickly and the three of them ignored pleas from Sine. Stroma took her hand and they followed Ross out of the door.

"Get Fiona out first," Ross said to Enya.

She went ahead and entered blinking as her eyes adjusted to the dim light.

"Fiona, your brother wants you in the great hall," she announced and looked at the two strangers. Enya smiled and they smiled back.

"What does he want?" asked Fiona asked but Enya didn't reply.

She threw a top on and went past Enya into the light to see Ross beckoning her urgently. Enya followed and closed the door. Ross looked up at the warriors along the stockade wall and ran up the steps. He came back with two swords and stuck them in the ground. The warriors looked on curiously as he pulled Sheena around the dwelling out of sight.

"I'll get them out, then you make an appearance. Enya stay here," he instructed and she joined Sheena.

Ross opened the door and went straight in.

"I'm Fiona's brother, come and join us," he said and they smiled thinking they were going to eat.

As soon as they came into the open, Ross slammed the door making them turn.

"Go and stand beside those two swords, somebody wants to speak to you," he smiled and they looked at each other. "Stand beside them," he repeated. Imogen's eyes narrowed as she obeyed.

Sheena and Enya came into view and Imogen caught her breath. She swallowed hard and stared as Sheena stood in front of her.

"Have you come to kill the Queen?" Sheena asked without raising her voice.

"The Queen is dead. She died with the King," replied Imogen.

Sheena grinned and drew her sword, pointing it at Kayra.

"You have a new partner. Where is Halfdane?" Sheena roared his name and Imogen grabbed the sword. She moved fast and thrust at Sheena who parried her away.

"The Queen lives and the Queen will have her revenge!" screamed Sheena, launching a savage attack on Imogen.

For a short period, Imogen parried everything Sheena threw at her, but the attack was merciless such was her hatred and eventually, her sword found Imogen's arm. Blood pumped from the wound. Screaming like somebody demented, Imogen came at her swinging wildly and Sheena thrust into her chest. Kayra screamed when Imogen dropped her sword but made no attempt to pick up the second one.

Blood came from the corner of Imogen's mouth and her eyes moved but she still stood.

"How? How did you know?" she asked weakly.

"Your Celtic butterfly," replied Sheena but didn't know if Imogen had heard or not, as she collapsed dead at her feet.

Enya now grasped the situation and pointed her sword at Kayra.

"You!" she roared and came towards her.

Kayra collapsed onto her knees and grabbed the sword by the handle.

#

"I don't want to die. I'm not a warrior. Fia knows me, Fia knows me," she repeated and suddenly killing the Queen didn't seem as important as saving her life.

Fia had come, hearing the commotion and the great hall was also empty. Enya looked at Sheena, who stared around at the faces and found the Smertae, Fia.

"Fia, come here!" commanded Sheena yelled and she timidly obeyed.

"I don't know her; she has nothing to do with me," Fia muttered, nervously.

"Then how does she know your name?" asked Ross.

"Who are you?" Fia yelled in alarm, knowing her life was in danger.

"Kayra, Kayra, I'm Colin's daughter, Colin the stiller, taken by the Norse. Fia, save me," pleaded Kayra and her head sunk onto her wrists.

Ross grabbed Kayra by the hair and pulled her upright. She let go of the sword and he marched her, screaming, to the body of Imogen.

"Look closely at her wound," he said, pushing her down. "She might not be dead."

Kayra stretched to look closer. Her eyes closed and her head rolled to one side and came to rest between Imogen's legs.

Ross threw a look at Fia and she took a step backwards.

"She's innocent, brother. She's been with me and she has nothing to do with them, I swear," Fiona yelled and put herself between Ross and Fia.

He sheathed his sword, scowled and spat. Then he addressed the bewildered onlookers who were stunned.

"Torridon was taken because of two spies, the one who has her head was one of them. She also killed the Struie sisters. The other was a Smertae, is that right Fia?" said Ross and Fia nodded. "They were

Norse spies, both of them!" he shouted and a murmur ran through the onlookers.

"Do you want to see the tattoo?" Sorsce asked Sheena, taking the sword from her hand.

"No, I don't need to see her tattoo, you were right," Sheena smiled.

Ross took Enya's arm and led her away.

"I know you don't like killing sheep. That was killing a sheep," he said, and she put her arm over his shoulder.

Sorsce passed the still staring Sine and remarked,

"That's your clothes they're wearing."

"What?" she yelled and ran to the bodies, cursing.

"Throw them into the sea," seethed Sheena. "Let the sea take them back to the ones who sent them."

# Chapter 8

Frazer agreed with Urquhart, Ross agreed with Stroma and Sheena didn't agree with any of them but KrIke's comment that they would be like a dog chasing its tail struck a chord.

"Explain exactly what you mean, Krike," she ordered.

"There!" he replied. "If they land between Little Ferry and Dornoch it's a disaster. Stroma can't charge across the beach. We can't move, because if she moves, their boats will go around her and into Brora. We move, they'll come across the water and take Mahomack. If they land a force at Nigg to draw us out, we won't go because they will come at our backs. We march the army to Dornoch, they would be cooking their food in Tain before we got there."

"So, what can the Norse do if they land there?" asked Sheena.

"The Norse can't do anything," answered Krike. "They either attack us directly by boat, or march inland, or attack us from the land. They attack by boat we will massacre them before they get off the boats. They go inland and cross the river we can hit them at the river as they cross. If they land their main force at Nigg we can meet them in open battle, and they won't have horses. They know we have, so that's unlikely. I would say we get ready and wait. Leave them to land across on the other side and wait for them to make a move."

"Krike makes sense," agreed Sheena. "We can't attack and they can't attack. It will be a standoff for long enough to get back here with the horses. Tomorrow, I'm going to lead an army against the Smertae with all the horses and now I know why," she announced and grinned at her father. "Smertae are four hundred strong, stronger than Lugi. If they attack Brora the Lugi will be caught between the Smertae and the Norse. If they go inland and attack us, we will be trapped between the Smertae and the Norse. We must attack the Smertae. A surprise attack and get back here as soon as possible. We crossed the river, and we won't have much time."

"Sinclair is expecting the Smertae to attack from the west, according to the messengers from Dougal," Frazer reminded them.

"We were looking north from Torridon," said Ross. "Sinclair is looking west from Thurso and Smertae sit on their arse and go nowhere. If the Smertae were a decoy and it worked, it's working again. Sheena is right, the Smertae can stab us in the back when the time is right. If they're going to move, they will soon, and so can we. We can move fast, a small army like last time. Mounted, we can hit them hard. Most of their warriors will be outside the Stockade."

Urquhart sat listening to all the opinions, the arguments for and against. Sorsce served them food. Sine sat quietly by her father listening only. She wasn't allowed to speak; several times Sorsce had to put her hands over her mouth to stop her. Urquhart stood up and held his hand up for quiet.

"When she said she was taking all the horses and three hundred warriors to attack the Smertae, I thought she had lost her mind. So, did you. If the Norse land on this beach, they know our strength already. They saw the horses at the Field of Rocks; they won't see any across the water and they wouldn't expect to see any. Defending a beach doesn't call for horses, it calls for men in the water; the sand is too soft for horses. We wouldn't need horses to defend this Stockade. Three hundred warriors would hardly be missed from two thousand. Do you agree?" Urquhart asked, and they nodded. "If you were Norse and saw an army coming from the north, what would you think?" he grinned.

"Smertae!" smiled Stroma.

"If Sheena rides north with all the horses," continued Urquhart, "and the Norse are here before she comes back, she's going to create some confusion, especially if she joins Stroma and doesn't come back to Tain. With a combined force, Stroma will have three hundred horses and they will think our horses are still here. If the Smertae joins the Lugi, Stroma will have a thousand warriors and three hundred horses, instead of four hundred warriors and fifty horses. I think we should start thinking about trickery like the Norse!" Urquhart grinned and they cheered loudly.

"Krike! The warriors are ready, the horses are here, and all we need is food. Pass the word that three hundred will leave at first light. Don't tell them where they're going. They have all night to get bundles and food ready. Stroma, if the Norse come, show your force but don't come past Little Ferry. A show, then we go back to Brora. Sheena! when you come back, follow Loch Fleet around to Little Ferry on the Brora side. Show your force and head for Brora. Then we wait, if we're still alive," Urquhart added.

In Tongue, Drest was nearly out of his mind. A hundred warriors and families had deserted him and those who remained did so because they thought the others had left too soon. The yellow was on the broom, but the ground was still too wet to travel into the mountains and the rivers were high. The arrival of the three Longboats had boosted Smertae morale, but it was short-lived.

Drest's rants about new land and great riches were wearing thin. The warriors thought the Norse warriors were the first of many who had come to join them. When the boats left after only one night and took all the Norse warriors with them, morale took a dive.

Drest knew he had to do something, but he didn't know what. Torridon had fallen. the King and Queen were dead and the King's army had been wiped out. The Smertae were safe and Frode had told him the Norse would attack Mahomack soon, but he didn't know exactly when. Frode was sorry the Smertae were stuck in the north and so far away. If they were closer to Mahomack, they could take part in the battle, but sending messengers wasn't possible. It would only take the Norse army half a day to reach Mahomack; it would take a messenger six days to get to Tongue and back. The battle would be over before the Smertae arrived.

Magnus had enough language to get most of Frode's message across to Drest with the help of Isla, but Drest still had to read between the lines. It was the bit between the lines that worried him. If he did nothing, he would deserve nothing. If he waited much longer, he would be able to do nothing. He had to act fast. Once they were assembled and away from nagging wives, the warriors would settle.

Drest had a plan and he had great knowledge of the terrain west of Tain, as did many Smertae. They claimed they knew these mountains better than the tribe who owned them. He summoned his leaders and put his plan to them.

They would keep well to the west of Bonner, cross into the high ground and come east along the top of the Struie. There they would be in a position to see everything happening below them. They could attack at the same time as the Norse and claim their just rewards. Drest's plan was greeted with great enthusiasm and the word was spread.

Meanwhile, to the west of Tongue, Dougal had been watching the water level for days. As it began to drop a little every day, he led twenty Carnavii west towards Torrisdale. Sinclair had ordered him to go, after hearing news of the three Norse boats loaded with warriors that had swept past Thurso and headed towards Tongue. They had to find out what was happening to the west. Dougal's spies had arrived screaming that the Smertae and Norse were coming. Nothing and nobody came. Sinclair was demented and Dougal jumped at the chance.

Dougal had been driven mad by young spies and old men. They arrived in Thurso panicked and out of control, sending everybody else into a panic. When no Smertae or Norse appeared from the west, questions were asked. Then it transpired they had fired the Stockade and dwellings because the Smertae and Norse might attack - not that they were on the attack and moving towards Torrisdale. Now they had to find out if they had moved anywhere at all.

To add to his woes, the olds were drunk when the youths arrived and only sobered up on the backs of horses. They had no idea if the fires they set took hold or went out. Dougal had left a small barrel of whiskey and he feared it wasn't used to fuel any fire.

The terrain proved challenging but they made good progress. Snow still clung to the North faces of the mountains, but the burns and small rivers were negotiable. Two scouts rode well ahead of the main party and they were his best warriors. The youths and the olds, he left in Thurso. The Scouts approached the river Naver, the main obstacle they had to cross and waited for Dougal to catch up. The river was in spate and running fast.

They had no choice but to head inland and find a crossing, but they knew that if they couldn't cross, neither could anyone else. They took comfort in that and spread wide when they left the track. The going was soft but only one horse stood on any one spot and they traversed the peat and bog without incident until they reached a wide section of river that was frothing. Dougal was pleased to see the white water marking the Ford. They crossed and followed the river north on the Torrisdale side until they re-joined the track. The diversion was good. They saw many cattle still on the Torrisdale side and they were their own cattle. Sheep had also gathered in clusters where grass grew and hadn't been rounded up, stolen or slaughtered.

The sight of the Stockade and its dwellings made them stop dead.

Dougal cursed loudly, but some cheered and galloped towards the settlement. Two dwellings had burned to the ground outside the Stockade and on entry, only a section of the living quarters was destroyed. Inside, the main ramparts were intact and damage, in general, was nothing compared to what it could have been.

Two warriors went on to the nest at Ben Loyal and the rest made camp for the night. Dougal didn't know if he was angry or should celebrate but finding the whiskey barrel empty, he decided to remain angry.

Daylight broke to clear skies and from the nest, the Stockade and settlement at Tongue slowly emerged along with the Kyle. No boats were seen, but many Smertae stayed around the Stockade. They waited until noon to see if any Norse appeared and none did, then they headed back to Torrisdale, tired and cold but happy their existence hadn't been erased. A sheep had been killed and a great feast awaited the Scouts. The news they brought didn't change anything, and two fresh souls were sent to replace them. They took the sheepskin and plenty of meat. Dougal ordered them to stay until something moved, but if nothing happened, he would have them relieved in two days.

They didn't have to wait that long. At first light the movement along the banks of the Kyle was unmistakable. They wouldn't move until the Smertae moved. Under threat of having their balls removed, they waited until around noon. A long line of warriors, led by horses, formed and headed south. The spies breathed a sigh of relief and descended from the nest carefully. Snow still lingered there and the entire mountain was slippery.

Dougal was ecstatic and sent messengers to Thurso with instructions to tell his people to come back with all haste and to bring fuel with them. The olds would know what that meant. His thoughts shifted to his kin at Loch Shin and he knew there was no way to warn them.

Sine rode beside Sheena at the head of the army. Ross and Enya came behind with Frazer, who had demanded he should go. They were entering Lugi lands and Stroma had backed Frazer's demand. They parted company at Bonner. Stroma went east with her escort and a heavy heart. Sheena led her force north with purpose, and the warriors urged speed. They had been frustrated long enough and felt ready for battle.

The urge for speed subsided quickly and the warriors were ordered to spread out. The ground wouldn't take two hundred horses in line, and this manoeuvre caused a rapid slowdown. They didn't skirt Lairg this time; by the time they reached there, it was getting dark and Frazer went ahead with ten warriors to calm the village. The Decantae were painted for battle and would have one if they arrived unannounced. Most of the warriors from Lairg were in Brora, but not all; around twenty remained to protect the settlement and its great herds of cattle, especially from Smertae.

They were made welcome at Lairg, and Sheena was glad Frazer had won his argument to join her. The Lugi warriors that were left to defend the cattle had bows and spears. Few had swords and Sheena asked why?

"When Smertae steals cattle, they come in the dark and they move fast," said Frazer. "You would never get near enough to them to use a sword and if you cornered one, it's like cornering a Wolf. They spear them or put an arrow into them."

Sheena looked at Sine. "You hear that sister? A cornered Smertae is dangerous. No sword, just your spear," warned Sheena and winked at Enya.

Frazer went to speak with the Lugi warriors and came looking happy.

"They say if we're going to kill Smertae, they want to go with us," he said. "No point in them staying here" and Sheena agreed.

A hundred of her warriors were double mounted and one hundred single.

"Tell them they're welcome," she responded to Frazer's questioning look.

"How many bowmen do we have all together?" asked Ross and nobody answered. "Find out and tell them to stay together. Tell the Lugi bowmen to stay with ours. Frazer! The Lairg warriors know this land. They can scout ahead in the morning." Frazer agreed.

Before daylight had broken, four Lugi were saddled and ready to leave. They had their own horses and Frazer spoke to them briefly.

"Make sure the old people are well, and then make for the Skew. I doubt if we can make it there before dark, but you might. If you don't see anything stay there until we come," he said and returned to the dwelling where he had slept. Cooking was well underway, and the army would leave after they ate.

Loch Shin shimmered in the sunlight and many insects rose from the heather as the horses passed. It hadn't rained here for three days and the high ground was good. It got softer as they neared the dwellings of the old people, and their coming had been noted. The two warriors were welcomed warmly. They were well known to the old people and visited them more than anybody else.

"You're painted for Battle, have the Smertae stolen any cattle?" they wanted to know, but when informed of the real reason, a stunned silence ensued.

They left after eating some soup and headed north. Their two companions were well to the east of them and they left the old people with something to speak about. They knew this terrain intimately, every crossing, every small glen; where they would be exposed and where to go not to be exposed. They had played the deadly game with Smertae many times and carried two spears each. They saw wolves in the distance towards the west and the high mountains, but no bears. Plenty of deer, Red and Roe and many hares, some with white snow-fur still clinging to them. Above, two great Golden Eagles claimed the sky and eyed what the horses disturbed.

Ross learned that the total amount of Bowmen was twenty-seven, five hands and two fingers by a warrior who couldn't count. He was pleased with that and repeated his order that the Bowmen stay together. This wasn't normal; weapons and those who owned them were mixed, but his order was passed.

"Any reason why you want the Bowmen in one bunch?" asked Frazer.

"At the battle in the river, the Smertae went mad. They were easy targets for Bowmen and a shower of arrows is more effective than one at a time," he grinned and Frazer nodded.

They left Lairg as quickly as they could and headed north. All day they tried to follow the most direct route to the Skew but were forced to deviate many times due to bog and raging water. As the day stretched on, they were back on track but it was unlikely they would reach the Skew before the light faded. To the north, both scouting parties met at what they called the slab. A place they knew well and where they camped if they were unable to get to the Skew. It was also a hidden glen with stunted trees and named after a great slab of rock that like the Skew, offered a little shelter. Good for ten but useless for three hundred.

Frazer knew this place and suggested if they couldn't reach the Skew, they would make for the Slab, but he wanted the Scouts to carry on to the Skew and gather firewood. They could also collect some from the Slab and take some timber with them if they had time.

They had time and set about collecting firewood. With a bundle each, they headed towards the Skew as the sun dropped down behind the nearest mountain, casting a great shadow across the land. They were riding with abandon and were high on the approach to the Skew when the lead rider pulled up fast and pointed.

Smoke was coming from the direction of the Skew. Not much but coming from two fires. The Scouts turned around and went slowly back the way they had come until they lost sight of the smoke then they headed west. A light breeze was coming from the east and they wanted to get downwind of the Skew and the smoke.

They stopped in a hollow and sat on the bundles of firewood while they waited for darkness. When it came, they headed north walking their horses until they could smell smoke. Then they knew they were in the right direction, and three went forward towards the source of the smoke, leaving the fourth with the horses.

Walking quickly, they covered the distance to the west of the small, deep glen where water seeped and spread causing a bog. They skirted the bog and crawled forward seeing the flickering of flames ahead. Smoke and the smell of roasting meat filled the air and the sight unfolding before them made their blood run cold. A sea of horses and warriors were camped along the entire length of the glen. The Lugi scouts stared transfixed at the silhouette of horses and warriors against the light from many fires, not just under the ledge but all along both sides of the Glen.

# Chapter 9

The shock subsided slowly but the threat of what lay before them demanded great caution. They backed away without taking their eyes off the Smertae camp, much in the same as they would back away from a mother bear with cubs, barely breathing and never blinking until they reached the bog. Then they breathed heavily and crouching, headed back towards their horses.

"Hundreds of Smertae warriors and many horses, we must get back and warn the army," they whispered and walked their horses well to the south before mounting.

They headed south as fast as it was safe to do so, agreeing they should head back to the Slab first. If the army wasn't there, they would have to go further south, but finding them in the dark if they had no fire would prove difficult, and they had no idea if they would light fires in the open. They would certainly be in some secluded glen but which one? Knowing the terrain well, they soon decided on a second and third location and headed straight for the Slab. It was late when they saw the fire, only one under the Slab and they grinned.

Now they were in great danger of being mistaken for the enemy and yelled loudly to warn the guards of their approach. Walking their horses forward cautiously, they quickly found themselves surrounded by spear-wielding warriors, who escorted them to Sheena. They found her standing by the fire with Ross and Frazer, swords drawn.

"What is it?" asked Sheena.

"Scouts!" answered Frazer. "They've come back, they must have seen something."

The Scouts approached unarmed, having given up their weapons to the Decantae warriors. Frazer smiled.

"Your warriors don't trust anybody, Ross!" he said and went to greet the Lugi.

They explained what they had seen to a stunned audience and stared desperately at the meat roasting on the fire.

"You eat and stay here," ordered Frazer, before addressing Sheena.

"You told us a Smertae army from the north might come behind us and we doubted you. What do you have to say now, Ross?"

"I'm not worried about what to say, I'm more worried about what to do?" he replied.

"What they saw was in the glen," said Frazer. "But there might be more they didn't see. We can't attack them in the dark, but we can attack them at dawn."

Several warriors had come to see what was happening and Ross told them to gather all the warriors close so he could address them. Then he explained what the scouts had seen. Many among the warriors knew the Skew and when they erupted into battle cries, Ross yelled for quiet. When silence eventually returned, Ross announced that from now on, any warrior who made a noise would be killed by the warrior next to him. As he intended, that got their attention.

"This is Lugi land; they know the terrain better than anybody," said Frazer. "The warriors from Lairg will lead the army. We will ride until we get close to the Skew, then dismount and walk the horses until the signal to stop. At the first rays of daylight, we mount and charge. The bowmen stay with me."

Silence prevailed but Frazer did not let them forget the threat.

"I repeat what Ross said, stay silent or die. Now, get mounted and follow the warriors of Lairg."

Sheena came to him grinning in the light of the fire.

"What are you going to do with the bowmen?" she asked.

"I'm going to get them close enough to pick Drest's teeth," Frazer replied gathering up his saddle.

They rode the horses into the night and the warriors of Lairg led them to the west of the Skew. It was a long way but they estimated they would get there well before daybreak. The sky was clear, daylight would come quickly. They had to get close and in position ready to charge. If they charged from a distance, the Smertae would hear them coming. They had to surprise them, even if it meant charging on foot. With horses single mounted, one hundred warriors would be charging on foot behind Enya's mounted charge.

The gentle breeze wasn't in Frazer's favour. He wanted to get the bowmen into position along the steep gully that abounded in blackberry bushes along its sides but decided the risk was too great. The horses would be alerted if they went upwind of them and he decided to position them in front of the overhang. They couldn't kill anybody under the overhang, but they would kill anybody coming out from under it and he suspected Drest's leaders would be favourite for the comforts of the ledge.

Had the Lugi not been leading, nobody would have known where they were. Even those who had passed this way before felt lost. They had no idea where the Lugi were taking them and when at last they stopped, they could see no reason why. All they could hear were the sounds of horses.

Two Scouts came back and gave Frazer clear instructions.

"We dismount here and go on foot. If you want to divide the warriors for an attack, you have to do that here."

Frazer consulted Sheena and Ross.

"It's still a long way to the Skew," he said. "But we need to organise here. Any closer will be dangerous if the horses make a noise."

They knew both would lead a hundred in the charge. Frazer would lead the bowmen, while Enya would lead one hundred to charge the Smertae horses and scatter them. They would ride straight through the Smertae camp and trample all who got in their way, then swing left and come behind Sheena who would charge upwind and along the Glen to join Ross, leading those on foot behind Enya and swing right towards the overhang.

"Five have gone ahead to kill the guards," said Frazer.

They informed the commanders that the Queen would lead one hundred singles mounted; Enya one hundred single-mounted; Ross one hundred on foot, and Frazer, the bowmen.

"Assemble those on foot first then sort out the horses," ordered Ross.

It took time to sort out things in the dark and they were glad they had that time. Frazer led the bowmen on foot to the right and held them there. Sheena led a hundred mounted to the left and Enya a hundred beside Frazer. Ross held a hundred back and the order was given to walk forward.

The Lugi warriors bellied towards the Skew and peered through the heather, looking for guards but knowing the Smertae, they were more likely to depend on horses raising the alarm than their warriors. They marvelled at the number of horses they had and wondered who they had stolen them from. Some would certainly be Lugi. They saw no guards; no movement and the fires were low under the ledge. They retreated slowly to join the approaching army.

Sheena had proposed they encircle the Smertae, but Frazer dashed that idea.

"We must leave them a way to escape," he explained. "You must leave the north clear. No warriors to the north. As soon as Enya charges through them, she must swing west. If they think they're trapped, they'll fight. If they can escape, they will escape. Don't go after any that escape, let them go. Drest is the one we want. This is his army; the rest are just obeying their Chief."

"He's right," said Ross. "We have no idea how many they are. If they run, let them, or we might regret it."

"I want Drest alive," snapped Sheena.

They decided they would split their forces, but attack at the same time. They needed a signal that all would hear, and Sheena grinned.

"You decide when to attack, I'll give you the signal," she said. It was the excuse she was looking for and she went to Sine.

"You must go with Frazer and the bowmen, sister. Give your horse to somebody. When Frazer tells you, I want to hear the call of the wolf loud and clear and keep howling until Frazer tells you to move. You will be giving the signal to attack," Sheena said and crushed her to her breast. "Go!" she urged and pushed her in Frazer's direction.

Sheena passed the signal to all those leading. Two bow shots from the crest of the glen they halted. A Lugi came to Sheena and told her to follow him to the left. She did so and her warriors followed her. Frazer moved next, taking his bowmen and Sine to the right leaving Ross and Enya in the centre.

It seemed to take forever until a shaft of dim light appeared to the east and even longer before a blood-curdling howl made everyone's hair stand on end and the horses lunge forward, snorting.

In several strides, the howling was drowned out by an eruption of battle cries that seemed to envelop the earth. Enya dug her heels into her mount as the warriors let out a great roar. They were at full gallop when they came over the crest and the startled Smertae scattered in all directions. So did their horses, already on edge by the closeness to wolves. They reared and whinnied in terror as Enya's horses thundered towards them. Many broke free and ran for safety, many turned and ran alongside the charging horses, trampling screaming Smertae and knocking them over, while swords slashed down on those who still stood and spears skewered those who crouched.

Sheena struck from the left flank and Frazer's bowmen ran to cover the ledge. Ross's warriors ran screaming behind Enya's horse and crashed head-on with the survivors of her charge. She had driven a furrow through the main body of the Smertae and Sheena drove another through their flank. Enya wheeled left when they cleared the north rim of the glen and fell in alongside Sheena's charge. Many Smertae horses followed her troop and others ran with Sheena. The Smertae scattered in every direction as more than two hundred horses attacked from their side.

Racing from under the cover of the ledge, bodies poured into the open and were met with a hail of arrows from Frazer's bowmen. Some fell, others scarpered back under the ledge. Smertae were being driven towards the ledge and by the Decantae on foot and bowmen shifted their aim. Arrows thudded into backs and many facing Ross fell.

"Take them as they come into the open!" screamed Frazer, seeing more Smertae dashing from under the ledge.

Sine launched a spear and caught one high in the neck. Another took two arrows through his shoulder and they turned, not to run under the ledge but weaving towards the steep gully.

Smertae headed up the north slope of the Glen. They feared another charge from the horses that had gone over the top. They had no idea it was the same horses now attacking their flank. They reached the top and stared north. Only some horses could be seen and they had no riders. The Smertae formed a battle group along the high ground and roared their war cries down at the battle raging below but made no move to join it. They would hold the high ground and the Decantae could attack them there.

More Smertae broke before the charging horses and the ferocity of the foot warriors. Some headed up, others ran for the steep gully and many fell before they reached it. A surge of bodies raced from under the ledge and Sine's second spear mingled with many arrows before skewering a Smertae through the head. Half of them turned back and many were exposed to another rain of arrows. Some hauled the wounded into shelter, but as soon as arrows were fired at the raging battle, they raced again towards the gully; many made it and dropped from sight.

The Smertae on the north ridge screamed for their warriors to join them and some did. That only made the task of defeating those who didn't, easier. The bottom of the Skew was torn apart, the soft ground churned into a quagmire of blood, bodies and mud. Sheena screamed at Ross. She had seen the formation taking shape on the north ridge and feared they would charge.

He parried a thrust from a female Smertae and smashed his shield into the side of her head. She fell and he went to Sheena.

"Fly your standard. fly your standard!" Ross screamed at her.

She dug into her saddlebag and pulled out the standard of the King. A warrior lowered his spear and held it in front of her. With shaking hands, Sheena tied the standard to the spear and the warrior raised aloft the cross of St Andrews. When the Smertae on the ridge saw the standard of the King, fear ran their length. Until now they were fighting Lugi and Decantae, not the army of the King. But the King was dead. Drest had told them the King was dead, and the Queen. Now they looked at the warrior beside the flag and many gasped that it was the Queen. Others thought otherwise, but the Standard of the King flew, and they couldn't argue with that.

The shouting gradually decreased and morale sunk along the ledge, but the Smertae remained ready for anything, except what happened next. The standard and the warrior with yellow hair and the one bearing the flag of the King came towards them protected by twenty horses. They walked and stopped halfway up the slope.

"The Norse are defeated, go back to your homes. Where is Drest?" asked Sheena, her voice penetrating the silence.

Several arms pointed towards the ledge, but nobody spoke.

"Take your wounded with you," she commanded. "Who will be

chief?"

She watched as a scuffle broke out among them. One warrior was pushed to the fore and Sheena beckoned him to come closer. Reluctantly he approached her and lowered his sword.

"What's your name?" she asked.

"Alastair!" replied the warrior.

"And why you? Why will you be chief?"

"Drest's sons are dead. Drest's sister is my mother."

"Tell them to stop doing battle, and lead them back to Tongue," she ordered and Alastair commanded his warriors to sound the retreat.

A hunting horn blew one long blast and swords were lowered. Eyes turned north and those who could run, headed up the hill fast but those who couldn't struggled, expecting to be cut down, accepting their fate. But Sheena turned and galloped east, clearing the way for those who streamed up from the hell below.

"Let them go! Let them go!" roared Ross and sat on a dead horse with his head between his legs. He looked at the warrior he had hit with his shield, she was alive but just lay there staring at him.

"You're not dead! Go home!" he shouted. She leapt to her feet and ran up towards Alastair, who stood alone.

"Find Drest!" ordered Sheena and the mass closed in around the rock ledge.

He had an arrow through his thigh, but Drest was far from surrender and came out screaming.

"Why do you attack your own people? I bring an army to help Urquhart fight the Norse and you attack me? My Queen, you live. I, your humble servant Drest, would never do battle with you, but it was dark and you attacked us!" he complained, wringing his hands.

Sheena smiled and looked at him with amusement.

"You tricked me once, Drest, then you sent assassins to kill me. The warriors Kayra and Imogen you sent are dead."

"Noooo my Queen, I sent nobody. The Norse must have sent them."

"Who told you I was dead?" Sheena grinned.

"The Norse said you died with the King in a great battle. They lied!" Drest stammered.

Frazer came close behind Drest and locked eyes with Sheena. She nodded.

"Drest! Alastair, your sister's son has replaced you as chief," she stated.

His eyes narrowed and his mouth opened as Frazer swung his sword at the back of his neck.

Sine recovered her spears and took hair from both warriors she had killed. She held the hair up for Enya to see and ran to Sheena who had dismounted. She stared at the head of Drest and jumped when Sheena spoke.

"The howling wolf has arrived," Sheena smiled and looked at what she held. "One or two?"

"Two," replied Sine proudly and headed for Frazer.

Behind them, the screams of the wounded faded and Ross waited with all the horses and warriors, while the Smertae moved their wounded to the hilltop. Alastair still stood there, proud of them and he knew why. Ten bowmen covered him with arrows notched. He would be the first to die if he ordered a charge.

As the Smertae cleared the battlefield, Sheena rode to Alastair alone.

"You will swear allegiance to the King and Scotland," she commanded and he obeyed on one knee. "Go, Alastair, and lead your people more wisely than Drest did," Sheena advised, dropping Drest's head at his feet. He took a sharp breath and kicked the head down the hill.

"I swear," he said and bowed.

Sheena galloped back to join Ross and Enya. They breathed a sigh of relief when the last of the Smertae vanished, but Ross sent warriors to the top to make sure they weren't playing tricks.

Battle fatigue descended quickly on the victors and Sheena gathered her command under the overhang.

"It seems everybody thinks I died with the King," she said. "The Norse think I'm dead. The spies thought I was dead. If what Drest claimed is true, that the Norse sent the spies and not him, and the Norse truly believe I died with the King, they sent the spies to kill my father."

"If they think you're dead, they won't hunt you down," suggested Frazer.

"Too many people know I'm still alive."

"We must leave here and head back to Stroma. I'll leave the Lairg men to bury the dead," Frazer announced and left them.

He soon returned, grinning and announced they had forty horses more than they started with and they were being saddled.

"How many did we lose?" Sheena asked and she didn't mean horses.

"Ross is counting."

Ross arrived with Enya. Both were mounted and covered in blood. They dropped to the ground wearily.

"We've lost about fifty and the Smertae half as much again," reported Ross and sat down heavily.

"That many! We need to bury our warriors here," replied Frazer and rose to his feet.

"I want to leave at noon," Sheena called after him as he strode towards their warriors.

She needed space and went under the overhang. Something caught her eye and she snatched it up, with a wicked grin she shoved it under her top carefully. She didn't want Drest's head, but this was even better.

The ride south was much faster than the ride north. The ground became firm along the tops of the hills and they had no reason to hide. They entered the forest above Loch Fleet and made their way down through the trees with Frazer leading. They reached the fringe of the forest around noon and stared across the rich lands and Loch Fleet. Eyes drifted in the direction of Mahomack and Tain, but they saw no reason for concern. Both were far away.

# Chapter 10

Two mounted warriors came galloping from the village on the shore of Loch Fleet and from their yelps, it was obvious they were glad to see Frazer and those he had with him. Sheena came beside him and they waited in silence, each with their own thoughts. The two riders reined in beside Frazer and nodded to Sheena, but it was Frazer they addressed.

"The Norse came at first light yesterday thirty-three boats and thousands of warriors Stroma wants you to ride along the east shore of the Loch and show yourself," the warrior rattled off in a panic.

"Speak slowly, man! Now start again," complained Frazer.

His companion spoke and he had himself under control.

"The Norse came yesterday at first light. Thirty-three boats and thousands of warriors. They're beside Dornoch, all their boats are along the beach and many have camped on the shore. Stroma wants you to ride along the east side of Loch Fleet so you can be seen," the messenger announced loud enough for all to hear.

"Are any on the east side of Little Ferry?" asked Frazer.

"Have any attacked Mahomack?" Sheena cut in, alarmed.

"No! They made camp beside Dornoch. They haven't attacked anywhere."

"Two boats are on the east side of Little Ferry," added the first messenger.

"Where is Stroma?" asked Frazer.

"She's at Galspie with fifty horses. She says to light the beacon at the village when you come, and she will meet you at the beach. Forbes is with her and the rest of the warriors are holding the Stockade. Everybody has abandoned their dwellings and they are all massed at Brora."

"Three hundred horses if we combine with Stroma. That's more than the King ever led. The Norse will think twice before moving away from Dornoch," replied Frazer.

"We rest first," said Sheena, "and then you can light the fire. We've come a long way and fought a great battle. We need to rest before we fight another," and she spurred her mount forward.

The army came clear of the treeline in one long column as Ross had ordered. Two abreast and keep a horse length between you, were his orders. If any Norse lurked in a position to see them, the force would look even more impressive than it already was.

Saddle-sore and weary, the army rested at the fishing village that had been abandoned. Sheena stared across Loch Fleet, her heart in the pit of her stomach.

Sigurd looked with satisfaction at the vast marching camp that had sprung up across the beach and onto the plain. The plain stretched as far as the timber-clad hills to the north. He had sent scouts to the abandoned village with orders to stay there and watch for any hostile movement coming from the north. They had water on three sides of the camp and only the north lay open to an attack from the land. The entrance that Frode couldn't identify proved to be the entrance to a large lake and not a river. It was deep and could only be crossed at slack tide. A great volume of water flowed through this entrance to their east. The sea was behind them to the south and what Ro-Sheen had identified as the Dornoch Fjord lay to their west.

Sigurd had taken six riders and horses across from Torfness on a Knarr. Two he dispatched to watch the area beyond the village. Two were along the shore of the lake with orders to report any movement of any kind no matter how small, reminding them that these savages could hide in a blade of grass; the remaining two he held at the beach.

Across the Fjord, Mahomack could be seen in the distance and Sigurd was impressed. The savages had used their big lumbering trading boats wisely and they were spread along the beach broadside on and grounded. Higher sided than a Longboat, they would be hard to take. Each one had become a stockade and would be swarming with warriors. The beach was long and they were easily avoided so attacking from the land was possible, he concluded.

Up until now, the savages looked from afar and the Norse looked back but neither made a move. Sigurd knew, and Frode knew, the strength of the force at Mahomack. What they didn't know was the strength of the force to the east; Lugi, as Ro-Sheen called them.

"They haven't taken your bait yet, Sigurd!" said Frode.

"Not yet, but they will," he smiled.

Frode had objected to putting two Longboats on their own across on the east side of the entrance to the lake. They were exposed and his army couldn't cross if they were attacked. He could see no problem in daylight but at night the risk was unacceptable.

Sigurd compromised and the two Longboats moved across to their side of the entrance as soon as it started to get dark, and returned to the opposite side at daylight. The crews didn't stray far from their boats and were ready to push them back into the water at the first sign of an attack.

This beach was firm and stretched for as far as anybody could see to the east. The terrain was the same as that at Dornoch and offered very little cover for any approaching force by day, but by night Sigurd had to agree with Frode, it was leaving a hundred warriors exposed.

Frode cast his eyes across the mountains behind Tain and sighed. Not until a signal came from there would they attack Mahomack. When the Smertae were in position, the attack on Mahomack would begin. The Smertae would attack from behind when all eyes were on the Norse. Sigurd also had another iron in the fire. Imogen, she would be there somewhere, and as soon as the attack began, in the turmoil, she would kill their leader or some of their command. As things stood now, the Decantae looked across at them from the nearest sand spit and they looked back. If the Decantae came by land with their horses the Norse would go to Mahomack in their boats, and they would get there long before the Decantae could get back. Sigurd knew they wouldn't be so stupid.

Reluctantly, Ross shouted the order to mount and weary warriors groaned as they stretched. They had rested and eaten but the long journey had taken its toll on morale.

"Light the signal fire!" ordered Frazer as he mounted. "Who is going to lead, Sheena?"

"Drest," she grinned and produced Drest's headgear they called a Bonnet. It had a bright red tassel on top and two eagle feathers stuck down the side, the sign of a Chief.

Frazer laughed and flicked his thumb at Ross who approached with

Enya and Sine. Sheena smiled then put on a serious face.

"You, brother, you look the same size as Drest. Try this on," she smiled and handed him the bonnet.

He grabbed it willingly and set it on his head. "A Chief at last!" he laughed.

"Chiefs lead, so, get to the front. Drest lives a little longer," roared Sheena.

Ross took a bow, sweeping his eagle feathers low before planting them firmly on his head. The warriors laughed and began to form a column. They followed the Loch around to the east and then it went south. Their enthusiasm increased as they closed the distance at a canter.

On the opposite side of the Loch, the west side, they spotted two riders heading south at the gallop, and they knew somebody had seen them. Soon after a shout caused Ross to turn and he watched as Stroma and her horses raced towards them across the grassland.

They slowed to a walk and Stroma turned her horses in the same direction some distance apart. She waved with her arm to go forward and Ross spurred his mount. Both columns headed for the beach at the gallop and warriors sensed they were going into battle.

Sigurd reacted swiftly and mounted, as did Frode and they galloped towards the two Longboats on the east side of the lake entrance. The messenger had warned the warriors there before heading for the camp and many warriors pushed the two Longboats into the water.

Sigurd cursed when he saw the great column of horses coming along the edge of the lake and the other column further to the east was going to reach the beach before the Longboats were afloat. However, the sight of what was approaching sent the Norse warriors into a frenzy and the Longboats slid into the water as Stroma hit the sand to their right. Warriors were pulled aboard and oars went out quickly, but several arrows found their mark before the Longboats were out of range of the Bowmen.

Ross was hard behind her but by the time half the column reached the beach, the Longboats were clear and the warriors on them cheered and jeered from safety.

"Look across the other side!" shouted Frazer.

Ross saw two mounted warriors, several bow shots to the west watching what was happening and he waved to them with his Tammy and yelped his way into the water to cool the horses. They followed Stroma's troop east along the beach and the two Longboats went west back to the safe area.

Sigurd and Frode had been shocked by what they saw and neither spoke. They had expected horses but not an army of them and where were the warriors with no horses? They watched as the last of the departing force cleared the beach and headed inland.

"You caught a big fish with a little hook," said Frode.

"That was a whale, not a fish. A little faster, they would have eaten the bait," replied Sigurd, knowing his warriors were lucky to be alive. He could have lost two Longboats. This force was more powerful than he or anybody imagined and he couldn't think clearly.

"In Mahomack, the sight of the two Longboats moving put everybody on alert. Krike had eaten with Aggie, the dog and Angus. Now they were on alert day and night and everybody was getting short-tempered. They had to split the force and let half of them sleep in shifts, something that was never done when the threat was staring you in the face.

He thought Urquhart would dismiss his proposal, but he encouraged it. They were too far away from Little Ferry to see what had happened there. Urquhart was feeling the strain, so Sorsce took over at night along with Fiona, when most of his command went north, and he fretted. Two of his daughters, his only two, were running wild. He couldn't have stopped them but that was no consolation. Urquhart still worried. Sleep had helped him, and he knew his warriors were badly in need of rest.

"Sort it out Krike, they need sleep. Half down and half up, whatever you decide," he declared.

A messenger came from the treeline behind Tain and told Urquhart he had seen smoke coming from Loch Fleet. He didn't know what it meant. Neither did Urquhart and after debating, they decided the Lugi must be signalling to each other.

"Why don't they attack?" complained Fiona.

"You mean the Norse? They wait, what for, we don't know?"

sighed Urquhart. Frustration was getting to all of them.

Close to the deserted settlement of Galspie, there was a great celebration and weary horses were led to rich grass. Warriors Lugi and Decantae danced in sheer abandon when the story of the battle at the Skew was told and the Smertae were neutralised. Drest's bonnet was placed on a spear and Stroma wanted to know why they hadn't taken heads.

"Too far, too heavy and they stink after two days. But plenty of hair!" smiled Enya, holding up her trophies to a great cheer.

Sine joined her in triumph and was lifted onto shoulders to parade her trophies. Now she would get two circles and she was indeed a warrior.

Whiskey and food abounded and the retreat of the two Norse boats was read by many as a victory. However not all shared this view, Forbes being the most sceptical.

"It doesn't make sense putting two boats on the wrong side of the channel at Little Ferry. It's deep and they would get no help from the main army. They moved quickly back to where they should have been. Bait! I'm thinking, to lure our force into the open."

"They did and shit themselves," Ross grinned.

Sheena put on a brave face and exchanged banter and ideas until the light faded, then sought solitude with the horses. Her mind was troubled. Only the Norse could have told Drest she was dead. According to him, he hadn't sent the spies and claimed the Norse had sent them. If the Norse truly believed she was dead, everybody south would think she died with the King and there was no safe way or means to tell otherwise. Somebody must have seen her escape from Torridon. Somebody must have lived who saw her in the Fort and somebody must have lied convincingly to the Norse that she had gone with the King.

Sheena knew if the King and Queen were both dead it wouldn't take long to put a successor on the throne. The southern tribes would jump at the chance and Eagan had blood amongst them. Bran was dead. She was stranded in the north and until the battle with the Smertae, nobody except the Lugi and Decantae knew she was still alive. If a new King had been anointed, not only the Norse would be after her head. She was deeply troubled. She returned to the celebrations when the sword dance started and watched Sine and Lugi warriors, male and female, perform to great cheer.

Stroma had warriors that could keep their eyes open and Forbes sent some to watch the beach and the approaches to Galspie. Decantae wounded had been sent to Brora. It didn't take long for whiskey to send more to sleep than dance. The Decantae had been riding for five days and had fought a great battle. All were exhausted and they still had to get the horses back to Tain without the Norse seeing them. There was only one way to achieve that and it meant traversing the Struie, approaching Mahomack from the west along the low ground or leading them down the deer runs through the forest, or both.

The horses that were captured from the Smertae would stay with the Lugi and Stroma would build her mounted force to close to a hundred. This was decided by Sheena and Ross had agreed. It made more sense to have a substantial mounted force east and west of the Norse and if they managed to return the rest of the horses to Tain unseen, the Norse would think twice about attacking in either direction.

The sight of the charging horses had stunned all who witnessed it and those on the receiving end felt shaken when they returned the Longboats to the west side of the entrance to the Lake. Sigurd summoned the two commanders and listened to their account in silence. Only two arrows had found their mark and both warriors escaped with flesh wounds, but the speed at which the horses had covered the ground from when they were seen until the alarm was raised was borderline for getting both boats to safety and shouldn't happen again.

Sigurd had no intention of repeating his ploy to get the enemy to reveal itself and assured them of that. He had nearly lost two boats, a hundred warriors, and nobody was more conscious of the fact than he.

Frode had hinted that Drest should wait for ten days after he left for Stromness, then to start south. He didn't know when Sigurd would attack. He proposed that if Drest reached the high ground before the Norse arrived, he had to keep out of sight until they came. If the Norse arrived before he reached the high ground, the Norse would wait until he signalled. Drest had to signal from the high ground the Norse army would be clearly seen from there, but the lack of communications worried both Sigurd and Frode.

Ro-Sheen was now protected like a jewel. Sigurd had asked for two Shield Maidens and Astrid had gladly supplied them; two of her best with orders to protect the interpreter with their lives. Frode surprised Sigurd when he suggested they should erect defences to the north. Sigurd had no intention of erecting anything, his defences were already built. All he had to do was kill the present owners and take them as he had done in Torfness.

The abandoned village close by offered some ready-made defences in the form of stone walls that separated fields. Frode set about improving this defence, more to keep his warriors occupied than for any real attempt to stop a horse charge. With four thousand pairs of hands, it didn't take long to dismantle a wall and rebuild it in a line of defence that stretched east-west that would halt any charge.

Sigurd smiled when he saw it, and encouraged its development, knowing it would send a message to the observers across the water; a message that he was defending not attacking. That message he warned Frode, didn't apply to his warriors. Frode quickly assured him they wouldn't get comfortable behind walls, but they had to be ready to attack or defend whatever came first.

Towards noon, Sheena led her two hundred horses east towards Brora with Frazer and Enya riding side by side. Father and daughter parted company at the entrance to a small glen that ran between two tree-clad hills, and Ross watched their parting with mixed feelings. She had insisted on going with him back to Tain when Ross gave her the choice that she could stay with her father or go with him.

She rode beside him and her eyes were dry.

"My father said if you get into trouble, you can head for Brora," she laughed and Ross laughed with her.

They had to traverse the high ground back towards the river crossing at Bonner and that meant a long journey through the forest and another well inland behind the north hills before they could approach the crossing without being seen. They knew they couldn't go up the track to the Struie in daylight with so many horses, for fear of being seen and in the dark, it would be suicide. The alternative was a long journey west until they reached a slope that would allow them to gain enough height before turning east back towards the track which they hoped to join at its highest point.

They camped when darkness was nearly upon them, but now rested and fed, they could have carried on, which was something Ross had considered, then dismissed. The moon was growing, and the skies were clear. It hadn't rained for days and the ground was firm. They would make time safely in daylight, but it would take the best of two days to get over the Struie the long way.

Sheena had explained to her commanders why they were going the long way, and why they had left the Smertae horses with the Lugi. That wasn't a popular decision, as many Decantae now had to ride double. However, getting warriors to Tain on foot in the dark wasn't hard. They would release those riding double, as close to Bonner as they dared, and they would make their way to Tain on foot. It was too dangerous to climb the mountain double mounted and they knew there would be stretches where even mounted would be impossible. The presence of snow added to their concerns.

Urquhart was more relaxed than he had been since the Norse arrived, they were building defences. That meant little and could be a ploy, but they could also fear an attack from the north or try and entice one. He had no intentions of attacking them from any direction and they could build a Stockade if they wanted. They were on Lugi land, land, that was good but wasted. The population of Dornoch was around ten families and they traded more with the Decantae than with the Lugi. Isolated on a long wide peninsula between Loch Fleet and the Dornoch Firth, the settlement was ancient and had given its name to the Firth.

No fires were lit at night, but many were lit during the day, as was the way with the Norse, and he played them at their own game. Warriors had gone into defence mode and no longer wanted to attack the invaders. Krike had sharpened poles dug into the mud at the low water mark, keeping everybody busy throughout the night. Now half were used to working in the dark and the other half by day.

They were stuck. Urquhart couldn't attack and the Norse didn't attack, and each day they delayed, taking Mahomack was getting harder for them.

Urquhart was fast asleep when somebody shook his shoulder and he looked into the eyes of Sine. He jumped up and grabbed her by the shoulders and shook her.

"Where the devil did you come from?" Urquhart rasped not sure if he was dreaming.

She laughed and struggled from his grip.

"She's come back with fifty warriors," said Sorsce, excitement in her voice. "Sheena and Ross are taking the horses over the Struie."

"Father, look!" shouted Sine, holding up two scalps for Urquhart to see. "Smertae. we did battle and we destroyed their army. I killed two!" she beamed.

"Let me get up and get some food and a drink, then you can tell me everything that's happened," Urquhart smiled and ruffled her already ruffled hair.

Sorsce dragged her away still speaking about horses and Lugi. Urquhart was keen to hear what she had to say and dressed quickly. A great dread had vanished, and he felt elated. He rushed into the kitchen and grabbed her around the waist. Spinning her around with great joy and hilarity.

"Tell me how you got here? Then what Sheena is doing. Start with that, then you can tell me the rest," Urquhart smiled and pointed to her two scalps.

Her excitement was infectious and Urquhart listened to a full account of her travels and battle in great detail, unaware she was a howler of great esteem. The news that they had lost fifty warriors in the battle was only justified by the Smertae loss being greater and the news that Drest had his head removed by Frazer, made Urquhart clap his hands in approval. The charge against the Norse and nearly catching two boats on the beach beside Little Ferry explained a lot and now Stroma had the Smertae horses. Great happenings she revealed in great detail, followed by her spear-throwing prowess, and he was delighted for her.

"How long until daylight?" he asked.

"Not long, can I start a fire?" asked Sorsce.

"Start the fire and get the warriors that came with Sine into the great hall; I want their story," said Urquhart and pointed to Sine's trophies. "Don't let Fia see them. They might be her kin!" he warned.

Deep in dangerous territory, the horses were halted below the great mountain and many fires were lit. This far up the river, bears and wolves prowled freely, undisturbed and unafraid of humans. Morning would reveal what lay before them, and they hoped memories of the hunters were correct. Few had ever been here and those who had, travelled down, not up.

Few slept, but many tried; wolves were heard not far away. The horses remained uneasy throughout the night and by the break of dawn, everybody was keen to go. When daylight finally revealed their challenge, they breathed a sigh of relief. Across the river Carron, the land was steep but not so steep; it could be climbed without traversing along the slope. It was as the hunters said and after crossing the river, they went straight up and soon found flat ground. The climb was stepped as had been explained to Sheena and they knew they were climbing in the right place, sometimes mounted, sometimes walking and they gained great height.

By noon they had reached the summit and were rewarded with a most magnificent view to the west and north. Not much snow remained on the west side and what remained was bypassed as they continued east along the flat tops and came across a track leading south. It had to be the Struie track and they picked up speed. With some luck, they would make it off the mountains before dark and ears that had popped incessantly on the way up, popped again on the long descent.

Before dark, they had reached the Struie sister's graves and Sheena was keen to keep going towards Mahomack. If they could get the horses back to their pastures and the warriors among their fellows before daylight, the Norse would see nothing. They would hear nothing also and she reminded all her warriors as they had already celebrated their victory in Galspie, there would be no celebration in Mahomack. They would melt into the defences as if they had never left.

Ross got the message across a little better.

"Celebrate again and you die," he announced and ordered them forward.

There was no argument against Sheena's thinking, and they set out along the track at a canter. This was heaven compared to what they had endured since leaving Tain. Two gallopers went ahead to warn the warriors along the track that they were coming, and Sheena guessed they would already know - if they were still alive?

"Are you all right, Sheena?" asked Ross, as they neared the rise that stood between them and a view of Mahomack. It was close to the junction where warriors had been standing guard.

"I think we should dismount here and go ahead on foot," she replied.

Ross relayed her request and the column came to a halt. He walked by her side towards the rise and suddenly a voice boomed out of the darkness.

"Hurry up, move yer arse, Ross!"

"Krike!" Sheena cried, greatly relieved.

From the darkness emerged many warriors. Riders handed them the reins gladly. Krike ushered Sheena and Ross to the side of the track where four horses were held.

"Where's Enya?" he asked.

"Here!" she said from behind him.

"Mount up. Urquhart wants you in Tain," said Krike.

They groaned but mounted.

"It's as black as hell," said Ross.

"No fires, only in the day. And the Norse are doing the same. We need to move before the moon gets up," urged Krike and they headed for Tain at a canter.

All eyes stared to the right as they went but they saw nothing. As Ross had said, it was black as hell, and on both sides of the Firth except for the pale light of the moon.

Their arrival at the Stockade in Tain proved anything but subdued. Many warriors came to welcome them and escorted them to the great hall where even more gathered, along with Sine and Urquhart who greeted them at the door. The Norse were far enough away for them to hold a party, but Urquhart demanded normal procedure and lectured family and warriors alike that no sign of anything having taken place should be shown.

Inside, fires were allowed, but none in the open and the great hall felt warm. Also, a great spread of food awaited them, which Sorsce stood guard over. The travellers were exhausted, and it showed. Even Sine didn't manage to stir them and conversation was abandoned in favour of food. Ross and Enya went to his quarters and he asked where Fiona was?

"She's at Mahomack. She'll come back at daylight," said Fia and they collapsed on a sleeping platform.

Sheena and Sine crawled onto another in her quarters and soon sleep enveloped them. Urquhart spent some time with Krike, and they went over recent events. They had the main details; the trivia didn't matter. The facts were that the Smertae were defeated and the Norse attacked at Little Ferry. The horses and warriors were back, and Stroma had acquired fifty more horses. How fooled the Norse would be, nobody knew, but the way Sheena had returned was, beyond question, impossible for any Norse to have seen.

They could speculate on the Smertae's intentions, but it was definitely not what Drest had claimed. And he was dead. Urquhart had his Bonnet and Eagle Feathers similar to his own, but Drest's feathers were bigger than his and he would swap them.

# Chapter 11

Norse Bowmen were on every boat and watched for any movement from the sea towards their beached fleet. It was something Sigurd feared more than anything. One small boat with two men could inflict serious damage to his boats and lookouts were posted throughout the night. They checked everywhere, especially between the beached boats, the only hiding place.

Something caught the eye of one and he poked it with a boat hook. It was soft and he called his companion to come and look. It was a body with no head, they concluded and pushed it away towards the sea. It stank and meant nothing to them. As they pushed it out between the boats, it turned over and they realised it was a female. The current took it and they washed the tip of the boathook clean.

This incident was reported to their commander and in turn, reported to Frode. It meant as little to him as it did to the warriors but proved his lookouts were doing their job. Sigurd received reports from all his commanders at first light and nothing was reported of any significance.

"Let them eat, and then march north," Sigurd frowned.

"Two thousand, the other two can sleep. Let me march them first. They can eat when they come back," decided Frode and started shouting orders to assemble the daytime warriors at the village. "Dress for battle!" he yelled.

His orders were greeted with great cheer and warriors, male and female, rushed to get armour on and headed the short distance to the savage village where Sigurd had taken up residence in a dwelling.

Across the water, their actions were noted with alarm from the sand spit and a galloper was sent to inform Krike as he ate at Aggie the Dog's.

"They're on the move! They head north!" the messenger screamed through the doorway, which was enough to spoil his breakfast and he rushed outside.

From this distance, the mass of warriors couldn't be seen and Krike mounted quickly. Urquhart had told him that if anything moved in that direction they had to head towards the crossing at Bonner with all haste. All haste meant horses and the horses had only been released to graze that night. Also, his men at Mahomack couldn't go. The warriors at Tain would go to Bonner. Mahomack had to remain defended.

Krike made a decision, right or wrong, it was a decision.

"Drive the horses to Tain," he ordered. "Get everybody that's got a horse and drive the rest to Tain. Send somebody to alert Urquhart."

His orders were met with yelps of action.

The messenger arrived at Tain around the same time as news reached Urquhart that the Norse were on the move along the east shore of the Firth. His cursing was short-lived when he was informed all the horses were being driven to Tain unsaddled, but bridles were being sent.

Urquhart assembled the warriors within the Stockade and addressed them.

"Horses are being driven here. Get bridles onto them, you have no saddles and get painted for battle. We head for Bonner!"

The roar from his men drowned out the rest of his encouragement to them.

By the time the first of the horses were driven into the Stockade, the bridles arrived and they worked quickly to bring the horses under control. Warriors mounted them and quickly headed for Bonner. Ross and Enya led. They had saddles and were glad of that.

Across the water at Dornoch village, Sigurd watched the horses being herded towards Tain and grinned at Frode.

"Looks like your bait has worked."

Frode scowled in reply.

"Go and tell the warriors to return and eat," Frode ordered a mounted messenger who galloped away towards the north.

Ross and Enya went slowly and soon many horses caught up with them, but nobody could see what had happened behind them. They had turned towards the Meikles ferry and were heading west. The last of the horses fell in behind and Ross ordered a canter. This sorted out the riders from those who thought they could ride and without saddles, many pulled their mounts up and cursed, deciding to run beside the horses.

Those trailing behind, received the order from Urquhart to return. The Norse had turned back and were no longer heading north. By the time that information reached the lead, they were nearing Bonner and cursed.

Panic for nothing, the warriors complained, but Ross wasn't so sure it was for nothing. If the Norse wanted to see how many horses they had this side of the Firth, they now knew.

That was exactly Frode's plan and he had proposed the idea to Sigurd alone. This meant if it worked, Sigurd would get the credit as he had done before, using the two Longboats as bait. Now, not only did they know how many horses there were, but they also knew the direction the horses had appeared from. It was a good morning's work. Before eating, and when the reasons were explained to his warriors, their anger subsided.

Sigurd returned to the Knarr Ship and his maps, summoning all his commanders to join him. As he approached with Ro-Sheen by his side he noted how high the Knarr ships were riding and knew he had to get them back to Torfness before the height of the tides, or they would be stranded at low tide. Nothing could push them back into the water, unlike the Longboats which warriors could handle, even taking them overland on occasions.

He noticed some activity beside one Knarr and he asked what was going on.

"The body of a female, Sire. They keep pushing it out to sea and it keeps coming back. It's got no head."

Sigurd told Ro-Sheen to stay where she was.

He climbed onto the Knarr's deck and went to look. Sure, enough the body was there and if it had a head, it would have faced him. Bloated and bruised with a great slash on one arm, all the signs said it died in battle.

"Turn it over," Sigurd commanded.

When the body rolled, Sigurd took a sharp breath. The Celtic Butterfly on its back told him who they were poking at with their boat hooks.

"That's Imogen!" he said. "Bring her to the shore and take her for burial at the village."

They stared at him, then at their revered ally and no longer viewed this as rubbish to get rid of.

Sigurd was more angry than upset. His first thought was if Kayra was still alive and could strike? He broke the news to Ro-Sheen and walked to the Knarr, with a glance towards the high mountains.

"Can Drest be trusted?" he asked Ro-Sheen.

She looked at him and smiled.

"Is that a question or are you making fun?"

"A question. Can we trust Drest?"

"Only the Norse trust Drest. Nobody else."

"Frode should have left warriors to make sure he marched south," said Sigurd with irony. Ro-Sheen didn't know what he meant.

Maps were spread and commanders assembled when Sigurd addressed them all.

"The Smertae, there's no sign of them coming. We must carry on without them. Imogen is dead. We don't know the fate of Kayra. They were going to penetrate the command at Tain and kill the leader. Now he lives and we need to re-plan starting with the Knarrs. They must leave and return to Torfness before they are grounded. I suggest they leave on the next high tide."

The agreement was unanimous and it was noon before he and Ro-Sheen returned to the village, having achieved very little in the way of progress. The Norse were safe where they were, and the savages were safe where they were. They were stuck and they had to find an alternative way to break the situation. They dismissed the idea of Drest and his army and Frode accepted his mistake of not sending warriors to ensure he kept his word.

They commanded six Skiffs to be sent from Torfness with orders to arrive as soon as possible at first light. Frode requested the Knarrs be replaced by something he could use but didn't elaborate on what that use was.

Ro-Sheen stripped and climbed into their sleeping platform. She lay there waiting. Sigurd stared at her then realised, Imogen was what was holding her back and his troubles dissolved.

Torf was informed that five Knarrs were heading towards Torfness and they were high out of the water, meaning all the supplies had been unloaded. He wondered what orders they had. They were on loan from Harold and would return to Norway as soon as they were no longer required to support Sigurd. Only one came close to the ledge under oars, the others went onto the sand, to wait for the tide to flood. The commander and navigator climbed the Rotten Rock steps and arrived by way of the small track to the main gate, where Torf met them.

Torf, and indeed the entire population of Torfness, was anxious for news from across the Firth. They could see neither smoke nor fire, nothing that would be associated with an attack, and concluded that, as at Torridon, the Picts were taken by surprise and hadn't managed to fire their defences. Never did they dream that across the Firth, progress was no more after seven days than it had been in one day, and the Pict army of Drest had failed to arrive on the high ground. Imogen was dead, and the fate of the other Smertae, Kayra, was unknown. That fact got his attention briefly but when it came to horses, the numbers east and west of Sigurd's position stunned Torf. He was greatly concerned, not about the army with Sigurd but with his own army; he feared the Knarrs had returned for his horses.

Torf felt greatly relieved when he discovered all Frode had requested were six Skiffs, to be loaded with as many supplies as Torf could achieve. The Skiffs had been busy to the east along the cliffs. They had removed the dead from the cave at the Collach and belongings from Hell's Hole before heading further along the cliffs to where the Savages called Cove Sea and there they found many Picts living in caves. They left them and didn't attack them.

They also found many traps at the Collach and set them. Fish were plentiful and so were lobster and crab. Four Skiffs were at the Collach, inside the small natural harbour they found to be even safer in bad weather than the shelter at Torfness. The rest remained on the beach below them and Torf sent a message to tell the navigators and masters to come to the Fort.

Two thousand warriors were deep in Moray. Sigurd had ordered a constant patrol split into two; five hundred warriors that could cover each other, as they traversed the base of the mountains east to west. And a similar arrangement with the patrol going from west to east. The only resistance they had encountered was from the warriors at the Stockade on the island. They had killed a scouting party that strayed too far from the main body and cut their heads off. Fifteen warriors died. They chased the Picts all the way back to the Stockade and onto the island. Another warrior died from an arrow fired from the Stockade and they retreated fast.

Knud soon realised Elgin stood between two main routes to Torfness, which could be reached by going east or west around the lake. He urged Torf to rethink his force which he stressed was only preventing Pict farmers from returning. He suggested reducing to one hundred on Lady Hill and patrols to ensure holding Elgin. He won his case and now led one of the patrols. His first task was to set Dallas ablaze as Sigurd had ordered.

As soon as one patrol returned, the horses were rested and the next patrol took its place. Torf had kept a thousand warriors in, and close to the Fort at all times, as ordered by Sigurd. Torf had more news to give than he received and felt disappointed at the progress north. He had expected Mahomack to have been taken, or at least something more than just a small, abandoned village.

Wives and children wandered the fort; the wives busy cooking and the children relentlessly exploring. Their favourite place was the Snake steps and they followed Torf's route up the steep path, up the Snake steps and barged onto the battlements with wooden swords just like Eogan and Bran had done, and it was great fun. But it wasn't the children who discovered the main reason why the Snake existed and what they thought was a shit idea, turned out to be just that.

Many warriors had scarpered down the snake to relieve themselves. On closer inspection they found a safe place cut out of the rock at the top of the cliff. The Snake took on a new meaning. It was an important part of the Fort. The only place they could relieve themselves without going all the way down to the beach and all the way up again.

Waifs and strays had returned to Torfness and were put to work. So too were many of the prisoners, and they were treated well by the invaders. It seemed the Monks were content to preach to the Norse in a language they didn't understand, and the need for communication was landed on them and the young. Imogen was cursed on many occasions for killing the only Monk who spoke Norse.

Torf had paired up girls of the same age, Pict and Norse, and in a very short time they were communicating; basic, but it was a start and they were even getting friendly. Not so the boys, who fought like cats and dogs. Torf had torn the place apart looking for the wealth of this place. Apart from ornaments of silver and some gold rings, they found little of value. There had to be wealth hidden somewhere and destroying the Fort to find it wasn't an option. They had plenty of time to find the treasures of Torridon.

Commanders and navigators arrived and were briefed on the situation to the north. They listened in silence and had little to say. They were given a map Frode had prepared, that would keep them clear of the point he had named Tarbat Ness. They would see their fleet once they rounded this point but if visibility was bad, they had to steer northwest and pass the entrance to the lake before beaching. Great emphasis was placed on the last point and all the beach to the east of the entrance was marked with crosses.

The Knarr ship left the ledge and two Skiffs replaced it. Immediately warriors started loading provisions and all the Knarrs waited for high tide, where they would beach where the Skiffs had been, at the Slappy. Sigurd wanted the Skiffs loaded quickly, and they had to cross as soon as they could. Killing animals for meat was a slow process and Torf went down to the Knarr ships as soon as they beached, to address their commander.

"We have hundreds of livestock. Every time the patrol comes back, they bring sheep, cattle, goats, pigs and everything they can drive and carry. The high ground is full of animals. Why don't you load them live and take them back across? The skiffs can't carry live animals."

The Commander thought for a moment. "If you order us, we will obey," he smiled.

From the Fort, the Monks watched the biblical scene below. Animals of all descriptions were led up ramps onto one Knarr ship at a time. Then the ramp was moved to the next one. Before long, four had their large holds full and were ready to float out on the next high tide. It would have taken many days to kill the animals and then they had to salt the meat. On the hoof, they could be killed on demand and were fresh. The flotilla left Torfness to great cheers and headed towards

Tarbat Ness. The Skiffs stayed respectfully behind the great Knarr ships.

The arrival of the Knarr ships and the Skiffs back at Dornoch created confusion among the Norse and panic among the Picts. The alarm was sounded in Mahomack and the relay all the way to Tain. Those closest to the Norse were on the great sand spit that jutted into the firth between Tain and Mahomack. It was close enough to see everything that was happening across the Firth and a possible landing site for the Norse, but it was unlikely they would be so stupid as to land between an army at Mahomack and one at Tain. Tain was protected by many sandbanks.

The spit was the forward observation post for the Decantae and the observers watched in dread as the first of the Knarr ships beached. Norse reinforcements had arrived.

Sigurd, Frode and many of his commanders went to the beach as soon as the flotilla was spotted, and their concerns were great. What had happened at Torfness that made the Knarr ships return? It could be nothing good.

The lead ship's bow ground onto the sand and ropes were thrown down to the waiting swarm of warriors, hundreds of them. The Picts stared as the big boat was turned to face them and lay side on to the beach. Sigurd pushed his way through warriors and saw the boat's crew struggling with something on deck. The end came overboard and with much screaming to keep clear, the heavy wooden ramp landed violently on the beach. He held back as orders were given to position the ramp and once it was secure, Sigurd with Frode right behind him raced up the ramp. The sight that greeted them made both laugh loudly as the smiling Commander bellowed,

"Torf ordered us back. He said if you have nothing better to do you, can feed yourselves!"

Sigurd shook his head and looked at the second boat being turned as with the first. He moved aside as sheep were grabbed and lifted to the ramp then released. Some went down, others fell off and into the water and there was great hilarity on the beach as the noise increased so much the Picts could hear it and a galloper sent to Urquhart. The galloper didn't have to go far and ran into twenty horses galloping towards him.

"They're unloading sheep from the big boats, hundreds of them!" the galloper yelled at Ross.

"Hundreds of boats or hundreds of sheep?" Ross fired back.

"Sheep!" shouted the warrior and spurred his horse after the troop.

They reached the end of the spit where the change of guard usually took place at night and made no attempt to hide. Mayhem ensued across the Firth and the noise of sheep was drowned out by the bellowing of cows and the squealing of pigs. Animals were being herded off the beach towards the village and Ross remarked this would be a fine time to attack the Norse.

"What are they doing?" asked Sine.

Ross looked at the two fresh interlocking tattoos on her thigh and grinned. She wasn't old enough to get that, but she had them. Now he would see if her brain was as good as her spear arm.

"You tell me. What do you think they're doing?" he challenged.

"Well, they're not going to ride them into battle," she said sincerely and Ross gave her a look. But she was thinking aloud as usual. "They can't start a farm in the middle of an invasion, so I think they're going to eat them," she concluded. "Eat them! Am I right?" she asked, her eyes wide in expectation.

"No, they're going to ride them into battle!" said Ross, taking a friendly swipe at her head.

Greatly relieved, they dismounted and watched the antics across the water. Two things they had all feared were the arrival of more Norse warriors or horses. The image of these fearsome warriors riding into battle on the backs of sheep with their feet trailing on the ground made Ross chuckle to himself, then share the joke. They all laughed except Sine.

Their presence on the spit didn't go unnoticed by the Norse, and Sigurd suggested they should send a messenger across and invite them to a feast. What the Picts would make of this development he had no idea, and would have to think about things, but not until the livestock was delivered to grazing and the pigs put into pens in the village left empty by the former inhabitants.

It took almost all day to unload the Knarr ships and the Skiffs.

Sigurd met with the commanders of all and congratulated them for their forward-thinking. He got in return the update from Torf and that explained where all the livestock came from. Tusk had killed his scouts and cut their heads off and they were a long way from his Stockade on the island. This man was a thorn in Sigurd's side and would be dealt with, he assured them. He had kept calm but inside Sigurd was furious.

Frode had requested the Skiffs for one purpose, scouting. Two would head east to the river they had launched the attack on Torridon from. Two would head west through the gap where the big drum beat and take a close look at the landing beach there. The two to the west were a decoy, the two going east had to find out if the river was still safe or now defended. Frode was adamant he could get there and back in one night if he left as soon as darkness fell.

All agreed the only attack they could make was against the Lugi to the east of their present position. To do that, they had to lure the Lugi into open battle and strike them from ahead and behind. Their land was small in comparison to the Decantae and so was their army, according to Ro-Sheen, but their land was also fertile and grew much timber. If they could destroy the Lugi, they could settle this land without fear of attack.

Now they were trapped between two armies. They couldn't launch a surprise attack against the Decantae. They watched every move the Norse made by day and by night, and they were the stronger of the two. But the Lugi presented possibilities. Sigurd had already lured them into the open. If he could do it again, they would be ready to exterminate them, but it would take planning and timing, Frode was an expert at that.

The first plan had gone to hell because of the Smertae. The spit between Tain and Mahomack, the Spit the Decantae used to spy, was the chosen battlefield. The Norse weren't going to attack anywhere. They planned to land on the Spit and wait until the army at Mahomack and Tain come to them as one. When the Norse crossed the Firth onto the undefended ground, the Smertae would move from the high ground and wait until the army from Tain and Mahomack combined their forces and marched onto the Spit. There the Smertae and the Norse would attack from two sides.

Now Sigurd had an army on two sides, both were cut off by water but one was within reach. He would try the same battle plan against the

Lugi but this time the Norse would come from both sides and the battle would be over before the Decantae could react. One enemy at a time where possible reaped rewards.

When darkness fell, Frode headed north with two Skiffs. He estimated it would only take him four turns of the time glass to reach the vicinity of the river. Staying close to shore he was confident he could find the entrance in the dark and the navigators agreed. Frode had connected the coastline that was missing and had seen no hazards that would force the Skiffs to stay well out to sea.

Around midnight, the moon would appear and if they were in position, the outline of the mountain, Morven, should be visible against the light even if cloud cover increased. They went seaward on the hunt for Morven.

Dead reckoning by the navigators was commendable, and the mountain with the missing top stood out proudly against the moonlight before it disappeared behind clouds. Morven, they established was on the correct bearing and the Skiffs headed towards the entrance to the river on the approach bearing, straight down the centre. According to the tides at Dornoch, they would catch the last two hours of the flood tide and be swept into the river mouth by the tide.

The one stern light they were using was put out and sails lowered. Two oars went out, one on each side, and they crouched low as the Skiffs picked up speed and came through the entrance fast. There was no sign of fires and no lights to be seen. By all accounts, the place was as deserted as they left it, and they breathed a sigh of relief, but still crouched low and stared across the flood plain and the east bank. They spoke in whispers and Frode asked the oarsmen to make for the east bank. He stood up and put his hand on the commander's shoulder then he fell on top of him.

"Get off," growled the commander and cursed, thinking Frode had lost his balance. As he pushed Frode away, his hand came into contact with something weird. He stared at the object as another embedded itself into the side of the boat by his head. Before he could shout a warning, an arrow found his shoulder and he screamed to the two seamen who were not on the oars. They grabbed shields to protect the oarsmen and shouted a warning to the other Skiff, too late, it was already under a hail of arrows and only two squatted hard against the boat's side as arrows thudded into the wood and flesh around them.

The current carried both boats towards the bend in the river and more towards the east bank and eventually out of range of the Bowmen.

The sound of arrows from the west bank was replaced by loud yelling and those who survived, pulled both Skiffs together and held them. They grounded on sand and two seamen jumped into the shallow water and held onto the Skiffs.

"Stay still. They can only see as well as we can," rasped the wounded master, his voice weak.

"Stay quiet and watch the water flow. As soon as the tide loses its battle against the river, push the boats out," hissed the navigator from the other Skiff.

The shouting across the river seemed to be on the move until one yell silenced it completely. Then the gurgling of the river mixed with the moans of the wounded and the shock of the attack struck home.

Across the river, Lugi warriors cursed as they headed upriver towards the Ford. They had let the two boats come close and were preparing to launch spears, not arrows when the boats suddenly turned towards the east bank. From their high point, where Forbes had insisted they stood guard, spears would have devastated the boats, and those that missed people would surely have had enough force to penetrate through the wood of the hulls and sink them. It was in desperation they fired arrows blindly and had no idea what they hit, if anything they fired at shadows. Now they had to cross the river and attack the Norse on the east bank, and they only had only a handful of arrows left.

Speaking in whispers, the Norse assessed the damage. Frode and three more were dead, two others wounded both with arrows in their thighs. They had six uninjured, enough to man both boats but not enough to lay a trap for the inevitable arrival of the savages. Were they all upriver or were some still waiting on the high ground across on the west bank? One thing was certain, they would push the boats out from the shore at the first sound of anybody approaching.

Two went as far as where a small stream met the river and waited there. It wasn't far but far enough to give them a warning.

Upriver, the headlong dash of the Lugi to get to the Ford slowed to a painful pace when they encountered blackberry bushes and broom, as they were following leaders who knew where the ford was, but not how to get to it. They had strayed too close to the river and suffered the consequences. Scratched and bleeding they eventually reached the gurgling water and cursed. The water level was way too deep to cross and they had no choice but to wait until the tide changed and the river level dropped.

The Norse waited and prayed to every god they knew; even the great Bull of the Picts got a mention. They prayed for the tide to turn and the clouds to stay covering the moon. The tide answered their prayers and the two returned from beside the stream, swords in hand and running.

"The water is running towards the sea," they gasped between breaths and their companions pushed the two Skiffs silently out into the river. They seemed to hang there for a little while before both drifted slowly towards the river mouth. Then, without warning a great rip enveloped both boats and they sped towards the river mouth at great speed. Oars were manned and the boats kept well away from the west bank. They cleared the land and went seaward for a long way before separating the boats and raising sails. The Skiffs sped west with the wind on their beam and a bone in their teeth.

# Chapter 12

Sheena summoned a meeting with her closest advisors, her father being the closest. She was under no illusions that the strike against the Smertae had prevented a greater battle. There was no other reason for Drest leading his force south, other than to support the Norse. They would never know what the plan was, but she was convinced there was one, and those in her company agreed. However, her calling those closest to her had little to do with the Smertae.

"How long has it been since Torridon fell?" she asked Ross.

"Forty-three days since you came here," answered Urquhart, to Ross's relief as he had no idea.

Neither had Sheena and her head jolted back. It seemed like yesterday to her and she had no idea how her father knew.

"We've heard nothing from the south. No messengers have come. We don't know what's happening there," she sighed.

"And they won't know what's happening in the north. The only people who know what's happening are the Norse. What are you getting at?" asked Ross, knowing she was leading to something.

"We didn't send messengers south because the two spies told us the Norse held Inver and the ground was too wet to go any other way. Now the ground is dry and the Norse may not hold Inver. We should consider sending messengers south, and where to send them, is why you're here," smiled Sheena.

"I've been thinking about that," said Urquhart. "Send them west into Caledonii country. The chances are the Caledonii know less about the Norse than we do. Send them south, they could be away for a long time. We know the dangers they face and travel in force. Anywhere east of Inver they're likely to run into Norse. That leaves only one destination but getting there won't be easy," he stated and looked at the faces listening to his every word.

"They must find Tusk," he continued. "I fear Munro and Anderson will already have moved their forces, but Tusk has a Stockade on an island. He told me when he was here what he was going to do, and he's had more than a year to achieve it, so I think heading for Tusk is the best option. If he's been defeated, the messengers will head over the mountains to Gordon. He will hold Bennachie. So will Mar and any driven from their lands, McDuff, Buchan, Grant. If an army is being massed it will be at Bennachie," announced Urquhart with conviction.

"Where's the map?" asked Krike.

Urquhart went into his chamber and came back with two. He spread one out.

"This is to Inver and as far east as Culloden moor."

He unrolled the second map and joined it to the first at the moor.

"What are we looking for?" asked Sheena.

The others thought there was nothing but lines drawn on the map and all going in circles.

"These are mountains, said Urquhart. "Here, south of the moor are the Monadhliath Mountains. Cross them, the foot of the Cairngorm Mountains, and Tusk is somewhere at the base of the highest mountain, Ben Macdui. He drew this, but he had only gone that way to Inver once and never again, he said. In my mind, that's the only safe way to get to Tusk, and if he's dead, get to whoever is still alive."

"So, what's so difficult?" asked Ross.

"Forest, that's what's so difficult. Tusk said he couldn't see his hand in front of his face. You can't see anything among the trees, and the mountain range is near wooded to the top. By the time you climb up to see where to go and back down, you're lost again, and if it's raining, it's more hell because you can't see anything above, or below. Plus, the place is full of wolves and bears. That's what's so difficult," Urquhart replied, smiling.

"Travel blind, stop and get eaten. Sounds like your kind of venture, Krike," said Ross.

"You can eat Drest's bonnet, Ross. No lobsters there. Sounds more like yours!" said Krike.

"Nobody here goes," stressed Urquhart. "We need to find warriors who we can trust to make it and come back. That means going through this forest twice."

Sheena locked eyes with Ross. He had seen that look on her face before and he knew she was deeply troubled. She took a deep breath.

"The messengers will go south. I am speaking to you as your Queen, so do not question my decision. The messengers will go south to confirm the Queen is dead," she announced and a murmur filled the room.

"The Queen is dead," she continued, "the wife of the King is dead. The Norse believe she is dead. The Smertae believed she was dead and the people in the south will believe the same. That is the reason why no messengers have come from the south. Forty-three days have passed. By now the tribes to the south will have crowned a new King. Eogan had blood there. Bran is dead, I am dead. They would have acted quickly. Now if I am alive, not only the Norse will be after my head, but all the tribes in the south too.

"My decision is final and the last order of this Queen will be that you obey her wishes. Now Sheena, daughter of Urquhart, has returned," she concluded and Sine ran to her side.

The rest stood and looked at each other stunned.

"We will go and find messengers," said Urquhart. "Sorsce, Fiona, Enya stay here." Urquhart indicated to Ross and Krike to come with him.

Outside, they breathed deeply and looked at each other.

"Where did that come from?" asked Urquhart.

"She's been acting strangely since she spoke to Drest," replied Ross. "He said she was dead. The only way Drest would think that, was if the Norse told him and if the Norse are convinced, the word would soon spread. She's right, but I think she's getting ahead of herself. She should wait until the messengers get back from the south and find out what's happening there before making such a decision."

"The decision has been made, Ross, and we must obey her command. If she's right, she would have no life and nowhere to hide. Now she will have a life, and we know where she can hide," Urquhart grinned.

"Tusk! Everybody calls him Tusk. Does anybody know what his real name is?"

"Mael Brigte, that's his real name," replied Urquhart.

"Mael Brigte? Tusk's easier but the messengers do need to know his real name," Ross grinned.

Krike was in deep thought and Urquhart clapped him on the back.

"I know what's going through your mind, it went through mine too. No boats, they wouldn't get far." Urquhart read his mind.

"Warlock!" Krike grunted.

Across the Dornoch Firth, there was great grief. In addition to Frode, one master and one navigator had been killed along with a seaman. Sigurd was distraught. He had suggested Frode send somebody else to the river to find out if it was safe to land warriors, but he had dismissed his suggestion with a statement Sigurd couldn't counter.

"I never take somebody's word for what's safe. I will know if they discovered our camp," he had replied but didn't elaborate. Now he was dead. Savage arrows were in three other dead and two wounded. Sigurd sought solitude and stayed inside the Pict dwelling for most of the day. The bodies were taken ashore and arrows removed but nobody had been given any orders.

Some thought Frode's body would be returned to Norway, but that decision rested with Sigurd, a decision he was all too aware of and wrestled with his options. What would Harold expect him to do? And just as important, what would Frode expect him to do? There was also the old way and the new way. Tormented, Sigurd finally emerged and ordered fire bundles to be prepared. He went to look at the Skiff Frode died on and nodded in approval. It wasn't a Longboat, but it only lacked in size. In all other respects, it was a Longboat.

"Prepare this boat for a fire burial," Sigurd ordered and waited for a reaction. Some cheered wildly, others fumbled the crosses around their necks, and Sigurd felt reassured. "Put a spar on the mast and make a cross. Tie fire bundles along the spar and on the mast," which received an even greater cheer.

He went to the bodies and ordered that Frode be laid towards the bow and the other three at his feet. He went to the Longboat Frode called his home and found Tarbat, the commander.

"Tarbat, you will take Frode's place. You were his commander, now you will be one of mine. For now, you remain as commander of this boat," Sigurd instructed and Tarbat bowed in obedience. The honour Sigurd had just bestowed on him was his right and restored the chain of command.

Sigurd himself had been one of Harold's Forecastle men, not even a commander. He was given the title, Jarl of Orkney, from his brother Rognvald Eysteinsson, the first Jarl, who had been granted the islands by Harold as compensation for the loss of Rognvald's son Ivar, who had died fighting for Harold. Harold treated the brothers as his sons and they looked on him as their father. Rognvald was now fighting battles south, in the land of the Angles, and Sigurd north in the land of the Picts. Between their two armies stood two much greater armies, and both Sigurd and Rognvald knew their limits.

At Galspie a galloper had arrived and informed Stroma that the Norse had tried to enter the Dale of Helm with two boats the night before, and her warriors had driven them back out to sea. That was as much information as the warriors from the Helm had. When they crossed the river, they found nothing. The boats had gone, and no trace of anything was to be seen. They didn't know if they killed any Norse or wounded any but assured Stroma the Norse wouldn't come back.

Forbes had been right. If the Smertae were on their way to attack Urquhart from the back, the Norse would be looking to attack the Lugi from the back. They had enough warriors and enough boats, and Forbes had insisted on leaving a force of twenty warriors, with spears and bows, to cover the river mouth from the high ground on the west side. If the boats were scouts, now they had an answer. The warriors from the Helm could now join her warriors at Brora.

Early morning when the tide was on the ebb, Sigurd was summoned by Tarbat. They had prepared the funeral boat and he had to light it as was the custom. Ro-Sheen went with him to the beach and the sight was incredible. Four thousand warriors lined the beach and many lighted beacons shone as reflections off helmets and swords. Sigurd took a beacon from Tarbat and climbed aboard the Skiff.

He stood with the beacon held high above his head and roared,

"Frode! Frode! Frode!"

His tempo was repeated and developed into a roar. Between each roar of Frode, the thunderous sound of swords being slapped against shields made them roar even louder. Sigurd climbed down into the boat and set fire to several fire bundles that ignited quickly. Satisfied the fire had taken hold, he quickly jumped onto the sand, and many warriors pushed the Skiff afloat. They held it there until the flames started licking the mast and with one mighty effort, they sent the boat out into the current. The roars of Frode and thunder were loud enough to reach the bewildered Picts on the sand spit. They stared transfixed at the boat going up in flames, with a great flaming cross above it and the fear of God went into them. They didn't know what this meant. Alarms were sounded and warriors rushed to the shore and stared at the spectacle.

The inferno drifted east quickly and as it passed the roaring warriors, beacons were thrown into the water. It drifted out towards the point and burned from bow to stern. Soon it went to its watery grave along with the dead. The chanting stopped when only smoke hung over the sea.

The funeral over, Sigurd went back to his dwelling, breathed a sigh of relief and lit the Stern lamp from the Skiff that Tarbat had given him. He needed more light. Everything had gone well and the boat had burned longer than some Longboats he had seen. In the middle of a war, burning a longboat was unthinkable and the Skiff had been a good substitute. His warriors were pleased with the ceremony and also pleased that Frode and the others would go to the afterlife with their heads.

The Monks at Tain had seen and heard the happenings across the water and to one Monk from the western isles, the burning boat meant only one thing, somebody important had died. That news was conveyed to Urquhart and he hoped it was their leader. His hope came close.

Krike arrived as they ate in the Stockade and he declined food, as Aggie the dog had fed him.

"Your messengers," announced Krike and Urquhart cast his eyes over the four young warriors.

He asked them if they had eaten. They hadn't, Krike had pulled them from the beach. Sorsce gave them food and Krike a dirty look.

Ross grinned as he had just crossed the Struie with them leading.

They had also excelled themselves in battle and wore the rings to prove it. One had a Bear, two had Eagles but the most muscular, called Hector, had both and three rings on his forearm. They were young, fit and ate like animals, tearing into a leg of sheep between slurps of soup.

"Mael Brigte," said Urquhart and they looked at him puzzled. "Mael Brigte, you all know Tusk?" and they all nodded. "His real name is Mael Brigte. Get that name into your heads and don't forget it. Your task is to find Tusk, or Mael Brigte. Ross will look out the four best horses we have, Angle horses, and you'll be armed with the best weapons. You find Tusk and find out what's happening in the south. Then get back here," commanded Urquhart and looked for a reaction.

Krike had already told them that, but not Tusks real name.

"Mael Brigte, strange name," Hector grinned.

"This journey will be dangerous," warned Urquhart. "After you eat, you'll study the maps. The Monadhliath Mountains (Mona-Leea) and Cairngorm Mountains. Get the lie of the land into your heads. If Norse hold Inver, you must go around the Inver Loch and approach the mountains from the west. That won't be easy, neither will crossing the Monadhliath Mountains. Thick forest and full of dangers, not just wolf and bear, cut-throats and robbers, this journey won't be easy."

They grinned. They didn't expect it to be easy. They knew that was why they were chosen. They were scouts, all four of them, and Hector had been with Ross on many occasions. They were hunters and used to facing most dangers of the wilds. The conversation drifted to the sight across the Firth, and they finished eating.

"Follow me," ordered Urquhart and headed into his private quarters. They followed and stared at Sheena standing in front of them.

"The Queen has orders for you," said Urquhart and stepped out of the room, leaving the four alone with Sheena. They shifted from foot to foot uneasily.

"My life is in your hands, so kneel and swear to me you will abide by my wishes and accept death if you betray me," she said quietly and they obeyed.

One at a time they swore their oath of loyalty, and she told them to rise.

"The Norse think I'm dead, killed in battle with the King. Scotland might have a new King, we don't know. If a new King has been anointed, and his supporters find out I'm alive, they'll come after me and kill me. If the Norse find out I'm alive they will hunt me and kill me. Do you understand?"

They nodded.

"When you go south, you listen. Find out what's happening at Torridon and the rest of the country. Tell them we hold the Norse at Dornoch. Only if the subject arises will you tell them the Queen is dead. If they tell you the Queen is dead, act surprised and aggrieved. You know nothing about the Queen. Do you understand?"

"You're dead, and we don't know?" Hector grinned.

"That's a simple way to put it," she snapped. "We have an agreement. You don't reveal to anybody that I am still alive."

"If another King is anointed, can he be unanointed?" Hector frowned.

"No! Once anointed, he becomes the rightful King. Any threat to his crown will be removed, like me! Now you understand. Stay here, Urquhart has maps to show you," Sheena smiled and left them looking at each other.

Maps were spread and the four messengers became engrossed in the planning of their perilous journey. Going around the great Loch of Inver would add two days to a journey that Urquhart estimated would take four days if they managed to cross the river at Inver. They would travel by day and make no effort to hide. They would have the best of Angle horses and would be able to outrun anything or anybody they couldn't kill.

Sorsce was preparing food for five days and they would bring their own bundles. Everything else would be supplied by Ross.

"You leave at first light," said Urquhart. "Go and get some rest, you might not get any for a while."

# Chapter 13

The Dornoch Firth was revealing its riches with every increasing tide as the moon grew bigger. Huge Mussel banks were revealed, and an abundance of Cockles was being gathered from along its shores. Sigurd sent his Scouts on a daring mission. They were to head north along the shores of the lake and keep heading north until they reached the fringe of the forest. They would follow the forest west until they could see the Fjord, then follow the Fjord back to Dornoch.

He set a time glass and warned them not to stop. They would canter all the way and only gallop if they were threatened. His objective was to calculate the size of the land he now commanded. The navigators would work that out by time and distance which they had set by a known factor, how long it took for the time glass to empty as the horses cantered between their position and the entrance to the lake. The Roman mile was used extensively on land and was easy to apply. One thousand paces measured one Roman mile. To the navigators, this was a new challenge, but they rose to it with genuine curiosity and worked out a way to apply the speed of a horse to the distance travelled. As with a boat, speed would inevitably vary but they were sure they would get as near to the correct distance as possible.

Sigurd left them to it. He had other things on his mind. The death of Frode was a great loss. Sigurd knew he couldn't spend much more time here. He had to get back to Torfness and secure the lands to the south. Frode would have taken charge when he left. Now Tarbat would take charge but Sigurd knew Tarbat could sometimes be reckless. He had to either instigate an attack on his position from either of the enemy or attack one of them. This scenario was dismissed by Frode. If the Norse attacked, they would be exposed to attack from two directions. Tarbat had been one of the commanders who suggested attacking east and west at the same time because they had twice as many warriors as the Savages.

Frode had pointed out to his second in command that he had forgotten about horses. But Tarbat was adamant, Frode had defeated the King's army and the King had many horses, Frode had none. Ambush and open battle have no comparison. The King's horses weren't in a battle charge, Tarbat was reminded but still wasn't convinced. This factor worried Sigurd.

When the navigators finally decided on their measurement of the land, they decided it was close to thirty Roman miles around and more if they went all the way to the forest. Sigurd gave them a doubtful look. He had estimated half that at most, not double and checked their figures and how they reached them. He couldn't fault their calculations and declared the land they circled was bigger than some of his islands in Orkney. The report on the land was also good; a lot of it was unused and most of it fertile. Some showed it was a flood plain and another lake existed close to the northwest corner next to the Fjord.

Now Sigurd could fill in some of the information he didn't have. With the help of his scouts, he made a map of the area they now knew. He made another with Tain, the land to the west, the Fjord, and the new land all together; now he could study strategy. He decided that the Knarr ships would stay and be anchored close to shore, a decision which raised a few eyebrows.

Three days had passed since Urquhart had sent the messengers south and this feeling of being stuck and inactive was beginning to frustrate even the most aggressive, Ross being one of them. Like his counterpart across the Firth, Urquhart's command studied their maps. The maps of the immediate area were in great detail, unlike those of Sigurd, but regardless of detail, they could find no way of attacking the Norse from the Decantae side of the firth. Stroma could attack with her humble force against more than four times her strength, but without support from Urquhart's horses and warriors, the Lugi would die.

Dawn broke across the Firth revealing calm water all the way to the Longboats and Knarrs. Fiona shook herself and, with three others went to the water's edge to walk. They walked to keep their eyes open. They had been on the spit all night and would be relieved soon. A shout from those who stayed behind shifted their focus towards the Norse boats and they screwed their eyes up against the glare of the sun. A boat was seen coming in their direction and they hurried back to their horses.

"Wait!" Fiona shouted as several warriors mounted.

They made out a figure on the bow of the boat waving frantically and then a white flag, waved more slowly. They stared at the approaching boat and counted only two oars on each side. It looked the same as the other boats but was much smaller, so they realised it was much closer than they originally thought, and panic seized some.

"Take the horses out of bow shot. Two of you stay with me. If anything happens, charge them!" Fiona ordered and seven warriors mounted and led the horses back as commanded.

The boat came closer and Fiona noted the tide was slack. She and her companions stood with spears and shields at the ready and realised a female was the one waving the flag. The boat came within shouting distance and the oars were shipped.

"I bring a message for Urquhart. I bring a message for Urquhart!" came the message across the stillness loud and clear.

Fiona was taken by surprise to hear it was her language but who was this?

"What is your message?" she called back.

"Sigurd, Jarl of Orkney wishes to meet here at noon, to discuss terms with Urquhart, Chief of the Decantae," shouted Ro-Sheen.

Fiona repeated the request, leaving out the title of Jarl.

"Sigurd will come in this boat, with only the boat's crew and under the white flag. He will expect Urquhart to honour the white flag," called Ro-Sheen and Fiona nodded. She was staring at the beauty of the messenger and her fine, Lynx cloak. Her hand tightened on her spear.

"I will give Urquhart the message."

She watched as the oars turned the boat and it went back towards the Norse.

Who was she? A thousand questions raced through Fiona's mind, but her brain was numbed by the encounter and she rushed to her mount.

Urquhart was eating when Fiona burst into the great hall, causing many heads to turn in alarm, including his.

"The Norse, they sent a messenger," she gasped. They froze in anticipation. "Sigurd wants to meet you under the white flag to discuss terms!"

"Where?" asked Urquhart.

"On the spit. They sent a small boat across and the messenger speaks our language," she replied excitedly.

"When?" he snapped.

"Noon! he wants to meet at noon on the spit!"

Urquhart looked at her for a moment.

"Take a seat, Fiona and calm down," he smiled. "Discuss terms, we don't discuss terms with an invader, but I'm curious."

"So am I. I'm curious about the messenger. She's very beautiful and speaks our language," she smiled and accepted food from Sorsce.

"Get the commanders who are relieved here and leave those on duty. You stay here," instructed Urquhart and Fiona nodded.

Krike found himself wrenched from slumber in Aggie the Dogs and arrived at the Stockade last. Urquhart herded them all into his quarters where Sheena waited with Sine and Fiona. Enya and Ross stayed on duty and would be informed of the decision, not involved in the making of it.

Discussions went on and Urquhart demanded they be conducted in an orderly way. As expected, some opposed the meeting with Sigurd and some agreed to it. Surprisingly, Sheena was in favour and explained why.

"They wouldn't ask for terms if they had a chance to kill us. They know we can't attack them, and we know they can't attack us. We have no answer. Father, go and listen to them, find out what they propose? We can always say No!"

"She's right," said Urquhart, "but it's a break with tradition. We fight invaders, not discuss terms with them. What say you?" he asked his command.

Krike replied for all of them,

"If Ross was here, he would say no. I say go and find out before he gets wind of it. Sheena's right. But you must decide, Urquhart."

"What would you do, young Chief?" Urquhart smiled and looked at Sine.

"Me! Me? I don't know, father, I've never been invaded before," she shouted in alarm.

"Get her dressed in her finest," ordered Urquhart. "They have a beautiful messenger; we can match that, and more. Their messenger must be Smertae. You will wear their chief, Drest's bonnet," Urquhart grinned as Sheena and Fiona grabbed hold of Sine.

Sheena watched with a lump in her throat as her father and sister rode out ahead of ten mounted bowmen. Sine held a spear with a white flag and rode upright as commanded. She felt petrified but Urquhart growled at her to act as if the bonnet on her head belonged to her. He was also dressed in his finest and together they looked impressive. So too did the warriors following behind; they had all removed their war paint on Urquhart's orders. He commanded them to stay out of bowshot, but if any trickery developed, to get into range immediately.

Krike had already gone to Ross, who as expected, expressed his fury that Urquhart had agreed to speak terms with an invader.

"Sheena orders you to stay here and don't move," said Krike.

"Madness! You should know better," seethed Ross, taking his frustration out on Krike who was enjoying having Ross by the balls.

Slack tide found Urquhart and Sine staring east from the shore and they watched closely as a single boat approached with only two oars on either side. They counted six people aboard. Two stood side by side on the bow, both had long blond hair, like Urquhart and Sine; one had a beard.

"Keep your head high and your eyes alert," Urquhart told Sine. "You see any sudden movement out there, get off your horse. The bowmen will come fast."

Whether Sine heard him or not he had no idea, she stared transfixed; about to face the hated enemy in person, and her heart threatened to leap out of her chest.

The boat drew closer and two oars were taken in. The oarsmen held the oars aloft so as they could be seen and soon the second set followed. The craft glided closer.

"We will beach at the high-water mark!" called Ro-Sheen.

That was a safe distance. Urquhart didn't reply and the boat grounded. The men dropped the oars into the water and dug them into the sand, holding the boat's bow on the beach.

Ro-Sheen stared at the beauty beside Urquhart and at the bonnet she wore and felt uneasy. It looked like Drest's bonnet, but she said nothing and took instructions from Sigurd. Then she stood tall and addressed Urquhart, in clear and ringing tones,

"Sigurd is offering you terms that you can accept with dignity. The lands he occupies will become a trading area. You have three days to discuss this with the Lugi. If you agree, three thousand of Sigurd's army will be withdrawn. If not, another five thousand warriors will come from Torridon and the Decantae and the Lugi will be exterminated. If the army withdraws and those who remain are attacked, the army will return in force, seize all your lands and kill every one of your people.

"I will throw a map onto the beach when we leave. The land chosen as a trading area is marked. You have three days to answer. Sigurd will receive the answer from the Chief of the Lugi at the entrance to the lake. You are free to send messengers across the trading area for three days; only ten warriors, any more will be attacked and the terms withdrawn."

As Ro-Sheen finished, Urquhart dipped his bonnet to her for sheer bravado.

"Tell Sigurd his message has been understood. You recognise the bonnet she wears, and you will make sure Sigurd sticks to his word. We will consider his terms. The three days will start from daybreak tomorrow. Today I will light a beacon if we agree to speak to the Lugi. If you don't see a beacon at Tain, your request has been refused."

"Ro-Sheen translated but didn't mention anything about a bonnet. Sigurd nodded.

"Daybreak tomorrow and send us smoke at first light if you go to the Lugi. Here is the map," Ro-Sheen called and threw the rolled-up document high up the beach.

Sigurd barked orders and the oarsmen pushed the Skiff into deeper water, turned and headed back towards the Norse fleet.

"Get the map," ordered Urquhart.

Sine jumped. She dismounted and grabbed the leather roll from the sand.

"Keep hold of it until we get back to the Stockade!" he shouted and spurred his horse towards the Bowmen. "One of you, get Ross from

Mahomack."

The galloper found him with Krike in Aggies and he wasted no time in heading back to the Stockade, still muttering about the wisdom of all this, and fishing for details from the Bowman. Trickery was afoot, of that he was sure.

When Ross arrived, he expected a full-blown meeting to be in progress, but they had waited for him. Urquhart hadn't even opened the map.

Urquhart passed the message from Sigurd as he understood it. They all heard it at the same time as Ross. Even Sheena had to wait. They looked at Urquhart in relative silence. Nobody had anticipated anything like this. They had expected a demand to surrender, nothing less.

"Before we go any further, we must look at the map," said Urquhart, "and see exactly what Lugi land he wants."

Sine spread the sealskin and they couldn't help admiring the precision of its lines, tattooed in blue ink.

"What trickery is this?" asked Ross, pointing out that the line at the north end wasn't joined to the lines east and west.

"The forest, they want access to the forest," replied Sheena, "and they don't know how big it is. That's something Stroma and her council can decide. He's left it blank."

"Or he wants the land all the way to the Sea of the Dead," scorned Ross.

"That land belongs to the people of Dornoch," said Urquhart. "There's nobody else on it and most of it is wasted. I asked Embo to put our cattle there years ago, and he said he would put his own cattle on it, but he never did."

"Some of it floods when the wind and the tide hold back the river but not very often," said Sheena. "The chances are, Stroma has never been on this land."

"This drives a wedge between us and the Lugi. It's trickery I tell you," insisted Ross.

"The wedge is already there if you haven't noticed," Fiona spoke for the first time.

"Wedge or no wedge, this can't stand," said Urquhart quickly. "They can draw what they like, we can still go anywhere we wish, on any land no matter who it belongs to, provided there is no intent of harm. That right exists as it has for eternity, we will never surrender it."

"Three thousand of their army. We don't know his full strength, so how can we tell if three thousand have left?" complained Ross.

They continued to thrash out the positives and negatives until they had exhausted every avenue. In the end, they agreed to take it to the Lugi and let them decide. In Sheena's opinion, with alterations, the Decantae would agree, so long as Ross witnessed the removal of warriors.

"What?" he yelled, staring back at her.

"That way brother, you won't be getting cheated," she smiled.

"Fiona, get that Smertae, Fia here!" demanded Urquhart suddenly.

She gave him a puzzled look but obeyed and left them.

When they arrived, Fia had a look of dread on her face when she saw Urquhart and Sheena.

"Relax, Fia, you're not going to be executed unless you tell me lies," grinned Urquhart. "That Smertae woman who knew you, what was her name?"

"Kayra," she answered nervously.

"She said she was taken by the Norse. Do you know why and was anybody else taken with her?"

"They weren't taken, they went to learn Norse, and one Norse came to Tongue to teach his language."

"Who went with Kayra?" he asked.

"Ro-Sheen, but I have nothing to do with them, they were young, younger than Sine when they left Tongue."

"What did Ro-Sheen look like?"

"Ro-Sheen was very beautiful. Her hair was like Sine's and she was very clever. I heard that she learned their language quickly," Fia announced with a hint of pride.

"Now we know who was with Sigurd. Her name is Ro-Sheen.

Thank you Fia, you can keep your head for another night," Urquhart laughed and Fiona shook her fist at him. "Double the guards tonight," he ordered.

# Chapter 14

Three days after leaving Tain, the four hunters crossed the moor at Culloden. No Norse was seen at Inver, but all the people they spoke to were on edge. Torridon had fallen and they feared the Norse would strike west.

Nobody had come from the south; only stragglers from Ardersier had arrived at Inver. They reported that the great Drums on the Black Isle had been sounded twice but they had no idea why. It seemed nobody took the route through the forest, preferring the easy route and everyone warned them, as Urquhart had, that bad people hid in this forest and many wild animals.

To ride horses as these messengers had, and be armed like they were, projected them to high status. They were treated accordingly and sent on their way with extra hides.

On the south side of the Moor, they entered the great Caledonii forest and almost immediately their world became smaller. Within a mile, they were checking directions against the sun and continuously ducking branches; progress became very slow. The horses pricked their ears and whinnied but the men saw nothing and nerves were on edge. They knew they would have to make camp in the forest for at least one night and were determined to get into the open any way they could before dark; the only way was up.

They reached a gradient that took them high enough for their ears to pop and they kept going. They caught fleeting glimpses of animals and birds through the thick foliage, but as they climbed, the trees began to get further apart and the light increased. So too did deer, which appeared in abundance.

They reached the treeline and felt greatly relieved when they looked back the way they had come and saw the lie of the land on the Black Isle, a thin strip of water just visible. They concluded this must be the Moray Firth. They were going in the right direction, but they hadn't travelled as far as they thought. The men followed the treeline around the east side of the mountain and found a small burn running through some rocks, where they stopped and made camp.

Hector took the precaution of marking the direction south with stones. They knew there was a likelihood of mist at daybreak, and they couldn't wait for it to clear. They lit a fire behind some rocks and used the hides the Caledonii had given them to block its light. The silence soon shattered after the sun went down, and they knew they were being tracked by wolves. The horses had detected them long ago, but now they announced their presence and Hector grinned.

"That should keep us safe tonight," he laughed.

When wolves had a hunger and were close, bears were seldom seen; they feared bears more than wolves. They hadn't lit the fire for cooking but to keep the wolves at bay. They gathered enough wood to keep it alight. If the wolves came too close, the horses would warn them, and they positioned their spears ready to grab.

The next morning, as Hector had anticipated, mist covered the mountain. They couldn't see anything and didn't care. They knew which direction to take and when they entered the forest, they wouldn't be able to see far even if the sun shone. The wolves had kept their distance and the men had slept. Now, they had to find the track to the east that would take them to Aviemore. Spending another night in this forest wasn't planned, and they pressed on. It was a long time later when the sun appeared and they felt glad to see it ahead of them.

They rested in a clearing and Andra, the youngest one, climbed a tall tree to get some idea of what lay ahead. The sight that met his eyes caused him to come down quickly.

"A big mountain, very high, with snow. That way!" he pointed.

Hector tapped the map Urquhart had given him and grinned.

"We're on track! That has to be Ben Macdui. There," Hector pointed to the circle that indicated a high mountain, a Ben.

Hector looked at Andra and decided to go up the tree himself. It was as Andra described, but the height was greater than Hector expected and that meant it was closer. They had to head directly east to get onto the track or they would end up at the base of the mountain. They rode back among the trees and headed east. If they didn't find the track soon, they would continue south to the mountain.

Gradually, the trees started to appear further apart, and smaller. The terrain ahead was still hidden, but they had the feeling they were getting close to the edge of the moor they hunted. After they crossed a second fast-flowing river, Andra came beside Hector and whispered,

"We're being followed."

Hector looked around slowly and saw nothing at first, then some movement to their left.

"We're being followed; ride on and don't change speed. Keep going the way we have been," Hector told the others.

The sight ahead came suddenly and wasn't expected. They cleared a low ridge with outcrops of rock and stared at the Loch that stretched across their path. A moment of panic ensued; they were trapped but Hector held his nerve and turned to face the followers.

"Stop! We stay here. Let them come to us," he said, drawing his sword.

They followed his example and released their shields from their saddles.

What emerged from the trees made their blood run cold, followed by the urge to gallop for their lives. Twenty mounted warriors painted for battle walked slowly towards them and more came from the left.

"Vacomagi," thought Hector aloud. "They must be Vacomagi.

From his left, another twenty warriors cleared the trees and started approaching them at a walking pace. Hector's eyes fell on the Bowmen who approached with arrows notched. They were on either side of the leader.

"Lower your weapons," Hector hissed and they followed his lead.

The painted warrior who led them waved her arm and the bows were lowered. They walked and only stopped when they were close, too close and those on the left did likewise.

"Speak for God's sake," whispered Andra.

"Who are you? Why are you on our land?" came the female voice, loud and clear.

"We are Decantae, messengers from Urquhart and we seek Mael Brigte," shouted Hector.

"Who?" she shouted back, louder.

"Tusk! We seek Tusk," Hector grinned as laughter ran through the ranks of the Vacomagi.

Their leader approached alone.

"I am Innes. Tusk is my father; you will follow us," she announced and informed her warriors.

She went east and Hector followed. The warriors that had been on his left followed behind. She came to a halt and held her arm aloft. Through the trees, the messengers could see clear ground ahead and waited. They heard sniggering and turned to find three female warriors, coming close to read them. The messengers read them in turn and realised they were amid equals. A shout from Innes spurred them into the open and they galloped south along the track they had been searching for.

The sight of the Stockade on the island impressed the Decantae, and they looked at Innes as she came close.

"Swim your horses to the Stockade. Only ten will go, the rest will go along the Loch in the water and come out on the hard ground. Then they go somewhere safe," she smiled and read the Decantae as two boats made their way towards them from the Stockade.

Tusk watched the approach of his boats with what appeared to be captives and waited at the back of the island where the boats would land and the horses climb out of the water. He scowled until he heard Innes's excited voice, shouting,

"Father they have come! The Decantae have come!"

He burst into smiles and rants as he waded into the water, hauling Hector from his boat and crushing him in a hearty embrace. Innes followed her father's example, and all four messengers were greeted like gifts from God. They were marched inside the Stockade and greeted by the inhabitants with great smiles and cheers. Never in their dreams did they expect such a welcome and they each drank freely of the ale thrust upon them.

"Prepare food!" yelled Tusk and bade the messengers follow him.

They paused in what they thought must be his quarters and were told to take their weapons off and anything else to make themselves comfortable.

"This is where you will stay," said Innes and they were impressed.

"Come tell me what's happening in the north?" urged Tusk, leading them into another room, much bigger, and with tables.

"The Norse are held at Dornoch," replied Hector. "They have the Lugi on one side and the Decantae on the other. They don't attack, neither do we."

"How many?" asked Tusk.

"We think about four thousand. They have thirty warships still on the sands at Dornoch."

"My God that many?" said Tusk, lowering his voice. "Our spies tell us they have two thousand in Torridon and another three thousand patrolling the lands. That's nine thousand if they form one army."

"Urquhart wants to know what's happening south. We've had no messengers since the fall of Torridon."

Tusk sighed a great sigh and banged the tabletop.

"Aye! What's happening in the south, that's what I want to know. Royalty is bastards. Still, I suppose it's their right, but they could have waited before grabbing the throne. This new King, he's set up his council in Kinghorn in Fife. Fife of all places, between two great rivers, the Tay and the Forth. Good to protect, but no good to attack," scorned Tusk raved and slammed his hand down again hard on the table. The messengers looked at each other but didn't speak.

"Tell Urquhart that Uurad, son of Bargoit, has claimed the throne. The chiefs have all sworn allegiance to him because he is the rightful heir," sighed Tusk.

"What about you?" asked Hector.

"Aye, me too, but not in person. I sent a messenger. So did the rest of the chiefs between the Dee and the Moray Firth. Gordon has rallied the warriors at Bennachie, but he expects no help from the south. The Norse are sweeping the area from the Monadhliath Mountains to the coast and killing anybody that stands in their way. You were lucky to get here. Who told you to come by the mountains?"

"Urquhart, he said you came that way once and never again," Hector grinned.

"He's got a good memory. He's right, but I was driving cattle and lost half to wolves and bears. The wolves scattered them through the forest and that was that. We've been abandoned in the north. They've wanted the seat of power moved south for years. Now they have the chance to do that, they'll wait and make sure there's no reason to move the power back to the north. They'll be content to hold the Norse at Bennachie. Anything north of that is abandoned for now; God knows for how long. All the time they delay, the Norse get stronger."

"So, what you're telling me is we can expect no help from the south?" asked Hector, quietly.

"You can expect no help, and I can expect no help. Let me explain Hector; if the army attacks Torridon, it will never take it. The Norse tricked the King. They won't be tricked and the defences there could hold off any attack. If the army goes north by way of Inver to attack the Norse, they'll get into their boats and head south. By the time the army gets back, they'll be fighting to get back into their own lands. North of the river Don is on its own. It's been abandoned for now, and like Urquhart and the other tribes, we're left to do what we must to survive.

"Tell Urquhart the warriors of Cluny managed to find the body of the King on the battlefield, but alas not the body of the Queen. He will be heartbroken, she was like a daughter to me also, but the Norse left the battlefield for so long, the wolves and crows and everything else that feeds on flesh, stripped the corpses and it was impossible to tell Norse from Pict. They burned them all together. The Cluny survivors came here with three cartloads of arms and the body of the King. He's buried here until we can get him to Iona," Tusk said quietly.

There was silence for a while and Hector changed the subject.

"How many are you here?"

"We were two hundred, now we're four hundred strong, and any Norse that comes close gets attacked. We've killed over a hundred of them so far and they can't touch us here. They thought about this several times then changed their minds. They don't like getting their heads cut off for some reason!" Tusk laughed and the messengers laughed with him.

Food arrived and they ate in relative silence. Innes joined them and got some approving looks.

"Do you believe we managed to kill one of the Norse with an arrow fired from the battlements of the Stockade?" she grinned.

"That's a long, long way for an arrow!" said Andra.

"When you finish eating, we'll go and look at the defences, announced Tusk, proudly.

This they were all keen to see and hurried their food.

"Go with Innes, she likes galloping up and down ladders," said Tusk.

She disappeared briefly into an adjoining room and came back with something cradled in her hands.

"What do you think of that?" she asked, showing it to them.

"A little spear, or a giant arrow?" replied Andra and took it from her, looking puzzled.

They each inspected it in turn and frowned.

"It's an arrow," said Innes, "not a giant one, an Angle one, to fit an Angle bow. Come, I'll show you. Bring it."

She led them into the courtyard. It was a bustle of activity out there, and they headed up the nearest ladder to the ramparts. The messengers stared at the number of weapons stockpiled and ready for use. So many spears and so many arrows. They had never seen the like. Many warriors gathered and Innes pointed towards the back of the Stockade to where they had swum the horses. Two boats overflowing with warriors were landing.

"That's the warriors coming back, the horses are all safe in the glen. The Norse think we keep them all in the Stockade because when they chase us, this is where we come, but as soon as they go, we take the horses to the Glen. If they besiege the Stockade, we can get warriors out in the night and attack them in the dark with horses. But they haven't taken the bait yet. I think they're afraid we will kill them on the side of the Loch from here," she smiled.

"With this?" Hector challenged in a doubtful tone.

Innes called down for somebody to get Cian and bring the Bow.

When Cian appeared, the messengers looked at each other and stepped aside as the huge warrior with a walking stick grunted and towered over Innes. They watched fascinated, as he placed the stick under his knee and knelt heavily on it, pulling one end towards him and placing the bowstring on the end he was holding. They looked at each other again when this thick cumbersome thing was turned into a bow and Cian grinned at them.

"You see that white rock on the shore?" asked Innes. "That's the range finder. If any Norse comes closer than that rock, Cian can reach them."

"You jest!" mocked Hector. "That's at least a bow shot and a half, or two."

"Watch," Innes replied proudly.

They stepped aside to give Cian room and stared as he drew the arrow back almost to its tip, then loosed it high into the sky and in a great arc, the missile flew until it stuck into the ground a horse length from the rock.

"You should tell Ross to go back to Angle-land and bring back a thousand of them. Then we could defeat the Norse," laughed Innes.

"Ross?" Hector asked curiously.

"Yes, he gave it to my father. He took it back from the battle with the Angles, but no arrows, I make the arrows. I have another ten but somebody will have to go for that one. They take a long time to make," she grinned and ran her fingernail over the eagle on Hector's shoulder. "You went for feathers. I wanted to go but father wouldn't let me."

Eagles' nests are not the place for female warriors," smiled Hector and Innes pouted.

"I'll launch a boat and get the arrow," she said. "That warrior with the burn marks is one who came from Cluny. He can tell you what happened until I come back."

She headed down the ladder and the messengers made for the warrior immediately, anxious to hear a first-hand account of what happened, and they got one. Despite the rain, the Stockade at Cluny had caught fire inside and out. They must have poured oil between the timbers. Once the flames inside took hold, the dry timbers exploded. They were a hundred years old and the fire spread quickly. Many were trapped where they slept. Only the ones who were on the battlements had a chance to jump, before the flames crossed the divide between the

Stockade and the forest, setting the entire hill ablaze.

"That must have been what we saw from The Field of Rocks. We thought it was just a forest fire," said Hector.

The warrior then went on to the gruesome discovery at the Kinloss burn. The carnage they found, and amongst it, the body of the King. They got as many weapons away as they could before the Norse came back. He described the gruelling trek across the Dava to eventual salvation by Tusk. They knew nothing about the fate of Torridon until days later, when stragglers arrived, most of them young. A Monk called Aethan had saved them from certain death and they were in shock.

They watched as the small boat went to the shore and Innes ran to the arrow, she waved it triumphantly above her head before heading back to the Stockade. They went to meet her at the landing area, and she was all smiles.

"It didn't break," she announced proudly.

"Why were you and your warriors in the forest?" Hector asked.

"I wondered when you would ask that. We were laying a new track for the Norse. They follow the old tracks. They can move faster and cover more ground, but when they reach this stockade, they stay out of range, then go away. Father wants a track made to a kill zone at the base of the mountain. If we can lure them there, we can kill plenty with spears and bows, but my track leads to Culloden. You were spotted long before you saw us," she smiled.

"I believe you. It looks like your band are the only thorn in the Norse's side this side of the Moray Firth!"

"When do you leave?" she asked.

"We must go back to Tain as soon as we can."

"You know where to come if the Norse drive you out," said Innes. "We'll escort you to Inver, we know the forest well. We hunt there now to keep away from the Norse army. I can get you to Inver in one day."

Hector frowned, that was a day less than they had taken to get here.

# Chapter 15

At Bonner, Ross and Enya led eight warriors across the river and headed east. Urquhart had lit a beacon at daybreak as the Norse had requested. Ross was still convinced this was a trick, but he failed to come up with a reason to prevent Urquhart from agreeing to speak to Stroma. It was up to the Lugi to agree to the proposal. It was their land. All they could do was present it to them, and even that was against his better judgement.

Nobody came anywhere near them as they traversed the disputed land and they reached the shores of Loch Fleet, unscathed and a little relieved, although none would admit it. They had left the Lugi at Galspie many days ago and suspected they would still be there or close by. They headed for Galspie and hadn't reached the end of the Loch before a party of Lugi warriors came at them from the treeline.

They reined in their horses and waited. Forbes led them and he was grinning from ear to ear.

"You lost your mind, Ross?" he said and pulled up alongside Enya. She took his hand and smiled.

"I'm looking for Norse to kill but I can't find any," replied Ross, looking around.

"Me too, they must be hiding."

"Where's Stroma?" asked Ross.

"Galspie! We're here, she's there, and Frazer's at Little Ferry."

"You'd better send somebody to get Frazer and come with me to Galspie. I bring a message from the Norse!" Ross said solemnly.

Forbes looked at him. All jesting stopped, and he barked orders to his warrior to go back to the treeline and watch every move the Norse made. Two were to get to Frazer and tell him to head for Galspie.

They took off at a canter. It wasn't far, but Ross knew he still had to make the return journey and that was far.

Stroma rode out to meet them and touched hands with Enya before falling alongside Ross and Forbes.

"Ross is carrying a message for you from the Norse," announced Forbes, and Ross gave him a look that stopped any further comment.

Warriors took their horses, and they entered a longhouse that smelled of food.

"We wait until Frazer gets here," said Ross.

They were given soup and Stroma looked curiously at the rolled-up skin on the table, but Forbes took her attention away from it.

"They came back to The Helm," he said. "Two small boats came in the night, right into an ambush. They were out of spear range but not bow range and they fired everything they had at them. By the time they went across to the east side, the two boats had escaped back out to the sea and nothing was left. We've no idea if they hit anybody, they were firing at shadows. They took the sword back with them. We don't expect them to come again."

"What sword?" asked Ross.

"They left a sword where they camped," replied Forbes. "Frazer said nobody leaves a sword by accident. They must have left it to see if anybody had been there and taken it. We think they were looking for it, and if it was still there, they would have sent warriors back to the Helm to attack us from the east. They won't be back," he finished, decisively.

Stroma went outside and came back cradling a sword and offered it to Enya. It was covered in rust, but they had cleaned it up, Stroma explained. The Norse sword was indeed a weapon of high quality and sharp. Enya passed it to Ross.

"I think my father is clever," said Enya. "No warrior would lose this. It must have been left. Somebody stupid would have picked it up."

Stroma blushed.

Ross suddenly banged the weapon on the table and stared at Forbes.

"When? When did this happen? How many days ago?" he demanded.

"Four, five? I don't know," Frazer replied.

"Six nights ago," said Stroma. "Why?"

"Why? because four days ago they had a funeral, a very big funeral; didn't you see it from the ferry? The fires, the boat on fire and the warriors chanting something?" Ross asked anxiously.

"We saw something on fire, but the ferry is a long way and around a bend from where they are. What you are getting at?" Forbes asked.

"Two boats went into the Sutors but when the Death-Drum sounded, they turned and went back. That was the same night your boats were in the Helm. They were looking for a safe landing area east of the Lugi and a safe landing area west of the Decantae. One at the Helm and one close to Nigg.

"Your men killed somebody very important, Stroma. A monk at Tain said he had seen such a funeral on the western isles. Somebody of great importance, a leader, or a Royal, gets such a funeral. I tell you, your warriors have killed such a person. Who, we don't know, but the death might have something to do with this!" Ross frowned and stabbed his finger on the rolled-up skin.

"What is it?" she asked, desperate to see what lay inside.

"You won't like it, so wait until Frazer gets here. Where are the people from Dornoch?"

"Here, why?" Forbes answered.

"You'd better get whoever speaks for them here when Frazer arrives," said Ross, quietly and Stroma took Enya with her to go and find the one they called Mother Dornoch.

Frazer finally arrived, his horse lathered in sweat and he grabbed Enya and swung her around laughing, before putting her down and grinning at Ross.

"The messenger said there was a messenger from the Norse here, you changed sides Ross?" he quipped.

"I thought *you* had. What took you so long?" Ross replied and slapped him on the back.

"Open the damned thing now!" Stroma ordered and stared at the map with a blank look when it was unrolled and spread.

"Frazer the boats that tried to land at the Helm," said Ross, "the ones that your warriors ambushed, we think they killed somebody important. So important that after his death, the Norse changed their plans. I believe they planned to attack you from the east and the Decantae from the west. Surprise attacks timed like the one at Torridon. They have enough warriors to land a thousand at the Helm, a thousand at Nigg and support both with the two thousand left at Dornoch. Whoever you killed was important enough to change their plans. This here is the proposal straight from Sigurd, Earl of Orkney."

"What is it?" stroma frowned.

"It's our land!" shouted Mother Dornoch, and all hell broke loose.

Frazer grabbed the Norse Sword and banged it heavily on the table, roaring for quiet, his face red with anger.

"Let Ross speak and remain quiet until he's finished!" Frazer roared and banged the sword on the table again.

"This is a message to you. to the Lugi," continued Ross. "It's your land and only you can decide. It has nothing to do with the Decantae, but I'll give you some advice, there is trickery here somewhere, believe me."

"Carry on Ross. Tell us what this Norseman proposes, and keep the yelling down," Forbes urged.

"The land you see that takes in everything between Loch Fleet and the crossing at Bonner, on two sides, and stretches open-ended into the forest, they want. He says that if you grant him this land, he will withdraw three thousand of his warriors. One thousand will remain and set up a trading settlement. They will not attack the Lugi, or the Decantae, and we won't attack them. Once the trading settlement is built, he will leave warriors to protect it and the people who will settle there and withdraw the rest.

"If we don't agree, another army will come to join the one he already has here. He threatens to exterminate the Decantae and the Lugi. We have three days to decide and Stroma has to give her decision to Sigurd at the entrance to Loch Fleet, the morning after tomorrow. So, the choice is no choice. Agree or die, that just about sums it up."

"He wants to build a Norse Colony between our armies. Does he think we're stupid?" said Frazer, straining to contain himself.

"I don't know what he thinks," replied Ross. "But one thing is certain, these open-ended lines could stretch to the Sea of the Dead."

Stroma stared; she had never been on this land apart from passing through it, but it was that fact that triggered her to speak.

"If they have this land, we can't travel west."

"Urquhart says the right of way exists in all of Scotland and one day it will become Law. That is what you have to demand, freedom to cross this land. The right of way as Urquhart calls it," Ross said adamantly.

"Except Smertae!" Enya added and they laughed.

"Would you go back?" Ross asked looking at the old woman, and she recoiled at the thought. Her mouth opened but nothing came out.

"I think if Stroma agrees to this proposal, you and yours should demand to go back," said Ross. "From what we can see, Dornoch still stands. Your dwellings are all there and now you have hundreds of sheep and pigs and some cows. We can see your boats."

"Any reason they should go back?" Frazer asked.

"Freedom of movement. We have people among them, we'll know exactly what they're doing. We have no people we won't know. The Norse have no idea who was there, so they won't know who comes back. Just a thought," Ross smiled.

"You've had this for days. We just learned of it. Go take Enya for a walk and we'll discuss this among ourselves," said Frazer.

Ross leapt to his feet glad that somebody had taken the responsibility away from him.

Meanwhile, in Moray, Tusk had ridden to the edge of the forest with Urquhart's messengers. Innes and ten warriors would escort them to the outskirts of Inver and leave them there. Tusk had given Hector something sewn into a small leather pouch. He was to deliver it to Urquhart. He checked that Hector knew the name of the new King, and all four of them had to repeat the name, Uurad son of Bargoit. Satisfied, Tusk offered them safe haven if they were driven from their lands and safe haven to any who wished to join his fight against the Norse.

With that, they parted and Innes led them at speed through what they thought was hell on earth, but soon discovered animal trails had been cleared of branches and a network of them kept the party heading north. They crossed the Find and Nairn rivers more easily than they had before, and saw much wildlife including bears and wild cats but no wolves.

Deer were in abundance and would be hunted on their return journey, Innes informed them. She gave three of them a kiss on the cheek as she bade farewell at the edge of Culloden. The fourth, Hector, she kissed on the lips and his heart leapt.

Tusk's warriors headed into the forest. They would spend the night there, but the messengers had beds in mind and galloped towards the settlement at Inver.

As night fell on Lochindorb, Tusk poured a Whiskey and rattled his fingers on the tabletop, reflecting on a conversation he had with Hector about the young girl from Torridon who was saved by the Monk. She said she saw a warrior with long black hair spearing Norse, then she and a man went out through the great gate with somebody who had yellow hair. Tusk's remark to Hector that the Queen would still be alive if Ross had been in Torridon, was answered with a shrug a sigh and a delay.

"It is what it is. She's dead," Hector said eventually.

"It's as well because, if she wasn't, she soon would be if this new King got word of it. Or the Norse, they would hunt her down," Tusk stated staring into Hector's eyes, who dipped his head, understanding.

A shrug, the visions of a traumatised young girl, a delayed response and picking his words carefully. A glimmer of hope survives. Tusk grinned and downed his drink in one gulp.

At Galspie, if Ross had any thoughts about getting back to Tain the same day, they were dashed when a galloper was sent to Brora to get Callum. Stroma would have her full council. To make such a decision without one of them would be unwise. He found Enya among her warrior friends and they were in a giggling mood.

"You lot been at the whiskey?" asked Ross and was hauled to the ground by blue-painted, would-be rapists.

Enya laughed hysterically at their antics. Ross surrendered gladly and they had their fun.

"Ross! Get lost, she's staying here with us," one chirped.

"That's what I came to tell her. We stay here tonight. They just sent a galloper to get old Callum. It'll be dark before he gets here. How many of you are keeping me warm tonight?" Ross grinned and Enya threw an oatcake at him. He caught it and took a bite.

He smiled at her and left them to their chatter. He went alone to a dry-stone dike and rested his elbows on it. He finished his oatcake and stared towards the sea, deep in thought. It didn't last long, and he headed back to the meeting.

They were silent when Ross entered, and Frazer held his arms out in resignation.

"Before you go any further," said Ross, "Urquhart has sent messengers south to find Tusk. If they find him, they'll come back. Then we should know if any help is coming from the south and what the situation is in Moray. They should return soon, but I don't know if that will be before the deadline the Norse gave us."

"Stay here," said Frazer.

"My father will go crazy if we allow the Norse a foothold on Lugi land," said Stroma, looking at Ross for support.

"Your father will be one of many," said Ross. "But the choice isn't between a foothold and no hold. It's between a foothold and total destruction of the Lugi and the Decantae. Forget about other people, they can deal with their own problems, we have to deal with this one. Either Sigurd is afraid to face us in open battle if we combine our forces or he wants his army somewhere else, or he wants to set up colonies and trade. Take your pick Stroma."

"Start with the last one first, trade," said Forbes.

"You start," quipped Stroma.

She was obviously not getting her way and Ross sat next to her and Mother Dornoch.

"OK I'll start," replied Forbes. "We've lost Torridon, most likely all of Moray and the trading routes we used for hundreds of years are no longer. Where do we trade now? With the Smertae?"

That changed the line of thought; even Ross hadn't addressed this fact and what Forbes had brought up demanded attention.

"If we're cut off from the south, even if no Norse are here, we wouldn't be able to trade. Our boats would be attacked in the open sea and that route would be closed. Make no mistake about that. The Norse have us by the balls no matter what we do. When they took Torridon they ruled the north. We fight them and win, they'll come back stronger. We trade with them; their boats can cross oceans and our trade would increase. The big boats came back with cargoes of livestock. If they bring livestock here, they can take livestock away.

"Stroma, your father can trade with the Norse. Drive cattle and sheep here, bring the harvest of the hunters here or ask the Norse to set up another trading post. Just an idea," Forbes smiled at her horrified expression.

"You sound like Callum," Frazer scorned.

Ross grinned and poked Stroma.

"You going to answer him?" he urged.

"Sinclair would rather die than yield to the Norse, and so would I," hissed Stroma.

"That's exactly the choice we face," said Ross, "until we know what's happening in the south. If all is lost, we can expect no army to take back Torridon or come and attack the Norse here. We either fight and die soon or fight and die later. Forbes is right, with all our warriors dead, who will look after the other half of the population? They'll be sold as slaves and the Norse will have all the land. We must wait until Callum comes. How long will he be?"

"Don't worry about Callum," said Frazer. "What you two are pointing out is what Callum would be pointing out. He'll be happy we're throwing everything into the fire. As he says, what burns, burns, what survives is a decision. You two carry on with the trading."

"If they want the land, they can pay for it," croaked Mother.

Stroma was horrified by that idea as were the rest of them.

"Sell them nothing. If they steal land and remove people, they should pay compensation. Mother! Your family should get compensation or be allowed to return to your land," Stroma stormed.

"Now we're getting somewhere," grinned Forbes.

"What do you mean?" snapped Stroma.

"It's called a deal. We make a deal with the Norse, one that's binding on both sides. We give something, and they give something in return. As it stands, they want everything, and we get nothing!"

"So, what else can we demand?" asked Frazer.

"Right of way," said Ross, quickly.

"What about the northern border, where do the lines join there?" Forbes asked, looking at Stroma.

"Urquhart says a Smertae by the name of Ro-Sheen is interpreting for the Norse," said Ross. "The other Smertae was executed by my sword. Two Smertae were learning their language. We need people who will also learn their language and some of them to learn ours. No communications could be a disaster."

Callum arrived and food was served. The discussions went on late into the night and Stroma's stance of total defiance began to wither.

Ross left them to debate and went to find Enya among the dwellings. He was led to one that was alive with chatter and peered through the open door. Enya lay fast asleep on some skins and he put his finger to his lips. They hushed and he picked her up and carried her to another dwelling close by, that Stroma said they could use. He laid her out on the sleeping platform covered with thick deer hide and found a plaid. Like her, he was exhausted and covered both of them.

# Chapter 16

In the four days since leaving Inver, the messengers returned to a greatly changed settlement. Three Norse boats had been sighted from Nairn and caused panic on both sides of the Firth. Many people had flooded into Inver carrying everything they possessed and were camped on both sides of the river. Across the other side of the Firth, the Drum had been sounded at Avoch but had gone silent. As usual, there was no sign of life on the Black Isle and people who had been depressed before, felt more depressed after the messengers confirmed that no army was coming to help them, that a new King had been anointed, and power was now held in a place called Kinghorn in the old Kingdom of Fife. Few even knew where Fife was, let alone Kinghorn.

Hector discussed their options and decided they would head for Dingwall and not stop at Inver. All four of Urquhart's messengers were natives of Dingwall and the chance to stay with families was grabbed even if it was only for part of a night. Indeed, it was in the early hours of the morning when they arrived at Dingwall, and they were shattered. So, too were their horses. Their arrival caused a great stir, and despite the time of night, an anxious audience scrambled for news. What they had told in Inver they had to re-tell in Dingwall and several drams later, sleep won the battle.

Hector cursed when finally, he was woken by his mother, who was delighted he had a good sleep. Frantically, he mustered the other three and saddled horses that were fresh, fed and slept. They parted with words of warning that if the Norse came, they had to head for Tain or head into the Black Isle. They assured the messengers they would head for Tain.

"When they start beating that damned drum, they're putting stakes into the ground," one muttered and rubbed his rump to get the message across.

Journey's end was in sight, but it would be late before they arrived at Tain, even at a gallop, but nights were getting longer and they were confident they could make it without killing their mounts.

The previous night, Urquhart and the entire Decantae force were in turmoil. The Norse had lit many fires across the Firth and movement on a gigantic scale was observed by the scouts from the sand spit. Sheena insisted the fires could be a decoy and gallopers were sent to rouse warriors who had stood guard all day. All night the Decantae force were put on high alert. It was a time of truce, but nobody trusted the Norse. By daybreak, it became clear the Norse were still in position along the beaches of Dornoch and Urquhart cursed. This night he fumed what was good for the Goose, was good for the Gander, and ordered all his fires to be lit at sunset.

Messenger's hearts were in their mouth as the loom of fires lit the sky ahead, and they feared they were too late and had missed the battle. They cursed their families for letting them sleep for so long. But when their eyes landed on the source of the loom, they scratched their heads in confusion. At the fork, there was a big fire and many in either direction towards Mahomack and Tain. Across on the Dornoch side, even more, fires burned.

"I don't like the look of this," said Hector and called a halt.

"What do you make of it?" asked Andra, in little more than a whisper.

"If we ride in there at the gallop, we'll get speared," said a voice behind them and they agreed.

"We go at a walk," said Hector. "I wish we had a horn."

As they walked out of the dark into the light, warriors rose from the vegetation on both sides and stared.

"It's us, the messengers from Urquhart!" shouted Hector in alarm as spear arms were drawn back.

"Aye, you make a fine target Hector!" said a voice close by.

"Aye, and you better hit it, Laing! Or you'll have a spear stuck up your arse!" replied Hector to his younger brother.

Laughter ensued and the warriors relaxed.

"We have a truce for three days. That's why the fires are lit," explained Laing without being asked.

"We have to move," replied Hector. "You have a new King, and no army is coming from the south. We'll tell you all about it when we get back."

He spurred his horse forward and when they reached the Stockade, they found it too was well lit.

The warriors inside the Stockade greeted their arrival with great joy and they went quickly to find Urquhart. Sorsce showed them to his private chamber, where he sat with Sheena, studying a map spread open on the table.

"Am I glad to see you!" Urquhart grinned, and Sheena went one better, kissing all four on the cheek.

"We don't bring good news," said Hector and Urquhart told them to be seated.

Hector looked at Sheena.

"It's as you feared, they have anointed a new King. His name is Uurad, the son of Bargoit. Tusk said to tell you this. And he said to me that if you were still alive, you would be in great danger because royalty are bastards."

"You told him I was alive?" Sheena frowned.

"No! But Tusk suspects you are. He said if Ross had been in Torridon, you would be alive. Somebody saw a black-haired female spearing Norse, and then she and a yellow hair female went out the great gate with a man. She was in shock. They were going to be slaughtered until a Monk stopped the Norse and they let them go."

Sheena nodded her head. In the heat of battle, even a Queen becomes just a yellow hair; she felt grateful for that.

"Do you know this new King, son of Bargoit?" she asked Urquhart.

"I know the name. Bargoit was kin to Eogan, but I don't know how. Ross might know him. He would have been at the battle with the Angles."

"He's set up a seat of power in Kinghorn Fife. Wherever that is?" added Hector.

"Now give us the real bad news," complained Urquhart.

"First, I have to give you this," said Hector and passed the small sewn pouch to Urquhart. He frowned and took it.

"Tell us everything you know and make it fast. We might have to send a messenger to Stroma before daybreak," Urquhart urged then cocked his head in the direction of a commotion outside. “Krike!” he said, as the door burst open. “Sit down unless the Norse have attacked!”

Krike sat down and stared at Hector expectantly.

“So, tell us, what happened after the battle until now?” Urquhart urged again.

They listened in silence as Hector gave the account, which he had repeated several times and had it off by heart. Sheena lowered her head when told the King was buried at Lochindorb until his body could be moved to Iona. The rest was lost to her and she stared at the floor as he continued his news.

“Go and eat we have things to discuss,” said Urquhart to the messengers.

He cut open the sewing on the pouch and tipped the contents onto the table. Whatever it contained was wrapped in woollen cloth and he unwound it.

“Sheena, this is for you, not me,” he said quietly.

She looked at the two gold rings, the gold crucifix, the lock of hair bound by strands of hair into a ring and the tears welled in her eyes.

“Come Krike,” Urquhart barked, grabbing him by the shoulder. “We have work to do. We must send a messenger to Stroma before she meets with the Norse.”

It was a chance; the only chance. They had to get a messenger to Stroma before daybreak.

At Meikle Ferry, three warriors rowed the small boat across, towing a horse behind. The closest Norse fires to the ferry were some distance away, but that meant nothing, warriors could be guarding the crossing. To get somebody to Stroma before daybreak meant talking the chance. They were all unarmed and they had a white flag with them in case they were challenged.

The boat beached quietly, but the horse was frisky and struggled to get out of the water. By the time the rider had settled it down and mounted, they realised the crossing was unguarded. Fiona headed east at speed. She knew this terrain and had insisted she should go. She was also one of the best riders. Sine had to be restrained from joining her by Urquhart and Krike.

The track ahead was good, but Fiona knew if she strayed even a short distance from it in places, she could land in a bog; some of the troughs she had to avoid were deep and a potential death sentence to her and her horse.

She reached the shore of Loch Fleet and breathed a sigh of relief. She was now on undisputed territory and knew the threat from the Norse was behind her, but she had no idea what lay ahead, nor where to find Stroma. Urquhart had instructed her to go to Galspie first; the Lugi would have warriors there but whether Stroma was with them, she would only find out on arrival. If not, she was to head for Little Ferry with all haste. Stroma would be there, he assured her.

That was all very well but Fiona had never been to Galspie. She knew where the track went right and led to it, but that was all. She found the track and the moon helped but not enough to go fast. It was a frustrating ride until she saw a fire ahead. Somebody must have lit it, but who would light fires at this time of day? She reined in and saw the outline of dwellings in its light.

"I am a messenger from Urquhart. I have a message for Stroma!" she called and waited.

From the side of a dwelling, a fat woman waddled towards the fire and threw more wood onto it. Fiona frowned and shouted her message again. The woman looked around and jumped when she saw the horse and rider, then squinted into the darkness as Fiona came forward.

"Who are you?" she said, alarmed, raising a burning stick from the fire.

Fiona dismounted and came forward with her hand up.

"I'm Fiona; I have come from Tain with a message for Stroma."

"Go away, Stroma not here, she go to the beach," shouted the old woman and pointed with her fire stick.

Fiona rolled her eyes and groaned as she heaved herself back into the saddle.

"How long ago?"

But the woman just looked at her and pointed again with her stick.

Fiona cursed and headed in the direction the woman pointed and hoped it was towards the beach. She hadn't gone far when the reflection of the moon on the water lifted her spirits and she hit the sand at a canter. The horse seemed to know the ground ahead was safe and galloped towards Little Ferry. Urquhart had told her it lay five miles distant.

Meanwhile, Ross rode behind Stroma and her council with Enya by his side. They were early but without a cloud in the sky, daybreak would come quickly and the moon was so bright they could see the way ahead clearly. Fires in the distance were read as belonging to the Norse. They had lit no fires but had given Mother instructions to have fires ready when they came back. They would eat on their return.

A commotion behind them made them turn in alarm and rein in their horses. Swords were drawn as all immediately suspected trickery. Fiona roared her way through the mass of horses until two warriors with spears grabbed her halter.

"Get me to Stroma!" she yelled at them. "I have a message from Urquhart."

They escorted her, still hanging onto her halter and "messenger from Urquhart" was repeated ahead of them until Ross picked it up and waited anxiously for the messenger to appear.

"It's Fiona," said Enya, as Stroma came beside Ross.

"My sister Fiona with a message from Urquhart? It must be important," he said. Quietly his heart was beating fast, fearing something bad had happened, knowing the risks Fiona had taken to get here.

"Brother, get me off this damned horse, I'm raw!" yelled Fiona.

"Dismount!" Stroma commanded her warriors and jumped from her horse.

Enya and Stroma helped Fiona down and she grimaced with pain. She was breathing hard as they walked her to the grass above the beach and sat her down. Ross gave her a drink of water and she hugged Stroma and Enya.

"I thought I would never catch you," she said between gulps.

"What happened?" asked Ross.

"The messengers sent to Tusk, they came back late last night. Ach, never mind the details, what you need to know is this: no army is coming north to help us. No army is helping anybody. A new King, Uurad has already been anointed and the power is now in the south. Torridon has been abandoned just like us. Urquhart says to make a deal with the Norse, we have no choice," she gasped, taking another mouthful of water.

Ross let out a long breath and went to Frazer.

"Well, now we know," he sighed.

"Now we know indeed, but that doesn't change anything," warned Frazer. "We still ask for terms; he can only refuse or accept."

"And we still have three thousand warriors that could make a big hole in his army," smiled Ross, slapping Frazer on the back.

"Let's get to the bastard. Mount up!" shouted Forbes and looked up at the sky.

"Send scouts ahead," ordered Frazer. "Search the land around Little Ferry."

Several horses went quickly past and galloped towards the distant fires. Fiona rode side-saddle between Stroma and Enya. Inside her thighs were raw, and her back ached but as they neared their destination, her ailments got less and like everybody, she looked at the first rays of light in the east. Scouts came to report all was well at the ferry and the Norse were already on the west side, waiting.

"This isn't going to work," said Frazer and Ross looked at him.

"What?"

"We're too far apart to discuss anything. The channel is wide just now with the big tides and it's nearing high tide. The channel will be more than a bow-shot wide," he sighed. "We didn't pick the meeting place, he did."

"Is there a boat here?" asked Ross.

"That's a good question. Is there a boat still at the ferry?" Frazer roared to the following warriors.

Some yelled there was, others that there wasn't. Then a warrior rode up beside them.

"If the boat was left, I know where it will be hidden," he said.

"Go ahead and find it if it's there," ordered Frazer and turned to Ross.

"You feel like a boat trip?" he grinned.

"I hadn't planned on one. What's the charge for the ferry?"

"You want it in guts or stupidity?" asked Frazer and they both laughed.

Stroma came beside them and she stared straight ahead, her face set in stone. They realised the light was upon them just as the warrior who went to look for the boat was seen coming towards them, two bow shots distant.

"The boat is there, and the oars are there," he told Frazer and got a weird look from Stroma.

"What boat?" she asked.

"A Little Ferry is a boat, not a place," grinned Frazer.

The scene ahead came into view slowly and out of focus, but as they neared, what awaited them was vast and intimidating. Only two horses stood by the entrance to Loch Fleet but behind them for as far as they could see stood warriors, and they were also massed deep along the west side of the entrance.

Forbes halted the horses and stayed in front of them with Enya and Fiona, while Stroma went ahead of Ross and Frazer. They followed close behind her and she went to the water's edge.

"Just stay still, don't do anything; let them make the first move," Frazer's voice reached her. She was shaking but not visibly.

Across the water, a horse went down to the watermark and stopped just as Stroma had done, and the rider raised both arms into the air and spread them apart. A very faint voice reached them, but they couldn't make out the words.

Frazer turned to Forbes and shouted,

"Tell them to get the boat!"

Stroma swallowed hard.

Four horses headed to their right and warriors dismounted. They disappeared into the sand-hills and reappeared carrying a small boat between them.

"The Little Ferry has arrived, Stroma!" said Frazer. "As soon as the boat's in the water, get into it and go to the front. Ross and I will get behind you and we will row. Keep looking at them and relax."

"Relax! Relax!" she seethed and was still seething as the boat was launched. "I'll kill you for this Frazer and you Ross!" she snapped as she stepped into it.

Ross grinned at Frazer, but neither made any comment. They took an oar each and the warriors pushed the boat out from the shore.

As they approached, Stroma realised the warrior on the horse was female with long golden hair and beautiful, but the warrior who walked his horse down to the water beside her and dismounted, looked anything but beautiful, with a long beard and long hair, plaited down both his shoulders, and he wore some kind of ornament on his head that stretched over his nose. Chain mail clunked against a mighty sword as the wearer neared.

"You keep your temper, Stroma and keep that Dirk in your belt," Frazer warned as they covered the final boat length.

Sigurd was impressed and waded into the water. He held his hand out to take Stroma's and she nearly died. He assisted her out of the boat and onto dry land.

"Did Sigurd forget to bring a boat?" Frazer shouted to Ro-Sheen, and she shouted the translation back. Sigurd laughed loudly and nodded his head. He said something in Norse and Ro-sheen advised the Picts to follow him. She dismounted and did the same.

They walked a little way and curious warriors craned their necks to get a closer look at the savages and mumbled among themselves. They had never seen any without their faces being painted and they looked like humans which surprised the superstitious among them.

Ro-Sheen came close to Ross.

"You must be Ro-Sheen. When you interpret, tell Sigurd exactly what we say, word for word, do you understand?" Ross said quietly.

"I understand," she replied, her tone decisive and walked on.

They reached a place where Sigurd had obviously waited as skins were spread over the sand. He beckoned them to be seated and took the lead.

"Introduce yourselves, I will interpret," said Ro-Sheen and remained standing.

"I am Stroma, Chief of the Lugi, this is my land," she said, and Frazer threw her a look.

"I am Frazer of the Lugi council; I speak for Stroma," he said and met her gaze.

"I am Ross of the Decantae council, I speak for Urquhart."

Ro-Sheen repeated their introductions then Sigurd spoke.

"He is Sigurd, Jarl of Orkney and he welcomes you to *his* land," translated Ro-Sheen and smiled at Stroma.

She knew not to take the bait and anyway Frazer spoke before she could say anything.

"You tell Sigurd that the Lugi and The Decantae agree that he can start a trading area here, but we have conditions that must be discussed."

"They watched for any change in expression as Ro-Sheen translated but there was none, and Sigurd spoke again.

"What conditions?" Ro-Sheen asked.

"The people who you chased off their land, they get compensation, or they can come back," proposed Frazer.

"They can come back," Ro-Sheen said in translation of Sigurd's answer.

"Tell Sigurd that we are three people among four thousand warriors. If he's not afraid of us, why does he have Bowmen with arrows notched pointing at us? Tell him," insisted Ross.

Sigurd grinned and waved his arm. The bowmen lowered their bows.

"The east and west boundary that goes into the forest," said Frazer, "it doesn't meet. How far into the forest does he expect to go?"

Sigurd spoke for a considerable time when he answered, and Ro-Sheen smiled.

"Sigurd says he needs timber to build the trading area and houses for those who will remain here. Once the dwellings have been built, he will pay for timber cut from your forest, but he isn't going to pay for timber to build a trading post. You decide how far into the forest the boundary should go."

They looked at each other. They hadn't expected to be asked to decide anything. Sigurd spoke again.

"Sigurd says the further into the forest you go, the more of his land you will have to go around to get from east to west. He wants enough timber to build the settlement," Ro-Sheen smiled.

"You tell Sigurd we won't be going around anything. Right of way exists in this country, it's a tradition, travellers have free passage across any land, provided they are travelling and do no harm to the land, or anything on it," Ross barked.

She rattled that off and Ross looked expectantly at Sigurd, but he said only one word,

"Unarmed?" asked Ro-Sheen.

"No, not unarmed. If an army wants to cross any land, they're free to do so, unless they are at war with the owners. Free passage, armed or unarmed, as long as no harm is done to the land, or anybody or anything on it," Ross repeated adamantly.

Sigurd gave this great thought before he spoke again.

"Sigurd says this is a strange custom. In his land, if you trespass you will die. But if his land is the only land where people can't cross, how will he let people know? The solution is very complicated and would demand guards. That's expensive and a waste of warriors. Do you swear to abide by such an agreement? He asks."

"We don't need to swear but he must," replied Frazer.

"If Sigurd swears, then you must also swear. The Norse way is to swear by the sword," she translated.

"So be it, we will follow his lead," agreed Frazer.

Sigurd stood up and drew his sword. He nodded and they drew theirs. They crossed swords and touched each.

"Sigurd swears to follow tradition and allow passage over his lands," said Sigurd.

Each of them said, "I swear" in turn, and sheathed their weapons. Now that they knew no army was coming, and Sigurd's army didn't want to fight one, the idea of holding them here lost its significance.

They discussed everything they had spoken about at their meeting, including interpreters, and all was agreed. Ro-Sheen would supervise that. Then Sigurd spoke.

"The Norse will need supplies of wood, of wool, of meat, fish oil, fish and many people will work the land and grow many crops. The drink that drives everybody crazy they will take to the lands to the south. You have many seals; they will need sealskins and your people will prosper trading with the Norse far beyond the lands you know," Ro-Sheen interpreted.

"When do they leave?" asked Ross and she spoke to Sigurd.

"He stood up and roared something at his warriors and was rewarded with a great cheer."

"Tomorrow, two thousand warriors will go. As soon as the ships return, another thousand will go. You can send somebody here to check, Sigurd says," Ro-Sheen smiled.

It was on the tip of Ross's tongue to ask where they would go but decided against it. Sigurd stood up and approached Stroma. He towered over her, but she held his eyes. He took her hand and kissed the back of it and mumbled something in Norse.

"It's time to leave," Ro-Sheen said quietly.

The trip back across the narrows was a bit more hair-raising than the first as the little boat was swept seaward by a vicious outgoing tide. Frazer and Ross rowed like demons to get back to shore as the Norse looked on, amused.

Sigurd took hold of Ro-Sheen's hand and kissed it.

"I didn't believe you when you told me such a tradition existed," he said. "Right of Passage, I like it, I like it more because they have sworn to uphold this crazy practice. Now I can wander all over their lands with their blessing!" he laughed.

# Chapter 17

Urquhart had paced the battlements all night. He was worried to death about Fiona and regretted sending her alone. Before daylight, he was out on the spit watching the Norse from as close as he could get. Fires had gone down or gone out, much like his hopes of an army coming from the south. The news the messengers had brought back took a while to fully digest, and the threat to Sheena's life that Tusk had outlined, certainly existed, but there was a worse scenario to consider, that of Civil War.

If the man across the water found out the Queen was still alive and only a few miles from him, and a new King had been anointed, would he kill her, or use her to divide the country? If the Norse supported the Queen and wanted to reinstate her even as a puppet ruler, the tribes would rise up against each other and divide the country north and south. They still had allegiance to the Queen as long as she lived and declared the new King a fraud. Urquhart's mind was in turmoil. But he decided if he was in Sigurd's position, he would use her, not kill her and reap the benefits of divide and conquer.

Sorsce found him and knew his mind was tormented. She had left Sine to sleep with Sheena. The rings of the King, her wedding ring, and the Ring of State were in her hands. It was the ring of Eagan's hair that fractured her resolve, and she wept openly for the first time.

"One problem at a time, Urquhart," said Sorsce and he grinned.

"Which one first?"

"That one," she replied and pointed toward the Norse army.

They were too far away from Little Ferry to see any activity and when daylight arrived, nothing seemed to have changed. They gave up and spoke to Fiona's warriors who still kept vigil on the spit.

"Anything happens over there, if you see any movement, come and get me," ordered Urquhart then headed back to the Stockade. Sheena and Sine met them at the gate, and both were smiling.

"The lovers return," Sheena quipped and took Urquhart's horse. Sine took her mother's, and they rode them to the stables.

They wasted no time in returning to the kitchen. They hadn't eaten yet and Sorsce usually ran things there. That's where they found her and questions were fired.

"We're too far away. They could be fighting a battle at the ferry and we wouldn't know, even if it was in sight. Anything happens, the warriors on the Spit will let us know. Are you feeling better?" Sorsce asked Sheena.

"I feel great. They never mutilated the King. He'll be buried in Iona, and I'm glad a new King has been anointed. I don't want to be a Queen without a King. Now I have to decide which way I am going to die," Sheena smiled and Sorsce caught her breath.

"You die and I'll kill you!" she raged and they burst into laughter.

Sorsce took food to Urquhart, but he was fast asleep. She left him sleeping and yawned herself. It had been a long night.

"Father, father, father!" Sine yelled and shook Urquhart.

"What is it, Sine?" he growled without turning around.

"The Norse, father they're going away, they're going away on big boats!" she cried and ran from the room.

Urquhart was close behind her, and on reaching the courtyard found Sheena holding two horses and surrounded by warriors.

"You'd better go and look, father," said Sheena and handed him the reins.

Sine mounted in one bound and the warriors let out a yelp and followed them through the gate. They galloped quickly back to the Spit and found many warriors gathered there with Krike.

"Two boats have already left and warriors are being marched in single file onto another two," announced Krike and grinned.

Urquhart didn't reply. He just stared at the huge Knarrs and the line of warriors boarding the one closest. He cast a glance at the tide-line.

"What's the tide doing, Krike?" he asked.

"On the ebb. It's near half tide."

Urquhart shook his head. It was half tide when he left here, and now it was half tide again. He thought he had hardly slept but half the day had passed. He said nothing and watched the spectacle unfolding with mixed emotions.

"Where do they go? That's what I would like to know," said Krike.

"They can go to hell as long as they leave here. I don't care," sighed Urquhart.

"And what price do we have to pay for this?" asked Krike.

"We'll find that out when Ross gets back. Whatever they agreed to, we must accept. If there was any hope of the army coming from the south, Krike, we could hold them here, but we've been abandoned. So why destroy what we have for nothing?"

"Aye, Urquhart, they knew what they were doing when they took Torridon first, I'll grant them that," he replied, gloomily.

"Ross said to watch for trickery," said Urquhart. "This Sigurd has foresight he's not thinking about now, he's way ahead. I think this is his second plan. I'd like to know who he burned in that boat. He certainly never came here with this size of force to negotiate, and now they go away. Unbelievable!"

The troop that galloped towards the crossing at Bonner hoped to get to Tain before dark and were on track to achieving their goal. Decantae and Lugi escorts rode with Stroma, Forbes, Enya and Ross. Fiona was saddled on a pile of fox skins that hardly eased her pain, but she had to endure, she had no choice.

Warriors came to the Stockade to alert Urquhart that a troop was seen heading towards Bonner, and he asked Sheena and Sine to go and greet them.

"A horse! If she fell off a horse and broke her neck, she would be dead," suggested Krike, now that Sheena had left the room.

"It's no problem getting her dead. She's got to be seen to be dead," insisted Sorsce.

"I think drowning is the best way," argued Urquhart. "It's often that bodies aren't found. The other problem is getting the word out and in secret. She's supposed to be dead now, so having her dead twice and letting everybody in the world know she was alive, that's not easy."

Sorsce agreed with him.

"Just get her dead and I'll do the rest," growled Krike.

"Ask her what she wants, that's the easy way," suggested Sorsce.

"That's what we'll do. What are you going to do?" Urquhart threw at Krike suspiciously, who just touched his nose in reply.

Food was ready by the time the troop arrived, which was the main reason for alerting the Stockade that they were coming. Fiona needed help getting down from her horse and walked painfully to her dwelling. Asked if she had caught a salmon between her legs, she shouted back at Sine, that what she suggested wasn't funny.

"Ahh! Fiona, you've been raped!" screeched Fia, running to console her.

"By a horse?" scorned Fiona.

"They shouldn't have sent you alone. I knew the Norse would get you!" raged Fia.

"Not the Norse, Fia, a bloody horse," groaned Fiona.

"How did it manage that?" she demanded and Fiona left her to figure it out.

Once fed and watered, they gave Urquhart a detailed account of the negotiations with Sigurd and he nodded approvingly, especially concerning the return of the people to Dornoch. That was unexpected and they had done well to get an agreement on that and closing the boundary to the north in the forest. A bow-shot into the trees meant they wouldn't have far to go to get around the Norse ground. He was happy with that and said so.

"Don't have to go around; the tradition of passage exists. We can go straight across. Sigurd agreed to respect our traditions and swore to abide by them," declared Ross, with a sense of achievement.

"And did you swear to abide by them?" asked Urquhart.

"Certainly," replied Stroma. "We all swore to abide by them. Sigurd insisted."

"Ross, you said trickery was afoot. Now you know what it was," sighed Urquhart. "But it's too late to do anything about it now."

They looked at him bewildered.

"Right of passage has been granted to you by the Norse. And you swore to abide by it. That means the Norse have the right to cross your land, as much as you have to cross theirs," he said and waited.

The rest of them exchanged looks, not of alarm but guilt. Urquhart was right, they had fallen into the trap, with their eyes wide open.

"Might be a good thing, might be bad," grinned Urquhart. "There's nothing you can do about it now. The Norse have already left with four big boats loaded with their warriors."

"We're staying here until they come back, to take away the rest," Stroma told him. "We can't see anything from Little Ferry. The Smertae, Ro-Sheen, wants young girls, two from you and two from me, to teach their language. She wants girls because they're more intelligent and will pick up the language quickly. She's going to teach them in Torridon. It's called Torfness now and Tarbatness is the name they use for the point of land east of Mahomack."

"You say a thousand warriors will remain and three thousand will leave?" asked Urquhart. "A thousand is too many. They don't need a thousand warriors to build a trading post, and if they leave a thousand, we must keep a thousand of ours. Tomorrow, go back and speak to this Sigurd. He can leave a hundred or two hundred at most. Stroma! It's better if your people work. If they don't work, they'll look for any excuse to attack the Norse. I'll go across by boat from Mahomack and speak to the Smertae."

As Urquhart finished, there was a great sigh of relief because nobody would have to go back by horse.

Sheena walked the battlements and stared across the water at the many fires that burned like the fire in her heart. Urquhart had no choice but to accept terms with the Norse, but she would never accept them. She knew what she had to do and climbed down the ladder. Hector handed her the reins of her mount and Andra opened the gate.

Together, they walked the horses towards Mahomack. Both were painted for battle and Sheena had her long hair tucked under her leather top and out of sight. Her bundle was big and sat across the saddle. In front of her, Hector had one also, but it belonged to Sheena, not him. Decantae fires lined the route to Mahomack and the travellers waved as they passed. At the crossroads, they turned right, away from Mahomack and once clear of the warriors along the track, they began to canter. They disappeared into the night heading in the direction of Invergordon.

After they had eaten and finished their discussions, Urquhart insisted it was a time to celebrate.

"The Norse want to trade, we trade, we get rich, we get rich we can raise a bigger army. This is not over; it's just the beginning!" Urquhart toasted and downed his whiskey.

Musicians arrived and a party atmosphere developed. Sine joined in and danced to the pipes, followed by Enya and then Stroma.

"Where's Sheena?" asked Ross.

"Leave her, Ross," advised Urquhart. "The messengers took back the King's Rings and his hair. She's been in solitude since. She spent all day yesterday in the Abbey with the Monks. She just stares and doesn't speak to anybody. I'm worried about her."

"She'll speak to me," snapped Ross. "If she's that depressed, the Monks will only make her worse. She can't stay here, Urquhart, she'll die. You know that."

"Leave her! Tomorrow's another day. We've had drink and might make things worse. A clear head, Ross, and wait till she's had a good sleep, then we'll speak to her. But not tonight," Urquhart ordered and poured another bowl of whiskey.

Ross reluctantly agreed and took the offering. He went to Enya and Sine, tipping some into their respective bowls, and the music started again. They were in fine fettle when Andra entered the great hall and went straight to Urquhart with a look of death on his face.

"Sheena has gone to the water," he said.

Urquhart leapt to his feet.

"What?" he yelled, and everybody stopped to look at him.

"Sheena has gone to the water!" announced Andra loudly.

Ross rushed to Urquhart, drinking vessels cast aside.

"Get to the beach!" screamed Urquhart. "Sheena's gone into the water!"

There was a mad rush for the gate. Many warriors joined them and they headed towards the shoreline, including Andra. It was he who found the folded skins, with the Crucifix on top, beside the water.

Urquhart knelt and wept beside it and Sine joined him. The current was strong and they knew their beloved Queen had perished.

Krike rode back to Mahomack, after a "hair of the dog" and headed for the other hairy dog. Aggie was up and about and so was Dog. He licked Krike's hand as he put on his best sad face and looked at Aggie.

"What's the matter with you?" she asked.

"Oh, Me Aggie! A terrible thing's happened, but it's a secret," Krike whispered and she came close. "The Queen did away with herself last night. She went into the water and we fear she's drowned. They're looking for her body now, but we can't tell anybody, because if the Norse got wind of it and she's found alive, they'll kill her. So, it's a secret. Where's Angus?"

"At the smoker," she replied, stunned by the news.

"I'll go and tell Angus," said Krike and left her.

He grinned as he watched Aggie shuffling to the next dwelling, Dog hard behind her. He could rest assured that news of the Queen's death would reach every ear, as a secret, and spread faster than fire.

"Angus! We'll need enough for breakfast," Krike announced.

Meanwhile, Sheena and Hector spent the day hiding at the dwelling of the Struie sisters, and as darkness fell, they headed west towards Dingwall. They would keep clear of the settlement and head for Tore, eight miles to the south of Dingwall and deep into the forest. They had a long ride ahead of them and knew they had to reach Tore unseen in the dark. They could go no further and would wait there for daylight. Hector felt nervous, but Sheena assured him he wouldn't get a sharpened stake. Nonetheless, he had stayed away from this forest all his life. He knew where the track led to Tore, but that was all.

A chosen few had access for trade, but so few that the track was little more than an animal trail, and as the forest engulfed them, they were slowed to a walk. Horses were nervous and shafts of moonlight cast dancing shadows adding to their unease. They went at a walk for what seemed an eternity until there was nothing ahead, the trail had disappeared and the horses stopped. Not sure if they had reached their destination or not, they dismounted and looked to left and right for any sign of the track but found none. They had reached a dead end.

"We must wait here for daylight," whispered Sheena and stiffened as a timber wolf howled in the distance. Through the branches overhead, the sky looked bright, but they didn't know if it was moonlight or daybreak. They would if the dawn chorus started, and soon afterwards a blackbird burst into song. It was joined by more chirps and wolves started howling far to their right. Daylight crept up on them slowly and being able to see their surroundings revealed very little until they saw a track leading back the way they had come and running parallel to the one they arrived on. They followed it for a long way back before it suddenly turned sharp left and back the opposite way.

They continued until they came to a clearing and stopped dead. Facing them stood ten warriors painted in colour and carrying weapons. All were naked except for loincloths. The females among them came armed with spears, the men had swords that were broad and curved at the tips.

"Sheena!" called one.

She walked forward and a warrior came alongside her horse. They clasped hands at the elbows.

"Where is your hair?" he asked. "Urquhart said you had long, golden hair?"

He smiled as Sheena pulled her hair out from under her top. Two females came to either side of Hector and read him. He froze and closed his eyes tightly. He had heard about these beauties; if you looked into their eyes you were doomed.

"Hector!" shouted Sheena and he opened his eyes in alarm. "Follow!"

With a painted beauty on either side, Hector followed, his eyes firmly glued to the backs of those ahead.

Close to noon, they descended a steep trail and water came into view on their right side. They had seen no other warriors since meeting the ten, and they rode in silence, without stopping and at a steady lope. The forest was thick and had only been trimmed around the edges by the look of the many stumps that were evident between the riders and the sea. Up and over a steep climb they could see sea ahead again and when they descended towards it, smoke clung to the hillside. Across the water, they could see Nigg on the east Sutor.

Warriors lined their approach to Cromarty and all bowed their heads as Sheena passed. Young and old they smiled and greeted her warmly. Two old people waited at the end of the line and Sheena reined in, in front of them.

"Sheena! Daughter of Urquhart, Chief of the Decantae, Sheena, Chief of Cromarty, we welcome you!" the old man howled in a voice that rose and fell.

"Urquhart, Chief of Cromarty, I have come to join you," she replied, and a great cheer went up.

Hector was dumbstruck and didn't know where to look. A busty maiden took his leg out of the stirrup and bade him get off his horse.

"You are not afraid of eagles, you should not be afraid of me," she smiled, and Hector choked.

Sheena was led to the dwelling of Urquhart; the old man took her right hand the old woman took her left. Two girls carried her bundles behind them, and a young boy came with her horse.

Hector stared across the Firth at the land. He couldn't believe it had taken a night and the better part of a day to get from there to where he stood. It was so close. He knew Urquhart had sent Andra to take a message to old Urquhart on the Black Isle, but he had been instructed to go to Nigg and cross by boat. Andra had been back in Mahomack for several days before Hector had received his instructions to stay away from all settlements and let nobody see Sheena entering the Black Isle.

Old Urquhart offered Sheena food and drink and it was gladly accepted.

"Your father has two daughters," he said. "We have no children. When I die you will become Chief of the Cromarty Decantae, when your father dies, Sine will become Chief of the mainland Decantae. One tribe with two Chief's, one tribe with two different ways of life. It's a good arrangement your father makes!" he chirped and Sheena smiled.

Hector wasn't smiling much. He was taken towards a fire on the beach and had to pass four stakes standing upright; they were the thickness of his forearm and were pointed and greased. The females with him giggled and wiggled their arses and everything else that swung free. Hector reached the fire and they sat him down on the sand. Some warriors came with fish and bread and grinned.

"You can eat Hector. Don't take any notice of them, they wait for a prisoner. My name is Iain," said the warrior and smiled. His friendly voice and posture didn't reflect the outer story tattooed on every part of his body.

Hector found his voice for the first time and asked if they had any whiskey? That request was met with a roar of approval and he got a clap on the back from a female who then ran from the beach.

Towards dusk, the search for the body of the Queen was abandoned. Ross was adamant they should search across the other side of the Firth where the Norse were, but Urquhart would have none of it. They returned to the Stockade as darkness fell and rode to the stables together.

"Thank God that's over; this has been the worst day of my life," sighed Urquhart.

"The worst day of all our lives," agreed Ross.

"I knew she was greatly loved, Ross, but not so that warriors wept."

They went towards the great hall and Stroma arrived with Frazer, Enya and Sine.

"Sine, bring Fiona and you three come to my chamber," ordered Urquhart.

Fiona was much better, physically but she felt broken-hearted. She came with Sine out of sympathy for her and her father.

"Close the door," said Urquhart. "I'm going to speak softly so listen to what I have to say, and after I stop speaking, you will remain silent. Do you understand? Silent, not a word, then you will go ahead as if nothing has changed. You know that if the Norse found out that Sheena was alive, they would come for her. This new King would do the same. Sheena would be killed one way or the other, sooner, or later. She would have no life."

"We would have protected her," insisted Ross.

"Every breath, every day, every night, for the rest of her life? I don't think so, Ross," replied Urquhart. "Sheena the Queen had to die. Sheena, daughter of Urquhart lives," he said and held his finger to his lips. "Apart from you who are here, only Sorsce, Krike and Andra know she's alive and one other, Hector who is with her. Hector has taken her to the Black Isle. I arranged it with old Urquhart three days ago, and they have gone by Tore so nobody at Nigg would see her cross.

"Sheena will stay on the Black Isle when Urquhart dies. She will become Chief. When I die, Sine will become Chief. Sheena says no matter what agreements are made with the Norse; she will fight them for the rest of her life. She will never surrender to them. Now she can fight them. The choice she had to make was either Urquhart or Tusk. She chose Urquhart and she chose the manner of her 'death'.

"She says sorry to all of you for deceiving you and welcomes you to the Black Isle to fight the Norse," Urquhart smiled and looked at the stunned faces, all except Sine who was beaming.

Ross grabbed her around the waist, and she burst out laughing.

"I'm going to kill you, you little shit! I thought you were weeping all over me all day, but you were laughing!" he said and spun her around.

# Chapter 18

Torf was taken by surprise when the Knarr ships arrived at Torfness, crammed with warriors. He thought many things might have happened but never expected the news brought by the commander. The untimely death of Frode, and how he died. Sigurd's decision to establish a trading settlement and the procurement of land without a battle was unheard of, as was the arrival of two thousand warrior's surplus to requirements, with the prospect of a thousand more.

The camp at the Clarkley doubled in size in one day, and suddenly Torf found himself with enough warriors to secure the lands east and west but he needed boats, not Knarrs. The Longboats were still with Sigurd, and now Tarbat. Torf had no love for Frode, but he respected him. For such a warrior to be ambushed and killed by an arrow in the back was something Torf couldn't get his head around. However, the influx of warriors demanded his full attention. They had to be fed and command established. He was grateful that Sigurd had sent some of the Shield Maidens, but not Astrid. They would move the domestic front.

The commander had orders to take the warriors to Torfness and return as soon as the weather allowed. The weather complied and the following morning all the Knarr ships sailed towards Tarbat Ness, passing Little Ferry by noon.

Urquhart had launched a small Yole at Mahomack and went across to the Dornoch side under a white flag. Together with Krike and Frazer, they lay offshore until they were beckoned to land by the now infamous beauty from Tongue.

"Now! that would get me into the stables, Krike," whispered Urquhart.

"Urquhart! Sigurd welcomes you," said Ro-Sheen.

"You know Frazer and this is Krike," Urquhart introduced and Ro-Sheen bowed to Krike in greeting.

They followed her to a tent adorned with shields and weapons outside, as many were, and Sigurd stood at the entrance with two warriors by his side.

"Tell Sigurd we have come to further the agreement," stated Urquhart.

He gave them a curious look but waved for them to go into the tent. Frazer noticed he didn't have any of the trimmings he had worn at their first meeting and didn't look so intimidating dressed in casual skins.

"Begin!" said Ro-Sheen when they were all seated.

"Tell Sigurd I request that he remove more warriors, and I will explain why," said Urquhart.

The discussions went on and food was served, roast sheep and the guests were impressed that it tasted the same this side of the Firth, as it did on the other side.

Messengers arrived and announced something, which Ro-Sheen explained was the return of the big boats from Torfness. Sigurd spoke to her then smiled at his guests.

"You can see how long it takes to get warriors here on slow boats," translated Ro-Sheen. "The Longboats are twice as fast. No matter how many warriors are left here, if they are attacked, the army will return in force and battle will commence. Sigurd can get warriors here faster than you could assemble your own." She pressed that point home, and it was a fact they couldn't deny.

"Krike will stay here," said Urquhart. "He will represent the Lugi and Decantae. I will send four girls; you can choose two to teach and two will return. Stroma will send two and they must be picked up at Little Ferry. Tell Sigurd these girls are under his protection. His honour is at stake if he fails them."

Sigurd listened and smiled. He didn't speak, he just held his arm out and Urquhart clutched arms with him.

"Krike! Two hundred will remain. Mother Dornoch and her family will come back to their dwellings. I'll return with the girls as soon as we find four willing volunteers," said Urquhart and grinned at Ro-Sheen. "Watch him. He likes Smertae women," he quipped and got a smile in reply.

"How the hell did the Smertae produce that?" asked Frazer, as they rowed from shore and hoisted the sail.

"Beats me!" replied Urquhart. "One thing is for sure, she never got her manners from the Smertae!"

He was highly impressed with Ro-Sheen. She didn't speak down to people and was very respectful, as well as being very beautiful and a traitor.

Krike watched them go.

"Take your bundle to the dwellings in Dornoch," said Ro-Sheen. "The Shield Maidens will show you one that's empty," and pointed towards the cluster of dwellings.

Krike stared at his surroundings and cursed Urquhart. Warriors were staring at him as they lined up to board the Knarrs and he wanted to disappear. He went to the first dwelling and looked inside. A warrior jumped to her feet and rushed to the door. She took Krike by the hand and led him to the next dwelling. She smiled and ushered him inside gibbering something he didn't understand. He threw his bundle onto a sleeping platform and cursed Urquhart again, before taking a stroll around the rest of the settlement and was surprised by the amount of livestock in sties and pens. Mother Dornoch never owned anything like this, he thought.

The commander came out of Sigurd's tent and headed back to the Knarr, where he assembled his own commanders and navigators.

"We go to Kirkwall, and then we go to Tongue. Two Longboats will come to Tongue with us, and Magnus will lead the army. We load timber in Tongue and bring it here. Then we take the Knarrs back to Norway for settlers!" announced the commander and a great cheer went up.

The Knarrs left before dark and Sigurd bade them farewell. Krike listened but didn't understand.

"Where are they going?" he asked Ro-Sheen.

She smiled but didn't answer. Krike threw her a look and went to get more food. This Norse food was good, he thought, and the scenery was good also. He was served by a Shield Maiden on a plate made of pewter and given a spoon made of metal, not wood. The urge to plunge an iron Sword into one was fading.

Ro-Sheen came and beckoned him to accompany her after he had eaten, and he went back to Sigurd's tent with her. She translated

Sigurd's news.

"When the Knarrs come back, they will be loaded with timber, enough timber to build most of the trading post. When that timber has been used, the Lugi must supply more, and warriors to haul timber from the forest. Norse warriors will be reduced to one hundred, as soon as the trading area is ready. You can tell the Lugi to start felling trees and get them ready to haul here. They'll be paid in silver for their labour and the timber."

Krike grinned and nodded in understanding. This man didn't waste time. As Urquhart said, he plans ahead, way ahead.

In Torfness, peace had returned to the battlements. Every solution had been looked at, every alternative addressed, but finally, Torf had given up. There was no alternative. He ordered the Snake steps un-blocked and warriors tore at the timbers and rocks that blocked it. Torf had ridiculed the builders of such a stupid stairway. It had led to the downfall of the Fort once and it wouldn't happen again. However, it seemed the shit design was exactly what it was. Warriors had a long journey in the dark to reach the beach.

A well-worn path extended from the bottom of the Snake steps to the edge of the cliff and on inspection, it looked like a huge chunk of rock had broken off as the sandstone wasn't even weathered. This was confirmed by the great slab of rock below the cliff. Whatever had been there wasn't now, and some warriors set about erecting a Thunder box. Now the guards could go down the steps and relieve themselves over the cliff, sheer luxury compared to the headlong dash from the battlements to the beach that often ended in a beach too far. The warriors were relieved, in more ways than one.

Torf's forces patrolled the interior relentlessly. Sigurd had insisted they must keep the pressure up with what force remained until he could return. Then the occupation of the fringes would start. Where that would end was unknown, but as far as Sigurd was concerned, he would expand until he reached the limit of his army. The limit of his army would be the ability to secure what they had seized and no more. Greed didn't come into his thinking. He knew if he couldn't protect the land he seized, there was no reason to seize it, and the Picts could be playing him for a fool. No resistance would tempt him to stretch his forces too thin, and then they would strike.

The return of two thousand warriors was a great relief to Torf, but without Longboats, they were unable to attack to the west into the narrows that Frode had encountered. Cluny was strategic and now manned by five hundred warriors. Little remained of the Stockade, but what remained was reinforced and they camped there. Also, at the east end of the high ground where the Picts called Covesea. The Skiffs had reported many Picts living in caves along the cliff face. Fifty or even more but dealing with them could wait. They seemed to stick to the beaches and sending warriors to their deaths for a few caves would be hard to justify.

However, where the cliff met the silver sands of the beach it was easy to seal and the Lake was close on the west side. This represented another strategic position and was also manned. A surprise attack from east or west was expected from the Picts, and their outposts at Cluny and Covesea were utilised. Above the cliffs, they discovered many small fields with crops growing and along the entire length of the high ground many fields appeared green with crops but with nobody to attend them. Torf wanted many more settlers before it was time to harvest the bounty already appearing from the land in many directions.

The thorn in Torf's side lay along the base of the high mountains to the south. His men had been massacred by the Picts. They would flee when any force appeared but killed any scouts that strayed too far from the main force. Always the tracks led back to the Stockade on the Lake, and the name Tusk infuriated Torf, as it did Sigurd.

At the mouth of the great Salmon River to the east, they established another camp, and the beginnings of a stockade were taking shape. They also discovered this river ran through the lands Tusk hunted and was known to the Picts as the Spey. Along this valley, they found great wealth in farmland, and whiskey-making seemed to be the main occupation of these people, but none had been captured who knew how to operate anything and the language problem was becoming as much a thorn in Torf's side as the hated Tusk.

With more warriors at his disposal, Torf gathered his commanders and told them to come up with a plan to destroy Tusk and his band of assassins. If he could do this before Sigurd returned, it would be a great achievement. His commanders were as keen as he was to wipe out the resistance and now, they had greater knowledge of their surroundings, they compiled a map which all agreed to be accurate.

If it wasn't for the fact Tusk's Stockade was built on an island, it would have been turned to ash by now and he would be dead along with his entire band. Attacking the Stockade would be suicide even with boats and they dismissed the thought. They all agreed they had to lure Tusk's warriors from the island and prevent them from getting back onto it when confronted with a Norse force. Getting even some of them would seem a victory; so far, they hadn't even killed one that they knew of.

Norse losses had been great, and the biggest loss wasn't warriors, it was horses. Every Scout killed was mounted, and Tusk got stronger with every horse he stole. Nobody knew exactly how many warriors Tusk had. Estimates ranged from two hundred to three hundred, and some thought fewer. It was impossible to tell. Despite many suggestions on how to lure Tusk's force into the open and destroy them, they reached no agreement that didn't involve high risk. Torf decided to restrict the Scouts to one mile from the main force, and all would carry hunting horns.

If any were attacked, they could sound the alarm. Help could get to them quickly. Only if chasers got within sight of Tusk's force were, they to chase them down and prevent them from getting back onto the island. Then, they could be dealt with. When Sigurd returned, he would decide how to dispose of Tusk. In the meantime, caution remained paramount. Commanders were warned not to lose any more horses.

The Norse had a problem with horses, but Tusk had an even greater one: where to keep them. It was only a question of time before their holding area was discovered. And the Norse could not only recover their own horses but Tusk's as well. The decision was reached to establish a second camp and keep the bulk of the horses there. Only twenty horses would remain close to Lochindorb.

Glenmore forest and the Queen's forest at the base of the Mountain Cairngorm was the chosen location. Tusk's warriors knew this place like the backs of their hands. The location was their primary hunting grounds, and a food supply came with the terrain. Also, a short gallop to the west, the upper reaches of the River Spey could be reached. There, salmon were spawning by the thousands, and bears were also in abundance. But the main reason for locating them close to the mountain was to escape. A day on foot would see refugees on the south slopes and the downward journey to the River Dee and safety. It was a hard climb, but the north face of Cairngorm was tame in comparison to the adjoining peaks of Ben Macdui, which were near vertical, and snow-clad all year round.

The population of Grantown had sought shelter with Tusk when the Norse sent a large army south along the Spey Valley. There they found great fertile lands with crops well established. They didn't destroy the crops along the valley nor at Grantown. Buildings were also left intact, but much livestock had been driven north when the army retreated. Tusk's most recent clash with the Norse was with the Scouts of their army, and ten more horses were taken along with weapons and heads.

Torf had gone crazy when the loss was reported, but Sigurd had warned him not to fall for a trap. If he laid siege to the Stockade, a Pict army could cut him off, and if they came, they would come in thousands. Cut off from retreat, the Norse army would be caught in open battle and destroyed. It was this warning and it alone that kept Torf from hounding Tusk in his own terrain. But now he had an extra two thousand warriors at his disposal, the temptation was great.

Four days after the warriors arrived at Torfness, lookouts on the battlements reported movement to the north, and Torf joined the observers. Many sails were seen in the direction of Tarbatness and the huge sails of the Knarrs were easily identified heading east, but all eyes stayed on the Longboats, and a great cheer went up when they came directly towards Torfness. Two had gone east with the Knarrs and Torf counted eight heading towards him, and the smaller Skiffs numbered three.

Great excitement filled Torfness, and horns were blown in celebration. They didn't know what they were celebrating, but the return of their fleet gave cause enough. Skiffs drew alongside the ledge long before the food was even slaughtered for the feast Torf was determined to have. Hundreds of warriors lined the beach, the ledge and the battlements. Great cheers greeted Sigurd when he stepped ashore with most of his commanders. Torf welcomed them all. Ro-Sheen was easy to see and with her came four females who looked young, and stared up at the Fort towering above them, with wide eyes.

At Dornoch, Krike marvelled at the speed the Norse had abandoned their stronghold, and he felt very uneasy. At least when the Smertae woman was here, she could translate. Now he was on sign language and the warrior Sigurd had left in command, named Bjorn, which the Smertae told Krike meant Bear, had the same temper as his namesake.

Two hundred Norse were left. Two Longboats and two of the little boats Krike couldn't take his eyes off. His breakthrough with Bjorn came as a drawing on the sand and Krike cracked what the Bear wanted, rollers to put under the keels of the longboats, so they could be hauled out of the water. There were plenty of rollers in Mahomack and at last Krike found himself on a Skiff. It covered the short distance to Mahomack fast and he guided it into a clear part of the beach. He was met with notched arrows and spears at the ready, but when they saw who was aboard, the weapons were replaced by laughter.

Loaded with rollers, the Skiff headed back, and the Bear was delighted. So too were the warriors and set about laying out the rollers as soon as the tide was high. Krike watched amazed as one great Longboat was pulled completely clear of the water by fifty warriors, and chocks were positioned behind it.

Now the reason was revealed, and much marine growth grew below the waterline. The shape of the hull was what fascinated Krike, and the shallow draft of such a large boat was unbelievable. A Pict boat of the same length would be three times deeper in the water and three times heavier. Now he knew why these boats flew so fast, but he found it difficult to work out why they didn't capsize.

One who stayed her distance from this Pict was Astrid. Ro-Sheen had explained to her, that the Picts had no written language and what they wanted to portray was either tattooed on them or carved in stone. She had explained some of the tattoos, and Astrid knew the four interlocking circles on Krike's bicep meant four warriors he had killed, and two looked fresh. She wondered if one represented Bente. She wasn't far out; one represented her saviour, Eirik.

Tattoos on the Norse were a complete mystery to Krike, but he did read something he thought he could exploit and that presented him with another excuse to get into the little boat.

Fiona had healed and gone back to the Spit with instructions to watch for anything suspicious. The Skiff that approached was such a happening, but the man on the bow made her smile. Krike passed his request to Fiona and she laughed. She sent two gallopers to Tain and

Krike waited. He gave her a full report on happenings across the water, and when the horses returned, they had four people on their backs.

"Stop your complaining or I'll dump the both of you in the water. Get into the boat!" Krike screamed at the two Monks.

Reluctantly they obeyed and sat with their books on their laps staring at the water sloshing around their feet until the skiff grounded on the far shore.

"Roast monk for supper tonight!" Krike yelled and hauled both of them to their feet. The sight that greeted them made them stare in wonder.

Norse warriors kneeled and crossed themselves when they saw what cargo the Skiff had delivered, and they triggered a great outcry in a language Krike didn't understand from the Monks, who couldn't get among the flock fast enough. The Bear gave Krike a great smile and joined his warriors on his knees. Not to be outdone, Krike joined them and received a glare for his effort. He never went to their Abbey and he had a Bull on his back.

# Chapter 19

To the North, the Smertae Chief Alastair went to his knees also when the great Norse horn announced the arrival of the Longboats. It was his worst nightmare and he had two choices, stay and plead for mercy, or run.

Only about one hundred warriors were scattered around the Kyle, and fifty at most around the Stockade. The rest of his people had gone on their travels, scattering far and wide. Panic engulfed the young Chief and when he heard his name yelled loudly, he nearly jumped over the rampart.

"Alastair!" shouted Isla and he turned. "Sound the horn, sound the horn!"

Her shouting reached the warriors closest to them and as a great blast on the horn sounded, Alastair looked at her in confusion.

"If they were going to attack us, they wouldn't announce their arrival," said Isla. "We must go to the beach and meet them."

She grabbed his hand and by the time they reached the gate, Alastair had himself more under control, but with no idea what to say to the Norse.

Isla recognised Magnus standing on the bow as the Longboat came closer and she waved to him. He waved back and barked an order to the oarsmen. Their oars dug in and the boat came faster onto the sand and ground to a halt. Magnus lowered himself into the shallow water, followed by many warriors all armed and with shields.

Isla spoke to Magnus, who looked at Alastair. He frowned and looked him up and down again.

"Magnus says you must tell him what happened, and how Drest was killed?" she translated and Alastair nodded. "In the stockade!" she urged; Alastair seemed in a trance.

Ale was served and food offered when Magnus asked why the Smertae had betrayed Sigurd? Alastair started rambling on about being attacked by a great army and Drest's head being cut off, and Isla was having difficulty following his story. It wasn't what the survivors had told her and she decided to tell Magnus her own version of events.

He listened unimpressed, and when she mentioned the army of the Queen, he knew she was lying. However, contrary to Alastair's fears, Magnus didn't care. Drest was dead and this young Chief seemed inexperienced in all matters. Had Drest been alive, Magnus had orders to kill him and any who resisted, then take over the Stockade at Tongue. Magnus had taken note of the amount of timber the Smertae had on the beach and it was enough for one Longboat to carry. He called to one of his Warriors and he left.

"Tell this chief that Sigurd will support and protect him and his people," he commanded. "The commander of our army waits in the deep water. He will come soon. His name is Tarbat. He will tell you what you must do. If you refuse, the army will take over all your lands and any who resist will die. Tell him!"

Isla stared at Magnus. She had grown in confidence since Drest was killed, and he couldn't belittle her or anybody else anymore.

"Magnus! Before this man comes, you must promise to protect us," she said. "Drest is dead. He is the one who failed Sigurd, not Alastair and not our warriors. Only Drest knew what Sigurd wanted, nobody else."

"Tell him he can do this the easy way, or the hard way," smiled Magnus. "Either way it will be done. Tell him to agree to everything Tarbat demands, and no blood will be spilt."

Tarbat watched anxiously from a Knarr Ship anchored in the deep water. Magnus had argued long and hard that he had to try and negotiate with Drest before any warriors were landed from the Knarrs. Their presence was critical, but warriors would only be landed if any resistance was shown by Drest, or the longboats were attacked.

Only a handful of warriors had gone ashore with Magnus, and when Tarbat saw a Longboat leave the shore and head back towards him, he expected the worst and cursed Magnus for his caution. It was with a mixture of anger and curiosity that Tarbat boarded the Longboat and headed for the shore. Many Smertae warriors watched from a distance as he was escorted by twenty Norse warriors to the Stockade.

Alastair pulled himself together with encouragement from Isla.

"Tell him to offer his arm to Tarbat," Magnus whispered in her ear.

Isla obeyed and Alastair did as she asked. This gesture took the wind out of Tarbat's sails and he frowned at Magnus.

"Drest is dead. They knew nothing about his orders from Sigurd. This new chief has no experience. He doesn't know how to lie," Magnus laughed.

"Tell him what is in the past, remains in the past," said Tarbat to Isla. "Now is what matters."

"We don't make the same mistake again. Tell him to assemble his people, and this time, they will all know what Sigurd's orders are," said Magnus and looked at Tarbat. "All discussions with Drest had been in private. The people outside his close circle wouldn't know anything, and if they don't know, they have an excuse. We address them all, and they will have no excuse."

"Tell me what you want to say. I can't translate if you speak fast," cried Isla in alarm and Magnus grinned.

"Let me speak, Tarbat, they know me," he said and Tarbat grunted.

He explained the happenings at Mahomack. The setting up of a trading post. Peace between the Lugi the Decantae and the Norse was secured without a battle. Also, the right of passage was being upheld by all.

"Sigurd now requests a similar trading post be set up here at Tongue," continued Magnus. "One hundred Norse will remain here and under the same conditions as imposed on the two other tribes. If they are attacked, the army will return in thousands, and they know what the consequences will be."

He spoke slowly, and eventually, Isla got the main gist of his message. She nodded her head and asked Alastair to sound the horn to gather.

The horn was sounded three times on the battlements and people started to head for the Stockade. It was the signal that the Chief was going to speak and the initial fears that the Norse were going to attack had subsided. They waited until the courtyard was full before Magnus spoke, and what he said wasn't on her script.

"Ro-Sheen stands at the right side of Sigurd. Ro-Sheen is one of you. Ro-Sheen asks you choose wisely," Magnus finished and Isla passed his message to the sound of many murmurs. She continued to outline what this was all about, and they stared at her in wonder and silence.

"What will we trade?" Isla frowned.

"Everything! Not just timber, everything from your land and most likely everybody else's land," Magnus chuckled.

Isla got the message and started mentioning everything she could think of until Magnus stopped her.

"Tell them Ro-Sheen wants two girls to teach our language. You will also teach two girls here. She wants girls because they are the most intelligent," Magnus grinned, and Isla wasted no time in getting that message across.

"Do you agree?" Isla yelled and a great cheer went up.

"They agree," she informed Tarbat and Magnus.

"Alastair, you must agree in person, and clasp arms on the agreement," Isla beamed, and greatly relieved, Alastair did as she suggested.

"Before they go, tell them the wood on the beach must be loaded onto a Longboat as quickly as possible," Magnus smiled.

"I think Alastair can take care of that," Isla grinned and told him the request.

Alastair raced from the company, glad to get away from them and glad to have something to do he was familiar with.

"We will leave one Longboat here and one hundred warriors, they will build a new settlement and trading post. They will need your help," Tarbat said to Isla, and she smiled.

The two commanders left the Stockade and went to the beach along with Isla and watched as timber was loaded onto the Longboat.

"Whoever killed Drest has done us a great service," Magnus grinned.

Three days later, the Longboat beached at Dornoch, and its cargo was quickly discharged. The two commanders decided to spend the night there and went to see how things were progressing, nodding approvingly at the two Longboats with their bottoms cleaned and oiled. Both of them had the same thoughts and ordered the Bear to launch one, and pull the one they had arrived in up the rollers and have it cleaned. They would leave it here and take the other to Torfness.

Likewise in Torfness, all boats were being cleaned on the hard sand beside the Slappy. Sigurd knew they would need speed, and removing marine growth was a guarantee of that, provided they had wind.

Torf still hadn't managed to unearth the riches of the Fort, and where they were kept remained a mystery, but he would find out eventually and he had more important matters to attend to. The return of Tarbat and Magnus would trigger the invasion of the west, and preparations for that were well advanced. One thousand warriors would follow the Longboats and use the Skiffs to ford any rivers they encountered. Horses would be swum across, or if a ford was found close to river mouths, they would use it.

Maps stopped at the west river, the Find, and new blank maps were drawn for the south and north sides. Tarbat was the only one who had gone into the narrows with Frode, but that was in the dark. This journey would be in daylight. All boats had two anchors aboard, and all stern lights had been removed and taken to the Fort. In addition to the Norse boats, two of the largest Pict boats had been launched, when required they would act as supply boats, with food and weapons aboard.

It was with a great cheer that the Longboat was sighted soon after it cleared Tarbatness and Sigurd watched it close the distance quickly. Two turns of the time glass were all it took before the oars went out and the craft slid alongside the ledge. When he saw both commanders on the Longboat, Sigurd was greatly concerned. Magnus should have remained with the army at Tongue.

"Your Knarrs are in Norway by now, or on their way back with settlers," Magnus smiled but Sigurd gave him a vacant look.

They quickly briefed him on happenings in Tongue and Magnus didn't elaborate on Drest's death. He didn't care how he died, and they all agreed his death had prevented what could have turned out to be a running battle with any supporters he had. Now, unbelievably, they had a trading post on both ends of the north land, and with tact, it would expand.

Sigurd was delighted, but his attention was drawn to two young girls who looked frightened to death and were holding small bundles under their chins and staring with big eyes.

"What's this?" he asked and pointed.

"That is a surprise, but first they need clean and new clothes," Tarbat grinned and lifted one onto the ledge. She was followed by the second, and Sigurd frowned.

"Don't ask," Magnus grinned, and took both by the hand. He led them up to the fort and Sigurd followed close behind shaking his head. He couldn't fathom how two young girls could be a surprise.

Two Norse women took the girls and Magnus instructed them that he wanted them looking like God intended, not the Devil, and the women laughed at the challenge. He then went with Sigurd to his quarters and maps were laid out.

Soon the mystery of the girls was forgotten as the challenge ahead was revealed and Tarbat had plenty to say about the tide rip that had caught his Longboats in the dark. He was assured no voyage into the narrows would take place except in daylight. The shore army would also be left behind. The Longboats could carry one hundred warriors each and the suggestion was to reduce the shore army and increase the marine one. They were in deep discussion when one of the women knocked and entered.

"They are ready," she announced.

Both Tarbat and Magnus hurried to the door and outside stood another woman, holding both young girls by the hand. Magnus whistled and the girls giggled. They looked nothing like the dishevelled waifs they had been given, and both smiled.

"Where is Ro-Sheen?" asked Magnus.

"She's in the Abbey, teaching. Why?" asked Sigurd.

"Keep them here, you'll see why shortly," grinned Tarbat and headed for the Abbey.

Ro-Sheen was teaching six children, and four Monks, and threw Tarbat a curious look when he interrupted.

"Sigurd wants you immediately," he announced, and Ro-Sheen sighed.

She followed Tarbat to Sigurd's quarters and stared at the two young girls dressed in Norse clothes and grinning.

"Hello! Who are you?" asked Ro-Sheen in Norse.

"You'd better ask them in your own language, I don't think your two sisters speak Norse," said Magnus.

Ro-Sheen stared, then let out a scream. She gathered her two young sisters in her arms and burst into floods of tears.

Meanwhile, on the Black Isle, Sheena felt she had gone back hundreds of years; the aura that surrounded the place wasn't fiction, these people lived as their ancestors lived and had no wish to change. They felt content with what they had and would fight to preserve it. For days she tried to come to terms with her new surroundings and failed. Hector was faring better and had gone hunting in the forest. His hunting skills were put to the test and he impressed his hosts by stalking a Roe Buck and killing it not with an arrow, but with a spear from above.

Sheena had been taken to the west Sutor and climbed high above the sea. She sweated in the heat but declined the temptation to undress like her hosts. She wasn't ready to run around bare-breasted and with only a loincloth like her companions. One of them was the girl her sister Sine had met before and her companion Adair. The three of them reached the summit of the steep incline that was covered in trees and they rested breathless.

The warrior Sine pointed out to sea and Sheena looked. At first, she could see nothing then a small dot of land came into view.

"Torridon," Sine announced and Sheena realised why they had taken her there, or so she thought.

What faced her on the top made her stop and stare. A solid wall of timber stakes resembling the wall of a Stockade but much lower, blended between the live trees and she was urged to follow to the right by Adair who let out a series of yelps like a dog as they moved.

Two warriors confronted them when they rounded the end of the stakes and more people gathered behind them. Children looked at the visitor and clustered together.

"Come, Sheena of the Decantae," a warrior smiled and beckoned her towards some kind of dwelling. It stood only waist-high but was thatched.

Sheena followed and smiled at the children who smiled back and giggled.

Steps led down and she realised this dwelling was a dug-out with as much below ground as above it and there wasn't just one, there were many. The inside resembled the dwelling in Cromarty and she gladly took a seat and accepted a dark liquid which she smelled suspiciously. It was blackberry juice and she drank it gladly.

"The climb up here is hard, that's why we live here. We are thirty strong," their host announced.

"They watch over us day and night," said Sine. "If they see anything that threatens, they sound the drum; it has many beats but slow means the threat is east, faster means the threat it south. Balblair has only one beat. Drink and rest, there is much to see here, among the trees."

"What is the wall of timber for?" asked Sheena.

"Windbreak. In winter you couldn't live here, you would be blown away. The wall of timber shelters the village, and as you can see, half the dwellings are underground. Timbers go from the bottom to the top and they don't get damaged in a storm," Sine smiled.

Sheena could see that the timbers were stout and the construction looked stronger than any dwelling she had ever seen. Apart from this, the dwelling resembled any other.

"We will go and see the Drum," said Adair.

That, Sheena wanted to see. She had heard of this great drum all her life.

"What's it made of?" she asked.

"A horse," grinned Sine.

"A what?" Sheena gasped.

"A horse."

"How can a drum be made from a horse? You tease me."

"The skin of a horse not a whole horse," laughed Adair.

Sheena shook her head; even the thought of such a big drum didn't fit into her imagination. But that wasn't her main concern.

"Can everybody hear it?" she asked.

"No. Sometimes they can and sometimes they can't but as long as the threat hears it, they think the alarm has been raised, whether it has or not. The same as a horn depends on the wind."

"And nobody comes into the open. Nobody can be seen so an enemy has no idea of your strength," smiled Sheena.

They nodded. She knew this but there was a lot she didn't know, such as how to get around on the island, which was the most important.

They went from the dwelling towards the sea and two warriors came with them, along a narrow path that ran parallel to the windbreak that ended abruptly above a steep drop into the sea far below. To their right, two females appeared and looked at them curiously.

"Somebody is watching from here day and night, winter and summer," said Sine and called to her friends to uncover the Drum.

Sheena waited while skins were removed from what looked like a big barrel and she stepped closer to inspect it. The skin across the top was fastened by many thongs of what looked like pigskin, but it was the metal on this Drum that Sheena took note of; it was Bronze and the wood wasn't Pine it was Oak.

She spread her arms across the top and could just reach both sides. The observers grinned at her inspection and she tapped the drum skin tentatively.

"I want to bang it!" she said.

"You do that, and you will get into trouble. The drum is never sounded unless it's to give a warning. We use this," Sine said and handed Sheena the striker.

She took it and the urge to use it got stronger. The wooden striker was bound in leather and had a knob of solid pigskin on the end.

"A little bit?" Sheena pleaded and they laughed.

They agreed and she tapped the striker on the middle of the skin, quickly withdrawing it. Her 'little bit' sounded much louder than she thought it would.

From this point, the view was commanding and nothing could enter the Sutors without being seen. Also, across the Moray Firth, the land was clearly visible and to their right, it came even closer before turning west.

"Ardersier is in that direction," said Adair and pointed.

"We saw a Norse boat today, heading for Torridon," said one of the warriors and Sheena came back to earth.

"Come, Sheena, we have much to show you," said Sine, taking her hand.

They headed west for a short distance and Sheena began to feel anxious.

"We're not armed," she said. "We can't go into the forest unarmed."

"We don't intend to," replied Adair and led on.

The dwelling they came to next had no sign of habitation but was like the others along the high ground, semi dugout. Adair ran down the steps and opened the door. She came out with three spears and headed back inside again. She re-appeared with two bows and a handful of arrows.

"You want more?" she asked.

"No!" said Sheena and laughed.

"We don't carry weapons every time we come up here. We keep them here; it makes the climb easier. We'll put them back when we return. Take a look inside," said Sine. "There is enough to arm twenty warriors. Swords, Shields, Bows, Spears and hundreds of arrows," she beamed.

"I'm impressed," said Sheena.

"Ten places like this are on the high ground," said Adair. "They're not easy to find. We all know where they are and you will too, but that will take a long time. From here, we follow the high ground west until you can see our farmland, then we will go back to Cromarty."

Adair slung a bow over her back. Sine did likewise and each took a spear. Sheena was left with a spear and the arrows.

Sheena felt the sweat streaming from her as she tried to keep up with the two ahead and she was glad when they stopped and put their fingers to their lips. Sine pressed her spear into the ground and slid the bow off her back Adair followed and Sheena handed them arrows.

"Caper," whispered Sine.

Sheena stayed still as the two warriors crept forward, arrows notched and bending low. She peered ahead of them into what looked like a bank of gorse. She was looking for the Caper, the great Black Grouse that was abundant in all the forests. It fed on pinecones and it was big enough and slow enough to be taken by an arrow, especially on the ground as they preferred to run rather than fly.

Sheena spotted it before the two hunters. She could do nothing, but she breathed out when she saw Adair pull the bowstring back. Sine followed suit and both arrows were loosed into the gorse. An almighty flapping followed, and the two hunters raced towards their target. The Caper was hit but was far from dead. The bird went wild, flapping madly and shaking an arrow clear, it raced through the trees trailing a wing.

They raced after it and Sheena cut it off when it turned right. Adair was nearly on top of it and yelling wildly. It dodged her dive and ran straight into Sine's outstretched bow, its neck jamming between the bow and the bowstring. She twisted hard to keep it there and Adair grabbed it, then spun it vigorously by the head and its neck broke. The wing that worked went berserk and then went limp. The hunters collapsed on the ground laughing loudly and Sheena gathered up the unlucky bird; it was big and black with scarlet eye rings and a good catch. They recovered both arrows and went south into the sun.

"We don't have to go any further, we can see the start of the farmland from here," said Sine and they lay on an outcrop of rock that stood clear of the forest.

Sheena marvelled at what she saw below, many fields rich in crops and many people tending them. They were far away, and the land turned to their right obscuring what lay around the bend but directly across the waters of the Moray Firth was land and it was close, very close.

# Chapter 20

In Torfness, the plans for the invasion of the west were being agreed upon, blank skins for maps prepared, boats cleaned and rigging repaired. Tarbat warned the navigators and commanders about the narrows and made it clear to all why they would be making no forays into the unknown in the dark. It wasn't a great sacrifice; darkness was very short, but the days were also starting to get shorter. Sigurd knew he had to move quickly if he wanted to secure his western flank before the good weather ended. It remained surprisingly still and hot enough to make sleep uncomfortable.

Torf had demanded to lead the land army. He had been stuck in the Fort long enough. Sigurd agreed. He had more faith in Torf than in Tarbat but didn't say so. However, Tarbat was also pleased with this arrangement and was glad he would command the warships. Magnus got the task of protecting the Fort and keeping the relentless patrols along the interior active. Now they had more maps of the interior, it was possible to divert the patrols and not take the same route all the time. This had resulted in fewer Scouts being killed and horses lost.

Since the arrival of her two young sisters, Ro-Sheen had gone into mother mode and had arranged with a Norse family to keep them. They also had two girls and the hope was they would communicate as only children can. Ro-Sheen had also been warned by Sigurd that when the invasion of the West began, she had to accompany him. She was critical for negotiations, and there was no other. She had been well rewarded for her contribution so far, and the death of Imogen meant Sigurd had silver to spare.

The first hurdle was close and the river Find had to be crossed and the army assembled on the sands at the west side of the river. Getting warriors over wasn't difficult but getting horses across meant either swimming them or crossing at a ford further upriver. Salmon crossing the shallow Ford were unnerving the horses. It took a long time before they had them all across and their camp had been established for two days before Sigurd was satisfied and Torf took command.

Tarbat requested that the Skiffs could go ahead of the Longboats and scout the narrows. They could turn and manoeuvre quickly and alert the Longboats of anything threatening ahead. Sigurd had to think about this, Skiffs weren't in his plans. They had served their purpose and their last foray into enemy territory had ended in disaster, with the death of Frode. However, what Tarbat suggested made sense and eventually he agreed that two Skiffs would accompany the Longboats for scouting purposes only.

Ro-Sheen's class in the Abbey wasn't going well. All doors and windows stood wide open, but the place was still hot enough to make the habit-wearing Monks pour with sweat and they complained. Children, stripped to their bare skin was one thing, but Ro-Sheen had to side with the Monks.

"Is it always as hot here in summer?" she asked, wiping sweat from her brow.

"No, we will pay for this," grumbled a Monk. "Last time it was as hot as this, the sky went black and hail came with a storm.

Ro-Sheen silently wished it would hurry up, but there wasn't a cloud in the sky. By noon, they'd had enough, and she sent the children to the beach. They scattered with great abandon and she grinned at her two sisters, hand in hand with their new sisters.

Sigurd was alone when she entered his quarters, and he was stripped to the waist.

"The Monks say there is going to be a storm," she announced and flopped down heavily.

"At last! Now I have a weather connection to God. Did he tell them we were going to have a storm?" he asked sarcastically.

She smiled and took her top off.

"I don't know what the weather's going to do but I know what I'm going to do," said Sigurd and carried her to his sleeping platform.

The movement of warriors across to the west side of the Find River had only one meaning and Tusk had prepared for it. It wasn't long before news of the army crossing reached him, and he sent a galloper to Loch Morlich to bring horses. Norse patrols were getting smart and changing their routes and strategy. Scouts stayed a safe distance from the main force and didn't stray far enough to kill. News that many Longboats loaded with many warriors had returned to Torridon from the direction of Mahomack had puzzled Tusk, but now he knew what their intentions were, the invasion of the west.

The army had a two day start on Tusk and he wasted no time in assembling thirty warriors. They had enough Norse armour and weapons for each warrior and deception would get them close to their quarry. Innes led the troop through the trails they had cleared towards the moor at Culloden and even Tusk was impressed by the work that had been done. They breathed a sigh of relief when they reached a viewpoint overlooking the Moray Firth and there was no sign of Longboats. They were ahead of the Norse and headed back into the forest to make camp and wait.

Sigurd was in two minds whether to go with the Longboats and Tarbat or with the land army and Torf. He knew either one would look on his presence as being a lack of trust in them, but he had only two choices and not going wasn't one of them. He chose to go with Torf and took him aside to explain why and the reason he searched for was looking him in the face.

"I must go with you because we will need an interpreter. Ro-Sheen will come with us," said Sigurd. Torf had hoped she would.

They set out towards the Find River in one of the Skiffs. Their horses were already across the river and Sigurd marvelled at the speed of the small boat, despite only a breath of wind and even the little wind they had felt hot, coming from the south and half west.

Sigurd had assembled all navigators and commanders before they were dispatched and emphasised this wasn't a race. They had time, plenty of time, and keeping the army at sea and the army on land as close to each other was demanded. The Longboats could cover ten times the distance of marching warriors, but they could also go slow or stop. They must not get too far ahead of the land army. Skiffs were different, they could go quickly and get back quickly. They had a free hand but were forbidden to land anywhere for any reason. They would Scout and come back to report to Tarbat.

Everybody knew exactly what was expected of them and the Skiffs would leave the Find at daybreak the following morning. Longboats would leave Torfness at the same time and the land army would move out as soon as their camp was dismantled.

Sigurd had the map Imogen had prepared. She had traversed this terrain and despite much of her travel being at night, she had a good knowledge of her surroundings. Her map indicated much desert between the Find and the next west river and from what Sigurd could see, her map was correct. The land on the west side of the Find, called Culbin, was even more arid than the east side, with huge sand hills as far as they could see, and the only route west was by the beach. Her map also showed this arid land lessened at the next river. This river was the objective, not just to reach it but to get the army across it and camped on the west bank ready for an advance the following day.

Tusk sent four Scouts east at daybreak. They were to locate the Norse army and return without being seen. Innes pleaded with her father to go and after being hounded for half a night, Tusk relented with a warning not to engage with the Norse under any circumstance and they were to return after noon, no matter if they found the army or not.

It took little time for Torf to get his men moving and six Scouts headed along the beach ahead of his horses that totalled only fifty. Barren and windswept, they soon discovered the riches below the beach as horses' hooves threw up hundreds of cockles which the following warriors scrambled to pick up. The tide was low, and horses spread out to reap as much of this harvest as they could without stopping. The land they traversed was known to the Picts as Culbin. The Culbin sands Ro-Sheen had found out were shifting sands and feared by the Picts, who claimed whole villages were buried under these sands and the people in them.

Before noon, the Longboats were seen offshore and Torf laughed. Now the shoe was on the other foot. There was enough breeze to allow the Skiffs to sail but not the Longboats and all were under oars. Now they would struggle to keep up with the land army. Scouts reported nothing ahead, no sign of humans but as they passed a great sandbank that was isolated from the shore, they had seen hundreds of seals along its length. More riches from this desert.

It was as Imogen had drawn and the River the Picts called Nairn was reached long before dark. The scouts returned and Sigurd thought they had run into a Pict army by the speed they galloped towards him.

"The river is shallow, we can cross easily and it's alive with Salmon, hundreds of them and easy to spear!" yelled a Scout excitedly and Torf sent twenty mounted warriors with them back to the River. By the time the marching army arrived, they should have fresh fish to eat and conserve their provisions. The Scouts had also reported a small settlement with about twenty dwellings, but it looked deserted and was on the west side of the river.

They would deal with that when the main army crossed, and the mounted warriors were told to retreat if they saw any Picts approaching the river. By the time the main army came close to the river, the sky above the entrance was black with seagulls as Salmon were gutted and a great feast served. Two Skiffs were also on the beach and Tarbats's Longboats were keeping pace close to shore. Sigurd's army arrived fresh. They could have covered three times the distance in one day, but strategy demanded they go slowly, slowly enough to allow any Picts time to escape. There was no point in killing them and being killed if they were going to evacuate the land and Sigurd wanted land, not dead Picts.

On arrival, two hundred warriors attacked the dwellings and reported not a living soul was found, not even livestock and that pleased Sigurd. Better the Picts were lumbered with Livestock than his army. They wouldn't be far away and when eventually they found Picts, they would have all the livestock in one place. That was his thinking and great satisfaction was enjoyed when they set up camp and dined on the fruits of the sea.

Innes and her Scouts had gone as far east as Cawdor and were surprised to find the settlement still intact and all the villagers still there. When they were told a Norse army was heading their way, they already knew and would move if it came inland. They informed Innes that the Norse army had camped at Nairn and many boats also lay on the beach at Nairn. As her father, Tusk, had instructed, find their boats and you will find them, then get back. After resting and eating they learned that most of their warriors had perished at Cluny. The few that remained were following the Norse advance and they would come back long before the Norse. Innes advised they should head south towards the Cairngorms and not go west towards Inver.

Tusk digested the information they brought back. They had done well and now he knew he was at least a day ahead of the Norse army, but would they follow the beach all the way around to Ardersier or cut straight across the peninsula? That was his dilemma.

Morning broke to great cheer and warriors laughed as Longboats were pushed afloat and oars deployed. Every Norse warrior wanted to be on the Longboats and those who succeeded mocked those who failed. Now they had to row all day while those they had mocked took a leisurely walk along a pristine beach. Those who believed whistled for wind and those on the shore drowned out their whistling with ridicule.

The Skiffs had sailed and although their progress was slow, it was still faster than if propelled by oars and the six men on each felt truly thankful. They could see the land ahead, turned towards the north and checked the copy of Imogen's map. She had gone overland but had drawn what she saw behind her and it appeared this land was a peninsula. They would go around, following the coast, while Sigurd would go straight overland heading west.

They had agreed on this during the feast of salmon and unless the wind got up, Tarbat had to stay away from the area where he suspected he had met the strong riptide. Under sail and with the tide behind the Longboats was the only way he would enter this unknown area, but the Skiffs could and must. Tarbat's force would wait in the shelter of the east side of the peninsula for however long it took for conditions to become favourable. Sigurd's force would wait at the village the Picts called Ardersier and stay there until the Longboats arrived.

Around noon, the great Drum on the west Sutor sounded and in the stillness of the air, the Drum could be heard far and wide, but not as far as the Skiffs. Those aboard heard nothing.

Sheena stared wide-eyed at old Urquhart as he listened intently.

"Listen carefully to the beat," he urged. "If it stops, the threat is going up the Firth; if it continues it's coming towards the Sutors."

She felt as if the earth stood still; people listened intently as the haunting drumbeat continued then suddenly stopped.

"Whatever it is has gone into the Firth," he told her. "Danger on our south shore. Come, Sheena!" he shouted and she jumped to her feet.

Outside they found a scene of feverish activity as warriors, some mounted double, rode west along the shore of the Cromarty Firth. Adair had brought Sheena's horse and handed her the reins. She mounted and Adair climbed up behind her. Hector had Sine behind him and they hit the beach behind the warriors.

"We go to Balblair, then head south through the forest!" Adair yelled in Sheena's ear.

She didn't need to ask why, the terrain around Balblair was more accessible to horses and she concentrated on catching up with those in front.

"It will take a while to cross over, but we will come out above Chanonry Point," continued Adair.

Sheena now had an idea of where she was heading. She knew of the crossing point close to Ardersier and that little bit of information spurred her on.

The two Skiffs reached the point and turned west. The navigator marked the map and took bearings on the Gap. The tide seemed to be in their favour, and they continued until the tide took the Skiffs and propelled them faster towards what looked like land ahead but according to Imogen's map, was a long spit of land, reaching south from the north shore and they concentrated on keeping the boat going in the right direction.

They passed a short section of coastline that looked no more than a small bay; ahead the land appeared more pronounced. They kept well out of bowshot as they neared the bay that opened up to their south. Imogen had seen smoke rising from here and it could only be a settlement. However, no smoke appeared today, from any direction.

From a vantage point high to the south, Tusk's lookouts spotted the two craft as they neared Ardersier and he came to look. This was expected but not two little boats. Where were the Longboats? Where was Sigurd's army? They couldn't move until they had answers to both.

Halfway across the peninsula, a shiver ran through Ro-sheen and she shook herself thinking it was her, but Sigurd looked at the sky.

"The temperature is dropping. Do you feel it?" he asked.

"I feel it. I thought it was just me," she smiled and shivered again as a cold breeze brushed her body.

She reached into her bundle and brought out a leather top. As she put it on, she stared curiously at the nearby mountains directly ahead. The tops which had stood at different heights suddenly appeared to level.

Sigurd stared also and then let out a roar that made Ro-Sheen's horse rear in fright.

"Storm!" he shouted. "Storm coming, find shelter!"

Torf took up the call along with a thousand others and led the way to the right, heading towards a ridge with trees, lying lower than their current position but still a considerable distance away. On horseback and on foot, the orderly column splintered into a heaving mass of humanity, scrambling madly to reach shelter, all eyes turned to the black sky forming over the mountains, while the sun still shone down on their panic.

Tarbat saw what was coming and immediately turned the Longboats towards the shore and into the on-coming wrath. Oars dug deep and fast. The Longboats approached the shore and before the sun vanished, the first bow beached at speed with the rest close behind. Large stone anchors thudded down and warriors used anything they could dig with to bury them deep into the sand. Others threw ropes from the bows to teams squatting below, holding the ropes tight, while more carried shields and made a windbreak behind them; then they waited.

The two Skiffs were on the west side of the point of land when they saw what was coming and made a desperate attempt to turn back and get the land between them and the oncoming storm. The tide stood against them and they made little headway. If anything, they found themselves drawn closer to the land and in sheer panic, to avoid being set onto a lee shore and totally at the mercy of the elements, they hoisted the sails. These were expert seamen and knew what fate awaited them if they failed to round the point and reach shelter. However, they also knew that the one thing that could save them could also kill them, the wind.

Hail the size of eyeballs preceded the white froth that raced towards the two craft and darkness descended as clouds enveloped the sun. The wind and sea hit them like a battering ram and within two breaths, the sail of one Skiff split before it could be lowered. On the other, they managed to lower the sail, but it blew out of their grip and overboard. Broken waves the height of a man pounded both boats, snapping the oars. One Skiff broached and went broadside on to the onslaught; its sail went under the boat and caught the water, pulling the lee side down while the weather side was pounded with waves that seemed to have no distance between each one. The ferocity of the wind against the tide was fearsome and they prayed for salvation.

Salvation approached in the form of white turmoil, that was the spit of land they were trying to get around and now they would be thankful to crash onto it. Both boats filled with water faster than they could be bailed out and the one with the sail overboard heeled over precariously to port, but the little craft refused to go over until the sail snagged something on the bottom and it went over so quickly the crew were thrown into the air, all of them having gathered on the starboard side. Screams were snatched by the wind and the sea crashed over them.

The crew of the other Skiff cut the sail from the mast and left the halyard attached. In desperation, they cast the sail into the sea from the bow of the boat and tied the rope to the bow. As soon as it took the weight of sail and water, the bow swung into the tempest and the crew hung on as spray lashed their faces like whips. Eyes filled with water and nobody could see, then a tremendous crash announced they had made contact with the beach on Chanonry Point and the boat was doomed. Three jumped from the port side into the tempest and were immediately swallowed by the sail now at the mercy of the sea and heading towards the beach. The three that went over the starboard side were cast onto the beach like driftwood and pummelled into the pebbles.

Inside the Black Isle forest, above Chanonry, the scene was one of fear and destruction as branches snapped and came crashing to the ground hitting horses and warriors alike. The sky suddenly lit up and lightning flashed so close they could hear it crackle, but when the thunder roared it seemed to punch into their bodies. Many rubbed the bull on their backs and prayed for salvation, believing the end of the world had come. Hector grabbed Sheena and Adair and hauled them under a fallen tree. Sine was already there and he raced to grab two more warriors. The whistling of the wind changed to a loud moaning that put the fear of God into all of them.

On the opposite side, Tusk and his band had been caught in the open with nowhere to run and hauled their horses to the ground. They hung on tightly to halters and lay in the thick heather waiting for the onslaught. They didn't have long to wait and as soon as the hail hit, the horses wanted to get up and run but a warrior hanging onto their heads made that impossible. They resigned themselves to their fate, with some soothing words and even more curses.

Sigurd crossed himself and prayed for those at sea and thanked the Lord for keeping him on land. He also promised he would always abide by his weather forecast in future, much to the amusement of Ro-Sheen who revelled in the turmoil.

The wind moaned ever louder through the trees above the army crouching under shields and lying in the thick heather. The ridge had sheltered them and the shields took the impact of the hail but now came the rain in horizontal sheets. The sky looked fearsome as clouds raced past what light penetrated but slowly, the light began to win the battle and the wind started to ease along with the rain.

"It's over!" Sigurd yelled to Torf who sprung to his feet. He issued orders for four warriors to head back to the beach and follow it until they found the Longboats.

"If they were caught in that they'll be halfway back to Torfness," said Sigurd but that wasn't his worst fear; some may have sunk, and the fate of the Skiffs weighed heavily on his mind. "We make camp here until we know what's happened to the Longboats," he ordered Torf.

Torf agreed. It would make no sense to put more distance between them and the Longboats, they had to wait here.

Apart from a few kicks and bites, soaked to the skin and covered in heather seeds, Tusk's troops were unscathed and scrambled to their feet as soon as the wind died.

"What was that father?" asked Innes, wide-eyed.

"I haven't seen the likes of that since I was your age," Tusk replied and stared up at the sky. It was rapidly clearing and he pointed up to the clouds racing across the loom of the sun. "What's up there came down here. That's what that was," he grunted.

"The sky fell down!" Innes gasped and rushed to tell all what had happened.

"We go back to the forest," Tusk grinned and mounted.

Across the water from Tusk on the Black Isle, those who emerged from the forest looked like survivors from a battle, but they were more dishevelled than wounded. Scratched and with pine needles sticking into every crevice, they stared at the devastation before them. Crops were flattened and carts overturned as was everything not secured to the ground. Animals wandered through dykes that had been blown over and many people were heading for the point.

They passed an elderly woman who was waving her arms in despair and they asked her why the people were heading for the point.

"Boats! Two boats, they were in trouble out there. Look at my oats!" she seethed.

Sheena spurred her mount towards the point along with the others. Many warriors were walking, and they passed them, but some riders had already reached their destination and dismounted.

Hector passed Sheena with Sine on the back and yelled to go faster. They galloped towards the warriors who were grouped around something on the beach and curiosity made them dismount quickly. Bodies! They could see three on the beach but the warriors were looking at two on the grass.

"Two are still alive," said Hector after pushing his way through the crowd.

Sheena stood behind the group and they made no attempt to move. Sine yelled at them to move aside and let their Chief through. That got their attention, but they had never seen this new Chief before.

"I am Sheena! What happened here?" she asked and they quickly stood aside.

She looked at the two young survivors, both of them no older than her sister. They were in shock, covered in wet sand that stuck around their eyes and most of their exposed flesh and matted their hair. As she looked, a spasm ripped through one and water streamed from his mouth. The other shook uncontrollably and Sheena turned away. If nobody helped them, they would die. But what was the point of letting them live, just to kill them?

"What shall we do?" asked Sine.

Sheena stared at the broken pieces of boat littering the beach and the bodies lying there. It was a miracle they hadn't been killed. She had heard the Monks speak of such things and was about to say so when she remembered where she was and thought quickly.

"They were not supposed to die. But they still might. Will their God save them, or our God?" she asked. "Take them to shelter and let your God decide if they live or die."

Her reading of the signs was greeted with great approval.

Tarbat's initial fears that the Longboats would be driven off the shore were ill-founded. The wind was so strong it created a tidal surge, pushing water ahead of it and the water left behind was sucked into the void. The Longboats lay high and dry on the beach and bow to the wind, safe from danger. Tarbat knew they had escaped certain disaster having rowed as fast as they could to catch the tide. If they had been caught in the narrows, wind against tide and with little room to manoeuvre would almost certainly have resulted in boats being driven ashore. No anchors could have held against that tempest.

The Skiffs would have seen the storm coming and taken shelter, he felt sure of that. There was nothing they could do now the tide would have turned, and the Longboats had been beached hard. If they floated, they would pull them off the beach, if not they had to wait until the next high tide and so far, the tide seemed reluctant to move in any direction. He threw his hands in the air and ordered his warriors to make camp. Already they were gathering cockles from along the low water line.

The gallopers from Sigurd were elated when the Longboats came into sight and laughed when they saw they were out of the water. They told Tarbat where the army was camped, and that the army would head for the settlement at first light. Tarbat told them he had no idea where the Skiffs were but assured them, they would have taken shelter somewhere.

The village of Avoch mostly housed fishermen who were also farmers and farmers who were also fishermen. Most of the warriors with Sheena came from Avoch and they took the survivors there. They gave them Toddy which made the young men throw up everything in their stomachs, but the Picts persisted and eventually, the Norse started gibbering and taking warmth from the hastily lit fire. They were covered with woollen blankets and the whiskey made them sleep.

Females kept watch over them should they be sick and choke in their sleep, but they didn't and most of the sand on their bodies fell off when it dried. Sheena and her warriors from Cromarty went to the largest of the longhouses and were fed. They also got a first-hand account of the boats trying to ride out the storm and their eventual demise. The conditions described made Sheena shudder. What they had experienced in the forest was trivial in comparison to the hell at sea. They accepted the whiskey gratefully and like the Norse, gave in to the need for sleep.

Through the night, the Longboats floated and were taken a short distance offshore, anchored and left with only a few crew members on each. Others slept peacefully until a hunting horn announced they had to eat.

Sigurd and Torf felt greatly relieved that the Longboats were safe. After eating, they ordered the camp to be dismantled. Warriors were keen to get moving. They were used to moving fast and the novelty of the slow march was wearing off, perhaps because they were going through thick heather and not strolling along a sandy beach.

Ahead lay forest; deer scattered as the army approached. They also spotted some sheep that headed into the trees and Sigurd felt greatly pleased with the look of this land. The forest proved easier to traverse than the thick heather and ferns grew rampant along the forest floor. They proceeded slowly but not by choice and outriders stayed close. By noon it became evident they could march past their target and when they reached a clearing, Sigurd noted high ground to the south. He sent six scouts up there to get directions.

The riders cleared the forest edge and headed uphill to a crest not far away. There they stopped and surveyed the scene below. They could see the Fjord clearly and Sigurd's suspicions were right, they had travelled too far west and needed to head north. They were about to return when they spotted ten Norse riders heading towards them from the east and frowned, wondering what they wanted or indeed where they had come from?

They raised their arms in greeting and the riders returned the gesture. Those leading had Norse shields but three behind rode with their right hand on the reins, in their left, a bow with arrow notched lay alongside their mount. They were on top of the unsuspecting scouting party before three arrows flew at close range and three Scouts fell from their saddles. The others grabbed for their weapons as swords and a battle axe sliced into them. Only then did they see the blue battle paint on the sides of the Norse helmets, their last view of life on this earth.

Sigurd grew impatient waiting in the forest and feared the worst. Torf sent twenty warriors to the crest to look for the Scouts and what they found put the fear of God into all of them. Six headless corpses stripped of weapons and valuables lay on the heather. Their horses were gone and so were their killers. The warriors returned to the army quickly and Sigurd fumed with rage. Picts would pay dearly for this; but the mystery remained, how six Scouts had been killed. According to those who found them they were all in one small area. They had been given orders not to engage; orders to sound a signal horn; orders to flee back to their own force, and they hadn't obeyed any of them. Why?

The army turned north, now on high alert. Torf gave Sigurd a wide berth but Ro-Sheen didn't, she rode alongside him for some time before breaking the silence.

"It's what they want," she said. "They want you to kill everybody. That way they can recruit many warriors to fight against the cruel Sigurd. What you do is the right way, if they resist, they are killed, if they don't, they live and prosper. Our people have no answer to kindness, but they do to cruelty."

By the time they saw the sea ahead, Sigurd's rage had subsided and his mind was back in command. Torf had mentioned Tusk as the source of the killings, but Sigurd dismissed this as unlikely; they were too far away from Tusk's hunting grounds.

Meanwhile, the Longboats reached the point where they turned west, and the tide was with them. On the west Sutor, their progress was watched but no great Drum sounded. It lay on the rocks far below in pieces, the wind had ripped it from its mount and it hurtled over the cliff.

# Chapter 21

The Norse army cleared the forest and Sigurd stared at the fields of crops that spread far and wide. Even from a distance, he could see the wind damage and most appeared flattened. The roofs of many dwellings appeared ahead and surprisingly a single column of smoke drifted skyward. Marching the army through the crops would certainly destroy what wasn't already damaged. He sent outriders to find another way.

In Ardersier, old Hamish and his two brothers stood their ground, watching the army from afar and wondering why they had stopped. They saw the horses swing west and watched as they found the track leading to Inver then they came straight towards them glittering in the sunlight, a sight to behold or fear, but no fear showed on any of the old men's faces as they waited.

Some roofs had been blown off the dwellings and straw lay scattered everywhere but when he saw the three figures standing on the track, Torf called a halt and Sigurd came by his side to find out why.

"Three on the track ahead, it could be a trap," growled Torf.

"Then we will circle the trap," grinned Sigurd.

Five hundred warriors circled the village along the beach and five hundred along the sides of the crops. It didn't take long, and they waited.

"They think this is a trap," smiled Hamish and waved his arm for the horsemen to come forward.

He frowned when he saw the blond female and six horses walk towards them.

"Don't make any sudden moves," he warned. "Bowmen are on the horses."

Ro-Sheen didn't go too close and called to them to come forward.

Hamish strode towards her and the brothers followed.

"That's close enough!" she shouted and they stopped.

"Speak!" she demanded after studying them closely for weapons and seeing none.

"Are you afraid of three unarmed old men?" Hamish challenged and after Ro-Sheen dropped her arm, the Bowmen lowered their arrows but kept them notched.

"Are you alone?" she frowned.

"We're alone and you must be Ro-Sheen. I'm Hamish, Village Chief," he smiled.

The mention of her name took Ro-Sheen by surprise, but she didn't ask how they came to know it.

"Where are all your warriors and your people?"

"In Inver. Do we have to shout all day?" Hamish frowned and Ro-Sheen waved them closer.

"Now I'm going to get a sore neck," he grumbled, looking up at the beauty on the horse.

"You're hard to please, Hamish," she smiled.

"No, that's where your wrong, lassie. I'm easy to please; all they have to do is leave the village the way it is and allow the people to come back."

"The Norse have just had six warriors killed up there on the hill and their heads cut off. Do you know anything about that?" asked Ro-Sheen.

"No, nothing!" Hamish exclaimed.

"Sigurd can kill all of you and kill all of your people in Inver and revenge would be justified. Stay here, I will deliver your request," she said and turned her horse.

The Bowmen didn't move, and she approached Sigurd and Torf alone.

"Three old men; the Village Chief asks that you spare the village and allow the villagers to return. They are all in Inver," smiled Ro-Sheen.

"Walk on," replied Sigurd and pressed his knees against his mount.

He stopped and looked down at the old men. His face looked stern as he spoke but he didn't raise his voice.

"Ask them why I should let his people return and leave his village standing?"

"We hear that people have moved back into Elgin and some even back to Torridon, and a trading post is being built on the banks of Dornoch," replied Hamish and Ro-Sheen translated.

Sigurd was impressed that news of his achievements had spread this far, especially concerning the trading post. He was considering his reply when Hamish cut in, emphatically.

"You tell him this is the trading post, here at Ardersier. This is where trading with the south takes place. If Ardersier is destroyed, trading with the south will stop."

This claim had never entered Sigurd's mind. Why was this a trading post? He could see no reason for this site to be selected by the Picts for trading. Ro-Sheen posed the question.

"You crossed two rivers to get here from Torridon," replied Hamish. "And the traders won't cross them. Everything comes here by boat and they trade here because here the boats can get shelter."

Sigurd nodded but the mention of boats triggered another question.

"Ask him if he has seen any of our boats?"

"Were they little boats?" asked Hamish.

"Yes! Two small boats," confirmed Ro-sheen and Hamish took a deep breath.

"The boats are destroyed, and everybody was drowned," he said quietly.

"What? What do you mean?" she shouted and Sigurd looked at her in alarm.

"The two boats got caught in the storm yesterday. They were on the west side of Chanonry point and couldn't get around to shelter. One capsized and sank; the other was smashed to bits on the beach. Nobody could have survived."

She translated and Sigurd dismounted without saying a word. He turned his back on all of them and walked to the beach. Across the water, he could see the point sticking out from the north shore and his heart ached; twelve dead and two boats lost, as well as six dead scouts, killed today. He crossed himself and prayed for the dead and returned to his horse.

"We will camp here, and he will go to his people and tell them to return," he said and led his horse towards the beach.

"You must go to Inver and tell your people to come back. Bring everything with them; no harm will come to them but if they don't return, the village will be destroyed. Can you ride?" she asked.

"We're not that old," grinned Hamish.

Ro-Sheen spoke to a Bowman who dismounted, took his bundle off the horse, and handed his reins to Hamish.

"Don't stand there, give me a leg-up!" he barked to his brothers. "I'll be back before noon tomorrow," he declared and cantered west.

Word that a great army was camped across the water at Ardersier reached the settlement at Avoch and a short time later, reports that a great fleet of Longboats had also arrived at Ardersier, prompted Sheena to join the many warriors who left on foot to get closer and look. She was warned not to go by horse. Nobody was mounted and they all ran, half-crouched along the flatlands, stopping occasionally to peer over hedges and dykes that hid them from view.

Sine and Adair stayed with the two Norse survivors while several elderly women nursed their wounds, mainly caused by the pummelling onto the beach. Their knees and hands had taken most of the damage, but one had a big swelling on his head and his ear ached. The cause was a small pebble and once removed, he stopped whimpering, but they were far from well and wouldn't eat.

They were stripped and their bodies washed to remove the fine sand that was beneath their clothes, which were also rinsed out several times and dried. Sine and Adair dressed them again while they slept and giggled when the boys opened their eyes and stared at the bare-breasted females with tattoos all over their bodies. They quickly closed their eyes again not knowing what world they were in.

Many fires were lit along the south shore of the Firth and Sheena stayed beside Hector. She stared at her hated enemy for a long time and her heart sank.

"Thousands of them," Hector repeated, finding conversation with a Queen difficult. Then remembering what tragedy had befallen the

King, he fell silent.

"If they come here, we will be defeated easily," she sighed and took a deep breath. "I came here to kill Norse and I end up saving two. It's strange. World, Hector."

"You said yesterday that our God might save them?"

"I think our God is saving them!"

"We can keep them as hostages," he said, "or we can stake them and leave them at the point, so the Norse will think twice before setting foot here. Or we could lure their Longboat to the shore to rescue them and attack it. We could do many things, but it wouldn't stop that army. No matter what we do with them, the Norse will take revenge."

"What's that got to do with Gods?"

"If they get better and we let them go back to the Norse, they will tell their story and soon it will be forgotten. Do you agree?"

Sheena nodded.

"If they have the God that saved them on their backs, it would forever remind them and the Norse who saved them!"

"Come!" she urged and headed back towards Avoch at the run.

As they entered the dwelling, the old women looked at them curiously because they were smiling.

"Where is the tattooist?" whispered Sheena, with her finger to her lips.

They took her to the door and pointed to a dwelling, with a carving of the great bull outside. Sheena ran there with Hector. An old man lay on a sleeping platform, snoring and he was naked.

"Get him!" smiled Sheena grinned and headed back to the dwelling where the Norse were. "Get lamps, the Tattooist is coming! Where are Adair and Sine?"

"Gone to look at the Norse army," replied one of the women.

"We can hold them down," Sheena whispered, and the women nodded, keen to see what was to be put on the backs of their charges.

The Tattooist arrived and flicked his wrist. They turned one over on his face.

"They won't wake up, they're full of Toddy," the old woman whispered, and he grinned.

It didn't take him long to put the bull on the Norse's back. His years of experience showed and he worked with great precision. The youth moved a little but stayed asleep and the watchers marvelled as their God appeared. The second was done after the Tattooist had a drink of whiskey himself. The second Norse also slept soundly, opening his eyes only momentarily and shutting them again. The women washed the tattoos with warm water and left the victims in peace. They would feel the pain when they awoke and sobered up.

Darkness was descending before the warriors returned to the village and word of what Sheena had ordered was greeted with great cheer. When she saw a great swathe of fires across the water, she ordered her fires to be lit and feasting to commence.

"If we hide, they'll think we're afraid of them. Let them see we're not afraid," she said.

They lit fires beyond Avoch and all along the north shore.

Norse commanders gathered in Sigurd's tent. They had the loss of the two Skiffs and the killing of six Scouts to discuss, along with the surprising revelation that this place was a trading post.

"We get the people back and leave a force here, after we take this settlement at Inver," said Sigurd. "Then we will deal with the savages on that Island. Ro-Sheen says they are true Picts and will fight to the death and if they get you alive, they will stake you and cut your head off before the stake comes out your mouth. They sound like people we can do battle with!"

The listeners laughed with Sigurd, all but the Navigator of Tarbat's Longboat; his son had died on one of the Skiffs. For some, it was going to be a long night.

Sheena awoke between Sine and Adair and looked around. Her Companions also looked around and a voice made them jump.

"You have to wake up, you're wanted in the forest!" said a warrior and closed the door before they could ask why.

They got dressed and drank water before coming out into the sunshine. Their horses were already saddled, and the warrior handed Sheena the reins.

"Keep clear of the fields and go into the trees," he grinned and ignored their questions.

Adair jumped on the back of Sine's Horse and Sheena rode alone. She followed the two who seemed to know where they were going, and they didn't hold back; they galloped.

Sine entered the trees first and Sheena followed. Now on a steep hillside, they walked the horses and Sine stopped. Sheena looked ahead of her and stared in amazement. A line of warriors stood a bow shot into the trees and spread as far as the eye could see. Iain came forward painted for battle.

"Urquhart thought you might need help," he smiled and stretched his arms in both directions.

Sheena stared, not at him but at what was behind him.

"You sleep all day, sister?" came a familiar voice.

Sheena let out a scream and raced past the grinning Iain then screamed again when she saw who was standing with Ross. She grabbed Sine and swung her around, then dropped her and threw her arms around Ross and finally Enya before grabbing Sine to her breast and yelling,

"How, how, how did you get here? How did you get here?"

"I think she's glad to see us," said Ross to the two bare-breasted women who had arrived with Sheena and when Sheena stopped crushing Sine, her namesake took over.

"Do you remember me? I'm the other Sine!" she said and they laughed.

"My God, Ross, how many warriors are here?" gasped Sheena.

"Urquhart has a thousand and Urquhart has another thousand," he grinned.

Sheena jumped for joy and grabbed Ross.

"Tell me, tell me, what happened?" she pleaded.

"The great Drum was destroyed by the wind," he said, "and they saw the Longboats before they turned back. Nigg sent word to your father and he decided the Norse wouldn't know if a thousand warriors who were being stood down were taken here. The Norse think this is an Island. When they see our horses, they'll think the horses were here all the time. We just show our strength along with the warriors of the Black Isle, then return to Mahomack. They will be none the wiser we ever left!"

"So, we fool them with the same horses, twice. Ah, I'm so happy!" Sheena stomped her foot and spun around. "Iain! Iain!" she called and ran back down the hill to him. "What are we going to do?"

He stopped her headlong dash with both hands on her shoulders and laughed aloud.

"You tell me, you're the Chief!"

"Can they see us from the other side, or do we have to get closer?" she asked.

"We can only go to the edge of the Forest. If we go down, they won't be able to see us. We are lined and your father's force is lined behind us; you have to do something to make them look this way."

"It must be on the point. That's the closest to them and they can't see the flat land. Let me paint for battle and take the horses we have in Avoch to the point. Will that get their attention?"

"It should," replied Iain, "and we can see you from here. Do that and I'll let Ross know when to come out into the open."

Sheena grabbed her reins and shouted for Sine and Adair to come quickly. They galloped back to Avoch and yelled for all the warriors and anybody else who could sit on a horse to paint for battle and to hurry. There were great yelps of glee and people ran in all directions. The column that assembled was a mix of genders and ages from the old to the young, but they all had a mount and were all keen to do what Sheena asked.

They galloped towards the point, making sure they kept off the crops and scattered sheep with their haste. Only when she saw the bodies still on the beach did Sheena remember about the two Norse who were sick, but they and the bodies could wait. She had never been all the way to the point before and feared there wasn't one, as the land across the Firth got closer and closer. Then she saw the water ahead and slowed the horses.

The Norse had already spotted them and Sigurd alerted. Together with Torf, they rode east towards the closest place to this point that had caused such loss of boats and men.

"Walk the horses around in a circle!" directed Sheena and they laughed. "God knows what we look like from over there, but we even look like fools from here!" Sheena laughed and Adair raised her sword above her head and let out a blood-curdling war cry. That changed things and they all yelled and waved their weapons wildly.

Sigurd grinned when he saw the antics of the fools.

"They scare me to death, Torf, what about you?" he smiled and they stopped to watch.

They were joined by many warriors from the Longboats who were camped close by and Tarbat appeared waving his sword and screaming at the top of his voice,

"Show them you can see their great army!"

And a roar of laughter met that statement. Swords were drawn and waved.

Meanwhile, in the forest, Iain shouted to his right and left.

"Now! Walk ahead now," and the line moved forward.

"When they stop waving their weapons, head back to the village," ordered Sheena and Sine echoed her instructions.

The distance to the forest was great but so too was the line of blue warriors that came out into the sunshine. Sigurd caught the movement out of the corner of his eye.

"Torf, look at the forest," he said quietly and stared as the sunlight glittered off the weapons of the Picts who had deliberately positioned themselves in the sun's glare.

More eyes caught the spectacle and drew attention to it. The sword waving stopped, and Sheena retreated with her warriors. All eyes were focused on the forest.

"How many?" asked Sigurd.

"A thousand or near enough," replied Torf then gasped as another line of warriors and horses lined up behind the first, doubling the reflected sunlight.

Sigurd stared in silence. He knew this show was being put on for him and he hastily dissected the lines.

"Two thousand and at least three hundred horses. That's an army as big as ours," he declared; nobody argued.

As they stared, the top line of warriors and horses melted back into the forest, closely followed by the lower line and then there was nothing but the performers moving along the point and then they stopped. Sigurd watched curiously as some went onto the beach and began hauling things onto the firm ground.

Sheena had the three bodies laid out and their faces covered with skins and they put rounded stones on the skins to keep the birds from pecking out the eyes of the dead Norse. She gave the Norse a smile and mounted. She didn't head for Avoch and Sine followed her as they rode for the forest at the gallop.

Ross, Enya and Sine had stayed behind with ten warriors. The horse army headed back towards Mahomack at the gallop, while warriors on foot headed for Balblair. They would cross to Invergordon by boat as they had done to get onto the Black Isle. They were double and triple mounted on Black Isle horses.

"What did it look like from the point?" Iain was desperate to know.

"It looked like the edge of the forest was alive with sparks. All the weapons were reflecting the sun. You didn't need us. They would have seen you from the moon!" Sheena beamed and cradled her sister in front of her.

"What were you doing on the beach?" asked Ross.

"Three Norse bodies, we pulled them onto the grass and covered their eyes to stop the birds, but since the storm, I haven't seen any birds," Sheena answered.

"You killed three Norse?" Iain exclaimed.

"No! Two of their little boats were wrecked in the storm, and they were dead when we found them, but two are still alive."

"Two Norse prisoners," Iain grinned.

"Don't get any ideas with stakes," Adair shouted to Iain.

"What are you going to do with them?" asked Enya.

"If you stay here with me, you'll find out," said Sheena.

"I'll stay," came a voice from her neck and she squeezed Sine.

Enya looked at Ross and he nodded.

"If you get back to Nigg in three days, you can stay," he grinned.

"What? You want me to swim a horse across to Nigg?"

"You won't have a horse. I'll take it and leave it at Nigg," he chuckled.

Enya retrieved her bundle and shield from the horse and looked at her two spears stuck into the ground.

"You might need them," said Ross, seeing her indecision.

"I thought I was in another world, but you are all so close. Come back and tell our father he missed a great battle of wits. Come, you! Get on your horse before I keep you," Sheena urged and pushed Sine towards her mount.

Iain went alongside Ross and locked arms.

"We won't be far away," he said. "We'll stay in the forest until we see what the Norse do."

"We won't be far away either," said Ross. "If they cross the Inver, we might be side by side soon enough."

"The Caladonii will join us if the Norse cross the Inver."

This was news to Ross and he frowned.

"I thought they would just retreat to the west?"

"They might," said Iain. "But not before they front the Norse like we just did and with our forces supporting them, they might even stand!" he laughed.

Sheena and Sine said their tearful farewells and those watching were touched by how close the two sisters were, but glad to be galloping back to Avoch.

"Watch where you stick your spears!" Sheena shouted to her passenger.

# Chapter 22

Sigurd and Torf returned to the village and Ro-Sheen met them with a questioning look.

"You should have come to look; you were too far away here," said Sigurd.

"I saw them on the point and I'm close enough to that Island," she replied.

"Ro-Sheen doesn't like Black Islanders because they put Smertae on stakes and cut their heads off. Isn't that right?" Sigurd teased her, but she wasn't amused.

"You don't believe they stake people. You'd better hope you are never a prisoner over there," she scorned.

The jesting over, Sigurd had seen an opportunity. There were more people on that Island than he thought, and people meant trade. Mid-morning a galloper came from the west to inform the commanders of many people heading their way, some on horses and others on foot.

"Hamish!" said Ro-Sheen and headed for her horse.

She rode west with the warrior and spotted the line of people and carts approaching along the track. The guards were ready to intercept and Ro-Sheen knew she had to act quickly. She told her companion to wait and headed towards the approaching column.

She went just close enough to identify the travellers and she could see the white hair of Hamish in the lead. She galloped back and spoke to the massed guards.

"Stand aside and let them pass. Give them space. The village people are coming back. That's Sigurd's orders!" she shouted for all to hear and a murmur ran through the warriors.

Her shouting attracted the attention of Hamish's two brothers, and they came to her.

"Your brother brings your people back," she said and they both headed west along the track on foot.

"It's the Village Chief and by the look of things, he has the entire village with him," she smiled and Sigurd smiled with her.

"I expected conditions," said Sigurd and Torf just grunted.

"We had better go and greet this Village Chief and look our best," Sigurd grinned, and Torf flinched; he hated getting dressed up for anything.

"Would it be better if I go and greet them first, then you can speak to the Chief in private?" suggested Ro-Sheen and Torf immediately agreed.

"Tell the villagers they are under our protection," ordered Sigurd, "and tell them to go to their dwellings and continue with their lives, but all arms are to be left inside their dwellings. Then bring this Chief to me."

Ro-Sheen galloped west and Hamish saw her coming. She was alone and her long blond hair was blowing in the wind when she circled her mount and came alongside his.

"You did well, Hamish," she said by way of a greeting.

"Aye! We'll find that out soon enough."

"Don't worry," she stressed. "You and the villagers are under Sigurd's protection. No harm will come to them. Ride back and tell them they must go to their dwellings and get on with their lives. The only condition Sigurd demands is that all weapons must remain inside their dwellings."

Hamish gave her a look then turned his mount.

He came back before they reached the guards who were well back from the track and she could see he was smiling.

"The women say that's agreeable and if Norse try and get into their dwellings, they can kill them," he laughed.

"I don't think that was what Sigurd had in mind, but stick to it as a term," Ro-Sheen smiled.

The village was empty of Norse, not even one warrior remained near the dwellings and villagers scrambled to their homes, taking what livestock, hens and ducks they had into the dwellings with them. The two brothers came and stood in front of the horses and Hamish passed on the Norse conditions. They grunted their consent and Sheena told

Hamish to follow her to Sigurd's tent.

Across the water, Sheena was pleased to be told the Norse youths had taken soup and were trying to stand up. They laughed but Enya looked at them quizzically.

"What's so funny about trying to stand up?" she asked.

"Not on their feet," explained Sheena. "But when they get the urge to breed, they're fit enough to send back."

Adair giggled.

"That's a new way to judge people's health," chuckled Enya and poked Sheena.

"We can't speak their language so we must read their body language," shrugged Sheena. "We must get them, and the bodies back soon or we will have to bury them here. I think tomorrow morning we can take them and the bodies to the point and light a fire. We'll leave them and let them signal their own kind."

"If they manage to 'stand up', we could do that later today," suggested Enya, grinning wickedly at Sheena.

She met her eyes and read the challenge.

"I'm sure we can find some local clothes to wear, for a short time!"

Adair got up from the fire where they were roasting fish and ran to the dwelling where the youths were.

"They're asleep," she reported back. "But when they awaken, the Mother will come and get you in my dwelling," she chuckled.

"After we eat, we can get some warriors and move the bodies to the point. I'm sure they will stand up this day," Sheena grinned and looked at the beauty of Enya.

They used two poles tied to each side of a horse and trailing on the ground to move the bodies. They were stiff and two were fat. It took a long time to move the three of them to the point and all three were laid out with their faces covered as before. That chore out of the way, they returned to Adair's dwelling and then the fun began.

"If Ross could see us, he would kill us," laughed Sheena, standing bare-breasted with just a loincloth and Sine put her arm against Sheena's breast, comparing the colour.

"Are you both sick? White like snow!" Sine fretted.

They both had to agree and looked at the bronzed skin of their companions with envy.

"Mother comes!" hissed Adair and the old woman entered with two bowls of soup. She stared at the white breasts of the maids and laughed.

"I have to watch mine don't drop into the soup. You would have to bend over to get yours anywhere near it," she chirped and handed them a bowl each.

At times, the two youths weren't sure if they were dead or alive. They had pains in their legs, arms, hands and back but the soup they had eaten had stayed down and they hungered for more. When the two figures arrived with bowls, they looked in the gloom and thought the women who fed them before had come back. Enya sat on the sleeping platform of one and Sheena sat on the other and the patients propped themselves up on one elbow as the wooden spoons found their mouths.

Slowly the image of who was feeding them came into focus. Their long hair hung down across the youth's thighs. Now they knew they were dead and getting fed by an angel but when Sheena pulled her hair back and revealed her nakedness, something stirred within that wasn't soup.

"I'm first!" announced Sheena, triumphantly.

"No, you're not! You just said it first," replied Enya.

"After they've eaten, we can tempt them to their feet," whispered Sheena and spooned in another mouthful.

Sheena put the empty bowl under the sleeping platform and stood up. The youth stared at her and made to grab her hand, but she stepped back and waved with her wrist for him to follow. He growled and whimpered a few times but managed to swing his legs over the end of the platform and stared at her with pleading eyes.

"Now I'm first; my one is up," Sheena scoffed.

"So is mine, well almost," said Enya and Sheena looked in her direction.

Her youth had indeed 'stood up' and was finding it hard to sit up.

But at last, his legs came over the platform and it was time for their tormentors to leave.

"Go, Mother!" Sheena shouted on entering Adair's dwelling and Mother rose stiffly.

"Are they up?" she asked and judging by the giggles, she didn't need to ask twice.

"I'll go and refresh my memory," Mother grinned and left them.

Dressed in their tops and having spent time with their eager audience explaining every detail of the resurrection, Sheena went to the warriors who were by the boats and gave them orders to take firewood to the point and prepare a fire, a big one.

"You two can take care of the youths," she directed. "We're going to stay out of sight. You might need some help to get them to the point, so get some warriors to help you. it doesn't matter if their legs work, put them on horses and sit them on the ground when you get there. Once the fire is lit, you know how to signal across to Ardersier, we don't. Make sure no warriors are on the point, just you two and the Norse. Stay on your horses and when you see a boat coming, retreat out of bowshot then watch what happens."

They repeated what she had said and rushed off to get warriors.

Sigurd had finished with Hamish and was having a discussion with his commanders regarding their next move. Hamish had revealed the savages on the Island always traded with this village and brought skins, wool and fish that was smoked but he never went onto the Island. Goods were traded from the boat to the beach for no other reason than that was how it had always been done. The mass of seals around the point was highlighted by Tarbat who claimed to have seen hundreds when they entered the narrows, as well as small whales. Trading with the south was also something to be considered carefully.

Inver remained highest on Sigurd's priorities and the reason they were here. He had to secure the western flank of his lands. He was reluctant to send the Longboats ahead, without knowing what awaited them. The army could march to Inver then the Longboats would come. He didn't want to lose more men or more boats if it could be avoided. Also, following the success of the Village Chief to bring his people back, Ro-Sheen suggested sending messengers to Inver to tell the population that if they resisted, they would be killed; if they didn't, they would live.

A rider arrived and entered the tent to report something was happening on the point across the water. It was a good reason to disperse and they all went to the beach. Hamish was also informed that a fire had been lit on the point and he hurried to the beach with his brothers.

A warrior found Ro-Sheen with some children feeding hens and sent her to the beach. The children followed her.

"What is he saying?" asked Sigurd and pointed at Hamish.

"He says they are signalling but we need to get closer to see what they want," she interpreted.

They rode east past the Longboats and Hamish commented on the size of the fire. He had never seen a signal fire that size. Straight across from the fire, they could clearly see two riders on horses and somebody standing alone on the shore.

Adair and Sine turned their horses towards the onlookers and reached out to grasp each other's hand. They stood with their hands held and Hamish read the signal.

"They want us to send a boat across," he told Ro-Sheen and she passed the message to Sigurd.

This could be a trick; he could see no reason why they would want a boat after displaying their intentions to resist with their army? It didn't make sense.

"I'll give them a boat all right," grunted Tarbat, "a boatload of Bowmen."

"Do it!" snapped Sigurd. "They challenge us but don't go on the beach. Take shield maidens with you."

Tarbat roared his orders to the watching warriors and a great cheer went up. They scattered to get weapons and headed for the nearest Longboat, making no secret of the boat being filled with Bowmen. But the two warriors across the water stayed where they were and still held hands.

The Longboat was manned and many warriors shoved it out into the current. Oars dug deep and it sped towards the far shore. The two mounted warriors turned and walked their horses away and Sigurd cursed.

"Cowards, they run!" he spat and stared when the horses stopped a short distance away and the riders turned to face the approaching boat, but he frowned when he saw the figure on the beach waving arms frantically.

Tarbat frowned also and stared at the lone figure then made out another sitting beside him but his attention was still on the horses. Fearing trickery of some kind, he ordered arrows notched. The yelling from the shore increased and many frowned as it sounded Norse.

"He's calling for help," said a Shield Maiden.

"It's one of our warriors!" said another and Tarbat screamed for silence.

"My God," he said and crossed himself. This required caution as bait came in many forms, and this could be one.

The figure on the beach yelled frantically and the one beside him struggled to stand. He helped him to his feet and together they yelled that it was safe to pick them up and their dead. Not convinced, Tarbat guided the Longboat to the east of the point where sand could be seen and almost in line with the horses. He scanned the terrain for any movement and could see nothing. Suddenly the two riders waved in the air as if waving good-bye and walked their horses inland.

Now they approached with every bow drawn back and Sigurd screamed as the Longboat hit the beach. He cursed Tarbat for disobeying his orders and threatened if one man died, he would have Tarbat executed.

They stared as warriors poured overboard from the Longboat and headed onto the Point. They passed the fire and headed to the closest part of the beach and the observers heard a distant cheer go up from the Bowmen as they carried something, then many things, back to the Longboat.

Tarbat was on the bow screaming when the boat returned, and warriors rushed to meet it.

"What's happening, what is it?" Hamish asked Ro-Sheen.

"They bring back two we thought were dead, and three that are dead," replied Ro-Sheen quietly.

"From the boats that were wrecked?" Hamish queried in hushed tones.

"Yes!"

"That's a miracle, nobody should have survived. It's a miracle," said Hamish and crossed himself.

"Do you have anywhere we can take the two that've survived? They say they're injured," she asked.

"Take them to my dwelling. Don't leave them on the beach," he insisted.

His offer was conveyed to Sigurd who agreed it would be wise.

Ro-Sheen made a move to go and look, but Sigurd put his hand on her shoulder.

"Wait, stay where you are," he said. "They come to me."

# Chapter 23

Inver was in turmoil and couldn't believe the population of Ardersier had returned to their village, but Hamish had convinced them that it would be impossible to resist the Norse army. The main settlement stood on the south side of the river. They had no defence that would slow the Norse, let alone hold them. Hamish had argued that even if they held the Norse, no army could come to their aid. The only one was from the north and on the wrong side of the river. To hold Inver was impossible.

The Caledonii were caught between two Norse forces. Their lands ran all the way to the west coast and inner Islands. They had been doing battle with Norse raiders from the western isles for many years. They feared taking their forces from the west. That would leave them exposed and it might be the intention of the Norse to strike the west while another army was on the east. Their dilemma, stark as it was, demanded action of some kind but not total commitment.

Led by a chief named Stuart, six hundred Caladonii warriors had massed at Clachnaharry on the north bank of the River Inver. Gallopers had been sent to Urquhart on the Black Isle and he had sent messengers to Urquhart in Tain. Word that Tain had an agreement with the Norse was met with disbelief, but the Black Isle had no such agreement and would support the Caledonii, but only if the Norse attempted to cross the river.

The other alternative the Caledonii had was to retreat west and draw the Norse deep into their territory along the Great Glen. Then, they would have an advantage in the forest and mountains. But to try and hold the settlement of Inver against such an army that had the ability to sail around any force and get behind it, would be madness. Their lack of knowledge regarding the lie of the land might make the Norse think twice about sending their army into the unknown, and how much land the invaders could safely hold would also play a major role in what they decided when they arrived at the river.

The river Inver was wide, deep, and fast flowing. Fed from the great Loch to the west, it split the land from north to south for more than two days' ride to get around the Loch. Crossing places between the river mouth and the Loch were few in times of drought and non-existent in normal times. Crossings were made by boat between the settlement on the south bank and the opposite bank called Thornbush, so named after the swathes of gorse that grew there. Clachnaharry lay beyond the Gorse and close to where the great forest reached the Firth of Beauly. In the forest and out of sight, Stuart camped with his warriors and awaited developments.

Across the water from Stuart's position lay Kessock on the Black Isle. Eyes on the high ground there could look straight up the River Inver and any attempt to cross it by the Norse would be seen by them even before Stuart's spies could reach Stuart.

Iain had orders from old Urquhart to shadow the Norse army when they moved west and block any moves they made to head north. The Black Isle warriors had no choice; if the Norse headed up the Beauly Firth, they would know this wasn't an Island and the land bridge was vast. Until the Norse managed to go all the way into the two Firths, the Cromarty Firth and the Beauly Firth, they wouldn't know that the waters of the two Firths didn't meet and discover the land between them was the land bridge to the Black Isle. That knowledge could lead to disaster. The Norse had to be stopped at Clachnaharry and there would be time to get the three Pict armies massed to meet them. They had no choice, they could no more cross the river than the Norse.

Inver would be taken; that couldn't be avoided but would the Norse stop at Inver? Those who knew military matters could find no reason why Sigurd would risk crossing the river. That was when his forces were vulnerable. Marching west along the south side of the river and the Loch, then east on the north side would take six days to cover a distance of two bow shots that was the width of the river. If he didn't cross, he wouldn't cross that was their verdict.

The happening on the point had taken everybody by surprise. Tarbat's navigator hadn't stopped thanking God for hours when his son Toke was identified as one of the survivors and Birger, his fellow survivor hadn't stopped speaking about naked angels, bulls and naked warrior women until he fell asleep. Both had been given a bowl of Toddy before they were taken to the point.

Sigurd came after getting de-briefed by Tarbat and the story about the nude warriors was confirmed by Tarbat, who had been close enough to see they had nothing on except tattoos.

"Now we go and look," Sigurd grinned.

Hamish welcomed Sigurd and Ro-Sheen to his dwelling, and they looked at the two sleeping survivors by lamplight.

"They have to be cleaned," said Sigurd, angry, that they hadn't already been cleaned.

Ro-Sheen laughed and translated to Hamish who also laughed.

"What they have on them is a healing compound, not dirt. It's a mixture of Bees Wax and fresh butter. They melt the beeswax and add a little butter then mix the two. It forms paste that they can spread over the wounds, but first, the wounds are cleaned with whiskey. Believe me, Sigurd, your warriors have been given the best treatment anybody could wish for. Their wounds will heal."

He felt the compound on Birger's knees and frowned.

"If their legs drop off, so will yours. When they can speak send them to me," Sigurd grinned, and Hamish didn't know if it was a jest or not. Neither did Ro-Sheen.

Bowmen had already killed four seals along the beach and they were brought back to be skinned and butchered. The abundance of fresh meat triggered a great feast on the beach. After eating, commanders gathered and plotted their next move. Sigurd was adamant that if the Picts used this village to trade with the south, they must have had good reason. It was so close to Inver which by all accounts was a much bigger settlement. However, if trading was done here, Inver lost its significance. There was only one way to find out.

Meanwhile, at Tusk's Stockade, Innes pleaded with him to let her take warriors north again. They had only killed six and she wanted to kill more, but Tusk held his ground and refused. His deception had worked well, and no Norse had escaped to warn others that their Scouts had been attacked by Picts, dressed as Norse. Now Sigurd's army would be on high alert and it was unlikely that scouting parties of just six, would stray far from the main army again. Innes wasn't convinced.

"If his army crosses to the north side of the river," he raged at her, "he'll be sending messengers back to Torridon, and messengers will be sent back to him. We can kill them, but for now young Innes, you wait like the rest of us!"

"Wait, wait, wait," she muttered.

"You can wait here in comfort or wait in the forest with our spies and get bitten by midges, soaked and have nothing cooked to eat. Please yourself," he said. "Don't be impatient! When we get the word, they're at Inver, we'll go back and read it as we find it. Fresh, and ready to do battle. Not spent by days of surviving in the forest. The spies will be relieved and come back here. If you want to join them, go ahead," he challenged and she stomped out without answering.

Tusk grinned; she was on fire this one. But she would learn - if she lived long enough, he thought.

Sigurd knew when something wasn't right, and the return of the villagers bothered him. He didn't know why. They had done what he wanted and returned but it was too easy. They all came back according to their Chief and none wanted to stay in Inver. Why? That was bothering Sigurd. Apart from the obvious reason, he suspected there had to be another.

Fifty scouts would now travel together and another fifty would shadow them. He sent the first west with instructions to get to the high ground and see what lay ahead then come back and report.

Tusk's spies watched from the fringe of Culloden Moor as the first fifty headed west and they were on the verge of getting mounted to follow when the second fifty made them rush back into the forest for cover.

Ahead of the first scouts, the terrain cleared and they marvelled at the beauty of it. The Fjord passed a narrow place and turned right around the west side of the Black Island. But straight across from the narrow place, fingers of land jutted out into the Fjord and they could see water between the fingers, some stretching inland. They sketched what they saw with charcoal and headed back to Ardersier.

Sigurd was surprised they had returned so soon. This Inver was closer than any of them thought and they studied the sketch carefully.

"Bring their chief here," Sigurd ordered Ro-Sheen.

She went to get Hamish and smiled at the two survivors who looked a lot better than the last time she had seen them. They thought the same about her. They knew who she was but had never seen her up close and she rivalled their dreams.

Hamish came after cleaning his hands on grass.

"I hate cleaning birds; I'd rather gut a horse than a hen. What does he want me for?" Hamish growled as he followed her.

"Tell him to correct this!" Sigurd instructed and handed Hamish the charcoal.

Ro-Sheen explained Sigurd's request and Hamish stared at the sketch.

"Inver," was all he said and drew the river going inland. He elongated the fingers of land jutting out into the Moray Firth and stood back.

"We can cross here?" Sigurd asked and pointed to the mouth of the river.

Hamish shook his head vigorously then chuckled.

"That's Thornbush, nobody can even walk through there, but I wouldn't cross anywhere if I was him."

Ro-Sheen didn't translate, just asked why.

"Use your head woman. Do you think the Caledonii would defend their land with a river at their back?" Hamish replied?

Now she translated and Sigurd nodded.

"He will tell lies but ask him how many warriors defend the north bank of the river?" Sigurd asked.

Hamish shrugged. "I don't know what's on the north side, all I know is Stuart has the Caledonii Army from the west, and they added six hundred along the Great Glen," he said sincerely then added urgently. "Whatever happens over there has nothing to do with us. We've done as he asked and the villagers are all here. None of our people is over there!"

Sigurd stared at Hamish when Ro-Sheen translated and then stared at the sketch. Hamish was ignored as the commanders studied the sketch with strategy in mind. The old man was right, no army would hold such a position with their back against a river they couldn't cross.

"If you don't need him, he would like to return to his dwelling," Ro-Sheen cut into their thoughts and Sigurd waved his hand in dismissal.

#

Hamish gave a sigh of relief when he left. He had passed the message Stuart had given him and they shouldn't suspect anything. He went back to his hen with a sense of achievement. How he was going to get the message to the Norse without raising suspicion had alarmed Hamish, but Stuart assured him an opportunity would arise. If not, as a last resort, he was to warn the Smertae woman that an army waited on the north bank.

Ro-Sheen noticed something and went to look. She instructed a warrior to cut part of the bush and she took it back to Sigurd.

"That is what we call Thornbush," she explained, and he looked at the spike half the length of his finger and grinned.

"We call it Gulltorn. Now I understand. It's good to hear it's on the north side, not the south. Tomorrow you will go with Torf and a hundred warriors to this settlement. Take a white flag with you and tell their leaders I want them to come here to discuss terms. If they refuse, the settlement will be destroyed and everybody in it," he said and Ro-Sheen gave him a questioning look.

"I'll decide what I'm going to do when I can see this Thornbush for myself," he grinned.

Sigurd returned his attention to the maps and placed the sketch beside the map between Torfness and Ardersier. This location at Inver looked like a meeting place, a crossroads made of water. Any force holding this position could control movement to the north and south. His concern was that an army coming from the west could attack his forces on the flank. From Inver, he could control three directions. He stabbed his finger at the sketch, his mind made up.

"We hold this! If we have to do battle so be it. But they will come to us," Sigurd declared and the commanders uttered their approval.

Now the tables were turned. If the Caledonii wanted to do battle they could cross the river and get slaughtered instead of the Norse. It was the thinking Stuart had hoped for but getting his message to the Norse presented a big problem. When Hamish arrived, Stuart briefed him and encouraged the people to return before he returned to the north bank.

Across on the Black Isle, Sheena and her three companions were with Iain and the army in the forest. Iain had watched every move the Norse made and he had seen the two troops heading west onto the high ground and concluded they were scouting.

"Why don't they move?" asked Sheena.

"They will when they're ready," replied Iain. "They sent scouts west, now they look at the information the scouts collected. Then I expect decisions to be made. Stuart has the Caledonii army at Clachnaharry. Our warriors at Kessock report the population of Dingwall, Muir of Ord and Beauly are on the move," he grinned.

"They run, for safety I don't blame them," she said.

"They run to join Stuart's warriors, not safety!"

"What?" exclaimed Sheena in disbelief.

"Pitchforks, scythes, spears and anything they can lay their hands on, and they'll outnumber Stuart's force. When the Norse see the force on the north side, they might think twice about crossing the river but if they do, we'll join Stuart. Ross will bring back the Decantae. Then we'll outnumber the Norse two to one. I hope they cross; we have a chance to destroy Sigurd."

"He has thousands of warriors at Torridon, this is only part of his army," she warned.

"I know, but he doesn't have another Sigurd in Torridon. We kill this one, the Norse will be in turmoil, the same as we are. Then the south might rally."

"I want to go to Kessock, to look," Sheena announced with an edge of excitement in her voice.

Iain called to some warriors close by and they mounted.

"Follow them, it's not far but it's not easy," Iain grinned as the four females mounted.

They cursed many times before the world emerged from the trees and suddenly, they looked down at the mouth of the river. Warriors came to greet them and horses were led back into the forest.

From their high vantage point, they could see everything that was unclear before. Smoke from the settlement at Inver identified its location and a warrior pointed to the right of the river.

"Clachnaharry! That's the Caledonii smoke and the other smoke is where the people have set up camp."

"It seems water is stopping the Norse," said Sheena. "It stopped them in Mahomack, it's stopping them getting onto the Black Isle and it might stop them here."

"Why do you think that?" asked Adair. "They have plenty of big boats."

"A Monk once told me a Norse strike comes out of the blue," said Sheena. "Savage and surprise like that at Torridon. Now they have no surprise and everywhere armies confront them. This Sigurd is clever, he knows what he wants, security and trade. From there, he can protect his west side," she pointed at Inver.

"From here the two camps look the same. You can't tell warriors from warrior's mothers and fathers," laughed Sine.

"Stuart is clever He's got warriors in the forest. Horses go back and forth between the camp and the forest. What the Norse can see might be less than what they can't see. They think we have two thousand in the forest; they saw our warriors, but they'll have no idea what Stuart has in the forest."

"I want to stay here with you," pleaded Enya.

"You must go back. You promised Ross," Sheena smiled and Enya sulked.

Tarbat assembled five hundred warriors, most were from the Longboats, but he left enough to get them into safety. Sigurd led over a thousand warriors as they left Ardersier at dawn. His plan to send Ro-Sheen with an ultimatum to the inhabitants of Inver was scrapped, as his commanders argued that the soft approach was demoralising his men. That had always been a fear and starved of action, morale would collapse and leave them vulnerable. However, that wasn't the main reason Sigurd headed his army towards Inver.

He was more convinced than ever that this junction of nature held the key to his security. The north side could go to hell, he wanted to secure the south side and the river. Scouts had reported that great mountain ranges lay to the north and the west. They had left great mountain ranges in Norway and didn't want any more. To the east, and only to the east, the land was flat and fertile. To the south lay high ground swathed in forest as were much of the lands to the north and west. Hunting grounds trade would come from these mountains and they would come to Inver or try to pass. His mind made up, he rode with Ro-Sheen by his side with only one objective, the capture, surrender, or destruction of Inver, whatever it took before this day was done.

A finger of land between the river and the Fjord was his first observation and he called in his commanders.

"This Ness will be our reference point, Inver Ness. We will approach with the Ness behind us. Tarbat, stay on the left flank and be ready to secure the river," he ordered.

The army swung north towards the watching warriors on the Black Isle. Iain had seen the Norse move at first light and his warriors had shadowed them towards Kessock. The bulk of his force waited at Tore, ready to join the Caledonii at the first sign of the Norse trying to cross the river, but the fact their Longboats were still at Ardersier made the likelihood of that slim.

They watched impressed as the Norse fanned out on the opposite bank from Thornbush and headed towards the settlement, three deep with horses leading. Hearts hammered in chests as the army neared their objective and swords were unconsciously clenched by the watching warriors. Enya held her spear tight and stared.

Sigurd scrutinised the west bank of the river and the sight of so much Gulltorn sent a shiver down his spine. It was worse than the old man described, much worse and stretched a long way inland. Bad, if you had to go through it, but good if somebody had to go through it to attack you.

Up ahead, all looked quiet and Sigurd didn't like quiet. He halted his army and Tarbat carried on along his left flank. As expected, the defences in Inver faced east and now they revealed themselves as no more than ditches and a small Stockade that was so close to the dwellings, it might have been one. Nothing stood between Sigrid's army and the Stockade and those in the ditches ran for cover.

"We stop a bow shot from the Stockade, you go forward with Torf and demand their surrender," Sigurd ordered Ro-Sheen.

She looked at him and he smiled.

"Last time you said that an arrow went over my head," she pointed out.

"That is so, but this time if an arrow is fired, we attack. Get your white flag ready," Sigurd instructed.

"Come!" urged Torf and Ro-Sheen went with him.

He held the white flag on a spear and from the battlements of the small Stockade, many figures peered as they approached.

"We stop now," Torf ordered and they waited.

It seemed to take a long time before the gate opened and two horsemen came out facing the warriors of Tarbat, but they swung around and approached Ro–Sheen and Torf. They also had a white flag and stopped several horse lengths in front of the Norseman.

"Surrender your forces to Sigurd, Jarl of Orkney, or be destroyed," Ro-Sheen called out to them and noted they weren't painted for battle. One was female and young, the other bearded with grey hair.

"What terms do you offer?" replied the female.

"Surrender and your people and village will be spared. Do not surrender and they will be destroyed," answered Ro-Sheen and frowned when the young one yelled into her companion's ear repeating what Ro-Sheen had just said.

"My father asks how can we can trust your word?" she asked.

"Ardersier stands and the people have returned," Ro–Sheen answered and looked at Torf.

"Tell them they have a great army on the wrong side of the river, and this is their only hope of saving themselves," instructed Torf and Ro-Sheen passed on his message.

"We will return and put your offer to the elders," called out the young woman. "If they agree, the flag will fly from the stockade."

"Don't take long, your lives depend on it," warned Ro-Sheen, then turned to Torf. "Do we go back to Sigurd or wait here?" she asked him, nervously.

"We wait," grinned Torf.

A short time later, Sigurd smiled when he saw the flag flying from the Stockade. He signalled to Tarbat and he led his five hundred warriors along the river, heading inland.

Ro-Sheen and Torf came to him and they were all smiles.

"Now we get them out before we go in," said Sigurd and cast an eye across the river. "Ro-Sheen, you must tell them to bring all their weapons outside and stay outside. Leave their weapons by the gate."

He got another look from Ro-Sheen.

"Go! You're in no danger, they won't harm you. If they do, they will die," he assured her, but that was of little comfort to her.

Tarbat had his warriors on the run as they raced upriver. The foliage was thick and didn't allow for more than two warriors abreast. Ideal for ambush and his speed reflected his thoughts. The sooner they reached the lake, the better, after that there was no urgency. If a force was hidden on the south bank, it would reveal itself and if a few warriors had to die to flush it out, that was the price you had to pay, but there was no sign of anybody and when he spotted a bear on the opposite bank, Tarbat relaxed and a more orderly march ensued.

At last, ahead of them, he could see the trees spreading out. They had reached the lake. They stared in disbelief at the vastness of it, stretching as far as the eye could see to the west and surrounded by high hills, the sides of which dropped steeply into its waters.

Tarbat spread his five hundred warriors along the length of the river with the command to make camps and stay there until they received further orders. By the time he returned to the settlement, Sigurd had assembled a vast camp on the east and north side. Some elderly Picts were with him and Ro-Sheen.

They stopped speaking when Tarbat arrived and gave Sigurd his report.

"We call a lake, a Loch," Ro-Sheen corrected, and Sigurd repeated the word, Loch several times.

"Then we call this Loch Inver, Loch Inver River and Inverness, is that correct?" he grinned and looked at Ro-Sheen.

"Or Loch Ness, River Ness, and Inver Ness," she laughed.

"You're right, that sounds better all connected and with the great lake—Loch at the head," he agreed.

"Tell them that Inverness will be the name of this trading post and they must spread word to the north, that trading will begin before the leaves fall from the trees," he told Ro-Sheen.

The listeners nodded and asked what Ness meant? Headland confused them, but she explained the point that stuck out into the Firth and they understood.

Sigurd fired questions at the elders for some time while the settlement was searched for weapons and any warriors that might have been hiding. Shield Maidens found seven teenage girls hidden for fear they would be raped. This discovery fired up Sigurd.

"Tell them the Norse who raid and rape on their west coast are our enemies. We're not the same as them. Tell them to send a message to the commander of their army across the river to return to the west. Tell him the word of Sigurd is honourable. My word will not be broken. We will not cross the river," Sigurd instructed and the elders listened.

"Release them and let them go to their families," Sigurd then barked at the warriors who held the teenagers as if signing his pledge with them.

That single act changed attitudes. Shield Maidens escorted the girls back to their families and gratitude was rampant.

The only boat Iain saw crossing the river was a rowing boat. No smoke billowed from Inver, no sign of battle and the Norse camp was seen to be established outside the settlement. There was a movement of warriors back towards Ardersier, all were mounted and much movement among the Caledonii Army. Iain sent gallopers to Stuart to find out what was going on when he saw people start to move north back towards Beauly.

The happenings at Inver were closely watched from the south also and Tusk's spies were closer than those on the Black Isle. They bellied out of cover and made their way back to their horses. What had happened at Inver raised more than a few eyebrows and they didn't know what to make of it. They had no idea what was on the north side of the river, all they knew was Inver had surrendered and was now in the hands of the Norse and they headed back to Lochindorb to break the news to Tusk.

Sigurd left Torf in charge of his forces at Inver and returned to

Ardersier with Tarbat, Ro-Sheen and fifty warriors. Hamish was happy that no slaughter had taken place but sad that Inver had been taken. When Ro-Sheen came to get the two survivors Sigurd wanted, she explained what had transpired but Hamish said they had gone to the Longboats and were much improved.

She sent a warrior to get them and returned to Sigrid's tent. This had been a good day; they had taken a major crossing place without losing any warriors or boats and it was boats that were uppermost on Sigurd's mind. This river Ness was fast flowing and would need to be entered only when the tide was coming in. Timing would be critical for getting any Longboats into the shelter of the river. The alternative was a short distance away at Ardersier, and the Longboats could come and go as they pleased once they came through the narrows beside the point. This might be the main reason Ardersier was chosen for trade, it was easier to access.

Toke and Birger entered the tent and bowed to their lord. Sigurd nodded at their gesture and told them to sit.

"Now you're back in this world, tell me exactly what happened to your boat and the other boat. Then tell me what happened to you," Sigurd requested and like Tarbat, lay back comfortably. Ro-Sheen did likewise; this could be a long story.

They spoke fast and in nautical terms and lost Ro-Sheen quickly. By the time they reached what happened to them, Sigurd and Tarbat no longer lounged back, they leant forward, listening intently. The hell of the storm was given to them in graphic detail. There was nothing the masters could have done, everything rose against them, but the failure of the sails was the main reason for their loss not the stability of the Skiffs.

They spoke more slowly and Ro-Sheen listened as accounts of naked angels and tattooed Shield Maiden, mingled with Bulls and a drink that made them sleep and soup that was made from smoked fish but was white like the skin of the most beautiful. And the listeners looked at one another, imagining they weren't as well as first thought; they were still in another world.

"Our backs were painful and the Picts put the healing paste on our backs to make them heal and the pain went away. The warriors on the longboats took it off and then we saw what they had done," Toke said quietly and lowered his head.

"What did they do?" demanded Sigurd.

Birger pulled off his jacket and turned around. Sigurd gasped. Ro-Sheen stared at the Bull then stared at Sigurd. He rose from his seat and flicked his finger at Toke.

"Take it off, let me see how the savages have marked you!" he seethed and threw Ro-Sheen a look she didn't like. He stared at the great bull on both their backs. Both were identical to the many around the Fort at Torfness.

"What does this mean?" raged Sigurd. "What message do they send? You're marked for life by a God who-,"

"Saved their lives?" Ro-Sheen offered and Sigurd turned on her with his hand raised. He had never hit her before but came close. He lowered his hand and stared again at the tattoos.

"You think the message they send is to let everybody know their lives were saved by this God?" Sigurd muttered.

Ro-Sheen didn't know if he was speaking to her or himself and stayed silent.

"Tell me, woman, what message this is?" he asked, his voice less threatening.

"I heard them say they would have died if they were left on the beach. The warriors on the Black Isle saved their lives. This is their God. They honour your men. The God they worship saved your men and it's now on them. To protect them for the rest of their lives," Ro-Sheen said quietly.

Sigurd was well versed in the rituals of the Norse gods and tattoos were common. What he thought was an insult suddenly became clearer and the reason they were delivered must also have meaning. This he would have to think about.

"Get dressed, I won't have to skin you," he quipped, and the youths hurriedly obeyed.

Sigurd's mind worked swiftly and he looked at Ro-Sheen.

"If they learn the language, they can be useful. When we get back to Torfness teach them your language. Their tattoos could open many doors," he smiled.

Sigurd knew this God was good, he had eaten some of it before! He learned the Wild Bull on the high ground was a God. Now, it came back to haunt him. He would tread carefully around this beast.

# Chapter 24

Torfness was a hive of activity, both inside the Fort and beyond. More dwellings had been put up along the Seller area and further, with more under construction towards the Clarkley. The great Dale of Clyde Horses, harnessed between the shafts of carts, hauled timber from the settlement at Cluny, where hundreds of dead trees were felled. Fire had only scorched the trunks but burned off most of the branches and the bark, making the task easier.

Magnus was under great pressure to accommodate settlers who arrived on the Knarrs, fifty families at a time. Sigurd had instructed they settle the fertile land between Covesea and Torfness first.

The concentration of Norse warriors along the high ground would deter any would-be attackers without allocating specific warriors to protect them. When Moray was finally under control, they would branch out and settle the prime lands and a large swathe of this land had already been cultivated. Magnus had orders to allow farmers to return to their land unhindered. Many crops would rot in the fields if left unharvested and a large number of farmers had already returned around the largest settlement at Elgin. Others would follow.

The storm that had hit the army to the west had mostly blown itself out by the time it reached Torfness and no damage occurred there but it had hit Cluny and felled many trees before heading inland, raising the river levels with torrents of rain. Salmon had taken advantage of the rise in water level and most had headed into the upper reaches of the rivers but enough had been speared to last the winter and many smokers belched smoke from the wood chips that were abundant at Cluny and filled the gaps of every cart.

The fishermen at the Collach had strings of pots the Picts called Creels and they were yielding great catches of lobster and brown crab. The Norse had replaced the Pict ropes with their own that was much stronger. Fishing lines were baited with the black worms abundant by the Slappy and all along the west beach. Lines of as many as fifty hooks were set at low tide for flatfish. The Picts called this a Scuntac and the fishermen who had been captured to the east, were let loose to undertake their profession, while their wives and children slaved inside the Fort.

There was no shortage of food and supplies were sent across to Dornoch to support the fifty settler families who had landed there. The cargo of timber brought from Tongue in the Longboat was quickly turned into the major part of a longhouse and by the time that timber was used, Lugi warriors had hauled as much again from the forest.

Mother Dornoch and family had more livestock than they had ever owned as compensation and their flock of sheep required two sheepdogs to keep them under control. The Norse marvelled at the intelligence of the black and white sheepdogs that answered to whistles, but everybody was getting sick of eating salmon and Krike ordered that white fish be brought from the Field of Rocks.

This request was frowned on, to begin with, but when the fishermen received payment in Silver, the frowns soon disappeared. Aggie the Dog fared well as the smoked fish of Angus fetched even more Silver and was in great demand. Thus, the field of Rocks and Balintore smokers went into competition. Trade was established at Dornoch long before the trading post was built, and long before it was established at Torfness.

The Norse had selected their families well. Those who had no warriors already in Scotland were restricted. They could bring as many children over the age of twelve as they liked but no younger. Some swapped young ones for those old enough, in the rush to get good land. The objective was interbreeding and the sooner the better. It had worked in many places, including Orkney and the more the blood of the nationals mixed with that of the invaders, the sooner lasting peace would prevail. Krike had already seen a Shield Maiden and a Lugi warrior come hand in hand from the dunes at the side of Loch Fleet and he had a sudden desire for a Smertae.

The time that Ro-Sheen had abandoned her teachings in the abbey wasn't wasted on her young pupils. They played on the beach, caught crab and lobster, gathered Wilks and drank from the magic place where the water came from the rock. Everything in Pict it seemed had a name in Norse, except Aethan. The two sisters were now asking for something to eat and stubbornly refused to get washed in Norse.

The return of Sigurd in triumph, and befittingly on a Longboat, heralded a great celebration. Horns were sounded and hundreds of cheering warriors lined the Fort and the beach. Gallopers had been sent from Ardersier to warn of his coming and he arrived like the conquering hero he was. Resplendent in his best attire and with the helmet he used on such occasions polished and gleaming in the sunlight. No wet feet this time; he was carried shoulder high to the Slappy and placed on the ground with great reverence.

Magnus and the commanders were also dressed and greeted him by bending the knee and taking his hand. Ro-Sheen felt something seize her legs and looked down. Two small faces stared up and she grabbed them.

The celebrations went on for two days and were soured only by the loss of the Scouts and the crewmen of the two Skiffs. However, the two who had survived were in great demand and showed off their trophy at every available opportunity. They also repeated their tales of angels and nude warriors, to everyone demanding to hear. If they lied, they would tell a different tale each time, but they told the same story without fail and many were jealous of their experience.

Sigurd was delighted with the progress Magnus reported, and he had lost no men or horses to the hated Tusk since Sigurd's departure. Magnus proposed that Sigurd go on a tour of the lands that were under his control. It would be good for the morale of his warriors and put the conquered in their place. He agreed to that suggestion and ordered Magnus to arrange an entourage that would impress but Magnus would not be going. Sigurd decided he should return to Orkney and rule until Sigurd returned. He would recall Torf from Inverness and put Tarbat in charge of the west. It was a promotion for Magnus, and he felt highly honoured.

Sigurd went to the battlements and looked north towards Mahomack. He would go there soon, but from all accounts, everything was on track to establish the trading post and the tribes were in compliance with their agreement.

Below him, two warriors had run down the snake steps, yelping and raced towards the thunder box overhanging the cliff. One made it, the one who hadn't started hopping from one leg to the other, pleading for the first to hurry up before he shit himself and Sigurd laughed at his antics. These steps weren't as stupid as first thought.

As he turned to go back to his quarters, something caught his eye.

He went closer and looked at the slab of sandstone with the great Bull carved on it. It leaned against the plinth that held the signal horn and wasn't attached in any way. He ran his finger around the deep carvings of the loins and thought for so long, that the two from the thunder box returned to their posts on the battlements and gave him a strange look.

Eventually, Sigurd went down to the building of the Smiths. He knew what he wanted but doubted he would get it. They bowed and muttered as he entered and told the slave on the bellows to stop.

"Have you any weapons from the battle left?" asked Sigurd.

The Smith looked up and pointed to a shelf.

"The swords have been repaired or turned into spears; broken spear points into arrowheads, all that's left is there," he said.

Sigurd went to look and fished out two broken sword hilts with only short remnants of a blade attached. One was Norse, the other Pict and both breaks had occurred in battle.

"We were going to re-use the hilts," said the Smith.

Sigurd thanked him and left with the two relics.

Meanwhile, still painted for battle, Sheena returned to Cromarty with Enya, Sine and Adair who wouldn't let her out of their sight. All four crossed to Nigg as passengers. Approaching the dwellings from the sea, they noticed four horses tied outside one and the oarsmen let out a shout. Sheena nearly jumped into the water when her father came to the door and waved. The boat hit the beach at the same time as she did and he nearly fell over as she threw herself into his outstretched arms.

"Me next!" cried Sine and when Sheena peered into the gloom, she saw Fiona next to her and she embraced both at the same time.

"We came to get Enya, but father said you would come," said Sine and hugged her tight.

"Where's Ross?" asked Sheena which brought a chuckle from Fiona.

"He changed places with Krike at Dornoch," grinned Urquhart.

"You jest! You mean he's in amongst the Norse?" Sheena gasped.

"He's unarmed and he's among the Norse," replied Fiona. "His curiosity got the better of him. As soon as word reached us that Stuart had retreated west and Inver had fallen, he cursed for a night and threw his sword onto his sleeping platform in disgust. When Krike arrived, he insisted I came here to meet Enya."

"Leaving Krike and the Smertae alone, in your dwelling? When is he coming back?"

"Tomorrow. Krike just wanted a break He enjoys it over there," smiled Fiona.

"Sounds like they worked this out well to me," Sheena grinned.

They had until the tide fell to the second marker on the beach and it could be seen from the dwelling. They exchanged everything they knew about the Norse actions. The arrival of settlers at Dornoch sealed the fate of that land. In Sheena's mind, however, she had lands with no Norse and was determined to keep it that way.

"Hide your hair and cover up," advised Urquhart. "Nobody will be any the wiser it's you. Wait till after winter and come back to visit in Tain."

Sheena said her farewell with tears.

Iain met the party when they returned to Cromarty village and they were surprised to see him.

"Urquhart says you must go back and take command on the south side until we make a new Drum," he said. "That's going to take me a long time if I can't find parts of the old one; but even if I find the bronze fastenings and hoops, it will still take a long time to shape the staves," he moaned.

"Why you?" asked Sheena.

"You'd better ask Urquhart that question. I think he wants you to take command of an army to get the feel of it," he grinned.

"I have led two armies into battle and won both battles. Get the feel of it!" she scorned.

"He knows that," agreed Iain. "He also knows also that I haven't led an army into battle, so either you repair the Drum, or I repair the Drum!"

Sheena threw her arms around him and laughed loudly.

"You repair the drum!" she said and kissed him on the cheek.

"You can have a horse each if you take mine. I won't need it getting down the cliff," he said despondently.

Sheena dashed in to see old Urquhart and her new mother for a brief period. The nights were long and they had a long way to go to reach Avoch. Adair handed her a spear and armed with one each, they headed towards Balblair.

Sheena knew the warriors were getting restless. They had spent many days in the forest and she decided to change the routine. Instead of food coming to them, they would go to the food, but in the dark. They would sleep in dwellings and go back to the forest before daylight. This change was greeted with great cheer. She had to tell them all about the battles with the Smertae and before long they were eating out of her hand. She still refused to remove her top but came close a few times when urged on by the female warriors.

On the third day of her command, they reached the forest as the first rays of light rose in the east. Shortly afterwards they saw something else in the east, the unmistakable square sail of a Norse Longboat. Sheena and a hundred warriors moved east above the point to get a clearer view and waited. Only one Longboat had appeared, five remained at Ardersier. They could see the boat had a full complement of warriors, as it went into the beach at Ardersier and they watched them go onto the shore.

Sheena went back to her horse and pulled her bundle off the saddle when a shout reached her and she returned quickly to see what had happened.

"The Longboat, the one that just came in, it's heading for the point," said Sine.

"Shall I get the rest of the warriors here?" asked Adair anxiously?

"They would hardly put their warriors onto the shore and attack us with an empty boat," retorted Sheena.

They watched curiously as the Longboat neared the sandy side of the point and sure enough, it beached on the sand. They waited with eyes glued to the craft and picked out activity on the bow but not an invasion by any stretch of the imagination.

"Mount up, we'll get closer," Sheena ordered and there was a mad rush to the horses.

Tarbat wondered if Sigurd had lost his mind and screamed at his men to be careful. The stone was heavy and they slid it down from the Longboat on thick planks, ones they had used to haul it into the boat at Torfness. Once on the beach, they put a litter under it and carried it up onto the track leading to the point and set it upright. Tarbat placed the two broken sword hilts on top and looked at the approaching riders. They were still a long way from being a threat, but he ushered his crew back onto the Longboat and oars pushed it afloat.

"They're leaving," said Sheena.

"They're running away," Sine corrected.

The Longboat pulled out into deep water and turned its bow into the current then it just seemed to stay still. Sheena held her hand up and the horses stopped. They went forward at a walk; the boat lay out of bow range, but it could still be a trap. She saw somebody go into the bow of the boat and wave. Ahead of them, they could see nobody, and no movement and she concluded whoever was waving was waving at her Then she saw the obstacle ahead on the track and stopped.

"What is it? What's that on the track?" hissed Adair but Sheena took no notice.

Throwing caution to the wind she spurred her mount forward and the closer she came, the more she recognised what lay ahead. She stopped a bow shot from the slab of sandstone and her warriors came alongside.

"Now we walk," she instructed and they moved forward.

Several gasped as they saw the outline of the Bull, others stared nervously at the Longboat that seemed to be staying in the same position.

Sheena dismounted and the others followed, leading their horses. They all stared at the great Bull. Sheena knew this stone; she had seen it many times, but it was what lay on top of it that amazed her. The others stared at the two broken swords, confusion written on their faces, then looked at her for an explanation.

"What does it mean?" asked Sine.

"I think it means you can all go home. The Norse will not attack the Black Isle. A broken Norse sword, a broken Pict sword and both broken in battle," Sheena replied and mounted her horse.

She drew her sword, raised it high above her head and waved it slowly at the Longboat. Tarbat drew his sword and returned the gesture from the bow. Then the boat turned to port and oars dug in sending it back towards Ardersier.

Sheena felt numbed. She and her warriors were still staring after the Longboat. At the side of the track, she noticed the litter and sheathed her sword. She got off her horse and put her arms around the shoulders of two warriors. They looked at her in wonder as she walked them to the litter.

"You had better take our God to somewhere better than here," she smiled and they grabbed the litter.

The procession that entered Avoch looked like the arrival of a victorious army and the villagers streamed out of their dwellings in sheer panic, only to find their own warriors approaching with great cheers and many war cries.

Sheena left them to celebrate in their own way and went to sit by the boats and watch. A warrior handed her a bowl and she grinned; it was going to be a victory celebration but whether a victory had happened or not she wasn't quite sure. She toasted the Bull and took a sip of Whiskey. It triggered a desire to join the others.

Her offering of life to the Norse had been returned. Sheena had a great feeling of satisfaction without winning a battle.

# Chapter 25

The Stockade at Huntly had been re-built to hold more warriors than it was originally designed to hold by the Picts. A garrison of five hundred prepared to guard the western approaches to the great fertile valley that stretched east. Another Stockade would be erected close to the sea. The location of the second Stockade remained undecided but the settlement of Banff, where the Pict Stockade had stood, offered the best option. The river entered the sea there and positioned close to the beach, the Stockade could only be attacked from the north and west. Sigurd controlled the north and west, but other sites also offered some degree of natural protection.

In the interim, the garrison would camp at Banff until a decision was made. The river was rich in Salmon and hunting along the fertile valley yielded many deer. The Picts had cleared vast stretches of the valley and crops grew in abundance. Was this a reach too far? Could they hold this much land with the forces they had? Would they need more or bring in warrior settlers? These principal concerns piled up. Sigurd had to consider all of them, knowing that if he made a mistake, he would pay dearly.

He needed the ability to reinforce outposts quickly and two ways were better than one; by sea and by land. Huntly could only be reached by land but a landing place at Banff would save a day's ride overland from Torfness. The commanders under Magnus were tasked with making a final decision while Sigurd was in the west. He could change their decision, but he never did, ten minds being better than one. And he had hammered into them the need for foresight.

Banff became their final proposal. A plan of the Stockade site lay spread in front of Sigurd. He liked what he saw and fired many questions at the commanders. They gave answers that proved they had taken everything into consideration. The distance to the settlement being built at the mouth of the fast-flowing River Spey was half that of Banff to Torfness and offered a faster supply of reinforcements by land to either Huntly or Banff.

Everything considered, Sigurd heartily approved of their choice. They would beef up the standing force at the mouth of the Spey and rapid response to the southwest became possible from this location. The Spey garrison would be strengthened and Longboats taken onto the beaches there, forming the backbone of the east. The centre would be Torfness and Cluny, while Inverness would protect his west flank. Second only to implementing them, Sigurd loved making plans, especially defensive ones and soon two Skiffs were sent to Banff to announce construction could begin.

Sigurd had much to see, much to discuss, people to meet and form alliances with, spread throughout his new kingdom. He prepared for many long days on horseback with an entourage of five hundred. They finally set off for Elgin via Backlands and Covesea, passing through the heartland to Keith and Huntley. Sigurd chose his route carefully. He was surprised to find crops standing tall and ripening, unlike those to the west. He saw no sign of storm damage and many Picts had smoke coming from dwellings. They came and stared at their new master but stayed their distance.

Ro-Sheen was impressed by what had been learned in her absence and her two sisters showed little disappointment when she told them she was leaving again, and wouldn't be able to teach them until she returned. After much cuddling and hugging, Ro-Sheen said goodbye.

"Ha Det!" they replied.

"Ha Det!" shouted Sigurd back to them and laughed. "They learn quickly; did you teach them?"

"No! They must be learning on the beach," smiled Ro-Sheen.

Although warriors had ravaged the settlement at Keith, when they arrived most of it had been re-built and the strange smoking buildings back in operation making the crazy water that Sigurd now looked on as a valuable trading commodity. Greatly enlightened by Ro-Sheen, he had ordered the repairs to be undertaken and slowly the Picts returned. He was offered a small barrel of whiskey by a toothless woman who said it was good for his teeth. Ro-Sheen translated and Sigurd roared with laughter but what he did next surprised many. He dug into his pouch and handed the woman a silver coin.

"Take it!" instructed Ro-Sheen.

She took the coin hesitantly then looked at it in wonder. She had never held silver before and didn't know what this gesture meant.

"Tell her we buy what they make," said Sigurd. "We don't take it for nothing," and he walked his horse away.

The woman ran back to those too afraid to come close and brandished her coin like a battle-axe above her head, shouting that she was rich.

The winning of hearts and minds had begun. It would lead to trust and interbreeding and within a short period Norpicts would appear. Ro-Sheen had suggested that name for Half Norse, Half Pict, children. Sigurd just smiled and insisted trying to make them was better than making them.

Ten days later, after spending enough time at various locations to discuss issues with commanders and Pict leaders alike, the great column which had now been joined by the Norse patrol and numbered fifteen hundred warriors reached the settlement of Grantown on the banks of the fast-flowing River Spey.

This was Tusk country and they now moved with extreme caution. They found crops in the fields, not ready to harvest yet, but little sign of life around the settlement. Buildings that had been damaged remained damaged. They saw sheep but no cattle and the riverbanks stank of rotting guts, fish scales and fleshless heads. A massive catch had taken place here and whoever carried it out, had made sure they cleaned the fish well away from where they were speared.

Traversing the land between Huntly and Grantown and as far as they could see towards the high mountains, they came across prime hunting ground, the best Sigurd had ever seen. He vowed this Tusk wouldn't deny him hunting on his own land. That night, they sat around a large fire and discussed how best to kill this most stubborn of enemies and the debate stretched far into the night.

Those in Lochindorb saw the glow of fires from the Norse camp. Tusk knew of their approach well in advance, but not their intent. His scouts had watched the Norse since they left Keith but had stayed a safe distance and stuck to the forest. When the Norse headed west, Tusk's warriors were a day ahead of them and crossed the open moorland as if on a deer hunt, killing two Roe bucks in the process.

Tusk's band evacuated the Longhouses on the side of the Loch and stowed themselves safely inside the Stockade. All eagerly awaited the arrival of the Norse. Weapons were sharpened and the battlements bristled with spears and arrows. Innes had sixteen made for the Angle Bow, which she lay in a dry place, she had made from skins, along with its deadly missiles. Now she insisted it would stay on the battlements. Three more warriors had managed to draw the bow back, but she wouldn't let any loose an arrow. Innes insisted they wouldn't need practice and when they fired the next arrow, it would be into a sea of Norse. They hoped that the sea had arrived.

Ro-Sheen sought the company of the Shield Maidens when the Norse commanders got together. They had six main subjects, boats, battles and sex; closely followed by hunting, fishing and the weather. They spoke so fast and changed subjects so often, one time she thought they were having sex with a fish. She sighed with relief hearing the pole snap, and the fish got away. The Shield Maidens could match the men at most things; they could fight and were experts with bow, spear and sword as well as covering warriors' backs with their shields. But when they were together, they spoke girl talk and swapped ideas about how to look more beautiful. They washed each other's hair and made it into fascinating styles and Ro-Sheen relaxed in their company. She was held in great esteem being so close to their Jarl and she knew many things they didn't. When she came to them, she was welcomed with open arms and bone combs.

Sigurd had listened to all opinions relating to the hated Tusk. None had come close to reality and Sigurd was a realist. He had reached a decision before leaving Torfness, but he had kept it to himself and urged commanders to come up with solutions. Nobody had changed his mind, but he felt gratified that several suggestions unwittingly fell in line with his own decision.

"A wolf on the loose is a dangerous animal," Sigurd advised his men, "a wolf in a cage is not. This wolf has built his own cage and he sits in it. He's no danger to us and we're no danger to him as long as he stays there. And until we can tempt him out, we will only feed his ego by even showing any interest in him. Each time we go to its cage and each time we leave is a victory for the Wolf. Tomorrow, we march north along this great valley. We follow this river to our garrison at the river mouth, and then head back to Torfness."

"Do we burn the crops here?" asked one of his men.

"No! If we burn crops here, they'll burn more crops in revenge. We have more to lose than they have."

His main crop was slowly materialising. It would take time but the lure of their land intact was more of an encouragement to the Picts to return, than the prospect of burnt fields.

The Sea of Norse that Tusk had hoped for, failed to appear and as the day wore on, he suspected trickery. They could be lying in wait, out of sight and ready to pounce on anybody who left the safety of the Stockade. Disappointment spread amongst the warriors but Tusk dismissed any thought of going after them as foolhardy.

"We wait!" he roared and stared in the direction of Grantown.

His concern was for the crops there. Like Sigurd, he knew if the crops were burned here, it would start a war not fought with weapons, but with fire. That kind of war brought only losers no winners.

Two days later, Sigurd and his entourage returned safely to Torfness and Tusk held fast in his Stockade. It was only hunters from Loch Morlich who appeared on the banks of the Loch and Tusk launched a boat quickly to find out what was going on. He cursed when they told him the Norse had gone north days ago and they thought he knew.

Tusk quickly sent gallopers to Grantown. He knew the crops hadn't been burned but such an army could trample crops into the ground with ease. The gallopers returned with news that no damage had been done to anything in Grantown that hadn't been done previously and Tusk wondered what game this Sigurd was playing.

"What does it mean, Father?" asked Innes.

"This Norseman isn't stupid," sighed Tusk. "When they came the shoots were barely out of the ground. No chance to burn crops that hadn't grown. Scorched earth, burn everything, but even Torridon escaped that fate, their attack was so sudden. Now the crops grow and the Norse are many, they need to be fed as we do. If he destroys our crops, we will destroy his."

Innes hadn't thought about it like that. She could see no logic in allowing your enemy to eat. And according to their scouts, the crops were untouched in most places. The Norse would have more than enough to eat with what they could protect, without fear of it being burned. It didn't make sense to Innes.

Sigurd was greatly pleased by what he saw on his travels. Even the

Cave People at Covesea were tending their crops above the cliffs, indifferent to the nearby Norse encampment. They didn't come close, nor did the Norse approach them and they were gaining in confidence. Crops were also being attended by Picts in places he visited on his tour of conquest; his commanders reported many were returning from the south and even more coming out of hiding in the dense forest.

Timing and foresight leave nothing to chance and seasons were critical. Sigurd could never bring in enough settlers to reap one-quarter of the harvest of Moray. Word of his kindness and the fact their crops were undamaged spread fast and those who had been left behind, namely the old the young and the sick, were joined by the more able who had run to swell the ranks of the army that would counterattack the Norse and drive them back into the sea. When this army failed to materialise, warriors slipped back to their families and dwellings in the dark and unarmed. They would have arms hidden somewhere but their presence was more important than the location of their weapons and many had horses.

They needed horses to plant the following year's crop and nobody made any attempt to take those horses from them, adding to their sense of security. Some even came into the seller area to trade. Silver changed hands there and in the north at Tongue and Dornoch for timber, fish, wool and labour. Sigurd was getting a reputation for being generous and by all accounts a fair and honourable man. Even his warriors were looked on with respect; they didn't harass anybody and helped where they could. The Picts had no idea that the Norse warriors were under sentence of death if they harassed the returning Picts unless they were attacked first.

The first harvest looked to be a good one. All Norse settlers had been settled between Covesea and Backlands. All were protected by the sea and the Laich. They could also get back to Torfness quickly.

The second harvest also grew steadily and promised to be much more valuable than the first. Harold would be paid handsomely in slaves. A steady stream of Picts came to tend the first harvest, oblivious of the fate that awaited them. Sigurd was well aware of the enemy within; the Picts would have a hidden agenda above and beyond crops. Sigurd played a dangerous game, but it was the only way to entice the second crop back into his domain. He had a toe-hold in Tongue and Dornoch but a stranglehold on Moray and the surrounding lands, except those belonging to Tusk. He would strike before the Picts could, but first, Picts would plant the next harvest ready for the hundreds of settlers that would take their place when the Picts were enslaved.

When word reached Torfness that the trading post was ready at Dornoch, Sigurd headed across the Moray Firth to pay a courtesy visit to his colony. A Longboat loaded with many ingots of iron, clay, bricks and bellows went first to warn the Lugi and Decantae that the next Longboat would bring Sigurd, accompanied by a hundred warriors, not extra warriors above his agreed number, but to change with the ones already there.

Krike and Forbes understood the explanation drawn on the sand. One hundred in, and one hundred out, it wasn't complicated to them but appeared more complicated to the Norse. Astrid had selected and staked out the land for her family and they had come with the first settlers. Astrid chose the best land she could find that ran into the place they called Loch Fleet. Warriors who wanted to stay were each given three hundred paces wide by five hundred long. Families were expected to erect shelters before winter and Sigurd would pay for timber and labour.

It was a generous offer and taken up by many warriors besides Astrid. She had two brothers and one teenage sister who had sweated since their arrival, realising Astrid had handed them a new life. The Lugi delivered wood for their dwelling and some stayed to help with construction or to be close to the Shield Maidens. Either way, they worked hard, and the dwelling would be ready long before winter.

The family of Glo were next to Astrid, her mother and two teenage sisters. Astrid had also selected land for them and staked it out. Female Lugi warriors were helping Glo's family and the aspiring Lugi bucks were kept at bay. This integration of nationalities and sexes without any communication between them was sometimes hilarious but words were being picked up daily, especially by the young bucks from Brora who had reason to impress. Even Sigurd had adopted several Pict words and didn't try to change them. A Ben he learned was a mountain. A Lake was a Loch, and a valley, a Glen.

As on his tour of Moray, Sigurd dressed to impress when he stepped off the Longboat at Dornoch. His helmet polished to gleaming stood proud of his cloak of Gold and Blue, edged with ermine, the colours of Orkney. In his left hand he carried a shield with a blue field and gold Longboat on one side; on the other, a red field with a gold crowned lion, the crests of Orkney and royal crest of Norway. His right hand rested on the silver hilt of a great sword and he smiled broadly as warriors bowed in his presence.

Krike and Forbes stood at the side of the welcoming party and glowered at the antics of the Norse.

"If he wants me to kiss his arse, he's out of luck," growled Krike.

"What about her?" asked Forbes as Ro-Sheen appeared looking resplendent.

"That? That Smertae would kill me. She's more your age, Forbes!"

"She can kill me any time she likes," grinned Forbes and then stiffened as Sigurd approached down the line. As he neared them Ro-Sheen came close to interpret.

Sigurd nodded his head and they both returned the gesture.

As he spoke to them, Ro-Sheen smiled.

"Sigurd is pleased with what you have achieved here and has brought silver to pay both your tribes for everything they have provided. He wishes that you go and invite your chiefs to come here for a feast and to settle accounts," she said.

"Tell Sigurd we can ask but don't be surprised if they refuse," replied Forbes.

Ro-Sheen raised her eyebrows and told Sigurd, but he grinned before speaking.

"They can bring a hundred warriors each. They can bring two hundred, but I think four warriors each will be enough. They will be under my protection and my word is honourable. No harm will come to them. No harm has come to you. We are one hundred you are two thousand. Tell them to come tomorrow at noon."

Ro-Sheen translated and what she said was true. If anything happened to their chiefs, Sigurd would be slaughtered, at the very least all his settlers would be slaughtered, there was no doubt about that.

"You go the hard way; I'm going by boat. Are we still going for her?" Krike asked.

"We go for her," Forbes replied and went to saddle a horse for his journey.

He watched as Sigurd discarded his regalia and mounted. He was with Ro-Sheen and Astrid as they rode along the beach in the direction of Loch Fleet. Sigurd was on a mission.

Astrid waved as she passed her dwelling and her brothers waved back and bowed as they recognised who was with her. Sigurd waved at them and looked ahead. Beside a half-built dwelling stood three women, one old, two young and they wrung their hands in front of them nervously.

"The mother and two sisters of Glo," Astrid announced and Sigurd reined his horse in and dismounted.

He didn't seek introduction; he went to the mother and kneeled in front of her. On one knee he took her hand and kissed it.

"Glo died in my arms. She was a brave warrior we owe you much," he said, then turned to the two sisters. "Your sister was a very brave warrior. She died in the great battle for Torridon, and she avenged Bente. You should be very proud of her. Glo gives you this land and this dwelling. I give you this," Sigurd said quietly and handed the mother a small pouch of silver.

"Buy what you need and prosper on this land. I will come back and visit you again. Astrid must go back to Torfness with me, but I will ask somebody else to watch over you when she's gone," he assured them and mounted.

He headed into the expanse of the new ground with Astrid leading and continued his tour of the settlers, under the curious gaze of some Lugi warriors who had no idea who he was.

Meanwhile, Forbes had reached Brora and found Stroma.

"Payday!" he announced and Stroma looked at him as if he had gone mad.

"What do I have to pay you for?"

"Payday for you, not me. Your invader has come to pay his debts, Sigurd is here."

That made Stroma sit up and take notice.

"He invites you to join him tomorrow at noon along with Urquhart. He wants both of you to go to Dornoch," he grinned.

"With an army?" she quipped.

"An army of four. He's guaranteed your safety. You have his word."

"He's testing us, to see if we fear him. I don't fear him, I hate him," she seethed.

"We have over a hundred warriors working with the Norse. He took a Hundred with him from Torridon and he's sending a hundred back, apart from the ones staying with their families. Only one Longboat remains and three small boats. He wouldn't try anything and Urquhart will have two hundred all ready to cross at the first sign of trouble. We can mass the mounted warriors at the head of Loch Fleet. I don't think he's stupid enough to try anything," Forbes assured her.

"If we show that much strength, he will think we fear him!"

"What do you suggest?"

"You suggest," she said. "You've had more time to think about it than me."

"I suggest you make yourself look like the beautiful Chief you are and act like one. I spoke to Krike before he went to see Urquhart. You want to hear more?"

Stroma threw him a suspicious look and nodded.

"Sine and Fiona will represent the Decantae, along with Ross and Krike. Enya and you together with me and Frazer will represent the Lugi. Urquhart won't go; he'll use this as an opportunity to send Sine. I think between the four of you, Sigurd might take his eyes off the Smertae, Ro-Sheen. Krike has to sell that idea to Sine, Enya and Fiona as well as Urquhart. I only have to sell the idea to you. Are you ready to accept the challenge of the Smertae?" he laughed.

Stroma looked at him and frowned.

"What will happen if we kill him?"

"As you say, I've had more time to think about it than you. Killing him wouldn't be difficult. We kill him, then kill the rest of them, then wait. Wait for what? His longboats and the ones they call Knarrs, where are they? He has an army of many thousands and boats to get them here. Without destroying his boats, killing him would unleash his army to seek revenge and they can be here within days. Yes! There would be great battles but without support from the south, we would perish and not only our warriors. If we kill the settlers, the Norse will kill all our people. He knows it, we know it and that's his strength. Kill me if you dare? Do you want to dare, Stroma?

"He can't lose, as long as he holds Torridon. He can't lose. Time! Stroma that's all we can play for, time for our own forces to attack from the south, then we can attack from the north. You must play for time, humour him but show him you're not afraid of him. You're not going to like what I have to say next, so hear me out before you erupt."

"I haven't liked anything you've said so far, so tell me."

"The Smertae, Ro-Sheen, she's the way to Sigurd. She's his voice and ours. Get on the right side of her and that's the reason we think it's best that you, Enya, Sine and Fiona will get closer to her than a delegation of men. The more women there, the better chance you will have to befriend Ro-Sheen."

Stroma opened her mouth to protest.

"Uh-uh," he warned her, then continued. "She's a strange one; there's no airs or graces with her, no indication she thinks she's better than anybody. Indeed, she's gracious and knows her place. She's also very beautiful and held in great esteem by the invader. Ro-Sheen is the link to Sigurd whether we like it or not; what we say, she translates and also what he says. Ro-Sheen is in a powerful position and I don't think she realises how much power she has. Sow some positive thoughts in her mind. Get her alone and praise the rewards you get from the bastard she works for. Do something to put him at ease, anything to buy time."

"You want me to kiss the arse of a Smertae?" she growled.

"I would, but she wouldn't let me," he said.

Stroma threw a wooden bowl at him and burst out laughing.

"Let's hear what the others have to say about yours and Krike's crazy plan. I think Ro-Sheen has bewitched you both!"

Krike was having the same challenge trying to sell their plan to the women but Urquhart was in agreement with him and pushed all three of them to agree. In the meantime, water was boiling in kitchens and the Smertae, Fia, was looking out for the best attire Fiona owned and Sorsce the best for Sine. Enya owned very little but Sheena had left belongings with her father and Ross encouraged her to join the delegation in support of Stroma.

Paying homage to a Smertae wasn't in their blood but killing them was. Convincing them that they could reach Sigurd through Ro-Sheen took tact, something Krike greatly lacked but fortunately, Urquhart did not.

"I think they fear her beauty more than they fear Sigurd," said Urquhart.

This caused a riot among the competition that resulted in strenuous denial that in turn, resulted in the desired decision. There was a frantic race to groom and ready themselves for the confrontation with the Smertae and the presence of Sigurd was moved to the side-lines. Ro-Sheen was a challenge and they rose to it.

"Father, I don't understand," complained Sine.

Urquhart grinned and looked at her; she had been beaten to the hot water by Enya and Fiona and had to wait.

"Then let me explain," he said. "You go and confront this Sigurd. Hold your head high and don't be intimidated by him. Show him your strength but the Smertae is the only one who can tell you what's in his head. Befriend her, loosen her tongue, let her speak her mind, not something she has to translate. Let her speak her own thoughts and you will find out more from her than you will from Sigurd. Whiskey will loosen her tongue; all you have to do is get her alone and let her speak. Encourage her to speak and in turn, you will let her know our strength can be doubled quickly if the Caledonii joins us. That will get back to her master. Let her drink, but you do not drink, understand?" he ordered.

"So, it has nothing to do with beauty. You tricked us," she scoffed.

"It has everything to do with beauty. The four of you get Sigurd's attention away from Ro-Sheen. Get him merry and get her away from him and see what you can find out. What's happening in Torridon, what's happening in the south, in Inver? Find out anything you can, Sine, especially who was killed at the Helm. We need to know!" he thumped his hand on the table in frustration.

"I'll try father," she promised and headed for the kitchen quickly.

# Chapter 26

From the stockade at Banff to the Stockade at Inver, the colour of the cleared land changed from green to gold as crops ripened in the heat of summer. Self-preservation rose uppermost in the minds of families who had abandoned their lands and dwellings ahead of the Norse invasion. Life in the forest had proved harsh and dangerous; they had lost people to wolves or killed by bears, but some were also on the brink of starvation and knew they would never survive a winter.

The return to their fields and dwellings started slowly but as crops ripened and word spread that the Norse had left those in peace who had returned to harvest their crops, the more confident the Picts became that they could return safely. What started as a trickle turned to a flood as the vanquished returned to their own lands.

On the South slopes of Bennachie below the great Hill Fort and south towards the river Don, the bulk of the Picts had held their ground. If the Norse came south, they would have to cross the river Don. Stopping them before they reached the Don became the focus but as time passed and reports came from north and south, their situation remained confused. The Norse didn't come south, and the King's army didn't come north. Gordon Grant Munro and many Chiefs including MacDuff were holding half an army and that hold grew less as the weeks turned to months.

The fact that their new King had abandoned them took a long time to ram home but after sending many messengers south, the truth slowly sunk in that this King had no intentions of attacking the Norse. Power had shifted to the south and that's where it would remain.

They had to make decisions and act on them quickly. First, they had to arm and supply the Hill Fort. It provided a formidable defence but defence it would remain. Unlike Torridon, Bennachie could only be re-supplied by land and could hold out no longer than one winter if it was put under siege. Six hundred of the youngest and fittest warriors would hold this Fort. The rest would return with their families to their respective lands and all arms would be hidden somewhere safe except those for self-defence.

MacDuff led his people east to the coast from there they spread out along the glens of Fundy towards Huntly. Grant was in his own lands and Gordon a stone's throw away. Munro and Anderson released their people with instructions to keep to the forest until they were within the area held by Tusk.

At Lochmorlich the exodus was the same and hundreds returned along the great Spey valley. Tusk had also seen his numbers reduced and arms were left at the Stockade buy those who left to tend their crops.

Most of the crops that had been flattened by the freak storm, had time to stand erect again and what couldn't received help, with the result that three-quarters of the crops survived. Norse patrols were getting predictable and faster. Now they were familiar with the terrain they knew exactly where to go and where not to go. Many Norse warriors were mounted and formed tight formations of a hundred that included warriors on foot or double mounted. Picts ran for cover when they first swept down on them, but the Norse didn't stop they just kept going. All knew what Sigurd's intention was and all knew that much of the crops the Picts were harvesting would be traded at Norse Stockades or Torfness.

The Norse settlers included many craftsmen and they wasted no time in setting up their business. The Seller area that used to hold a market became a market and expanded towards the Clarkley along with many dwellings for the traders and with the expansion came work and the need to employ Picts. A steady stream of timber arrived from the great forest and forges turned out nails by the hammer strike.

Boat traffic to and from Ardersier, Banff and Dornoch was in full swing. Warriors spread in a defensive arc that stretched from Inverness to Banff. Only one area remained hostile and unsecured, the lands of Tusk. Sigurd's strategy of ignoring his existence, keeping Norse Scouts close to the patrols and strengthening his grip on the land instead of chasing shadows, was paying dividends. Many settlers had arrived and were dispersed to the rich lands of Moray. Norway was awash with Iron and much already smelted came in the form of small ingots many of which had been sent to Dornoch along with Smiths who would turn the ingots into trade goods.

The land between Mahomack and Balintore was also rich in grazing and crops. Many of Urquhart's warriors had returned to reap the rewards of their labour knowing to leave the crops to rot in the fields would lead to another disaster, one they couldn't fight with weapons. Starvation was a real threat that couldn't be ignored and like the crops along the south side of the Black Isle, fields were turning golden. Sigurd injected himself into this shift in priorities with an air of humility that he judged would encourage normality and subsequently acceptance. The Norse had arrived and intended to remain. The Picts could accept that or fight. Sigurd prepared himself for either.

The arrival of Stroma and her escorts via the head of Loch Fleet was cheered by the many Lugi warriors labouring on the dwellings of the Norse. Frazer noticed several Shield Maidens with Lugi warriors and passed on his observation to Stroma.

"It won't be long before the Norse are going to Brora to visit their relatives," he scoffed.

"I see," she said and left it at that. She had more on her mind than breeding as she spied four galloping horses heading straight for them.

Forbes came alongside her mount and eyed the approaching riders suspiciously. Frazer came on her other side and they rode on.

"It's Ro-Sheen and the leader of the female warriors, Astrid," announced Forbes, seeing the long blond hair of both.

The figures waved in greeting as they halted a bow shot in front of the Lugi Chief. Stroma urged her mount on and only stopped within a whisper of Ro-Sheen.

"Sigurd sent us to meet you. He awaits you on the beach at Dornoch," said Ro-Sheen and whirled her horse around before Stroma could speak. Her companions followed and the Lugi Chief fell in behind them as they cantered south.

"My father would kill me, Frazer, if he knew what I was doing," said Stroma.

"If killing was the answer, we would all be dead," he frowned in reply and she fell silent.

The journey towards the shore of the Firth brought many unexpected sights and the closer they got to the beach, the more populated the land became. Many Norse and some Lugi watched as the riders passed and waved in greeting, some at Astrid, others at Stroma. They saw dwellings of all sizes under construction and passing through a cluster they heard the unmistakable ringing of the Smiths, pounding iron into utensils while all around, smoke filled the air.

On the sand spit across from Dornoch, Krike and Ross waited with their three females for the arrival of the Skiff to take them across the water. Sine wore the eagle feathers of the Chief and no matter which way she turned, to both Ross and Krike she looked the spitting image of Sheena when she was young. Sine carried a sword and wore the dirk of Embo in her belt, just like Stroma.

"The Norse have driven a wedge between us and the Lugi, a wedge of land," Urquhart had warned before they left Tain. "Make sure they don't drive a wedge of silver between us. Don't let this Sigurd favour one tribe. It's Lugi land they take, not Decantae. Make sure the Lugi get paid in silver more than the Decantae and make sure Sigurd knows he cannot break our alliance with the Lugi."

They took his words to heart.

Sigurd realised that if Frode hadn't been killed at the river, a different situation would prevail, whether for better or worse he didn't know. What he faced now lay somewhere between the two, neither a victory nor a defeat and he would have to use tact to ensure he didn't lose his foothold on the north. As long as he held Inver, communications between the north and the south side of the Moray Firth would prove difficult if not impossible. In his many meetings with commanders, they had weighed up the situation from every angle and concluded that securing Torfness and Moray was essential. That had been their main objective and they had triumphed. Nothing should put the lands he had already conquered at risk.

News of the Picts returning in droves to harvest their crops changed the landscape in more ways than one. Sigurd now had an enemy within, and it was growing by the day. Before their return, Sigurd had many warriors he could dispatch to the north without leaving the south weak. Now the bulk of his warriors patrolled the conquered lands in a show of strength that would deter any thoughts of rebellion. Harold had warned Sigurd not to bite off more than he could chew and now he found himself on the border of doing just that. The situation didn't call for threats, it called for diplomacy and like Urquhart, Sigurd had addressed the distribution of Silver with great care.

Krike let out a grunt when he saw the Skiff being launched from the beach at Dornoch and they awaited its arrival on the west side with more than a little apprehension. Sine started to shake and Fiona put her arm over her shoulder and squeezed her.

"Don't worry, he won't eat you," she grinned.

I'm worried I might eat him," retorted Sine, stroking the gem on her Dirk.

"Straighten your bonnet and lift your chin," said Ross. "You're a Chief just like him. He's no better than you; don't let him think he is."

Sine smiled, then looked behind her where her father sat with a hundred mounted warriors. She waved and Urquhart waved back.

"Come! We go to the beach," commanded Krike and led the party towards the shoreline. "I'm getting one of those boats even if I have to steal it," he growled for the hundredth time.

The sun was high and the air still, when the bow of the Skiff slid onto the beach at Dornoch. They saw much smoke and a hive of activity as they approached, and the smell of roasting meat reached them as soon as they set foot ashore.

Two warriors familiar to Krike eyed up the beauties with him, making no attempt to hide their lust. They followed the two warriors towards the Longboat, pulled up high out of the water and obscuring much of the beach to the east where the smoke came from. Sine and her companions stared in awe at the large and impressive building standing close to the shore. The men working on the roof stopped and stared when they spotted the beauties on the beach.

The party rounded the bow of the Longboat and saw the reception before them. Stroma stood up and went quickly to Enya and embraced her.

"Now we're equal and you're not getting her back," Stroma threw at Ross.

This broke the ice, together with the realisation that there appeared nothing formal about this gathering, something Sine had dreaded. But she froze as the big bearded Sigurd stood up and walked past Forbes with his hand outstretched.

"Take his arm," grunted Krike and Sine obeyed.

Sigurd's greeting made Ro-Sheen laugh before she translated it.

"Sigurd says the sun has come to the ground in four pieces. He thinks you are all very beautiful!"

Sine didn't know what to say and Ross stepped up.

"Tell Sigurd, Urquhart sends his daughter as a show of faith and he sends this as a drink to peace," and presented Sigurd with a small firkin barrel of whiskey.

He took it and a smile parted his beard when Ro-Sheen relayed Ross's greeting.

They all sat as Shield Maidens turned a roasting spit with half a pig above the fire. More Shield Maidens gathered nearby and Ross noted with suspicion as the one called Astrid positioned herself next to Forbes.

Sigurd wasted no time in bringing up the subject of payment and spoke for some time before Ro-Sheen took over.

"Sigurd is unsure how you want the payments to be made. The Decantae have fed his people since they arrived and the Lugi have provided labour and timber. Sigurd wants you to discuss between yourselves how the Silver will be divided."

Sine jumped to her feet before anybody could speak and they all looked at her. She directed her words to Stroma, not Sigurd.

"My father says only one-quarter of the Silver will be given to the Decantae, the rest will be given to the Lugi," she said and they all waited for Stroma to reply.

"If your father is happy with that, then so be it," Stroma smiled.

Sigurd observed in silence as the two young Chiefs spoke. He had watched as Stroma had embraced the black-haired beauty who now sat with her and taken note of the two knives both Chiefs wore on their belts which were identical and unique. The bond between these two tribes ran deep and turning one against the other would prove difficult, but not impossible. This was not the time. It would come but not now. When Ro-Sheen repeated Urquhart's wish, Sigurd nodded in agreement.

"Tell them the old Chief is very wise and his thinking is the same as mine," he added and stood up. "The two Chiefs will go to the trading post with me."

Ro-Sheen translated and Ross looked at Frazer in alarm.

"I will go with Stroma!" insisted Frazer.

"And I will go with Sine," demanded Ross, staring at Sigurd defiantly.

He grinned and waved his arm towards the building and they fell in behind him.

Most of the roof was planked but still allowed enough shafts of sunlight to illuminate the interior which looked even more impressive than the outside. An old man sat beside a table and he stood up when the party entered. In front of him lay a pile of Silver coins that drew their eyes away from their surroundings. They looked from the Silver to each other in silence.

"Tell the Chiefs, one of them take one coin, the other take three," Sigurd directed and Ro-Sheen passed on his request.

Sine went first and Stroma looked nervously at Ross.

"Go ahead, it's only fair, it's your land and your timber," he assured her.

She pulled three coins towards her and Sine took another. This went on in silence and the pile diminished quickly.

"Enough!" shouted Frazer and they jumped.

Stroma whirled on him with a questioning look.

"That's enough," he repeated. "Sine, take what's left. They didn't eat trees and the fishermen will need paying."

"We have enough, you take the rest," agreed Stroma with a smile and pushed the remainder of the coins towards Sine.

The old man handed two leather pouches to Sigurd. He bagged the pile of Sine first, bowed, and gave it to her. He did likewise to Stroma.

"We eat!" Ro-Sheen announced.

"And drink," added Ross.

They returned to the beach; Frazer carrying the Lugi Silver and Ross that of the Decantae. Sigurd came between the two young Chiefs and towered over them. In their absence, Krike had already removed the bung from the whiskey barrel and Forbes had signalled Astrid the need for drinking vessels. She returned with many small clay bowls and again sat next to Forbes.

Sigurd spoke and Ro-Sheen looked at Stroma.

“Sigurd wants to walk with you along the beach,” she said. “He has something to say to you in private.”

Stroma looked first at Sigurd then at Frazer.

“Go, find out what he wants,” advised Frazer.

Sigurd and Stroma, together with Ro-Sheen, went a short distance east then stopped out of earshot of everybody. When Sigurd drew his sword, Stroma grabbed the hilt of hers but he grinned and started drawing on the sand.

“Sigurd knows who you are. He knows your father is Sinclair of the Carnavii,” Ro-Sheen explained.

Stroma frowned wondering what was coming next. Then she watched as a land she was familiar with emerged on the sand from the tip of Sigurd’s blade. He drew from Tongue until he reached where they stood and looked at Stroma as he replaced his sword in its scabbard.

“Tell your father the Norse want to trade in peace, as we’re doing here. We have already erected a trading post in Tongue. That’s a long way from his east. Sigurd would like to set up such a trading post at Thurso, with your father’s permission, and avoid a war between the Carnavii and the Norse, a war only the Norse would win,” Ro-Sheen interpreted.

“Tell Sigurd I can’t speak for my father. He hates the Norse and will fight to the last man,” replied Stroma defiantly.

Ro-Sheen told Sigurd what she had said and he nodded in understanding.

“Sigurd says he offers your father peace and prosperity. Trading with the Norse will make life better for his people, not worse as you can testify. Before winter sets in Sigurd wants you to send his message to your father and bring his reply back. Will you do this?” Ro-Sheen asked.

“I can try but my father is stubborn and so is his council.”

"You have a long time to live. The future lies ahead not behind. You will become Chief of both tribes when your father dies. You must consider your position. The lands of the Carnavii will belong to you or the Norse. Sigurd says the choice is yours, not your father's."

Stroma swallowed hard; she didn't like this conversation and wished Frazer was with her or Forbes. She needed their opinion; she needed their support but most of all she needed time to think.

"I'll discuss Sigurd's offer with my council. Two are here and that will be enough," she replied.

Ro-Sheen informed Sigurd; he smiled and nodded in agreement.

They returned to some curious stares and when Stroma took Frazer and Forbes aside, it aroused even more curiosity, but nobody asked any questions.

Krike grunted and filled bowls with whiskey. He handed one to Sigurd who looked at the liquid with suspicion. Krike took the bowl from his hand, gulped it down then refilled the bowl and handed it back to Sigurd.

"It's not poison!"

Ross handed a bowl to Ro-Sheen which she declined but he insisted saying unless she drank it, their agreement meant nothing because she had voiced it. She had to think about that but concluded she had no choice and took it.

Meanwhile, Sine had an empty bowl cupped in her hands and they all waited for the return of the Lugi. They came and were handed bowls. Sigurd eyed Stroma and she nodded at him confirming his request would be sent to her father. Ross toasted to peace and good trading, which Ro-Sheen conveyed to Sigurd and he tentatively put the bowl to his lips but seeing the men and the women downing theirs, he resigned himself to fate and his eyes opened a little wider as fate slid down his throat.

Forbes threw a suspicious look at Krike and thrust out his bowl.

"I'll have a double to catchy up with you, Krike!" he demanded.

Ro-Sheen sipped her whiskey and eventually drained the bowl, by which time the fiery liquid took effect. When Sine suggested she go with her to show her the private place, Ro-Sheen gladly agreed. They took off along the beach and Ro-Sheen staggered slightly and laughed aloud.

Sigurd reflected on how far the Silver of Imogen and Halfdane had stretched. He still had plenty left and felt content with this day's work. Now he feasted his eyes on the savage beauty before him.

# Chapter 27

Across the conquered lands to the base of the mountains, an uneasy peace had settled by order of Magnus. He and all his commanders knew Sigurd's strategy and anybody who put that in peril would be punished. His warriors were spoiling for battle but even they accepted the fact that the crops must be gathered, or fire would consume them. Also, the fact the Picts were gathering most of it meant they weren't, a just reward for obeying orders. The silos in the lower fort looked close to empty; they removed what remained and cleaned out the silos ready for the new grain.

Tusk's band continued harvesting late into the night and no Norse patrols came close before turning north along the Spey Valley. There they left the Picts alone by skirting the small settlements and what they called Crofts. As confidence grew, Picts started to hold their ground at the sight of the invaders, instead of fleeing into the forest. Resentment and hatred waned slightly but was still strong. Now they had two sources of hatred, one for the Norse and the other for their King who had abandoned them. That hatred grew ever stronger than the first.

Along the coast, the fishermen landed great catches of cod and smokers billowed day and night. The Norse were trading for everything and along the Glens of Foundland between Huntley and Banff, the area Picts called the Glens of Fundy, the harvest was gathered with purpose. Trade with the Stockades east and west started slowly but gradually increased. Norse settlers began the construction of dwellings close to each Stockade and established markets at Huntley and Banff. Picts had one of their own at the settlement of Turriff that remained intact, the Norse not crossing the river to attack it as was feared. The warriors of the glens had massed at Bennachie and those who remained would hold the fort. Turriff market was central and traders bought there and sold to the Norse stockades to their west and east for profit.

Barley was abundant along the Spey Valley and stills in full swing, keeping the coopers busy making barrels, while the foresters felled the oaks to supply the coopers. Things had returned to some sort of normality and they agreed that life under the Norse wasn't as bad as some had feared.

A splinter group of young Pict warriors who ridiculed the collaboration with the Norse, ran wild and out of control, raiding their own people. At first, they demanded provisions in any form they could get but soon turned to killing for the provisions they wanted. They rode with impunity and looked down on all who collaborated with the Norse as nothing but traitors.

Grant tracked some and slaughtered them on the banks of the River Livet, close to the settlement of Glen Livet. Grant had set a trap there with many horses. The raiders took the bait and Grant was rewarded with nine more horses than he started with and ten heads. Those who escaped across the river were tracked to the Stockade at Lochmorlich. Those who remained there were cast out and the Stockade raised to the ground. Some went to join Tusk but others reluctantly returned to their own lands, some to labour for the Norse in the case of those deposed.

Robbers took advantage of the situation which Tusk described as a plague of Smertaes and his warriors tracked and killed several in the great forest to the west. However, such incidents provided a mere diversion from reality and Tusk knew they were in a race against time. As soon as the harvest had been gathered by the Norse, the truce would come to a bloody end.

Meanwhile, in Torfness, the great mystery remained. Only Sigurd and his commanders knew that the riches of Torridon, the treasury, had not been found. Somewhere in this Fort lay the wealth of the King but where? Despite many searches, they found nothing. The warriors believed such riches had already fallen into the hands of Sigurd and the commanders allowed them to think that. If the truth came out, it would cause a free-for-all to find the riches, and all could be stolen, so they kept their secret.

In the large stone building of the lower Fort, used by the smiths, the hammers rang out incessantly. Three Smiths worked there from dawn till dusk but unlike the Smiths who had set up forges outside the Fort and were turning out utensils to trade, the Smiths inside focused on the manufacture of only one item, leg irons. Sigurd had ordered that five hundred be made before the next harvest showed in the form of green shoots. It was a tall order and to date, they had made just over a hundred. Charcoal for furnaces was in great demand and many Charcoal pits were dug along the ground above the west beach.

Skiff captains scratched their heads in wonder when Torf ordered them to take the fishermen the army had captured back to the mouth of the Spey where their boats lay beached. The captives felt equally bewildered when they arrived at the river and were set free. It didn't take long for them to get ship shape and a flotilla of ten boats headed east towards Buckie, Cullen, Soy and Banff. Sigurd gave orders to roof and wall the compound in the lower fort that had served as their prison; little more than a cattle pen, nothing of any value could be kept there. Commanders were to use any means possible to lure the Picts into a false sense of security. They needed to plant next year's crops. Only then would the hammer fall.

Sigurd had a longing to return to Orkney but too much was happening in his conquest and he abandoned any thought of returning there, even for a short visit. Orkney was secure and Magnus would make sure it remained that way. As a gesture, Sigurd sent three Longboats of timber with him to Kirkwall. They were loaded at the Horn of Find that stood a lot closer to the great forest than Torfness. There, timbers were driven into the soft mud and a loading platform took shape quickly. The bay offered shelter in all conditions and Norse called the place Findhorn. The building of infrastructure meant work for idle Picts and with work came reward; food, shelter and protection.

Dogs were in great demand, especially what the Picts called Terriers. They were killed and skinned to make creel floats, marking the lines of hooks now used for codfish. Surplus sheepdogs were also used before they grew too big and the float makers were kept busy as old floats rotted after one summer and had to be replaced, as skins weren't treated with anything except salt. Turned inside out, the hair was on the inside. Plugged both ends and legs tied they were blown up and another plug hammered into the centre of the first. Now local and Norse fishermen combined their skills with hook and line and fish were abundant.

Sigurd left Dornoch and headed for Ardersier with a light heart. The red-haired beauty had pledged an answer from her father but couldn't tell him when. To get her answer he would return to Dornoch or send a representative before the days grew short. That pleased Stroma and gave her plenty of time to convince her father that compromise was the only way to stop a war and retain his command of Carnavii lands of Caith. Ro-Sheen had informed Stroma that Caith was known to the Norse as Caithness and Torridon was now Torfness It seemed they stuck a Ness on the end of everything.

Together with Frazer and ten warriors, Stroma headed towards Dunbeath. She had left old Callum in command at Brora and Forbes at Dornoch with the Lugi workforce who were well pleased with the reward for their work. So too were Urquhart's fishermen and like those at Torfness, they were joined by some Norse who had lines of cotton and used lures instead of bait. Krike convinced them to use a Skiff and was soon in command, showing them the best places to cast their lines.

Sinclair knew well what had happened south as Stroma suspected he would but the severe tongue lashing she expected on arrival at Dunbeath failed to materialise. Welcoming her with open arms, Sinclair noted his little girl was little no longer, she had blossomed into something special.

She carried herself well and had two rings on her thigh that Sinclair wanted the story of before he revealed the source of his own knowledge of what was happening at Dornoch.

Stroma listened wide-eyed as Sinclair explained the Smertae had sent messengers to Dougal in Torrisdale. They had informed Dougal that the Norse had established trading posts at Tongue, Dornoch and Inver. Also, the Carnavii could use the trading post at Tongue in safety. There would be a truce between the Carnavii and the Smertae.

Stroma marvelled at this news; as far as she was concerned there was more chance of her father declaring a truce with the Norse than with the Smertae.

"It's a long way to Tongue," Sinclair cut into her thoughts and she looked at him. "The battle with the Smertae at the Skew; it's taken the fight out of them. Norse are running the show at Tongue. This new Chief the Smertae have, he's not half the man Drest was. Dougal says the half he's lost is the conniving half. Times have changed," he sighed.

Stroma was lost for words, but not Frazer.

"What about your council, will they agree to the Norse setting up a trading post at Thurso?" he asked.

"Tomorrow you'll find out," smiled Sinclair. "They're in Thurso. Tonight, we celebrate the homecoming of the Chief and make merry. It's time we had something merry to celebrate!"

Stroma suddenly saw her father in a different light. He had aged much since the death of Donal. He was also more approachable and seemed resigned to fate, something he had fought all his life, preaching 'Your fate is in your own hands.' Now, it seemed, his wasn't.

News that Stroma had returned spread quickly and warriors descended on Dunbeath knowing there would be a great celebration. They weren't disappointed; music and dance continued late into the night, for some until the sun came up, not however those who were going to Thurso. They gulped down a hair of the dog at daybreak and together with Brody, Stroma her warriors and Frazer set out across the moors.

It was noon before the Sea of the Dead came into view and the sight of the Orkney Islands beyond made Stroma catch her breath. Despite the calm conditions, the sea was white with broken water obscured in places by a smoke haze that rose above the settlement at Thurso.

Brody sounded a hunting horn as they descended and many people gathered out of curiosity to see who approached from the south. There was a great cheer when they recognised Stroma, and the cheers brought out more onlookers. By the time they entered the Stockade, many warriors appeared, welcoming Stroma like a Queen. She waved her bonnet in the air so energetically, the eagle feathers threatened to take flight.

Frazer grinned with satisfaction. It seemed the young Chief was as popular among the Carnavii as the Lugi and Brody encouraged the onlookers with his yelps. Stroma noted Brody appeared more upbeat than normal and had gone along with her father as if they had agreed on something before, she arrived. Fergus met the troop and ushered them into the great hall to eat, barking orders to the cook to get something rattled-up quickly.

Stroma found herself surrounded by warriors her own age and they wanted her life story. The females dragged her to a dwelling close by and told Fergus to go to hell!

"Women, dammit, dangerous beasts!" he scoffed and clasped Frazer in an embrace.

"It's been a long time, Fergus since we hunted Smertae," Frazer grinned.

"Aye, those were the days Frazer, when Smertae were real Smertae. But now they're tamed, it would be more like hunting a chicken than a wild cat," sighed Dougal.

"Frazer has come about a trading post for the Norse," Brody grinned and Fergus cocked his head.

"Aye! And would that be about the trading post in Tongue, Dornoch or *here*?" Dougal enquired with an air of sarcasm.

"Here!" Brody grinned and Frazer looked at him with suspicion.

"There's no trading post being built in Thurso," said Fergus. "They can build it at Scrabster. I want to see what they're doing from a distance, not on my doorstep."

"You've all discussed this and made your mind up long ago by the sound of things. Explain!" demanded Frazer.

"I'll explain but first I have to do something," Brody laughed and made his way to the dwelling where the women held Stroma captive. He threw the door open and received a torrent of abuse and a few impossible suggestions.

"Stroma! You can stay with the mad people. The council have agreed the trading post will be built at Scrabster," he yelled and banged the door shut. He headed back to the others with yelps of glee ringing in his ears.

"The Norse has us all by the balls, Frazer," moaned Fergus. "Nobody in their right mind thought they could take Torridon."

"We resist, we die," replied Frazer. "Alive, we might be humbled but not defeated. Torridon was defeated in battle, the North has not been defeated in battle, not yet. That's the difference between cooperation and defeat. We invite the Norse to trade but we keep control of our lands and our people. Let me tell you something you don't know, something we only found out a few days ago."

That got their full attention.

"Gather around," ordered Brody to his warriors who were waiting to eat. "At last we're going to get the full story."

Frazer had a captive audience. He began his story when the army went north suspecting the treachery of the Smertae; the battle at the Skew and his beheading of Drest. Also, the trickery they played on the

Norse with the horses when they joined with Stroma at Loch Fleet after the battle and the subsequent reappearance of the same horses at Mahomack, after taking them the long way over the Struie.

"The Helm Brody!" said Frazer. "That's where they launched the invasion of Torridon from. Stroma sent two messengers to Sinclair and they ran straight into the Norse army. We found one washed ashore and went to look."

Frazer explained what they discovered and the setting of the trap by Lugi warriors. When two Norse boats went back to the Helm in the night they were met with a shower of arrows in the dark. He described the funeral with all the fire ceremony and the mystery surrounding it that followed the return of the boats to Dornoch and his audience listened, spellbound.

"Urquhart's daughter, Sine, found out only a few days ago that the man who was killed was Sigurd's top commander, the Commander of his army, and the man who planned the invasion. His name was Frode! Two other commanders were killed but we can be sure we wouldn't be here now if the man named Frode wasn't killed. We owe our lives to an arrow in the dark and we'll never know who fired it," Frazer looked around at the silent faces and continued.

"The Norse would have taken the Lugi from the east first. Then they could have attacked the Decantae from two sides. He could have sailed half his force to Nigg Bay and come back overland. The Decantae would have thousands of warriors to their east and west, the Norse had enough boats to achieve that and if that was their plan, I think the outcome would have been a lot different than it is now. Make no mistake, this Sigurd didn't land on the North to set up trading posts, he came to conquer. Has he changed his mind? Or just delayed? That's the question you must keep uppermost in your minds. Don't give him reason to attack. Show no weakness and no aggression. We need peace and time. Do whatever you must to secure both," urged Frazer.

The hammering of a ladle on a pot made everybody jump and the cook roared to come and get food.

"Sinclair is sick; he won't last much longer," said Brody. "And Katrion demanded we address the situation before Stroma becomes Chief. She can't live in peace with the Norse on Lugi territory and fight them on Carnavii territory, and if she just fights them, we either have to move south or the Lugi have to come north. In either direction, the Norse will have all of Lugi lands or all of Carnavii lands. If a Trading post is all they want, it solves a big problem."

"One Chief of two tribes," said Fergus. "It might be a first and God knows where it would lead? The Smertae are buying wool and cloth from all around Torrisdale and trading with Dougal. It's too far from here but two wagons of wool went three days ago and there's enough wool to fill another ten besides what we'll keep, and many hides, deer and sealskins."

Frazer was taken aback; he had prepared for an argument, prepared to try to justify the setting up of a Norse Trading Post against all his principles. Now, it seemed they wanted one and had even selected a location for it.

Suddenly the hall erupted in an avalanche of flesh and long hair that raced towards the kitchen pushing the men aside, as Stroma and her entourage burst in creating pandemonium and rumps received slaps that only made their merriment worse.

Stroma was abandoned after they ate. Frazer had never seen her so happy and left her with her kin. Together with Brody and Fergus, they rode down to Scrabster, a short distance to the west. Frazer was all eyes; he had been to Torrisdale many times but never to Dunbeath or Thurso.

When they arrived at the chosen site, Frazer frowned. It was hemmed in by high ground. The beach looked small and what sand it had was only a thin strip between high and low water and very little above high water.

"What's your thought?" asked Brody, remaining mounted.

"Do you have a second choice?" said Frazer.

"Dunnet Bay to the east," Brody replied and swept his arm back towards Thurso.

"Let me look. I think they're too hemmed in here. They need space and if you don't give them space to build dwellings and support themselves, they won't be happy, and we have to keep them happy until we kill them," Frazer grinned and followed his hosts east.

Not far past Thurso to the east, a large bay opened up and Frazer knew immediately they had a site fit for purpose. It had everything and a large sandy beach. It wasn't boxed in and the land around it supported some sheep and only one small column of smoke came from a dwelling on the east shore.

The three riders headed down to the beach and traversed it at speed. A boat was hauled up onto the sand beside the dwelling with the smoke and Dougal went to the door and yelled inside. Nobody answered and he mounted again.

"They must be on the headland," he growled and spurred his horse east.

They hadn't gone far when they spotted two men doing something that Frazer noted with some curiosity. They were digging in a large, flat and thin rock, standing it upright beside a line of similar slabs. Some stood as high as the man's chest and were both unusual and impressive.

"Shelter for the sheep in the winter," explained Brody. "The slabs are easy to get and do the job.

"I'll speak to them," said Fergus, dismounting. "You stay here or go look around before they start asking questions."

Frazer followed Brody east until they crested a low rise and Brody pointed.

"That land furthest out to sea is the island of Stroma. Now you know where she got her name. It means island in the stream and it's well named."

Frazer stared at the Island and asked if anybody lived there.

"No," replied Brody. "It's the closest to the Norse and cut off most of the time. The weather has to be calm before anybody goes there and even then, they have to stay clear of the whirling water when the tides are strong. The olds used to fish there and stay for long spells, but no more," he sighed.

They heard a noise behind them and turned to see Dougal galloping towards them and he was smiling.

"The brothers agree the Norse can set up a trading post in Dunnet Bay. Ten sheep is the price."

Dougal grinned and Brody gave him a cynical look.

"How much did they ask for?"

"Fifty but I convinced them they would be surrounded with the ones Frazer calls Shield Maidens and they dropped the price. We go back!" Dougal urged and led the way.

They spent the night at Thurso and Stroma mingled with her kin while Brody and Frazer drew a map on sealskin, the tattooist then ran over their lines with blue ink. It was an official document and had to be produced on the arrival of the first Longboat to enter the bay, with only one Longboat allowed to enter at one time. That restriction would be lifted when Sinclair saw fit and not before.

Any agreement was more than Frazer or Stroma had expected but this was far more extensive. Frazer watched as Fergus and Brody made their marks on the map. The marks of Stroma and Sinclair would seal the deal and it would be sent to Sigurd in Torfness on their return to Dornoch.

"Come! My island in the Sea of the Dead. If you stay with them any longer, you'll be dead," Frazer grinned and Stroma groaned.

# Chapter 28

Tusk looked at Innes and the warriors who accompanied her and drew his Dirk.

"The harvest is gathered, the hunting begins!" he bellowed. "Go!" and drove the Dirk into the tabletop.

There was an outburst of joy and excitement and warriors scattered in all directions to prepare for the hunt, knowing full well Norse were high on the list next to red Stags. Tusk had held them back for months now they were let loose but with a warning.

"You bring ten deer back here before you look at any Norse. Get your hunting skills back, you've been farmers for too long to fight. Bring back the deer. If you can't kill deer, the Norse will massacre you," said Tusk.

He was right, nobody had lifted a weapon in anger for months including him and he went with the hunters towards the mountains.

Those who ridiculed his warning soon realised the wisdom of it. After three days in the mountains, they had only managed to kill one deer. The herds gathered above the treeline and getting within bowshot was difficult; those who managed that feat failed to hit their target and cursed themselves. Tusk was merciless and drove them hard enough that the first deer had been consumed before the second one fell. Now they were alert and their senses had returned. Three more stags fell in the next three days and Tusk returned with three deer and a smile on his face, revealing his famed tusks.

He commanded warriors to come back with another six or stay on the mountains. Tusk had used the upheaval of the harvest to inject several spies into Torridon and Cluny. No Picts were allowed inside the Fort but the settlement outside the mounds thrived and traders abounded.

The young who had been thrust together at Torfness soon spoke both languages and the Monks had also risen to the challenge. So too had many Norse mothers who had to mingle at the market and trade with both Pict and Norse, especially for fowl, eggs and milk. Most of the trading was barter and very little silver changed hands.

The Skiff that took the sealskin from Sinclair to Sigurd had two most unlikely passengers aboard, one was acting as courier, Krike. With him came the beautiful warrior, Ainslee. They had left Mahomack at first light and would return the same day. The weather and wind were perfect for the crossing in both directions. Krike had been given the cold shoulder by all the Skiff commanders and knew he had to change strategy. This he did and when he appeared with his daughter, Ainslee, the commanders were throwing their boats at him to get close to her.

Who better than to take it across the Firth than father and daughter? He had to bribe Ainslee with two silver coins. A fortune Krike grumped but she had the desired effect and not only with the Skiff commanders, Torf also appeared fascinated by her.

Sigurd spread the skin out and compared it with his maps of Pictland Fjord. Ro-Sheen was amazed that the Smertae and the Carnavii had also declared a truce and were trading at Tongue. Krike had informed her as they waited for Sigurd and his commanders to make a decision.

The decision wasn't made hastily and they discussed the advantages and disadvantages of such a location concerning tide and wind. Sigurd ordered Ro-Sheen to take his guests to eat while they mulled over this new site. The land indicated looked generous and included the entire headland but whether good land or bad was unknown.

Krike could hardly contain himself. He needed to get outside to the battlements. What he had seen briefly was a mere glimpse of what Torridon had become under its new name and he knew his way around.

"You eat, I'm going to get some fresh air," he announced and left Ainslee with Ro-Sheen.

Norse warriors dressed in mail and armed stared at him as he went up the steps to the battlements, but none challenged him. Krike stared in every direction then concentrated his gaze on the Clarkley Hill where the Norse army had established their camp. The encampment was vast. Below on the beach, eight Longboats were hauled up at the slappy and another three at anchor. People thronged on both beaches, east and west, and smoke poured from beyond the mounds where he couldn't see. Torridon had grown and the Fort remained undamaged as Ross had predicted. That fact alone made Krike shake his head in wonder.

His sight-seeing spree came to a sudden halt when Ro-Sheen called his name.

"Sigurd wants you!" she announced and waved for him to come.

Sigurd was on his own and he smiled when Krike appeared. He spoke to Ro-Sheen and in his hand, he held a small wooden box.

"Sigurd says the commanders accept the location for a trading post and one Longboat will visit the bay within the next ten days," she interpreted.

Sigurd opened the small box and showed Krike the contents. He stared first at the gold bangles then at Sigurd who said something to Ro-Sheen.

"These are for the two young Chiefs. One is for Stroma the other is for Sine. Sigurd hopes these are the only Norse circles they will wear in the future," Ro-Sheen grinned.

Krike didn't know what to say and stared at the intricate Norse artistry. Some resembled Pict designs and they were beautiful, not chunky, just slender and feminine. Just what two sword-wielding Pict warriors would want, ran through his mind and he smiled broadly at their reaction to this peace offering.

Sigurd spoke again and Krike was glad of it.

"Sigurd says your daughter is very beautiful and is welcome in Torfness as are you," said Ro-Sheen and Ainslee blushed.

"We must return to Mahomack," said Krike. "We took three hours to get here and I expect three to get back. Tell Sigurd I want one of his little boats when he's finished with them," Krike chanced his luck.

When Ro-Sheen translated, Sigurd laughed and gave Krike a hefty slap on the back as he walked him to the door.

Ro-Sheen went with them to the ledge and waited there until the Skiff left. She looked longingly towards the north and wished she was going with them. She sighed in resignation and headed for the abbey, there was teaching to be done.

Ainslee hadn't spoken since arriving at the Fort. Now she stared up at the massive walls in wonder.

"How? How did the Norse manage to defeat the Fort? It's

impossible," she muttered to Krike.

"Aye, that's what we thought. How is what we would all like to know. We know how they got inside, but where they came from, we can only guess. They speak of a place called Hell's Hole; it's a cave close by, but I've never been there," Krike grunted and looked as several dolphins raced towards their plaything.

Stroma and Frazer had stayed at Dornoch and awaited the return of the Skiff. Sigurd had changed his mind about taking Astrid with him and the reason was by her side, Forbes! Stroma took note but kept her opinions to herself. Uppermost in her mind was the health of her father. Next was whether the Carnavii offering of a trading site would be accepted or rejected by the Norse and when she heard the horn announcing the return of the Skiff, she joined a line of Norse to welcome it back.

Krike made his way to her quickly and he was beaming.

"All good! Sigurd accepts the site, and he wants to seal the deal with this," Krike grinned and handed Stroma the bracelet.

She stared at it in amazement. It was pure gold and sparkling. Frazer stared at it over her shoulder and he too was impressed.

"He hopes that's the only Norse ring you wear in the future," Krike grinned.

"A bribe!" said Stroma and slid the bracelet onto her wrist. "Sine will be jealous," as she inspected the engravings.

"No, she won't, he sent one for her. He must have seen your matching Dirks and decided you should have matching bracelets." Krike showed her the second bracelet still in the box.

Stroma took it out and compared the two and as Krike said, they were a matching pair.

"Can we go across to Tain? I want to give her this," she said.

"No problem, Ainslee has many Skiffs, don't you?" Krike laughed and whacked her on the rump.

If Ainslee had little to say before, she made up for it now. She unleashed an account of her great adventure to eager ears as they headed west.

On the Black Isle, the crops were also gathered, and losses were minimal. Like most of the crops flattened by the freak storm they had time to stand erect again and what couldn't stand received help. Three times the Norse picked up trade goods from Chanonry Point and they seemed to get great pleasure from trips there. Hamish told them what they could get in return and barter took place on the beach. He had samples of his wares with him and bales of cloth foreign to all grew in demand, along with farm tools and skins of animals equally unfamiliar.

Sheena took a back seat and stayed far away. Reluctant to take her eyes off the Norse across the water, she still had commitments to old Urquhart and shared her time between Cromarty Village and Avoch. Her companions never strayed far from her side and as the temperatures began to drop, Sheena was glad to see them wearing some clothes. She also covered up after a short spell running free, as Adair described their way of life.

Tarbat dealt quickly with any squabbles and a few new graves sprung up around the Stockade at Inverness. Anybody armed crossing the river found themselves confronted by Norse warriors with orders to kill them if they resisted. After several Norse and several Picts lay dead, the message spread; trading continued across the river in the same way it was undertaken at Chanonry Point and peace prevailed.

Along the well-trodden track between Huntley and the River Spey, an arrow fired at the back of the last mounted warrior on the Norse patrol, hit the rump of his horse with such force it sliced the hide of the horse before burying itself deep into the rider's thigh. The horse bucked wildly, sending the rider high into the air then bolted between the two in front. It reared and lashed out with its forelegs unseating one rider and knocking another horse and rider over, before bolting back, the way it had come.

Several more arrows were fired into the melee hitting two Norse warriors and several horses, sending them wild and crashing into others. The troop spurred their horses away from bowshot and arrows followed them. The Norse stopped and re-grouped. Staring into the forest they could see no movement but charged with swords drawn. They didn't penetrate far before they were brought to a halt by thick foliage that defied vision and access. In disarray, they retreated and tended the wounded having to kill one horse with a broken leg.

They assessed the damage; two warriors were badly wounded, three others had flesh wounds. Counting the horse that had bolted back towards Huntly, they had lost only two horses and decided to press on towards the Spey before dark. Searching for Picts in the forest had proven deadly many times, and despite repeated requests to do just that, the commander ordered his patrol forward at the gallop. The Norse Patrols had made a track where no track had existed, and they could move fast.

On arrival at the Spey, four of the five hundred set up camp, the other hundred galloped towards Lochindorb. The commander felt convinced Tusk was responsible for the attack and travelling fast, they could cut off his men and kill them, if they could stop them from getting onto the Island. This strategy made more sense than searching a forest on horseback as Picts would have left their horses far away in a safe place and run to them on foot.

The Norse were out of luck; they were doing exactly what Tusk had predicted and Innes swung her band of twenty south, heading them for Loch Morlich, not Lochindorb and Tusk had the rest of his people safely in the Stockade before the Norse arrived. His warriors taunted them when they did arrive, and it became obvious to the commanders they had been tricked.

When the party arrived with two who had already died and one with poison spreading down his arm, Sigurd flew into a fit of rage. His ego had sustained a serious blow along with his false belief that he had achieved total victory and crushed the Picts. His first instinct was to round up Pict warriors and execute them, but Sigurd was a man who thought things through carefully before making rash decisions. He slammed the door on his chamber and stayed inside for half a day.

Now in control of his emotions, Sigurd summoned all his commanders and the commander of the patrol. He gave his account of the attack in detail and said he was convinced Tusk was behind it as the Stockade looked well-prepared for the arrival of the Norse warriors. There was no doubt in his mind.

"Cowards! They strike from the rear and run," said Sigurd. "This Tusk must be killed. Take steps to protect our warriors; split the patrols, avoid any places where an attack can be launched. Do something until we can come up with a way to lure this coward out into the open."

What he asked for could not be delivered easily. The forest was vast and the terrain rugged. Marching warriors would take weeks not days and try as they might, the ambushes went on with the loss of one or two warriors and some horses, but the fleeing attackers avoided every attempt to intercept and kill them.

Large flocks of geese were on the Laich and the weather had turned cold. It wouldn't be long before the snow fell and with it, the patrols would lessen. So too would the attacks. That was Sigurd's hope, but he also knew that when the deer came down from the mountains, his warriors had to hunt and expose themselves even more to Tusk's killers. He considered the options on Tusk. Kill him, he would be a martyr. Let him live to kill Norse, he would become a hero and a rallying point for rebellion. A defeat by him in open battle was unthinkable. Defeating him in open battle was impossible. Sigurd had to devise a strategy to degrade Tusk before he killed him.

One month passed before the next attack that saw eight Norse dead. A hunting party had strayed too far from the protection of the patrol and were massacred. They were also beheaded and their horses and weapons were stolen. With many mouths to feed at Torfness, salvation came from the west from the Black Isle and Inverness. As the temperature dropped and deer became more abundant on the lower slopes, entire carcases were traded instead of just the skins and taken by Longboat to Torfness, sometimes as many as twenty deer at any one time and the trade in meat soared by the time the first snow fell.

Hunting parties no longer needed to go into Tusk territory, and as a show of contempt, Sigurd ordered his warriors to wear their shields on their backs. A move that didn't go unnoticed by the Picts who watched them, then the rumour spread that Tusk was a coward and only attacked the Norse from the back. Sigurd had listened to Ro-Sheen, scarcely believing what she was mad about and she had to repeat herself several times before he grasped the seriousness of her accusations.

"If the Picts hate one thing more than the Norse, it's back-stabbers!" she raged. "I know my tribe has been accused of backstabbing for eternity that's why people hate Smertae. When Picts wear shields on their backs, it's an insult to us."

Ro-Sheen fumed and once she explained, Sigurd knew what he had to do. With Ro-Sheen and the Monks' help, his propaganda machine went into action and word was spread that Tusk was a back-stabber and a coward.

When the accusation reached Tusk, he laughed it off. As far as he was concerned, he had won this round; no longer did Norse hunt in his territory. He had no idea they had another source of deer meat and dismissed the rumours for what they were. They wouldn't fight him, so they tried to destroy his reputation. They were the cowards.

Ro-Sheen came to Sigurd and told him there was some trouble among the Picts, but she didn't know the cause of it.

"They want to go to the black stack on the mound outside the Fort and your warriors have stopped them, is all I know. Can I go and find out what they want?" she asked.

"Yes! Go. I'm curious. What do they want with a fire stack? Maybe they need to send a signal to their Bull God because nobody else will see it!"

Ro-Sheen went to the third mound with the warrior who had brought the news to the Fort. She found ten Pict warriors who were obviously frustrated with something.

She frowned when they explained that in three days, the New Year would fall, and they had to perform a fire ceremony that had been performed for so long nobody could remember how it started. They had to do it because it had always been done and they were afraid if they didn't, something bad would happen. The black stack was where the thing they called a Clavie would be burnt to cinders and the stack would also be set ablaze. There was a hole on top of the stack that the stalk of this creation fitted into and they wanted to make sure it was clear. They also wanted Sigurd's permission to build the Clavie and they needed a barrel.

It was all too much for Ro-Sheen to take in and she asked who the leader was? The Clavie King they corrected.

A balding man with many tattoos on his head stepped forward and Ro-Sheen shouted at the Norse warriors to let him through.

"You, come with me and explain to Sigurd what it is you want," Ro-Sheen instructed and led him back to Sigurd who frowned and looked at Torf.

"This will be interesting," murmured Torf.

"Draw a picture for Sigurd, showing what you are speaking about, because I don't know what your words are in his language," said Ro-Sheen, handing the Clavie King a piece of charcoal for him to draw with on the tabletop.

"He asks for a barrel. They will build something he will draw," she interpreted and the two Norse watched curiously as this strange thing took shape.

The Clavie King spoke as he drew, and she announced that when it was set on fire, warriors carried it around the settlement on their heads. They light it at sunset on New Year's Eve, every year at the same place. Then it follows a strict route."

The Clavie King quickly drew out the route and they recognised the lie of the land and nodded.

"Then it goes up onto the black stack and is burned to destruction. Only after this fire ceremony can the New Year be celebrated with music and dance."

"Tell him that to ask Norse to play with fire, is like asking a seal if it likes fish. Tell him to build it well and make sure he gets a barrel. Prepare some fire bundles Torf, it looks like we're going to have a celebration," laughed Sigurd and Ro-Sheen passed on his words to a grateful Clavie King.

"Come, Torf, we go and look at this black stack. I thought it was where they set a signal fire between Stockades, but I didn't see another one at Cluny," urged Sigurd and they followed the Clavie King through the Doorie Gate and up the mound. The Clavie King climbed on top of the stone structure and cleaned out the hole.

"It's clean and ready," he announced and jumped down.

Sigurd and Torf walked around the structure and couldn't see anything suspicious; it was just a rounded stone stack, shoulder high and blackened by fire.

"Go with him and get whatever he wants," Sigurd ordered Ro-Sheen. "Traditions are vital, theirs and ours. So, is religion and we must encourage both."

News that the Clavie would go ahead spread fast through the Picts and soon the children of the Norse were getting equally excited. Consequently, by the time the large square nail was driven into the stalk through the bottom of the barrel, as many Norse had gathered as Picts. Ro-Sheen's siblings pleaded with her to take them around with the Clavie and get some burnt bits which were said to be lucky, and she agreed. The Monks declined and shut the Abbey Door firmly. They were taking no part in a heathen ceremony, but the Norse flocked to see the lighting in droves.

Just after sunset, the barrel was lit. Slowly at first, the fire took hold and cheers rang out with every splash of oil that sent flames shooting skyward. More and more staves of barrels were fixed around the interior of the burning core and more oil poured into the centre. When it was well alight and billowing black smoke, they hoisted the Clavie onto a warrior's head with two more supporting it by the staves on each side. With screaming children on their shoulders, the mass procession headed down the slappy and across the bows of the beached boats then turned up to go around the route the Clavie King had drawn for Sigurd.

Many warriors inside the Fort waited, catching only glimpses of what was to come, and they cheered wildly when at last the procession headed towards them, spewing burning embers amongst the followers who scrambled to pick up bits that they could hold, and many hands were singed beyond bearing.

Sigurd stood on the battlements and surveyed the scene. Ro-Sheen with her handful of youngsters was let inside and joined him and the commanders, who immediately lifted the impatient children onto their shoulders, much to her relief. There was a time of small fire as the Clavie was lifted onto the Stone Stack and the stalk secured in the hole with wedges, then the barrel was re-stocked with fresh staves and showered with more oil that sent flames soaring high into the night sky.

This brought roars of encouragement from Norse and Pict alike until the Clavie King mounted the fiery stack and started hammering the barrel with what looked like an axe turned sideways. A gush of roasting hot oil spewed from the barrel and erupted in flames making the Clavie King jump for his life and immediately the Black Stack erupted in flames.

The onlookers were spellbound and children's shrill screams of excitement filled the air. Again and again, the barrel was attacked until at last it resembled a limp and defeated warrior with an arm dangling by his side.

Sigurd shouted to the warriors below him and they headed up the mound that was full of people and they started clearing them off the mound. The reason why became evident shortly afterwards when the first fire bundle was thrown into the dying flames and it erupted in a fire that spread down the mound at speed, igniting several more fire bundles on its way and within a few breaths, the entire section of the mound was ablaze, the heat hit the battlements and hands were held out to warm. More fire bundles erupted on top of the mound and the roar of the flames was equal only to the roars of the onlookers.

"The Picts had their fire and we had ours. Now they party and so do we!" Sigurd roared down to his warriors and a great cheer went up. "Let this continue, it's good for the soul, Torf," he said, smiling.

"So is the Pict firewater, and it comes in a barrel as well," laughed Torf.

The Clavie proved to be a great binder and was spoken about by Pict and Norse for many days. Burnt embers were in many dwellings and the black stack took on new meaning.

Winter had been kind at first, but when it came it came with a vengeance. Nothing moved on land or sea for many days and the snow covered all the mountains to the north, the south and the west. Patrols were scaled back and those that continued didn't stray far from the coast that remained free of snow, but ice could be a death sentence for both horses and riders and progress was slow. All the Longboats were pulled out of the water and work on them continued at a leisurely pace, stopping for the bad weather. The only thing in Torfness that continued at full tilt was the incessant hammering of the Smiths in the lower fort and the pile of Leg Irons grew steadily, as did stories around fires and back-stabbing became a favourite topic.

One year less one moon since the great fleet left the Helm, planting of the new crops began in earnest and a bustle of activity erupted all around Torfness and beyond.

It was time to put Sigurd's plan into action. They had circulated rumours that he had challenged Tusk to open battle with forty of his warriors against forty of Tusk's and the coward Tusk had refused to fight. Tusk went mad when he heard the news and denied any such challenge had reached him. News of Tusk's reaction circulated until it reached Sigurd.

The stage was set, and Sigurd knew if he couldn't prize the wolf from its lair with weapons, he might succeed with pride. He had discussed his strategy with his commanders, and they were eager to participate. He sent Ro-Sheen to assemble as many Pict warriors as she could find at the Slappy and together with Torf, he went there to address them.

"Tell them I want two strong young warriors to take a message from me to Tusk," he instructed Ro-Sheen and the reaction was instant, with many yelling to go.

"They are to tell Tusk that again, I challenge him to open battle. He will take forty warriors, I will take forty warriors to a place of his choice. If Tusk triumphs, he will rule this land. If I triumph, I will rule this land and his," proclaimed Sigurd, and Ro-Sheen translated.

Uproar followed and a fight broke out between two warriors. Sigurd grinned and once the fighters were separated, he pointed to them. They will both go, give them horses and food."

The warriors bowed in gratitude.

"Our warriors will escort them to the edge of the moor," relayed Ro-Sheen. "They will go to Tusk and return to their escort with his answer."

Now no doubt lay in Pict minds, the Norse had challenged Tusk and he had refused to fight. The rule of the land was at stake and if Tusk won, they would be free. He had to fight, or they would turn against him. Sigurd was delighted with this information which Ro-Sheen gleaned from angry comments.

At the edge of Dava Moor, the two messengers left the hundred-strong escort and headed south as fast as the terrain allowed. Tusk's lookouts spotted the riders long before they cleared the Moor and when they reached the edge of the western forest, they were confronted by ten warriors painted for battle.

They hurriedly explained their mission and were escorted by five warriors towards Lochindorb, the other five remained on the lookout. Tusk was warned of their approach and as no alarm had been sounded by the approaching warriors, he relaxed. They reined in beside a longhouse and Tusk eyed the two warriors. His first thoughts were that they come to join him; that wasn't unusual.

"Tusk, we bring a message from Sigurd. He says he wants an answer this time," announced one warrior, with a smirk on his face.

"Get down off your horse!" roared Tusk.

The Warrior ignored him and went to speak again then something cold and sharp rested on the side of his neck and he quickly left the saddle.

"Now, say that again!" Tusk demanded and approached him.

"Sigurd has a message and he wants an answer," said the warrior and shifted uneasily.

"You missed *'this time*!" Tusk bellowed and grabbed the warrior by the throat, then leered into his face and whispered menacingly, "there has been no other time."

Tusk let go and stood back. The warrior was shaken and showed it.

"Sigurd challenges you and forty warriors to fight him and forty Norse warriors in open battle," he explained, his voice noticeably more humble. "You win, you will rule. He wins, he will rule. You have his word of honour. He asks you to name the time and a place."

"That's better," Tusk growled and turned his back on the messenger.

He went into the longhouse and didn't re-appear for some time, but when he did, he was smiling, revealing his tusk in all its glory.

"You tell Sigurd he has my word of honour. We will do battle on the stubble field at Dallas, in four days from now, at noon. He should know where Dallas is, he destroyed it. If he doesn't, you know where it is, so take him there. Noon in four days; be gone!" Tusk yelled and the messenger mounted quickly.

The lookouts went with them to the edge of the Moor and they parted ways. The messengers were glad to be away from Tusk and laughed nervously as they headed north.

The escort of one hundred warriors had orders to take the messengers straight into the Fort and not allow them contact with any Picts before that. Sigurd heard of their approach and the messengers relayed Tusk's answer to Ro-Sheen with big smiles on their faces. Their smiles were not as big as Sigurd's and Torf's when Ro-Sheen passed on the news. They waited until the messengers were led away before erupting in celebration.

Fed and watered, the two messengers were taken to a small room under the battlements. It had a ring on the wall and when the door closed behind them, a lock secured it. Here, Sigurd ordered they would remain. If word got out about this battle, Picts would descend on the battlefield in droves. That had to be avoided.

At Lochindorb, spirits rose to great heights. Tusk could hardly believe his luck and his warriors were running around like madmen. They would have gone that moment to Dallas to do battle and they had no fear of the Norse. However, Innes brought a word of caution into their euphoria.

"It might be a trap or trickery, father?"

"Aye, now you're thinking like I thought," he replied. "If he had trickery in mind, he would have chosen the place, not me! The field in Dallas has forest close by on two sides and the moor on one side. He can only come from the west and our men will go into positions where they can see his horse coming from a long way. Any sign of trickery will be revealed before he gets to Dallas. Long before," he assured her.

"Tomorrow we select forty of the fittest warriors. They'll fight and get fit for three days. No mercy, I want them angry and we need to work on a strategy whether we fight in a cluster, four clusters of ten, or two lines of twenty. We need them drilled to know what they're going to do before we get there," Tusk said sternly.

Unlike Tusk, Sigurd and his commanders knew exactly what their battle plan was and the warriors who would do battle had already been selected. The theory was agreed upon but couldn't be put into practice until the time was right for Tusk to accept the challenge. Now, like Tusk, they had three full days to perfect their strategy and Sigurd told his commanders to muster the warriors at daybreak.

"Woden's day at noon! It's an omen, Torf. The god of victory smiles on us," laughed Sigurd.

Tusk dispatched spies to seek out the forest and the approaches to Dallas. The nearest Norse army was at Cluny and it was also put under observation. The forest all the way to Dallas was combed for any sign of anything suspicious and nothing was found. Vantage points along the track offered a view of any approaching horses and two spies were positioned there with instructions to count Sigurd's horses and make sure he was sticking to the agreed amount, then get back to Tusk at the field.

On Woden's day morning, Tusk assembled his warriors at the side of the Loch and again they checked their weapons. Most carried swords and dirks had been given by those who were left behind. Most warriors had two, one he would hold in the same hand as his shield, the other in his belt. Several had battle-axes they had taken from dead Norse as well as their swords and dirks.

The warriors were eager to go but Tusk was in no hurry and insisted they part company with their kin in an orderly way. He took Innes aside and her eyes said what she didn't dare ask.

"If we don't come back, you must make peace with this Sigurd," he ordered in a final voice. "Promise me!"

"I promise, father, but you will come back!" she forced a smile and gave Tusk a rare hug.

Tusk looked up at the sun then ruffled her hair, gently. When he made for his horse, they all followed and mounted. As Tusk led them north, the world behind them erupted into battle cries that made the hairs on their necks stand on end and those doing battle joined the crescendo as they picked up the pace. Eyes stared north; they didn't look back as was the way when going into battle.

Tusk wanted to be first on the field of battle but slowed his warriors, not wanting to be too early and they had plenty of time. For most of the way across the Dava, they spread out across the heather and cantered, disturbing many grouse that burst into flight before the blue swathe that yelped and howled as they neared the battlefield. Tusk was coming from the south, Sigurd from the north. Tusk would position his warriors at the east end of the battlefield. This would allow the Norse a clear run to their deaths.

Three riders came towards Tusk as they neared the site and reported no sign of Norse within the forest. Fifty Norse riders had come to look at the battlefield two days previously, then left. Since then, no Norse had come south of Cluny.

"When the lookouts come from the track, you will all go. I don't want even one man close to us or him," Tusk barked.

They reached the edge of the stubble field that Tusk knew hadn't been burned before being ploughed. His warriors had gathered the crop from here as nobody had returned to the destroyed buildings and the yield was great.

They dismounted at the east end and horses were led well away from the field of battle. There was much to do, and warriors tied one another's long hair tightly behind their heads. Those who wore skins and wool peeled off to the waist and swung their swords to loosen muscles. They had no fear and confidence soared, knowing the Norse feared them, more than they feared the Norse. Most of the many circles on the warriors represented Norse heads.

Two gallopers came into view at the west end of the field and galloped towards Tusk whooping loudly and waving their arms in the air. They were his lookouts from the track, and they reined in with great smiles on their faces.

"They come! And they come slowly with their shields on their backs. They don't trust you Tusk!" the spokesman yelled and laughter erupted.

It was a source of ridicule that warriors would protect their backs and leave their fronts exposed but it was also an insult that angered many. Tusk included.

"How far?" he demanded.

"Half a mile."

"Begone, all of you!" Tusk barked and waved his sword in the direction of south.

The spies didn't want to leave but Tusk had threatened to execute any that stayed within sight of the battlefield and the five of them left quickly.

"Stay close when we turn," Sigurd screamed at his warriors and the manoeuvre was executed exactly as they had practised.

At the first sight of the Norse, the Picts went further out into the field of battle and started hammering their swords on their shields. Tusk had two groups of twenty and they mingled as battle cries filled the air.

Sigurd halted his warriors a bow shot from the blue masses and shouted,

"Twenty left, twenty right!"

"He's counting you. A sign of fear!" Tusk scorned and watched as the Norse walked towards them.

They had to dismount to get their shields off their backs and Tusk judged where they would stop but when they walked on, alarm bells started ringing.

Sigurd stopped again only ten horse lengths in front of Tusk's warriors and raised his sword high.

"Frode! Frode!" reverberated through the forest and Tusk stared in disbelief as shields disappeared from riders' backs and he saw two legs on one side of a horse.

"Treachery! Treachery! Kill two each!" was all he managed to get out before the mass of charging horses made him and his warriors scatter in panic.

Sigurd's forty horse rode through them at speed with sword and axe taking down what the thundering hooves of his horses missed. Behind him, forty weapon-wielding warriors with shields fell on the stunned Picts with a vengeance. The horses wheeled around, riders dismounted and raced back to attack the Picts from behind. Tusk's warriors fought like demons, the treachery of the Norse made them fight with great anger and the clash of weapons resounded above the cries of "Frode!" and the battle cries of the Picts.

Outnumbered two to one, the battle raged and the stubble turned red. Tusk looked for the bastard who broke his word and that was a mistake. A blade sliced into his bicep and he dropped his sword. He grabbed a Dirk and plunged it into his attacker's face then dropped to his knees as an axe cleaved through his shoulder and blood spurted from his mouth. A warrior saw Tusk die but followed his orders to take two each and he was on his second two before he was slashed at from all sides and died beside his Chief.

One by one the Picts were slain taking a great toll on Norse with them to the land of the dead. Soon few stood on the battlefield as warriors sank to their knees exhausted, Sigurd among them and they fought for breath.

A hand fell on Sigrid's shoulder and he looked up.

"Find me the Tusk, I want his head," Sigurd muttered to a patrol commander.

A shout brought Sigurd to his feet and many more stood up. Only then did he realise how many men he had lost. He went to where the commander pointed and looked at the body of Tusk. He had died well and many of Sigurd's warriors lay around him.

Sigurd took an axe offered and severed Tusk's head with two blows. He lifted the head high.

"Now you can take revenge!" Sigurd roared.

His warriors beheaded every Pict, adding great pools of blood to the already sodden ground. Sigurd tied Tusk's head by its hair to his saddle and led his horse back to join commanders and warriors, busy with the same grisly tasks.

"Get the Pict horses and tie our dead to them. Leave the Picts where they fell. After we bury the dead where we agreed, we will return to Torfness along the beach, in triumph!" ordered Sigurd.

Satisfied all was ready, Sigurd mounted his horse and let out a yelp of pain as something sharp pierced the inside of his right thigh.

"You're dead!" Sigurd screamed at the head and lashed Tusk across the face with his reins. "He bit me! The wolf bit me!" Sigurd roared with laughter and the others joined him.

It was late afternoon before a horn on the battlements alerted Torf to warriors advancing from the direction of Findhorn. He narrowed his eyes and could just make out a black mass of horses coming along the beach.

He swiftly led two hundred mounted warriors to the Slappy and ordered them onto the beach. The tide was low and they picked up speed as they followed the low water line west, instigating Sigurd's next plan of action. If they were Picts riding towards Torfness, he would defeat them on the beach before they got near.

He crossed what the Picts called the Millie Burn and didn't stop to let horses drink. He urged his warriors on without taking his eyes off the approaching column and they were closing the distance fast.

Soon the large, round shields came into view and a pang of apprehension shot through Torf as if re-living a nightmare. He knew who the shields belonged to but who held them now? He had lived this uncertainty after the great battle and shuddered at the memory.

Torf halted his warriors by tall cliffs of sand and waited. If they were Picts they would stop and most likely take formation across the width of the beach, but they didn't stop. Suddenly a warrior with better eyes than him shouted,

"Sigurd!"

More voices joined the chorus at every stride of the galloping column until all were shouting his name and then they started chanting,

"Frode! Frode!" echoing the voices of the returning victorious warriors.

There was no holding the warriors back on either side and they met with great cheer, mingling with severed heads held high and covered in Pict blood; the victorious drowned in the praise of their companions and Torf made for Sigurd who was hard to find in the uproar.

"He's uglier than I thought," laughed Torf as Sigurd stroked the hair of his trophy.

"He bit me when he was dead. This is a prize wolf!" laughed Sigurd and they galloped to their welcome at full speed.

Word spread among the Picts that the Norse were returning. They knew of the challenge but neither the place nor the time. Tusk's head sealed the victory for the Norse, along with the heads of another forty displayed on spear points for all to see. The two messengers detained were released and shown the head of Tusk before they were let out of the Fort. Now they would spread the word of Sigurd's victory and one spat at Tusk for failing them.

Cattle were killed on the high ground and great feasting took place. They had crushed the last bastion of resistance and succeeded in delivering total victory. Sigurd had no qualms about tricking Tusk; as far as he was concerned, the man had brought about his own downfall by attacking his warriors from behind. It wasn't until Norse warriors started wearing their Shields on their backs, that the idea of two warriors on one horse came to him. A warrior could hide behind a shield and remain hidden until the horses stopped but only with discipline.

That was what Sigurd's warriors had practised for three days. Their training was savage and disciplined. He knew one mistake would result in the Picts charging him. He also knew if he hadn't tricked them, Tusk would have been victorious. Even outnumbered two to one, the Picts had killed more than thirty of his warriors and badly injured many more. With the help of the garrison at Cluny, they buried the Norse dead on the Battlefield close to the Kinloss Burn. Their souls would be among those who died there. They had learned of their resting place before the battle and were honoured.

Sigurd dispatched Tusk's head, to ram home to the Picts that their champion was no match for the Norse. Nobody had any idea what the cost had been to the Norse or that Tusk had been tricked and after a few days, nobody cared. News of Tusk's defeat spread throughout the surrounding area and beyond like wildfire. Warriors bearing their trophies of severed heads paraded again through Torfness but if the Norse had any intention of intimidating the Picts, they were very wrong. The Picts remained unfazed by such a parade and saw it as part of life. Hens laid eggs; warriors took heads it was normal. What wasn't normal was the amount of spitting at the heads for failing their people.

The victorious revelled in victory and the blood of their enemies stained all for many days as something they wore with pride. It wasn't until four days after the battle that Ro-Sheen noticed Sigurd favouring his left leg after all the celebration and drinking had driven her to seek shelter in the dwelling with her two sisters.

"What's wrong with your right leg?" she asked.

"It's nothing only a scratch where the Wolf bit me," he assured her, and she left it at that.

She had heard the story of Tusk's attack after death many times and had stayed clear of the warriors and Sigurd when they were celebrating, as many fights broke out when they drank whiskey. That was why she had gone to sleep with her two sisters and they made her welcome.

Two days later, she alerted Torf that Sigurd wasn't well. He wasn't eating and stayed in bed; he had also shouted at her to get out, something he had never done and she was concerned.

Torf went to Sigurd's quarters grinning, the effects of the celebrations were endemic but worse on some than others. His grin soon vanished when he looked at Sigurd, he was white, shivering and groaning. Torf pulled back his covering and cursed aloud when he saw the great red welt on the inside of Sigurd's thigh; black around the middle, fluid was trickling from the wound. Torf ran to get the Monks, almost knocking Ro-Sheen over in his haste. She stepped inside and gasped when she saw the wound then ran, without stopping to the market area, bought a honeycomb and butter then rushed back to the Fort.

Two Monks were attending Sigurd and when they saw what Ro-Sheen had come with they took it and ran to the kitchen. They melted the comb and mixed it with the butter then they came back with the paste smeared on a linen cloth and applied it to the wound, making Sigurd squirm with the initial pain. He grimaced and through short breaths spoke to Torf.

"Nobody dies from a leg wound. He couldn't kill me when he was alive and he won't kill me now he's dead," he panted.

For the next two days, the festering and fever grew worse and the Monks tended Sigurd day and night. He started going in and out of consciousness and on the third day a Monk summoned his commanders. They went together to Sigurd's chamber and he raised his head weakly.

"If I die, Torf will take command of my army," he whispered and closed his eyes.

The Monks came by his side and one put his finger on Sigurd's neck. They waited in silence until a long breath announced his last. The Monk took his finger away then pulled the covering over Sigurd's face.

Sigurd, Jarl of Orkney was dead.

---

# Footnote!

History records the cause of Sigurd's death as blood poisoning. Also recorded is the cause of the infection, a small wound inflicted by Tusk's teeth when his severed head was tied to Sigurd's saddle. The battle was fought against Mael Brigte of Moray, also known as Tusk, over a land dispute. Recorded also are the details of the deception whereby Sigurd brought eighty warriors to fight forty of Tusk's by double-mounting his horses. Where Sigurd is buried is not so clear and two locations are recorded as the most likely, Sigurd's Howe, close to Dornoch, or Burghead (Torfness) in Moray. Both are recorded by history as the two most likely locations. However, it is generally accepted that Sigurd is buried at Sigurd's Howe by Dornoch.

Alive or dead, Sigurd had debts to pay. Payment would tear the Picts apart when the Norse gathered their main harvest. --- Book Three

- G A Ross -

# Other Books in
# The Northern Wave Trilogy

### Book 1

The walled Fort of Torridon the seat of Pict power in Scotland in 800AD was the largest in the land and deemed impregnable. No surprise attack on Torridon was thought possible. Torridon and Moray were but a dream in the minds of enemies, a prize that was out of reach.

Decantae strongholds of Tain and Mahomack the lands of the Pict queen Sheena were within the grasp of the Norse. Sigurd, Jarl of Orkney with help from King Harold set his sights on what was achievable. Torridon, lay only three hours across the Moray Firth by Longboat.

Torridon could wait. An alliance with Drest, Chief of the Smertae to the north whose land bordered that of the Decantae allowed a surprise attack from land and sea on Mahomack and Tain.

Smertae were despised by all and were blamed for everything. Their land was the most beautiful but they couldn't eat beauty and felt they were hard done by. Drest saw a way of getting better land and riches. Plans were well advanced to take Tain and Mahomack until events took a twist and brought the dream of Torridon into the realm of reality.

### Book 3

With the seat of power now in the south with King Uurad, the north felt abandoned. The Norse had suffered their own tragedies but all was under control, except for Tusk's band, the last resistance in Moray. One harvest had been gathered and another one planted. Before the second Norse harvest could be gathered, Anvils would ring to the making of Leg Irons.

*Available worldwide from*
*Amazon and all good bookstores*

---

www.mtp.agency

Milton Keynes UK
Ingram Content Group UK Ltd.
UKHW040232210924
448566UK00005B/505

9 781800 943247